I AM JONATHAN S(

CLAUDE HOUGHTON OLDFIELD was born in 1889 in Sevenoaks, Kent and was educated at Dulwich College. He trained as an accountant and worked in the Admiralty in the First World War, rejected for active service because of poor eyesight. In 1920 he married a West End actress, Dulcie Benson, and they lived in a cottage in the Chiltern Hills. To a writers' directory, Houghton gave his hobbies as reading in bed, riding, visiting Devon and abroad, and talking to people different from himself. He added: "I like dawn, and the dead of night, in great cities." He disliked fuss, noise, crowds, rows, and being misquoted, or being told how much he owed "to some writer I've never read."

Houghton's earliest writing was poetry and drama before turning to prose fiction with his first novel, *Neighbours*, in 1926. In the 1930s, Houghton published several well-received novels that met with solid sales and respectable reviews, including *I Am Jonathan Scrivener* (1930), easily his most popular and best-known work, *Chaos Is Come Again* (1932), *Julian Grant Loses His Way* (1933), *This Was Ivor Trent* (1935), *Strangers* (1938), and *Hudson Rejoins the Herd* (1939). Although he published nearly a dozen more novels throughout the 1940s and 1950s, most critics feel his later works are less significant than his novels of the 1930s.

Houghton was a prolific correspondent, generous in devoting his time to answering letters and signing copies for readers who enjoyed his books. One of these was novelist Henry Miller, who never met Houghton but began an impassioned epistolary exchange with him after being profoundly moved by his works. Houghton's other admirers included his contemporaries P. G. Wodehouse, Clemence Dane, and Hugh Walpole. Houghton died in 1961.

MICHAEL DIRDA, a weekly book columnist for *The Washington Post*, received the 1993 Pulitzer Prize for criticism. He is the author of the memoir *An Open Book* and of four collections of essays: *Readings, Bound to Please, Book by Book* and *Classics for Pleasure*. His latest book, *On Conan Doyle*, won the 2012 Edgar Award—for best critical/biographical work of the year—from the Mystery Writers of America. He is a regular contributor to several literary periodicals, including *The New York Review of Books* and the *Times Literary Supplement*, as well as an occasional lecturer and college teacher.

By Claude Houghton

The Kingdoms of the Spirit (1924)

Neighbours (1926)

The Riddle of Helena (1927)

Crisis (1929)

I Am Jonathan Scrivener (1930)*

A Hair Divides (1930)

Chaos Is Come Again (1932)

Julian Grant Loses His Way (1933)

Three Fantastic Tales (1934)

This Was Ivor Trent (1935)*

The Beast (1936)

Christina (1936)

Strangers (1938)

Hudson Rejoins the Herd (1939)

All Change, Humanity! (1942)

The Man Who Could Still Laugh (1943)

Six Lives and a Book (1943)

Passport to Paradise (1944)

Transformation Scene (1946)

The Quarrel (1948)

Birthmark (1950)

The Enigma of Conrad Stone (1952)

At the End of a Road (1953)

The Clock Ticks (1954)

More Lives Than One (1957)

* Available from Valancourt Books

CLAUDE HOUGHTON

I AM JONATHAN SCRIVENER

With a foreword by
MICHAEL DIRDA

VALANCOURT BOOKS

I Am Jonathan Scrivener by Claude Houghton
First published London: Thornton Butterworth, 1930
First Valancourt Books edition 2013

Published by Valancourt Books, Kansas City, Missouri
Publisher & Editor: JAMES D. JENKINS
20th Century Series Editor: SIMON STERN, University of Toronto
http://www.valancourtbooks.com

Library of Congress Cataloging-in-Publication Data

Houghton, Claude, 1889-1961.
  I am Jonathan Scrivener / by Claude Houghton ; with an introductory
note by Hugh Walpole ; foreword by Michael Dirda. – 1st Valancourt Books
edition.
     pages cm.
  First published London: Thornton Butterworth, 1930 – T.p. verso.
  ISBN 978-1-939140-08-1 (*alk. paper*)
  1. Middle-aged men – Fiction. 2. London (England) – Fiction.
I. Dirda, Michael. II. Title.
  PR6029.L4115 2013
  823'.914–DC23

                              2012048968

Set in Dante MT 11/14

CONTENTS

THE QUEST FOR SCRIVENER

THIRTY or so years ago, I was sleepily turning the pages of
E. F. Bleiler's stupendous *Guide to Supernatural Fiction*—no
home is complete without a copy—when the entry for Claude
Houghton (1889-1961) caught my attention: "British author of psychological romances, often embodying personal mysticism and
a remote allegory. . . . Best-known work the fine psychological-
mystical-mystery story *I Am Jonathan Scrivener*." At that time I had
never heard of Houghton, but this brief description made *Scrivener*
sound intriguing. I read on. While discussing one of Houghton's
out-and-out fantasies, Bleiler commented that "like other of
Houghton's novels, notably *I Am Jonathan Scrivener, This Was Ivor
Trent* is essentially a description of the hollow man of the 1930s—a
person who is seemingly a successful, well-adjusted person, but
is internally empty, shattered and abysmally lonely." Houghton
sounded better and better. According to Bleiler, the writer had
even won the praise of Graham Greene for his craftsmanship. I
made a mental note to look out for *I Am Jonathan Scrivener* when
browsing through the fiction shelves of secondhand bookstores.

Several years then passed without my ever seeing a copy of
Scrivener. Not that I made any strenuous effort to track down the
novel. People who frequent used bookshops know that sooner
or later a wanted title will magically appear: One need only bide
one's time. *Ivor Trent* did turn up occasionally—for $10 or $15, often
in a handsome jacket—but I wanted Houghton's alleged masterpiece. Why start with the second-best?

Sometime in the late '80s, I traveled to Philadelphia on business
but naturally allocated Saturday afternoon for a little booking. I
duly visited antiquarian dealers, used-book emporiums, and even
one or two dingy paperback exchanges. In the rattiest of these last
I paused, just before leaving, to spin a revolving wire rack next to

the front door. And there it was, right at the top: *I Am Jonathan Scrivener*. Begrudgingly, I plunked down $2.95, convinced that in a just world the price should have been 50 cents.

Back home in Silver Spring, I studied my newly acquired treasure more carefully. Beneath the title was a woodcut of a Millet-like sower, backed by a rising sun. At the base of the front cover appeared the words "The Inner Sanctum Novels: New Fiction at $1." Though printed in 1930, the 382 thickish pages weren't brown or brittle in the least; the binding was actually sewn, though loose between a couple of the gatherings. Typically, the back cover outlined the action of the novel and listed other Inner Sanctum offerings. I recognized almost none of the authors or titles, many of which struck me as endearingly dated, even campy: *The Earth Told Me*, by Thames Williamson; *Beloved, O Mon Goye*, by Sarah Levy; *Denny and the Dumb Cluck*, by J. P. McEvoy; *Fifteen Rabbits*, by Felix Salten. Could this last, by the author of *Bambi*, be another children's classic? Perhaps a history of Thumper's offspring?

When I finally opened *Scrivener*, I discovered an unexpected notice, headed "To the Buyer of this Book": "The Inner Sanctum Novels are an experiment in book publishing. It is the thought of the publishers that the buying of new fiction has been seriously handicapped in recent years by two chief causes:

"1) The Price. Whereas many non-fiction books are bought not only to read but to reread and refer to, most fiction is bought for one reading only." (Such refreshing honesty, I thought.) "The price of fiction has remained relatively high because it has not been bought in quantities sufficient to enable a publisher to make use of the savings concomitant with large production." (Concomitant! You couldn't get away with that today.) "Meanwhile, unless the reader were certain he wanted to retain a book in his library, he has been content to borrow the book from a library or from a friend (whenever the occasion might arise) or else he has decided not to read the book at all."

"2) Library Space. This has in recent years become a serious problem." (Hoo, boy!) "More and more people live in relatively small apartments in which the area of library shelves is limited."

(Nowadays that last word would be "nonexistent.") "Where to put the books once they are read has become a real question. The book has been bought, but who wants to throw away a bound book? To meet these two factors, the publishers of this series of books have brought the price of all fiction . . . down to a dollar. You have now bought this book. If you do not wish to keep it, lend it to a friend, or send it to a hospital. Or, if you are clearing your shelves, throw it out with magazines." (!!!) "If, on the other hand, this is a book that you wish to keep bound in permanent form, take it to any bookbinder or send it back to the publisher with a remittance of one dollar, and it will be bound in cloth and returned to you post-paid." The notice ends by assuring the reader that this is "a first edition copy."

Needless to say, I found this announcement extremely ingratiat-ing, from the unsentimental method of book disposal to the pleas-ing tentativeness and lack of hype. I also wondered if Simon and Schuster would still honor their contract and bind the book for a dollar. And then return it postpaid.

Despite these winsome enticements, I didn't immediately find a sofa and settle back with *I Am Jonathan Scrivener*. I did read the first few sentences: "This book is an invitation to share an adventure. It is necessary for me to introduce myself as I am the only person in the world who can tell this story, but you will be wise to regard me simply as a mechanism for the narration of certain events. It is not necessary to know much about me, but it is essential to know something, since the adventure I am inviting you to share was the result of a dramatic and mysterious change which totally transformed the whole manner of my life." All this sounded cozily sinister and the invitation to share an adventure was . . . inviting. Nevertheless, I laid the book aside. I was pleased finally to own a copy, but there were other claims on my reading time.

For several more years *I Am Jonathan Scrivener* sat on a shelf in a little storage room for books, papers, and office supplies. Every so often I would pick it up and turn the pages. Once I had occasion to telephone E. F. Bleiler and mentioned Houghton's novel: He assured me it was a book that merited rediscovery. More and more

I thought about actually reading it, but somehow the moment never seemed quite right. Then, in the mid 1990s, I began to pack the book along with the mysteries and classics I usually take on vacation. *Scrivener* traveled to a house on Ocracoke Island, even visited Ohio a time or two. I moved the Inner Sanctum paperback to a mound of must-read books piled near my bedside. And finally, on the Saturday before Bill Clinton's inauguration in 1997, I casually picked up the novel, leaned back against the pillows on my bed, and read for three hours. Being a slow reader, I later finished the book on Inauguration night, just about the time the Clintons went toddling off to bed.

I Am Jonathan Scrivener proved to have been worth the twelve-year wait. In some ways it resembles a novel by Paul Auster, *City of Glass* perhaps, or *Moon Palace*, a blend of the spooky and the philosophical, with a twisty, slightly artificial structure. There are also flashes of Chesterton's *The Man Who Was Thursday*, early Evelyn Waugh, and the religious supernatural tales of Charles Williams. I liked it a lot.

Here's the plot: James Wrexham, 39 years old, has been living a life of demoralizing loneliness. Orphaned at 19, he has passed two decades working for a vulgarian entrepreneur, and gradually come to regard himself as one of life's spectators. Sitting in a barber shop one afternoon, he suddenly feels the overwhelming wretchedness of his existence—just as his eye notices an advertisement in the *Times*: "A gentleman of independent means who is leaving England requires a secretary to attend to his correspondence during his absence and to catalogue his library. The individuality of the applicant is of greater importance than his technical qualifications for the position." Wrexham immediately determines to apply for the job and sends in a rambling autobiographical epistle.

Rather to his surprise, he is invited to visit a prominent lawyer, who explains that Mr. Jonathan Scrivener desires him to begin employment at once. Mr. Scrivener himself has recently left for parts unknown. In due course Wrexham discovers that he has the run of spacious rooms in Pall Mall, a servant who cooks the best meals he has ever eaten, an exceptionally generous salary, and a written request from Scrivener to make himself comfortable, take a box at the theater, and in general follow his own inclinations. Not surprisingly, Wrexham tries to puzzle out the personality of his unseen employer. The books in Scrivener's library have obviously been read, but they reveal an improbable range of tastes and interests, from philosophy to pornography. Then one night, as Wrexham sits daydreaming among the books, he turns around to discover that a beautiful young woman has quietly let herself into the apartment with a latchkey.

The ethereal Pauline Mandeville claims to be a "friend" of Scrivener's, but then so does the vampirically glamorous Francesca Bellamy, whose millionaire husband committed suicide in Paris under dubious circumstances. As the novel proceeds, Wrexham encounters other friends of his elusive employer—the disillusioned, alcoholic Middleton, the playboy Rivers, the apelike Denvers. Each appears to have known a distinctly different Scrivener, and each is oddly obsessed with the man. Weeks go by. Wrexham grows increasingly convinced that Scrivener has embarked on some kind of bizarre experiment, using himself and this motley collection of humanity as guinea pigs. But to what end?

Throughout his story Houghton creates a sense of foreboding and psychological unease, even in his wittiest turns of phrase. "I've met a number of people who had endured agonies in their determination not to suffer." The soup in a Japanese restaurant "was neither hot nor cold, clean nor dirty, thick nor clear, and it had long weeds in it which looked rather like serpents who had died in youth." Says the desperate pleasure-seeker Rivers, "All people who are decent want to give. You have only to ask in the right way. . . . Here's an example. I met a marvellous girl at supper three nights ago. I drove her home. Naturally, I suggested that we should become lovers. That is, I gave her the opportunity of collaborating with me in the creation of beautiful memories. She's thinking it over. She's intelligent. She'll see that I'm right." "Most of us," says another character, "commit suicide, but the fact is only recognized if we blow our brains out." When Wrexham encounters the seductive Mrs. Bellamy for the second time, she appears to him "in evening dress and her beauty suggested a sword half drawn from its scabbard."

A biographical note at the end of my copy of *Scrivener* indicates that by 1930 Claude Houghton had already written a couple of volumes of poetry, a book of essays, two plays, and four novels. He'd been praised by Arnold Bennett for his dialogue and been called a genius. To little avail: Houghton is now almost completely forgotten. Nonetheless, *I Am Jonathan Scrivener* remains a tantalizing, highly diverting philosophical novel of rare elegance and wit. Given such merits, its disappearance for so many years invites mild despair. For the most part, we all read the same authors, the same old novels and stories, the same approved masterworks taught in school. Yet how many other really good books lie moribund, awaiting a reader to restore them to life? Happily, you now hold in your hands Claude Houghton's masterpiece and, thanks to Valancourt Books, you didn't have to spend years searching for a copy, as I once did. In fact, at this point all you need to do is settle yourself in a favorite chair and begin: "This book is an invitation to an adventure. . . ."

MICHAEL DIRDA
Silver Spring, Maryland, 2013

A NOTE ON THE NOVELS OF
CLAUDE HOUGHTON*

IT IS OFTEN said that in these days of awareness it is extremely unlikely that any novelists of real individuality and vigour will remain for long unrecognized.

Claude Houghton is, I think, an interesting example to the contrary. It is not true to say that he is unrecognized—everyone who is really interested in the contemporary English novel must know his work; but it *is* true that he has not had, as yet, the public acclaim and popularity that he deserves.

He has written seven novels and all of them are remarkable and, what is more important, they are all novels that could have been written by no other man alive. It must be further said of them that they are all extremely courageous both in theme and treatment. They would be courageous books in any time and in any country, but they are especially so just now because they have been written and published in an atmosphere opposed to their spirit. Houghton is a romantic and a mystic and his seven novels have appeared in what is the most realistic and unmystical period of the last hundred and fifty years. When I use romantic I mean of course none of the cloak-and-sword romance of the English novel of forty years ago. I mean something very much more important. I mean that attitude to life which insists that there are more spiritual worlds than this one in which we live and that it is man's chief business to discover his relation to these worlds.

This theme is implicit in every one of Houghton's novels. It is the whole subject of his first and most immature, *Neighbours*, which is the story (a very bold and remarkable one for a first novel) of a man who, living in an attic, conceives a hatred for the occupant of the next room. This occupant he never sees but always overhears. At last, when, in a frenzy of rage, he breaks down the

* This introductory note by Hugh Walpole originally appeared in the 1935 Doubleday Doran edition.

door and rushes in to slay his enemy he finds that this hated neighbour is himself.

Now it has been the creed of almost every important novelist in the last twenty years in England and America that *facts* are the only things of which we can be sure, the only things of which it is manly and sensible to treat. So facts we have been given—amusing, social ones by the women, hard, unpleasant ones by the men. Facts, however—material ones at least—are of minor interest to Houghton. That is not to say that he cannot give them us if he wants to. I know for instance no contemporary novelist who can give us so actual and peculiar a London as he. The flat in which Jonathan Scrivener's secretary lives, the little restaurant of *A Hair Divides*, the opening Piccadilly chapter of *Chaos Is Come Again*—these, and many more, are markably accurate, vivid and contemporary. His characters also are living human beings, not, as they almost always are in fantasy, shadows. It is not his business to transplant us altogether to another world—no, precisely the opposite, his object is to bring the other world into this one, a purpose in which he has now several companions—Charles Morgan, Geoffrey Dennis, Margaret Urwin and, incidentally, myself.

His method is, in fact, quite clear. He makes his backgrounds and his dialogue as real as the backgrounds of Theodore Dreiser or Somerset Maugham. His people talk as men and women of to-day *do* talk. But the things that his people perceive and the emotions that they feel are concerned always with their souls rather than with their bodies. Because this is so he is able to choose violent and even melodramatic plots, as one of his truest forbears, Henry James, did before him. The story of *A Hair Divides* for instance might well have been used by Conan Doyle or the author of *Raffles*. A man, jealous of his friend, murders him, remains undiscovered for twenty years and is exposed finally by the murdered man's lover. The murder itself however is of little account, and although the details of the story are perfectly realistic it is the *soul* of the murderer that matters, not his body.

This is still more true of the most remarkable of all Houghton's novels up to the present—*I Am Jonathan Scrivener*. So remarkable in truth is this novel that I cannot understand why it is not universally known and admired. It may be that it is one of those books like *Maurice Guest* or Forster's early stories that needs time for its full discovery. It is certainly true that, although it was published four years ago, I am constantly meeting people who have only just read and appreciated it. It is also true that I meet people who say: "It's all nonsense. I don't know what it is about"—but this is, of course, bound to happen often to novelists of the modern romantic school who write, very dangerously, of worlds that must seem unreal to those who are only conscious of this one.

This does not mean that *Jonathan Scrivener* is not a highly exciting story. Houghton has always, most remarkably, the gift of narrative and suspense. And this is the best of his novels up to the present for the very reason that he has not here yielded to one of his weaknesses, namely, the confusing of the issue. The theme is clear, the motive, the characters and the climax; the ringing final sentence is triumphant.

In his two latest novels *Chaos Is Come Again* and *Julian Grant Loses His Way* he shows more promise than in any of his others. At the same time they are actually less successful than *Jonathan Scrivener*. He is advancing here to really tremendous themes and his picture of the Petersley family in *Chaos* as a symbol of the post-War world is most memorable as are the opening and conclusion of *Julian Grant*. But in these two books his touch seems to me often uncertain and his characters sometimes unreal.

In fine, I believe Claude Houghton to be one of the most interesting and one of the most important novelists now writing in England. With none of his contemporaries can one compare him—his odd mixtures of reality and fantasy, his gifts of drama and of philosophy, his unusual and significant and courageous themes, his natural aptitude for narrative, this last one of the rarest of gifts among novelists to-day. The important thing is, I think, his uniqueness, and he has come into his full power at just the time when the English novel needs such a man as he.

HUGH WALPOLE

I AM JONATHAN SCRIVENER

PART ONE

CHAPTER I

I

THIS book is an invitation to share an adventure. It is necessary for me to introduce myself as I am the only person in the world who can tell this story, but you will be wise to regard me simply as a mechanism for the narration of certain events. It is not necessary to know much about me, but it is essential to know something, since the adventure I am inviting you to share was the result of a dramatic and mysterious change which totally transformed the whole manner of my life.

My name is James Wrexham. I am nearly thirty-nine. I was an only child and my mother died when I was very young. My father was an odd character, an enigma to everyone, and there was some mystery concerning the circumstances of his death. Personally I do not believe that he committed suicide but I may be wrong. He died when I was nineteen. I had just left school and discovered that not only was I practically penniless but that I had not a relative in the world. Moreover my father's eccentricities had alienated most of his friends. Hence my position was not enviable. Instead of going to the university, I had to earn a living and it was soon made clear to me that a public school education was not a passport to employment.

But a solution to my difficulties speedily presented itself. I received a letter from a man called Petersham in which he asked me to call upon him at my convenience. His note paper informed me that he was an auctioneer and estate agent. His offices were in the county town which was some twelve miles distant from my father's house. I visited him very shortly after I received his letter and I can remember the details of our first interview perfectly.

Petersham received me in his private room which commanded a view of the outer office through a glass partition. He was a small, alert man with a fiery moustache, a crooked nose, and the eyes of a lynx. He wasted no time on condolences, but looked me up and down with frank curiosity.

"So you're Oscar Wrexham's son," he said at last. "And now what are you going to do with all kinds of swell ideas in your head and no money in your pockets, eh?"

I told him I had no plans.

Petersham favoured me with his philosophy of life. It was a strange mixture of get-rich-quick and social servility. I did not listen with much attention for I was trying to imagine what link could possibly have existed between Petersham and my father and was therefore somewhat disconcerted when Petersham broke the thread of his oration and exclaimed:

"I know what you're thinking, young man. You're wondering what your father had in common with me. That's only natural, because your father was a gentleman and I'm not."

I imagine that I looked very embarrassed, but Petersham went on:

"Well, you can thank your lucky stars that I'm not a gentleman because if I were, you wouldn't be here. I started as an office boy, I did."

He shot out the last sentence almost viciously and as I did not know whether he required congratulations or sympathy, I said nothing.

"An office boy," he repeated. "I've had to fight, scheme, and work, and I've not done so badly, but I've missed a lot of business—and still miss it—because I am what I am. Now, as to your father, he once did me a service. It doesn't matter what it was. But I've never forgotten it, and that's why I wrote to you."

Then he explained his scheme to me. It was entirely logical.

Briefly it was this: I was to join his staff and learn the business. He would pay me a sufficient salary then, later, if we got on together, he would make me a partner and it would be my duty to open up and develop a better class of business than he had been able to attract. He ended by saying:

"I've capitalized my energy and you must capitalize your birth and education, then we can help each other. That's democracy, as I understand it. I shan't charge all your wages in the early years against Salary Account. I shall debit some of it to Goodwill, because you're going to prove an asset in the business one day. Now, what do you say? Mind you, it will seem dull at first. You'll begin by making and checking inventories and that sort of thing. You know what an inventory is, of course?"

I said that I had no idea.

"Good God! there's your public school education for you! Well, think it over. And if you come here, don't mix up with the clerks. Keep yourself to yourself in the office, but hob-nob with your own class outside. And make no mistake about me: I'm a snob, I am, and it pays to be a snob. I'm offering you this job because you're the son of your father and because you've been to a good public school. Think it over, and take your time."

There was really nothing to think over. Petersham was the only person who took any interest in me and it was essential that I should earn a salary. I accepted his offer.

There is no need to recount the loneliness and misery of the next few years. Then the war came and I escaped from Petersham but not from drudgery. I was wounded after I had been in the line for a week and was employed on clerical duties for the remainder of my services. At the end of 1918 I returned to Petersham.

During my absence his business had developed rapidly. I never heard any more of the scheme he had outlined at our first interview. This was a great relief to me for temperamentally I was incapable of making useful friends and capitalizing those social advantages which Petersham had regarded as potential assets. We saw little of each other. My work was dull, largely mechanical, and it made practically no mental demands. I lived in rooms on the outskirts of the town. I had no friends, and gradually I became what is called queer. I prefer to forget those years. If it had not been for books, I do not know what would have happened to me, but books are a poor substitute for life. For a long period I lived in a state of rebellion and the attempts I made to evade loneliness only led to degradation. Then something happened: I became content to be a spectator of life and at the same time I became convinced that my relations with Petersham would not last much longer.

It is curious how certain I was that change was at hand. I was so certain that I was not excited and the fact that there was no sign even of the possibility of change had no effect whatever upon me. I did not will it; I did not hope for it; I *knew* that change was imminent.

And then it came. The manner of its approach was remarkable and all the circumstances attending it were mysterious.

One Saturday I left the office as usual at one o'clock and went to a café at which I lunched frequently. It was nearly empty. After I had finished my meal, I became aware of two men sitting near me. An animated conversation sprang up between them and although I could not hear what was said I realized that one was trying to convince the other of the desirability of a certain line of action. As I passed them on my way out I heard the younger say in a challenging tone:

"Caution! That's always your cry! You've got to take risks, I tell you! If you look, you never leap."

I paid my bill and went out. The last sentence I had heard echoed in my brain: "If you look, you never leap." I crossed the road and went into a barber's. All the assistants were engaged, so I took a paper at random from the sheaf on the table, sat down and began to read. The paper was *The Times* and my attention was immediately arrested by an advertisement in the Personal Column. It read as follows:

A gentleman of independent means who is leaving England requires a secretary to attend to his correspondence during his absence and to catalogue his library. The individuality of the applicant is of greater importance than his technical qualifications for the position.

Directly I had read the foregoing I made a copy of it. I also made a note of the firm of solicitors to which applications had to be sent. My determination to apply for the position was immediate and that fact is noteworthy even in a series of events every one of which was unusual.

That evening I studied the wording of the advertisement and the next day I spent several hours drafting my application. It was difficult to assess the precise meaning which my prospective employer attached to the word "individuality." I imagine that I wrote about a dozen letters before lunch and I remember that each seemed more stereotyped than the last. By about six in the evening I evolved an application which satisfied me, but on glancing through it again later in the evening, I decided that it was hopeless. I tore it up, then sat down and wrote a long epistle about myself at red-hot speed. I sealed the envelope without even reading the letter through, posted it, and banished the whole question from my mind.

Over a week elapsed, then I received a communication from the solicitors. The name of the firm was Winkworth, Wolland & Williams and their offices were in Sackville Street, Piccadilly. Their letter was as follows:—

"DEAR SIR,

"With reference to your recent communication I am instructed by my client, Mr. Jonathan Scrivener, to say that he is impressed by your application and that he is disposed to believe that you would perform his requirements in an orderly and proper manner. In fact my client wishes me to add that, subject to a formal interview with the undersigned, you are justified in regarding your application as accepted.

"Subject to your convenience, I have to suggest that next Friday at 3 p.m., would be a suitable day and time for an interview and I shall be glad to hear in due course whether you could attend at this office on the day and at the time stated.

"Yours faithfully,
"WALTER WINKWORTH."

The wording, the whole atmosphere, of this letter were so unlike the commercial jargon in which Petersham indulged that

I was very much amused, but two facts were established: one was that I had been successful, and the other was that Mr. Walter Winkworth clearly regarded the decision to employ me as an act for which his client must accept responsibility. In fact, a second reading of the letter made me suspect that Mr. Walter Winkworth highly disapproved of the whole affair and I had considerable doubts as to whether he had even been consulted in the matter of Mr. Scrivener's secretary.

One thing was clear, however: I had to go to London on the following Friday and this involved an interview with Petersham. After some deliberation, I decided that I would tell him that I had obtained a post in London and sever our relations at the earliest moment possible.

Prosperity had not altered Petersham much. He had not moved to larger offices and he still lived in the same villa, but he was now very stout and had become extremely proud of the fact that he had started as an office boy. He had evolved into an ardent Conservative and often said he would go in for politics if his business activities permitted.

I saw him one evening at five o'clock. He was smoking a cigar; a cup of very strong tea was on the table. I came to the point immediately:

"I want to go to London next Friday," I began, "as I ——"

"What for?" he interrupted.

"I applied recently for a job in London and I've been successful."

"Never!" His amazement, if not complimentary, was profound. "God bless my soul! Well, I'll be damned!" Having uttered these rather contradictory exclamations he resumed his cigar and looked at me out of the corner of his eye as if he did not believe me. There was a pause, then he said: "Do you mean you want to leave here?"

"Yes," I replied. "I shall always be grateful to you for giving me a job when no one else would, but I've been in this town long enough and I want a change."

"But hold on a minute," he said, "what sort of a job have you got? This line of business, I suppose?"

"No, I am to be secretary to a man of independent means."

"Friend of yours?" There was a hint of sarcasm in his tone.

"No, I've never seen him."

Petersham turned in his swivel chair and faced me for the first time. I realized that I should have to tell him exactly the position. Unfortunately he evidently had time to spare. I explained briefly how I had obtained the post of secretary to Mr. Scrivener. When I had finished he looked at me with a mystified expression.

"And you mean to tell me," he began, emphasizing each word, "you mean to tell me you're going to give up a permanent job here for a fairy tale like that?"

"Just so," I replied.

"And when you've catalogued his library and he comes back to London, out you go, I suppose?"

"I really don't know," I said, then I added, "and I really don't care."

"Now we're getting to it," he said. "Do you know what's the matter with you? You're queer. I've watched you more than you think. You're queer, like your father."

"Look here, Petersham," I said in a tone which surprised him. "You've often made obscure references to my father and I resent them. If you know anything about him, which I doubt, either tell me plainly or do not refer to him. As to my being queer, as you call it, you simply mean that I am not like you. It would never occur to you that I might regard you as queer."

"Me! Queer! I'm a business man."

"Precisely." After a pause I added: "I know just as well as you do that the job I am taking is a risk."

"Now, look here, Wrexham," he said ponderously, "you don't want any advice from me, that's clear. There's plenty that do, so I'll keep it for them. But understand this; you can't play fast and loose with your job here. If you go, *you go*. See?"

"I understand perfectly. I'm afraid I haven't proved the investment you thought I should be. On the other hand, I hope I've earned the money you've paid me."

"Yes, you've done that. You haven't had much, but you've

earned what you've had. Our account is square. I think you're a fool to leave, but that's your business. Here!" he exclaimed suddenly, "what was the name of those solicitors you're going to see?"

"Winkworth, Wolland and Williams," I replied.

He repeated the name of the firm twice, then pressed a bell on his table. A girl appeared.

"Get me those papers about the Barnett mortgage, and don't be all night about it."

The girl disappeared and returned in a few minutes with some documents. Petersham glanced at them.

"There's a memory for you! Three years ago, my boy! Here we are! Winkworth, Wolland and Williams acted for Barnett. They're in a big way of business. I met one of the partners. No end of a swell! Well, I'll be damned! You'd better keep in with them—never mind Scrivener, whatever his name is. I expect they could buy him up. Here! If you get a chance to put anything my way, don't miss it through dreaming about the moon. You'll have to mention my name to 'em naturally, so just remind 'em about the Barnett business." He glanced at the papers again. "No, on second thoughts, *don't* refer to the Barnett mortgage. I see they say some nonsense here about my methods being pretty sharp practice. Well, mention my name anyway, and see how it goes."

"Supposing Mr. Scrivener wants me immediately," I managed to say at last, "would you have any objection ——?"

"Go when you like, my boy. Don't consider me, go when you like. But send me a line now and again and let me know if there's anything doing. It's like you to get in with the swells just when you're leaving me. Winkworth, Wolland and Williams! They're in a big way, there's no doubt about that. When that Barnett affair was on, I never thought I'd have any chance of doing anything else with 'em, or—Well, can't be helped. They've probably forgotten. They've got their fingers in a good many pies."

This was my last conversation with Petersham.

II

The following Friday I went to London. This visit was in the nature of an adventure as I did not know London intimately and the thought of the impending interview intrigued my imagination.

I arrived just before lunch. The sun was shining, streets and pavements were thronged, and in a second the life of the city claimed me. Another diminutive river had encountered the sea. I had lunch, then as I had an hour to spare, I sat down in the Green Park and speculated on the mysterious change which had occurred in my affairs and the certainty deepened in me that my old life was over for ever.

At precisely three o'clock I entered the offices of Messrs. Winkworth, Wolland and Williams. An immaculately-dressed young man received me and asked my business. His whole attitude suggested that it was not his duty to attend to me, that normally he was engaged on affairs of great importance, but that at the minute he was performing the unworthy function of recognizing my existence. He showed me into a large waiting-room in which the heavy furniture was arranged with grim precision. A table stood in the middle of the room on which virgin copies of *The Times* and *The Morning Post* were chastely displayed, flanked by copies of *Punch*, and a periodical entitled *Our Empire*. A volume of Debrett occupied the centre of the mantelpiece in aristocratic isolation.

I sat down and looked at the other occupant of the room. He was an old gentleman with snow-white hair and a pink complexion. He took no notice of me but continued to read the newspaper, from which occupation he apparently derived little satisfaction for he punctuated his reading with ejaculations which were not complimentary to the writer. "Bah! Rubbish!" he exclaimed loudly. He read a few lines in silence, then shouted: "Humbug!" I do not think he realized that he was speaking aloud. "Damned pack of scally-wags!" was his next comment. I became so interested in his criticisms that it seemed only a few minutes before I was summoned to Mr. Walter Winkworth's room. In reality half an hour had passed.

I was ushered into a room of great dignity. Everything was solid and impressive. A number of tin boxes were ranged round the walls and on each box was painted in white letters the name of the client whose documents it housed. It was clear that many members of the aristocracy entrusted their affairs to the firm of Winkworth, Wolland and Williams. A glance at those tin boxes was sufficient evidence as to that, and a glance at Mr. Winkworth would have dispelled the remaining doubts of even the most cynical observer.

He was rather tall, well-made, and wore a morning coat which fitted him to perfection. He had a white slip under his waistcoat and white spats over his patent shoes. His crisp hair, iron-grey at the temples, added to his distinction and a pince-nez dangling at the end of a black watered-silk ribbon seemed to proclaim that he was in practice in the West End, not the City. He took no notice of me, so I sat down and waited.

Mr. Winkworth was seated at a very elegant desk near the window and an attractive young lady sat by his side, note-book in hand. The silence was complete except for the ticking of a clock.

"Now, Miss Montgomery, be so good as to read that over, if you please."

His voice was, perhaps, a trifle over-ripe. He leant back in his chair and gazed at the ceiling while Miss Montgomery read the letter aloud. As I watched them, I felt that I was in a seat at the theatre.

"That meets the case, I *think*," he said when the reading was finished. "Please have it typed immediately and arrange that it catches to-night's country post."

She rose, put a paper in front of him, and glided noiselessly out of the room. He read the paper she had placed before him, then looked over at me.

"Ah! Mr.? Mr.?" He paused and I did not fill the blank as I was certain that he knew quite well who I was. "Mr. *Wrexham*. Of course! Mr. *Wrexham*." He looked down at a diary on his desk. "Three o'clock—Mr. Wrexham. Kindly take this seat."

I rose and took the seat indicated. He gazed at his highly polished nails with considerable satisfaction for several seconds, then he patted his tie and his hair, assumed a slightly stiffer attitude, then addressed me in a cold, formal manner.

"You wish to become Mr. Scrivener's secretary?"

"It was my reason for applying for the position," I answered.

"You did not state the salary you required," he said, turning slowly towards me and looking at me through half-closed eyes.

"I imagined that Mr. Scrivener would state the amount he was prepared to pay." There was a pause, then I added, "Perhaps I was wrong in thinking that to be the case."

He waved his hand. "We'll return to that later," he said, airily, as if I had introduced the subject. "What, exactly, are your qualifications for the position?"

"I have nothing to add, or to subtract from the details I gave in my application, Mr. Winkworth. I understood from your letter that Mr. Scrivener was favourably impressed by that application."

"We had a large number of applicants, a large number. Many from young men of considerable distinction." He rose and began to pace the room elegantly. "You were not at the university, I think, Mr. Wrexham?"

"Would it not save time if you read my letter again?" I inquired with a smile of genuine amusement. "All the facts concerning me are clearly set forth in it."

"No, sir, no!" he said irritably. "I have all the facts concerning this little matter in my head."

I said nothing, for I saw quite clearly that he was simply trying to hide the fact that Scrivener had already decided that I was to be his secretary. Why Mr. Winkworth thought it worth while to try to impress me, I could not imagine, but it was clear that he wished me to regard him as the arbiter of my destiny. Once I recognized this, he became a subject for study and I awaited his next move with interest. He returned to his chair.

"Mr. Wrexham," he began impressively, "you are, I take it, a man of the world."

"That's as good a description as any other."

"Just so. Doubtless, then, it has occurred to you that the negotiations between us have been somewhat unusual, and I tell you frankly I dislike the unusual, very much indeed. Very—much—indeed, Mr. Wrexham."

I bowed and waited for him to continue.

"My procedure has been unusual because the circumstances have been unusual. I propose to be frank with you. My client, Mr. Jonathan Scrivener, is slightly eccentric. He is a gifted man, a brilliant man, but on occasions a headstrong man. The present circumstances are an example. He has decided to employ you as his secretary. He has not seen you, he has not asked you for references, yet he has decided to engage you as his secretary." He made a slow, ample gesture indicative of disapproval.

"When you used the word 'eccentric' just now, Mr. Winkworth, did you mean that ——"

"Oh dear no! Certainly *not*. Mr. Jonathan Scrivener is highly connected and is very wealthy. When I used the term *eccentric* I did not mean to imply that my client was—Oh! most definitely not! Not at all! On the contrary, a brilliant man of quite exceptional intellectual attainments."

As I could think of nothing to say, I remained silent. After a pause, he continued:

"You understand that Mr. Scrivener wishes you to take the position immediately?"

"I know nothing," I answered, "except that I had this appointment with you to-day. I thought it probable that Mr. Scrivener would be present."

"Certainly not! Mr. Scrivener has already left England."

This news surprised me considerably. My employer was clearly an original since it certainly was strange to engage a secretary without seeing him.

"Not only that," Winkworth went on, "my client wishes you to begin your duties immediately and to take up residence at once."

I could not help laughing, a procedure which annoyed the lawyer very much indeed.

"I must apologize, Mr. Winkworth, but may I inquire what the phrase 'to take up residence' means?"

"It means, sir, that you will live in Mr. Scrivener's flat during his absence."

I stared at Mr. Winkworth's round, self-satisfied face in complete bewilderment. I remember that his large, glistening teeth impressed me unfavourably.

"Will Mr. Scrivener be out of England for long?" I inquired.

"As to that, I have no idea and I doubt whether my client has."

"All this is very interesting," I said lightly. "And where does Mr. Scrivener live?"

"He lives in a flat in Pall Mall but he travels a great deal and that, I imagine, is the reason why he has decided to employ a secretary."

Mr. Winkworth swung his pince-nez from side to side and assumed an exceedingly diplomatic expression. I was now convinced, however, that he knew little more than I did about Scrivener. I decided to obtain the bare facts of the situation without any finesse.

"Very well," I began, "then the position is this: Mr. Scrivener wishes me to live in his flat in Pall Mall and to begin my duties immediately. Naturally I want to carry out his wishes. There remains only the question of salary."

"The salary is ten pounds a week, sir."

"That seems very generous," I replied.

"It *is* very generous. It is exceedingly generous. I am instructed to add," he continued, in a lifeless but legal manner, "that my client wished me to tell you that his return to London, whenever that event occurs, will not necessarily involve the termination of your employment. Please understand that if I make no comment on these arrangements, my silence does not necessarily imply that I concur in them."

"I understand perfectly. I have already taken up a great deal of your time. Do I understand that it is Mr. Scrivener's wish that I should go to his flat to-day?"

"Certainly, if your arrangements permit."

"I can be in his flat within an hour. My luggage is at the station. Had a reference been required, Mr. Petersham of ——"

"A reference is not required, as I have already explained. That is the address." He handed me a paper. "There is a domestic on the premises and, I imagine, you will find a communication from my client. I think that is all."

I had already risen. I bowed to Mr. Winkworth and was about to leave the room when he said coldly:

"You will, of course, communicate with me, if necessary."

"Certainly, if necessary."

It was clear that he disliked me but I was far too excited to think about Mr. Walter Winkworth. I hurried through the outer office and was soon walking rapidly down a sunlit Piccadilly.

CHAPTER II

I

As I walked down Piccadilly I thought over the interview which had just ended. I discovered that the change in my affairs had proved more fundamental than I had anticipated. My life in Petersham's office, and the solitary life I had lived outside it, were over. I was now secretary to a man I had never seen. My salary was a generous one. I was to live in his flat in Pall Mall. I did not know what the duration of his absence from London would be, or what effect his return would have upon our relations. In fact, I knew nothing whatever about him.

The sunlight, the animation of the streets, the crowded pavements, fascinated me because they represented the background of the adventure upon which I was now embarked. Everything was unfamiliar. The contours of my world had been obliterated. Yesterday, the externals of my life had been rigid, mechanical, monotonous. Day had followed day like a recurring decimal. I had trod the treadmill of relentless routine. But now I was an instrument in the hands of Providence. And, to mortals, the operations of Providence are usually indistinguishable from those of pure caprice.

I rang up the hotel and cancelled the room I had reserved, then I went to the station, collected my luggage, and drove to Pall Mall.

I sat in the taxi and experienced the pleasant sensation that everything was beginning again.

Scrivener's flat was almost opposite St. James's Palace and was therefore only a few yards from St. James's Street. The buildings on either side of the entrance consisted of offices. I discovered that the flat was on the second floor. I paused outside the door for a moment surprised by the silence, then I rang the bell and half wondered whether anyone would respond to its summons.

The door opened almost immediately and I was confronted by a servant who evidently expected me.

"I am Mr. Wrexham," I said.

"Please come in, sir," she answered. "I had a message from Mr. Winkworth's office saying that you would arrive this afternoon."

I entered the hall and stood about while my luggage was carried into the flat. The hall was the size of a room and was somewhat sombre in atmosphere. It possessed a definite personality and produced the illusion that it was at least twice its actual size. So much so that I glanced round for the staircase, only to remember that I was in a flat. The walls were covered with a dark tapestry and on the wall facing the front door was a portrait of a remarkable looking man, evidently the work of an Italian artist.

I glanced at the woman who had let me in. She was instructing the taxi-driver where to put my luggage. She was deliberate in her movements and spoke in low, even tones. Her chin was rather pointed, her features were tense and tightly drawn, thereby giving a concentrated expression to the face, strangely at variance with the bright, almost psychic, light in the large eyes.

When we were alone, she said to me:

"Mr. Scrivener gave instructions that some of the rooms should be locked, sir, as he did not think you would require them."

"Are there many rooms in the flat?" I asked.

"There are more than you would think, sir. There are three bedrooms, two sitting-rooms and the library."

"Really! Well, I should certainly not require so many. By the way, what is your name?"

"Matthews, sir."

"Did Mr. Scrivener leave any message for me?"

"There is a note for you in the library, sir."

"I see. Perhaps I had better see my rooms."

"Certainly, sir."

I followed her down a broad passage, and she explained that the room at the end of it was the library. The two rooms next to it had been prepared for me: a bedroom and a sitting-room. The latter was a large room and both were furnished with distinction. I had never been in such luxurious surroundings. Wealth and refinement were apparent in every detail. It was so silent in the flat that speech seemed sacrilege.

As I stood contemplating this dignified magnificence, I felt that all this was a dream and that soon I should wake and hasten away to Petersham's office.

"Mr. Scrivener wanted me to say, sir, that he hoped you would alter any of his suggested arrangements if they did not meet with your wishes."

"Everything is excellent, Matthews. I am sure I shall be perfectly comfortable."

There was a pause, then she said:

"It was Mr. Scrivener's custom, sir, to give me orders after breakfast as to whether he would be lunching or dining at home and he suggested that perhaps a similar arrangement would suit you."

"Very well," I replied, then added, "When did Mr. Scrivener leave London?"

"A week ago, sir."

"And you have no idea when he will return?"

"None, sir."

I glanced at her but her expression revealed nothing, and I could see that she regarded Scrivener as a person so removed from her sphere that curiosity in regard to him would be an impertinence. It was quite evident that she would provide no clues as to the mystery of Scrivener.

"Would you like to see the library, sir?"

She opened the door at the end of the passage and I entered the room. I stopped on the threshold and an exclamation of surprise escaped me. I had never seen such a remarkable room. The walls were lined with exquisite bookcases from floor to ceiling: it was impossible to imagine the beautiful furniture in any other setting. Persian rugs subtly suggested warmth, glamour, and intimacy. But it was the atmosphere of the room, more than its actual contents, which arrested me. It vibrated with the personality of its owner; it awaited his return; it made one feel an intruder. Only the powerful can impress their individuality on the inanimate, and this library bore silent but eloquent testimony to the power of its master. The room was a creation, not an arrangement, and in one instant it told me more of Scrivener than Winkworth or Matthews had done. It told more and it knew more.

The rays of the setting sun filled the room with a soft radiance which caressed its beauty and quickened its colour. I stood motionless. The only sound was the low murmur of the fire.

"Would you like to have tea in this room, sir?"

"Yes, in about ten minutes," I replied.

I went into the bedroom, changed, and returned to the library just as Matthews appeared with the tea.

As I had tea I reviewed the conversations I had had with Winkworth and Matthews, endeavouring to remember every word that had been said. Did they know nothing of Scrivener, or were they deliberately hiding their knowledge? I felt that the answer to this question was of considerable importance, but the more I considered the conversations I had had with them, the more convinced I became that Winkworth professed a knowledge he did not possess, whereas Matthews made no attempt to disguise her ignorance. One thing, however, I felt definitely, and it stirred my curiosity: neither of them seemed surprised that Scrivener had decided to employ a total stranger as his secretary. Winkworth certainly had said that Scrivener was eccentric. Did he regard my appointment simply as another example of his client's eccentricity?

Or was there an explanation of an entirely different order? Was I necessary to the fulfilment of some plot of Scrivener's? Was he engaged in some underground activity in which I could be made to serve some end outside the range of my imagination? I knew of course that the promise of easy money is the bait which attracts recruits to the underworld. The façade which Scrivener presented to the world was reputable enough but that fact was of no significance whatever. No one believes in respectability nowadays, but most people, especially criminals, are careful to present an exterior of unimpeachable respectability. But appearances do not deceive me and for an excellent reason.

I have had little experience as the world uses the word: I have travelled very little and I have not met a great number of people. But I have known years of loneliness and there is a type of experience which is revealed only to the lonely. During those years I was forced to learn a good deal about myself and that knowledge taught me what to look for in others. If you have been behind the scenes, you never regain the illusion which belongs to a person who has always been simply a member of the audience. I have been behind a certain type of scenery, with the result that I am not to be deceived by appearances. The façade which people present to the world usually tells you only what they wish you to believe about them.

What did Scrivener wish me to believe about him? Presumably that he was an eccentric philanthropist. The normal man does not engage a stranger for a secretary without even seeing him, pay him generously, and let him live in his home. There was a mystery in all this and I decided to be on the alert for clues to aid me in its solution. I had no regrets, I had no one to consider. I had never experienced adventure of this type before and I welcomed it.

I had finished tea. It was perfectly still in the library. The light from the fire illuminated the titles of the volumes on the shelves. I sat, smoking a cigarette, and admiring the slender beauty of the Adam chimneypiece. I had the odd sensation that someone was in the room, and I felt that some drama was about to be enacted between me and this stranger. I do not mean that I felt that the room was haunted by some ghost. On the contrary, it was haunted by the personality of its living owner and the longer I remained in the room, the more aware I became of the power of this personality. It had set its seal even on the silence. I felt that it knew what I was, and that I was there by the election of its will.

Matthews appeared, and removed the tea. Dinner was to be served at eight o'clock. I had nothing to do till then, for I had decided not to begin work till the Monday. Moreover I was convinced that as my work consisted chiefly of cataloguing the books in the library, I should have ample time to complete it even if Scrivener returned to London sooner than I anticipated. For some reason I felt that it would be two or three months before he appeared.

Suddenly I remembered that Matthews had said that Scrivener had left a note for me. I had been so busy trying to solve the mystery of my engagement that I had forgotten the only tangible evidence at present available. I rose, crossed to the writing desk, and looked for the letter. I saw it immediately and was impressed by the clear, bold, handwriting on the envelope. I returned to the fire, sat down and began to read the letter. It was longer than I expected and read as follows:

"DEAR MR. WREXHAM,

"It was a great disappointment to me not to see you before I left London. It was necessary, however, for me to leave immediately and I do not know how long I shall be away.

"The instructions I have for you are few and may be briefly expressed. My wishes are more numerous and must be set forth in full. As to instructions: as you know, I want you to catalogue the books in my library. In no circumstances do I want any volume to be lent to anyone. The letters which come for me should be redirected. My address is written on the enclosed sheet. I should like the name of any caller to be sent to me.

"Next, as to my wishes: in the first place, it is my wish that you should live in my flat, and give orders to my servant as if you were in your own home. I realize that the work you will do for me will not occupy all your time—and there is no hurry for its completion. Now, I do not wish you to be dull. Should you feel inclined to go to the theatre, or a concert, please do so and obtain your seat at my agents. Also, it is my wish that you should get any clothes you require at my tailors. It is essential to have clothes for every occasion, even if one never goes anywhere. Should you require any *additional money at any time, Mr. Walter Winkworth has instructions to give it to you.*

"The fact that you are now reading this letter means that you have met Mr. Winkworth. I want to make it quite clear that he did not see the letter you wrote to me. Only I have seen it and, after reading it carefully, I decided that you should be my secretary. I mention these facts for several reasons: one is that Mr. Winkworth, in these circumstances, may not have received you with elaborate courtesy. Should this be so, do not let it disturb you. His attitude towards you may possibly alter. In any event, Mr. Winkworth is entirely normal and it is a dispensation of Providence that the normal have no insight of any kind. This fact makes life possible for the degenerate as well as the elect.

"One last word: you will write to me when necessary. The address given you—which is that of my bankers in Paris—will find me, but some days may elapse before a reply reaches you, as in all probability they will have to forward your letter to me. I shall keep them informed of my address, but I think it will be simpler for you always to write to them.

"I hope you will be comfortable and that you will follow your own inclinations without consulting me.

"Yours sincerely,

"JONATHAN SCRIVENER."

I read this letter twice. I looked at the sheet enclosed. The addresses of the bank in Paris, the theatre agents, and the tailors, were set forth in the same bold writing.

I rose and began to pace the room, the letter still in my hand. Was I concerned with a madman? The idea crossed my mind, but I dismissed it immediately. The letter was unusual, but it was entirely sane. But what did this man want with me? The letter admitted that my work was practically negligible. And why was he prepared to provide my amusements and my clothes, in addition to housing and food and paying me a good salary?

I found no answer to these questions. For a full hour I paced up and down the room trying to imagine an explanation, however fantastic, of the circumstances in which I found myself. It was useless. I read the letter again, analysing each sentence. His manner of referring to Winkworth clearly revealed that Scrivener recognized that both he and I were set apart from others and I felt certain that he wished me to know that he realized this. But *why* did he wish to establish this link between us? And why did he provide a means by which I could obtain additional money? And what logical reason was there to imagine that Winkworth's attitude towards me would change?

At precisely eight o'clock Matthews served the best dinner I had ever had. It consisted of entirely plain food of perfect quality, perfectly cooked. While I was having coffee, she gave me a latchkey for my use. In the course of a brief conversation I discovered that she did not sleep in the flat. She was married and lived near Victoria. At half past nine, she left the flat. I was alone.

I explored the kitchen and the bathroom and studied the hall again, then I returned to the library. I felt tired and decided to go to bed and read. I took a volume at random from the shelves. By an effort of will, I banished all speculations concerning Scrivener. His letter had served only to deepen the mystery. One thing, however, I decided definitely; he wished to provide me with amusements and clothes—he should do so. I must accept all the terms of his amazing offer to me, or reject them all. I must remain his secretary, or write immediately and resign. I was determined to continue the adventure, and so I decided to comply with each and all of his wishes—and await developments. His return would explain everything. And if he did not return for some time, possibly events would afford some indications as to why he required me in his service. . . .

I propped up the pillows behind me, switched on the reading lamp by the side of the bed, and opened my book.

II

A week elapsed. I must give a brief account of that week in order to indicate the background upon which events developed. I spent the mornings in the library, making a preliminary survey of the volumes I had to catalogue. In the afternoon I wandered about discovering London. It was a living library to me. I soon learnt that London is most beautiful at dawn and late at night; and that one can know a more intimate solitude among its moving multitudes than in the isolation of the country.

I visited Scrivener's tailors and ordered some clothes but I decided that for the time being I did not wish to go to a theatre. My own situation was dramatic enough and the hours I spent each morning in the library provided me with an intricate problem in the terms of actual life.

I know a good deal about books for the adequate reason that for several years books were my substitute for life. Nevertheless, the volumes on Scrivener's shelves were a new experience. In the first place there were books on most subjects, and yet no attempt had been made to group them systematically. This fact convinced me that, although Scrivener had read widely, he was in no sense a bookworm. My next discovery was that each volume bore on the fly-leaf Scrivener's name and that of the town in which the volume had been purchased, also the date. After I had glanced at a number of these inscriptions I realized the extent to which Scrivener had travelled. I found the name of every town of any note in Europe and it was clear that he had visited most American cities.

I spent my first two mornings in studying these inscriptions and evolved the idea of grouping the volumes chronologically. But a new discovery of greater significance temporarily diverted my attention. I found that several passages in each book were marked and often there was a marginal note in Scrivener's handwriting. But what awakened my curiosity was the fact that a passage marked in one volume—presumably as a sign of approval—was totally at variance in sentiment with that marked in another. It seemed quite impossible that the two passages could have been selected for emphasis by the same reader.

I soon discovered, however, that this contradiction did not apply simply to passages marked in different books. It applied to the books themselves. One group of books bore no relation whatever to another. It is necessary to make this clear. Scrivener's library might have been the result of mixing the libraries of half-a-dozen different men, each one of whom was separated from the others intellectually and temperamentally. One section of the books might have belonged to a scientist, another to a poet, a third to a philosopher, a fourth to a mystic, a fifth to a psychologist, a sixth to an occultist. And one section might have belonged to a mental sensualist. Yet each volume contained conclusive evidence that it had been studied by Scrivener. If the inscription on the fly-leaf of each volume gave proof of the extent to which Scrivener had travelled, the books themselves established the fact that his intellectual and imaginative journeys had been equally extensive. He had adventured far and wide in two worlds.

It was strange that I should be in the position to follow his tracks in the invisible world and yet remain entirely ignorant of him in the world of the flesh. Moreover, remarkably enough, I had long held the theory that access to a man's intimate library would reveal more, to a person of perception, than hours of the usual type of conversation in which the participants are concerned to conceal rather than to reveal the nature of their thoughts. In a somewhat dramatic manner I now found myself in the position to test my own theory.

I failed to test it. Had I succeeded, I should, perhaps, have offered an adventure different in kind from the one I have set out to present. I failed, and the following pages will reveal the cause of that failure, but it is essential to make it clear that after I had been living in Scrivener's flat for a week, I had made up my mind to group the books in his library chronologically. That is, I had decided that I would range together the books that had been purchased, say, in 1918, read each book carefully, then pass on to the books which had been purchased during the following year. I even began my task, and it seemed certain that nothing would prevent my finishing it. I had time, the books were within reach of my hand, I had no distractions. But I was soon to discover that I was not the only person interested in the mystery of Scrivener and I was destined to discover this fact in somewhat bewildering circumstances. Before narrating the first of these, a brief explanation is desirable.

If I were writing a novel, my task would be relatively simple.

I imagine that most novelists introduce each character at a point selected; elaborate that character's psychology on the background of a number of contrived incidents; then engineer that each component part of the jig-saw puzzle shall find its appropriate place precisely at that moment when the novel reaches its climax and its end. I have no such freedom. I have to record events as, and when, they occurred. I have to set down happenings which were, and are, a mystery to me. The persons I have to present are not persons chosen by me: they are people who appeared, and they cared nothing whether their entrances and exits fitted neatly into the scheme of a book.

Allowing for obvious differences, I am somewhat in the position of a novelist who had evolved a plot and characters for a novel. He was about to begin to write, when his characters suddenly became living human beings, independent of his will, who went their ways irrespective of the limitations imposed by an arbitrary plot. Whereupon the novelist became simply an additional character in a series of scenes and situations not of his contriving.

One final word. The rest of this book is already written. I wrote it at the time the events related therein occurred. I have only added a sentence or two. These first two chapters were written last, because I had no idea of publishing this book when I was writing the chapters which follow. This sentence is, therefore, the end of the book—for me. And the end of the introduction—for you.

CHAPTER III

I

I was sitting at the writing desk in the library with five or six of Scrivener's books in front of me. It was about four o'clock in the afternoon. For over an hour I had been studying a copy of Amiel's *Journal*. I knew the book intimately but certain notes of Scrivener's in the margin held my attention. To understand Amiel even superficially it is necessary to have been lonely, and there seemed a contradiction between the externals of Scrivener's life and the type of loneliness with which Amiel was too familiar.

I was sitting with closed eyes, striving to resolve this contradiction. Gradually, almost imperceptibly, the conviction deepened in me that I was not alone. At first I disregarded it. I knew that Matthews had left the flat nearly two hours ago and, in the second place, I had experienced this sensation several times during the last week. On each occasion, however, I had ascribed it to the atmosphere of the library being dominated by Scrivener's personality. But in the present instance neither logic nor experience could convince me. I was certain that someone was in the room. In order to prove myself wrong, I opened my eyes and looked towards the door.

A woman stood in the middle of the room regarding me with candid curiosity. I rose slowly and stared at her. I do not know which surprised me more: the miracle of her entrance, or the mystery of her beauty. I use the word "mystery" deliberately. She was slight and delicately made, rather tall, with wide-set grey eyes. Her short, golden hair clustered luxuriantly about her perfectly poised head. Her colouring and the strange precision of her features reminded me of a miniature painted by a great master. She was attractively dressed but clothes seemed accidental to her—a concession to necessity. The harmony of her body and the aura of freedom which invested her suggested speed, space, the rhythm of wind and wave.

For a full minute we gazed at each other.

"How did you get in?" I asked at last.

She opened her hand and I saw a latchkey. In spite of my surprise, I noticed the extraordinary delicacy of her tiny wrist. I must have remained silent for some seconds, for I was somewhat startled by hearing her ask:

"And how did you get in?"

I glanced at her quickly but she was not smiling. On the contrary she was looking at me with the gravity of a child eager to obtain information.

"I live here," I answered.

She turned away and looked round the room with evident interest.

"I have never been in this room before and I did not know that anyone lived with Mr. Scrivener."

She articulated each word perfectly: her speech corresponded exactly with the precision of her features.

"You have never been in this room before," I exclaimed.

"No, never. The door of the sitting-room was locked, so I tried the door of this room."

"Has the door of this room always been locked when you have been here before?" Some impulse prompted me to ask the question.

"Yes, always. Have you been living here for a long time?"

"No, just over a week," I replied.

"And where is Mr. Scrivener?"

"He is away."

"Away!" She turned and looked at me with great inquiring eyes. "He did not tell me he was going away. When did he go?"

"Do sit down," I said. "Mine is rather an involved story. You may be able to explain certain things which are mysterious to me."

She looked round the room again before accepting my invitation, then she sat down near the desk.

"Are these books yours?" she asked.

"No. They are Mr. Scrivener's. Let me explain briefly. I am Mr. Scrivener's secretary. He engaged me in that capacity just over a week ago. All the arrangements were made through his lawyer. I have never seen him." I paused, expecting her to express surprise, but her expression did not change. "He went away just before I came here. It was his wish that I should live here during his absence and I have no idea how long he will be away."

"What made him choose you for a secretary, if he did not know you?"

"I do not know," I replied. "I saw his advertisement in *The Times* and I applied for the position. I have to catalogue the books you see on these shelves."

Her next remark had no logical connection with my explanation.

"When he was here, this room and the room next to it were always locked. Now these rooms are open and the sitting-room, in which I used to see him, is locked. It's all rather mysterious, isn't it? But I am not surprised at that because I really know nothing about him at all."

I said nothing and for some moments there was silence. I could see that the necessity for explaining her possession of a latchkey had not yet presented itself. She began questioning me about the books and what sort of life I was leading in Scrivener's flat. Although she asked a number of questions and listened attentively to my replies, I felt that the conversation was only incidental and that her real interest in me was centred elsewhere. In fact I had the curious sensation that she was getting to know me in some silent region to which she had access, and that whether she gave or withheld her confidence did not depend on what was said between us. The sound of her voice, no less than her appearance, fascinated me. The passing of time, and the fact that we were strangers, seemed equally irrelevant. She could not have been more than twenty-three, but I felt that the essential in her had survived both education and environment and that she was strong, secure, in a power which was inalienably her own. I decided to ask no questions and to let the conversation go its own way.

"What will you do when you have catalogued the books?" she asked.

"I do not know. I shall write and tell Mr. Scrivener and do as he wishes. Anyhow, I am glad I came here. I have no plans of any kind for the future."

She sat quite still looking at me intently. Suddenly she smiled and instantly I smiled in reply. She had reached some decision and her whole body seemed to indicate the fact. She crossed her legs, clasped her hands round her knee and leaned back slightly.

"What's your name?" she asked.

"Wrexham. James Wrexham."

"I am Pauline Mandeville. I have known Jonathan for only two months. I always call him Jonathan. But I told you the truth when I said just now that I know practically nothing about him. He interests me very much—much more than anyone I know. But tell me this: why didn't you question me about him?"

"The only explanations worth having are those which are offered."

She laughed and I knew immediately that she laughed seldom. Repetition robs most things of their intrinsic qualities, and laughter of its music.

"But surely you must have wondered why I had a latchkey to this flat?"

"Where everything is a mystery nothing is mysterious," I replied. "Why should you explain anything to me?"

"But I want you to know. You are quite familiar to me. I haven't just met you—I have recognized you. Jonathan was brought to dinner at my home some two months ago by Sir Mortimer Dankin. Have you heard of him?"

"He's an actor, isn't he?" I asked.

"Yes. Jonathan defined him, in his presence, as an actor who had been knighted, who was of a most excellent family, who had been a Blue at golf, and who was the greatest snob on the English stage. He added that the last achievement was his greatest, as the competition was so desperately keen. He was extraordinarily amusing and brilliant that night. That was our first meeting. We talked a good deal after dinner. Then I came to see him here. I've been very frequently during the last two months. He gave me a latchkey so that I could come in whenever I wanted to."

"Have you ever met anyone else here?" Again something prompted me to ask the question.

"No, never. Why do you ask?"

"I wondered, that's all."

"I know no more about him than I did when I first met him. It's quite obvious that he could be very successful in almost any career. He is brilliant in so many ways. I wish you had met him." She paused, then went on: "I don't think my father liked him, but I have complete freedom at home, although I'm an only child, and I have several friends my parents do not know and of whom they would not approve. Do you know where Jonathan is?" she added.

"No. I have an address in Paris which will find him. I confess to you frankly that my whole position here is a complete mystery to me."

"You will solve it," she answered, "because you have surrendered yourself to it. I feel quite certain that Jonathan has a very definite purpose in bringing you here. I know only two things about him: one is that behind his actions there is always a definite purpose, and the other is that the past does not exist for him. If he does not meet me again, I shall be forgotten."

As the conversation developed, I discovered that her omissions were more significant than anything she actually said. I became more and more intrigued by the number and quality of unusual circumstances concerning which she evidently did not consider any explanation to be necessary. Thus, she ignored the fact that she was discussing Scrivener with a man who, after all, was his paid servant. Also, she was giving her confidence to a person of whose existence she had been ignorant half an hour ago. Something in her whole attitude suggested, however, that the conventions were meaningless for her. I felt that she was one of those people who could make no compromise between frankness and silence.

"Can I come here again?" she asked suddenly.

"Of course; whenever you like."

"Very well. I shall keep my latchkey. I think we shall get on together. Already we have one link in common."

"The mystery of Scrivener?" I asked.

"Yes. It's quite obvious that he knew that we should meet. He must have wanted us to meet. He's using us in some way. Perhaps he uses everyone."

"And are you willing to be used?"

She looked at me with a curious expression in her eyes before she answered.

"Yes. I feel that I am involved. I have never felt that with anyone else. There's a problem in his life. I do not know what it is but I feel that the way in which he deals with it affects me. I've told no one that and—like anything that is really true—it sounds quite ridiculous when it is put into words. It may be all nonsense. He may be simply amusing himself with me."

"In one sense, then, you don't trust him at all."

Again she looked at me before she replied:

"I shan't be able to explain, but I'll try if you like."

"Try," I said with a smile.

"It seems to me that here and there are people who simply cannot be judged by accepted standards. Because they are what they are, they have temptations of a different order from other people. This is partly Jonathan's theory. Sometimes the more highly developed they are, the greater becomes the attraction of the abyss. The sins they commit are different in kind from the sins of others."

"Perhaps they are the only people who are capable of sin," I interposed. "What passes for sin is merely ignorance."

"He said much the same," she said slowly. "I believe he is that type. He told me about a man he knew who founded some mystical or occult order. He appears to have been very remarkable. But what interested Jonathan was the kind of scandal which was associated with his name. No one knew anything about him, but Jonathan held that the *type* of scandal such a man's enemies invent is very significant."

"He discussed odd subjects with you."

"But you agree with what he said?"

Something in her tone made me certain that her interest in the subject was not superficial.

"Yes. And you think accepted standards are irrelevant where Scrivener is concerned?"

"I am certain of it," she said quietly.

She was not looking at me and I studied her carefully. There is in all of us a spirit of scepticism which remains with us all our lives. Our most treasured beliefs dwell in its shadow. It exists because we are all afraid of being duped. And with some of us, who have knelt before many idols only to discover eventually that they are things of stone made by men, this spirit of scepticism persists no matter how convincing the evidence may be that our doubts are baseless. For some of us it is not enough to see Lazarus raised from the dead.

And so, in this instance: was this woman—who looked as if a lie could not live in her presence—in reality an artist in deception, who was playing a part in some drama of which I was ignorant, yet one in which I was involved? I was certain she was not—until I remembered that one is never certain.

Logically, her story was ridiculous. Was it probable that the library and the rooms I now occupied had always been locked on her previous visits? It sounded melodramatic nonsense. Then her possession of a latchkey. She was extraordinarily beautiful. Scrivener was still a young man, and it was clear that he had considerable influence over her. Was it not possible that he simply employed greater psychology than other men in the art of seduction? Might not my engagement be in the nature of a trap?

Questions thronged through my mind. I know quite well the world I am in and the level on which most lives are lived. Knowledge does not cease to be knowledge because it is ignored. Men will still know how to make guns even if armaments are totally abolished. I knew that it was very remarkable to obtain the salary I received for doing practically nothing: so remarkable that the only logical explanation was that I was concerned either with a madman or with a man who in some unimaginable way was going to get value for his money.

These thoughts and a hundred others raced through my mind as I gazed at my visitor. Her very appearance seemed an answer to all my suspicions, but that answer was inaudible on the plane of logic. She rose and held out her hand.

"I must go, but we shall meet again soon. It will not disturb you if I come in here when the mood brings me?"

"Not in the least. Come whenever you like."

We shook hands and in another moment she had gone.

For the rest of the day I tried to construct a theory which would explain the circumstances of my situation, but I was soon forced to the conclusion that the additional data furnished by Pauline's visit had served only to darken the mystery. It was evident, however, as she had pointed out, that Scrivener knew that we should meet and desired that meeting. I remembered that in his letter he had asked me to communicate the names of any callers. I decided to obey the letter of his instructions and I, therefore, sent him a line merely saying that Miss Pauline Mandeville had called, but I gave no indication as to the nature of the conversation which had taken place between us.

I spent some time trying to recall every word that had been said during Pauline's visit and eventually I decided that nothing was so extraordinary as the fact that she had shown no surprise on learning the manner in which I had become Scrivener's secretary. Her reaction to that information showed clearly that she ignored traditional standards where Scrivener was concerned. It was also interesting that she entirely overlooked his lack of courtesy in leaving England without letting her know of his departure. She had not even taken the trouble to refer to this fact. It was abundantly clear that her estimate of him was such that it was not in his power to surprise her by the eccentricity of his actions. The more I considered her visit, the more convinced I became that if she had been his accomplice, she would have adopted a different method in her approach to me.

But I found it difficult to regard her simply as a character in a plot I was trying to unravel. She had attracted me as no one else had ever done, and the quality of that attraction, and the region from which it was exercised, evaded analysis. She was familiar to me with the elusive familiarity of a person encountered in a dream. Had she felt this? I remembered that she had said: "I haven't just met you—I have recognized you." And perhaps it was not unimportant that the headings under which we usually assess a person—age, class, means and so on—lost their significance when applied to her.

All the evening my thoughts continued to centre in her. I felt definitely that our meeting was only an incident in a drama about to begin and one in which I was destined to play a prominent part. I was excited, apprehensive, and impatient for further developments.

Just before midnight I went out into the Mall. It had been raining, but the rain had ceased and a great wind rushed through the

November night. The lights flickered and I could hear the trees rocking and groaning in the gale. The Mall was deserted and every now and again an eddy of dead leaves rustled eerily at my feet in piteous colloquy. Across the Green Park I could see the moving lights of the cars in Piccadilly; they looked like the eyes of invisible monsters. Then suddenly the clouds parted and a haggard and tragic moon reeled into view. Great menacing clouds raced past her like storm-tossed galleons helpless before the tempest. Then darkness and the wind claimed the night again.

II

Three days passed. I did little work in the library. A restless spirit possessed me and I spent much of my time studying the unfamiliar London which surrounded me. The days were fine, the nights frosty and hung with bright steely stars. Any memories I had of London were twenty years old and the contrast between the city I remembered and the one in which I found myself was nothing short of incredible—all had changed. The city I remembered had individuality; the city I was in had none. The difference is best established by the statement that where once everything had been *à la carte*, now everything was *table d'hôte*. Wherever I went, whatever the time, there were hordes of people—restless, irritable, or apathetic people—staring into shops, herding into 'buses, or waiting impatiently to cross streets which were congested with every type of vehicle, capable of every variety of speed. The gloom, particularly on the faces of the men, was remarkably apparent. In a thousand unsuspected places the results of ordeal by battle were unmistakably clear. These people were weary, sceptical, disillusioned. They sought for pleasure with all the feverish activity of the unhappy. Superficially, the women all looked alike but they were infinitely better dressed than they had been twenty years ago. The slut had disappeared, a fact frequently overlooked by critics of present day women.

I discovered that modern people never smile. They either shriek with laughter or look as if funerals were the order of the day. The dignity of which we English used to boast had vanished; everyone was slightly hysterical and seemed to be waiting for something to happen—half hoping that it would, yet half terrified that it might. The conversations which I overheard were always about money. It was quite obvious that no one saved sixpence, that Remorse was the shadow which dogged extravagance, and that a car of any sort was regarded as the highest pinnacle of human felicity. The garage has become our spiritual home.

Paradoxes were everywhere. For instance, it seemed to me that everyone was exceedingly class conscious when the plain fact of the matter was that classes had ceased to exist and that everyone now belonged to one vast undifferentiated mass. Democracy had triumphed at the precise moment when everyone had ceased to believe in it. Politics had become a longer word for chaos. At the time of which I am writing the Conservatives were in power. The Opposition was provided wholly by the supporters of the Government. The Labour Party was far too busy preparing its programme, or dealing with revolution in its own ranks, or explaining that it had not stolen its panaceas from the Liberals, to spare any time for effective criticisms of the Government's proposals. Meanwhile, as ever, the country was run by the Civil Service.

As to the Church, it seemed to exist precariously in the terms of a permanent earthquake.

My wanderings in London soon established the fact that its value as an antique was diminishing and that, as a modern city, it was a failure. Artists were no longer concerned with its welfare and everywhere the engineer was doing his splendid worst.

Only at dawn and in the depths of night was the city beautiful to me. In the hush of its silence were the voices of its memories. . . .

It was a Thursday afternoon. I had not been out all day as I had been absorbed in the study of a copy of Balzac's *Seraphita* which I had discovered in one of the drawers of the writing desk. Scrivener had obtained it some years ago, and evidently had read it more than once. This book, which was clearly one result of Balzac's sudden enthusiasm for Swedenborg, had always interested me but the passages marked by Scrivener, and certain of his comments in the margin, created an additional attraction. I was speculating on the remarkable diversity of the minds focussed in the volume before me, when the door opened and a woman came into the room.

She was entirely self-possessed and her assurance did not desert her on finding herself confronted by a stranger. She was wrapped in a fur coat which, even to my inexperienced eyes, was clearly of great value. But the dominating impression caused by her appearance was that I had seen her before. This sense of familiarity had nothing in common with that which I had felt in the presence of Pauline. It related to a definite background which momentarily I could not remember. She saw my perplexity and guessed its cause.

"Please have no hesitation in staring at me. I am quite used to it and it may help you to collect your memories."

She spoke in a light, ironical tone, as she thrust her face slightly forward for my inspection. I accepted her invitation and studied her minutely. In every way she was a contrast to Pauline: her hair was jet-black, her eyes were very dark, and her skin had something of the pallor of ivory. The features were proud, arrogant, fearless. Her red lips were provocative and her smile was a challenge. Only a glance was necessary to realize the power that such a type of beauty must inevitably confer. The admiration it awakes converts it into a weapon, to be used or ignored at the will of its possessor.

"I can see that you can't remember. Perhaps my name will help. I am Francesca Bellamy."

Directly I heard her name I understood why she was familiar to me. Just over a year ago her photograph had been in all the papers in regard to a tragedy which had been a mystery at the time and which still remained unsolved. I had been interested in the case and strangely enough it had been the photograph of the woman before me which had aroused my curiosity and impelled me to study all the available details. Briefly they were these: a well-known financier, Stanley Bellamy, shot himself in Paris. His name had often figured prominently in the papers in regard to various sensational financial deals and it was confidently anticipated that he had amassed a fortune. Directly the world learnt of his suicide, however, it was immediately assumed that revelations as to enormous losses would ensue. Editors were about to insert articles on the frailty of human nature, and the vanity of all mortal ambitions, when it was established that Stanley Bellamy's fortune had been underestimated and that he had just brought the biggest deal of his career to a triumphant conclusion. Everyone was amazed. Nothing shakes the foundations of our civilization so violently as the suicide of a millionaire. It is atheism in high places. Immediately, however, revelations on another level were eagerly anticipated. Blackmail, disease, remorse were all mentioned as attractive possibilities. But, to the disgust of press and public alike, no revelations of any kind were forthcoming. Bellamy had left a note simply saying that he was entirely sane and that he had taken his own life. By a will, made only a few months before his death, he left the whole of his fortune to his wife. It was her attitude, as reported in the press, which had interested me at the time. She had maintained that her husband's suicide was a complete mystery to her, that there had been no disagreement of any kind between them, and that she could only conjecture that eventually circumstances, which she could not imagine, would come to light and furnish an explanation of the tragedy. Her photograph was in every paper. It emerged like a beautiful mask from the flood of sensational conjecture surrounding it. Its pride and its beauty isolated it from the hysteria of which it was the centre.

A bitter smile curled her lips as she said: "I see that you *do* remember."

"I remember all the details perfectly," I replied.

She turned away and crossed to the fire.

"I'll take off my coat, if you don't mind," she said lightly. "This room is beautifully warm—a rare phenomenon in England. But I daresay there are excellent draughts to make up for it."

I glanced at her and became aware that there was something foreign in her appearance. It was only a hint, but it was there. She slipped out of her coat and I realized that the beauty of her figure, which had received every variety of journalistic attention at the time of her husband's suicide, had not been over-praised. She was tall, exquisitely developed, and there was sinuous grace in every attitude and gesture.

She sat down in an armchair and lit a cigarette.

"And now, as you know everything about me, perhaps you'll tell me who you are, why you are here, and where Mr. Scrivener is."

"I am James Wrexham. I am here because I am Mr. Scrivener's secretary. He is away. Do you mind telling me," I asked, "how you got in?"

"In the simplest way possible—with a latchkey. I start our conversation under a double disadvantage, you see. I shall, however, equalize matters somewhat by thinking the worst about you till you produce convincing proofs that such an attitude is unjustified." She laughed lightly, but I could see that she was not altogether joking. "How long have you been Mr. Scrivener's secretary, and why does he want one?"

I explained the circumstances under which I had become Scrivener's secretary and saw immediately that she did not believe one word of my explanation.

"All that is most romantic," she said when I had finished, "and would make an excellent opening for a novel." She looked round the room as if it would furnish a more satisfactory explanation of my presence than I had done.

"It's rather a pleasant room," I said impartially.

"You know quite well," she rejoined, "that I have never seen it before."

"I thought it possible, but I did not know," I answered.

She subjected me to a searching scrutiny before she spoke again: "When does Mr. Scrivener return?"

"What is the point of my answering, Mrs. Bellamy? It's quite clear that you don't believe a word I say."

She threw back her head and laughed with real pleasure. "Of course I don't," she exclaimed. "Would you believe a word that I said? Suppose that I told you that I had known Jonathan for only a month and that although I have a latchkey to his flat we are nothing to each other. Would you believe it?"

"Certainly," I replied.

"Then you're either a fool or a genius," she answered. "Do you always believe what people tell you? You cannot know much about this world."

"I don't," I answered, "though I think I am about to learn a good deal. But you overlook certain facts: I am a nobody; why should you take the trouble to lie to me? I am Mr. Scrivener's paid servant. At any time he may return and my relations with him may end. Why, then, should I take the trouble to lie to you?" She said nothing, and after a pause I continued: "Besides, is there much value in a conversation when one side is determined to think that the other is lying?"

"You're amusing," she said, "and I'm duly grateful. I agree with you too, but not because of the reasons you have given. All human relations are based on a false assumption, and so I must assume that you are not playing a part or, as you say, there's no point in our going on with our conversation. I want to go on with it for several reasons. It's pleasant in here, the draughts haven't turned up yet, and you are an individual."

"Then let me offer you one of Mr. Scrivener's cigarettes," I said handing her a box.

She put down the cigarette she had just finished and accepted my offer.

"Answer me one thing," she began. "But before I go on, is there anything you hold sacred?"

"There is," I replied.

"I knew you were an original, but it's fortunate as it happens. Answer me one thing and tell me the truth by whatever it is that you hold sacred: is it true that you have never seen Jonathan?"

"It is true," I answered.

"And you do not know when he will return?"

"I do not know that, and I do not know where he is. I have an address in Paris which will find him. I'm sorry to disappoint you, Mrs. Bellamy, but every word I told you as to the manner in which I came here was literally and exactly true. You have no need of your rapier where I am concerned. I am not interested enough in any human being in the world to tell lies at his or her bidding."

"You apparently do not mind then if Jonathan is using you for some obscure reason of his own."

"I believe more in intuition than in logic. Something made me apply for this job, something made me accept it, and something advises me to remain here. That may sound pretentious but it's true. Also I do not mind very much what happens to me."

She looked at me intently before she said: "All of which means that you have lived a lot alone."

"You are quite right. You already know my name. If you are interested enough, which is scarcely imaginable, you can verify the life I have lived." I then told her briefly my history since I left school till the day on which I entered Scrivener's service. I ended by saying: "Much that I have told you is easily verified."

"And why do you want to put all your cards on the table?" she asked.

"Because it is a waste of time for us to fence with each other. I will not allow humbug in my relations with others and I have the right to take that stand because I am prepared to be alone."

"You're an odd person," she said, almost to herself. "You have answered all the questions I have not asked and yet you have not cross-examined me. Perhaps you are about to begin."

I did not answer and for some minutes there was silence. Then she turned to me with a sudden movement which was indicative of the great vitality hidden beneath her mask of indolence.

"Do you know the only thing which makes life worth anything?"

"What do you think it is?"

She laughed. "That's a subtle criticism. It's this: the element of surprise. It's the only colour element left. I came here, opened the front door, expecting to find Jonathan. The sitting-room was locked, I find a stranger in a room I had never entered before. He tells me that he is Jonathan's secretary, that Jonathan is away for an indefinite period, and then he tells me the story of his life. The last being a feat which I could never accomplish in any circumstances whatever. Very well! All that is thrilling. You are now a friend of mine. That may not be a distinction. You possess, however, the only necessary qualification."

"And that is?" I asked.

"You interest me. Your technique in dealing with me was original. Shall I tell you what Jonathan is to me? Or shall I give you my latchkey and go?"

"I hope you will not go," I replied, "and I hope you will retain your latchkey."

"So you do not mind if I suddenly appear in this flat at any time, day or night?"

"Not in the least," I answered.

"You must lead quite a decent life," she said meditatively. "I'll make a compact with you. I won't discuss subjects concerning which I should be obliged to edit the truth. That is, I'll be frank where frankness is possible. You didn't mind, by the way, my calling you odd just now, did you?"

"It's happened before," I replied with a smile, "and I fancy it may happen again."

She rose, stretched herself, and looked down at me. She was a little like a lioness contemplating some queer object which had just appeared in her cage. It flashed across my mind what hell it would be to love her. For the first time I noticed her white, tapering hands and the long, slightly curling, fingers. I was certain that those hands had not trembled when she had heard that her husband had committed suicide. She still stood looking down at me, then she clasped her hands behind her head, and stared at the ceiling, her dark eyes bright with amusement. I have little doubt that she was aware that her attitude accentuated the magnificent lines of her figure.

"I think I'm a little afraid of you, Mr. Wrexham."

"I think you have already broken your compact, Mrs. Bellamy," I replied quietly.

She laughed, then went and settled herself on a sofa. "I'm going to tell you what I know about Jonathan. I only actually met him two or three months ago, but I had heard of him for years. It's a mystery that we did not meet long ago, but we both go abroad a good deal and possibly he avoided meeting me. You know, of course, that he's a very gifted person?"

"I know only what his lawyer told me. I gathered he was gifted but I was given no details."

"Was it Mr. Walter Winkworth?"

I nodded and she laughed softly.

"Isn't he the most perfect fool God ever made? I go to him sometimes because he's much more amusing than a comedy and only a trifle more expensive. What a butler was lost to the world when that man decided to become a solicitor! Where was I?"

"You were going to tell me about Mr. Scrivener's gifts," I reminded her.

"Of course. He could be famous as a pianist if he had wanted to be, or a writer, or an actor. You look surprised. It's perfectly true. Ignorant people imagine that he has not troubled to succeed because he is wealthy. That's nonsense. It may be pride; it may be that nothing that is easy attracts him; but it is not laziness. I knew, of course, that he had heard of me and I wrote and asked him to come to see me. He replied that my communication should have reached him through my seconds. It was very intelligent of him to recognize from the beginning that our relations would be in the nature of a duel."

She laughed lightly as she put another cushion behind her head.

"Either the duel has not begun, or you have not been wounded," I said with a smile.

"My defence is excellent," she answered.

"You found yourself on the defensive then?"

"Yes, immediately." There was a pause, then she added: "I don't think I'll tell you why. No, not yet, at any rate. I am far from convinced that you are not more subtle than any of us."

"I know nothing of your world," I answered. "I am absolutely ignorant of its ways and its weapons."

"That's what is so terrifying about you. I wonder what Jonathan's game is with you. You are certain there is no one who might have told him about you? He does not leap in the dark."

"There is no one," I answered, "besides, what was there to tell?"

She did not answer and there was silence for some moments. Then she said:

"I have seen a good deal of him these last few weeks. In some ways I hate him. He reduces one's other friends to shadows. You understand," she said with a trace of insolence, "that in saying what I have said I've made allowance for the possibility that you may be an accomplice of his?"

"Yes, I understand that," I replied.

"The fact that you ask so few questions is a little suspicious."

"Then let me ask you this: do you mind telling me what Mr. Scrivener looks like? I have no mental picture of my employer."

She looked at me narrowly. "Do you *really* expect me to believe that you saw an advertisement in the paper and wrote saying: *Dear Sir, I should like the job. Yours faithfully, James Wrexham*, that you were successful and are now living in Jonathan's flat, having seen only that old mummy, Winkworth?"

"I do not blame you for being sceptical. Of course I wrote a different letter from the one suggested by you. Otherwise, your summary is correct."

We talked for another quarter of an hour, then she rose impulsively.

"I must go. But I must give you an impression of Jonathan first. He is tall; he has the head of a composer and the face of an emperor. He is broad, strong, powerful. His eyes are eager, but death has kissed his mouth. He is an adept in arousing your curiosity and a genius in frustrating it. To listen to him is to watch God juggling with the worlds. To be silent with him is to fear him. He is armed at all points, and so is vulnerable everywhere. He is a challenge to your skill; a menace to your pride; an invitation to your vanity." She threw back her head and laughed long and loud. "Shall I go on?" she asked.

"If you can," I replied.

She laughed again. "I'm a good actress, as you'll discover. Shall I tell you his supreme achievement? It's this: when you are with him, this age does not exist. You feel that you are living in an epoch you cannot quite place: a time of great deeds, of compelling personalities; an age of colour, intrigue, crime; an age in which men and women dominated by the might of their wills; an age in which the people were slaves and their rulers were over life-size; an age in which the passions of the mind, the soul, or the body were the supreme realities—an age lit by the flames of ambition, an age in which to fail was to die." Again she laughed. "That sounds romantic, doesn't it? The hysteria of a schoolgirl."

"Hardly that," I protested.

"You will understand when you meet him. He fascinates me because he delivers me from this craven wretched little age; this nightmare of middle-class mediocrity!"

She spoke with passionate hatred. I felt that I was witnessing the performance of a great actress. She remained silent, so I gave her a cue:

"You find this age so repellent?"

"Repellent! The world's become an enormous fog, inhabited by millions of pigmies. There isn't a prize worth the winning. The greatest honours go to the greatest slave. An age of cripples so in love with deformity that the only god left is general paralysis. They are afraid of life and they are afraid of death and they loathe and fear anyone whose stature compels them to recognize their littleness. Don't speak of them! I must go."

I fetched her coat.

"We shall meet again and often," she said. "You interest me. I live in Bruton Street. I'm going away for a few days, but later you must come there." She spoke in the tone of one who is giving instructions. "There's a farce or a comedy to be played out and we find ourselves in the cast. I'll leave you to your books. If they are Jonathan's, they should be interesting."

"They are interesting," I said.

I went down to the street with her and saw her into the magnificent car which glided up as she appeared.

She gave me her hand. "Good-bye. It's been interesting, hasn't it?" A smile hovered on her lips.

"Very," I replied. The car disappeared and I returned to the library.

That night I wrote to Scrivener saying that Mrs. Francesca Bellamy had called.

CHAPTER IV

I

I T IS interesting to sit in a room, knowing that at any moment the door may open and your solitude be disturbed by the entry of a total stranger. It destroys the sense of isolation usually experienced when you are at home. It seemed probable that it was a hobby of Scrivener's to present each of his friends with a latchkey to his flat and if this were so, and his friends were numerous, it was evident that my life was going to be highly complicated but definitely interesting. Above all, there was the possibility that any day Scrivener himself might return and that the mystery of my engagement would be solved. In any event the visits of Pauline and Francesca had made me realize that my work in the library was of quite secondary importance. Scrivener had made that activity the excuse for my engagement. Of that I was certain.

Francesca's visit had served only to increase my perplexity. In the first place she compelled interest in her own right. She was poised on the background of mystery just as much as Scrivener. She had said that he was armed at all points and whether or not this was true about him, it was certainly true about her. I was somewhat in the position of a detective whose job was to solve the mystery of Scrivener. Pauline was one clue, Francesca another. But I found that my mind refused to regard either of them in this light. I discovered that I was thinking first about one, then the other, as if Scrivener did not exist. Each in turn captured my mind to the exclusion of everything else. Instead of one mystery I found myself confronted by three.

As to Matthews, I knew no more about her than I did after I had been in the flat for a day. She was always punctual, always efficient in the performance of her duties, never communicative, and apparently without curiosity in regard to me. Each day she ascertained my wishes as to meals and so on, and carried them out exactly, without troubling me with details of any kind. There was something of the aristocrat about her and I felt certain that the reserve and distinction which characterized her in the flat did not desert her when she left it. I learnt nothing from her and I refrained from questioning her directly.

However, long before I had had time to assess the data furnished by my visitors, and before I had evolved any theory in regard to Matthews, events occurred which occupied all my attention.

The first was a letter from Scrivener. It was very brief and informed me that it might be necessary for me to visit Mr. Winkworth in the near future in regard to some legal matters, the details of which he would send later. He suggested that I should ring up Mr. Winkworth in order to ascertain whether there was any likelihood of his being out of town during the next six weeks. The letter was written from Rome and was entirely impersonal in tone.

I rang up the lawyer's office and learnt that in all probability Mr. Winkworth would not be leaving London.

One night, a few days after Francesca's appearance, I was alone in the flat. It was nearly ten o'clock. I had dined at home and was becoming weary of the book I was reading when I heard a ring at the bell. I went to the door, somewhat amused by the reflection that a ring at the front door bell now caused me more surprise than the unannounced appearance of a visitor in the library.

I discovered a man evidently in a state of considerable bewilderment.

"I'm awfully sorry to disturb you," he began. "I'm afraid I've made a mistake. I wanted to see Mr. Scrivener."

"This is his flat," I replied.

"This!" He glanced round the hall. "Good Lord!" There was silence for a minute, then he asked: "Is he at home?"

"No, he's away. Won't you come in?"

"Away! That's rather odd." Another pause. "I say, I don't want to disturb you. I—I rather wanted to see Scrivener. Not that it matters, really."

"Well, come in, anyway."

He took off his overcoat and followed me to the library. Directly he entered the room I heard him give a low whistle indicative of surprise. Then he said to me:

"He's got a pretty decent place here."

"Yes," I replied. "Do sit down."

But apparently he did not hear me. He was wandering round the room looking at the books. He was fair, rather tall, and had the figure of an athlete. He wore a tooth-brush moustache and had deep-set, rather angry-looking eyes.

"Are *all* these books his?" he asked suddenly, evidently perplexed that one person could own so many volumes.

"Yes," I answered. "It's my job to catalogue them. That's why I'm here."

"I see," he said somewhat vaguely. "Look here, I'd better explain." He broke off and I could see that it was not easy for him to express himself in words. "My name's Middleton—Andrew Middleton."

As he did not continue, I said: "And my name is Wrexham—James Wrexham."

He gave a quick, nervous laugh which ended suddenly.

"That exchange doesn't tell us much really, does it? Well, look here, it's like this. You probably wondered why I seemed surprised about this flat. Fact is, I didn't think Scrivener was the type to have a show like this. I've met him only once, about a fortnight ago, and to be quite candid, I was a bit drunk at the time."

"Won't you have a drink now?" I asked.

Again he gave a short staccato laugh. "Thanks, I will. Damn it!" he exclaimed somewhat explosively. "I couldn't live with all these cursed books round me. I read a good deal myself, one way and another, but only the most frightful tosh."

He flung himself into an armchair and I mixed him a whisky and soda. Each night Matthews brought whisky and soda into the library before she left. I drank very seldom, but I had a drink on this occasion in order that Middleton should not drink alone.

He was smoking a cigarette and staring moodily at the Adam chimneypiece. He had clear-cut features and very sensitive nostrils. He moved restlessly in his chair and was clearly in a state of nervous irritability. I handed him his drink.

"Thanks so much. I say, it's damnably quiet in here, isn't it? I probably notice it because I've a dud flat off Oxford Street which is noisy as hell."

He evidently felt it necessary to talk and yet did not know how to approach the subject he really wanted to discuss.

"I say," he began again, "I suppose Scrivener went to the war, didn't he? I meant to ask him. Not that it matters, really."

"I don't know," I replied. "I know very little about him. You were in the Army, of course."

"Yes—France."

"How long?"

"Oh, about three years. I've really forgotten about it, though it was a better show than peace, don't you think?"

I told him that I had seen little of active service but that my brief experience of it had been sufficient to convince me that there were more pleasant activities.

"It's hell, of course," he said irritably, "but it has this great advantage: everyone knows it's hell. In war, everyone lies, and people show what swine they are. Sort of—naked and unashamed, don't you know. Gets rid of hypocrisy, anyhow. But you don't want to hear all that rot. I must explain turning up like this. I must seem pretty odd to you."

"Explain if you like, but you needn't. I'm only Scrivener's secretary—simply his paid servant. You're under no necessity to explain anything to me."

He sat silent for a minute then he got up and began to wander restlessly about the room. "Of course, you know him pretty well," he began. "He's a bit beyond me——"

"I don't know him at all," I interrupted. "I've never seen him." Once more I gave the explanation of my relations with Scrivener.

"Pretty queer bird, isn't he?" was Middleton's comment when I'd finished. "Probably a bit mad like all these people who've got brains. Well, now, look here, you've opened out about yourself. Wonder if it would bore you if I told you how I met him?"

"Not at all," I replied. "On the contrary, I'm naturally interested in him."

"You've probably noticed I can't explain anything very coherently. Anyhow, it was something like this: I've been all over the shop since the war, Canada, America and so on. I've been in South America for three years. Pretty good job in its way. I'm home on leave. Got back about a month ago." A long pause. "I—I took a bit of a punch on my arrival and I've made a bit of a fool of myself since." He broke off. "I say, I'll have another drink if you don't mind."

"Yes, do," I said. "Will you help yourself?"

In another minute he returned to his chair. "I simply filled in time knocking about this beastly town. You know what it is when you haven't anywhere to go. Well, one night, when I was a bit on, I went into some damned café in Soho." He broke off as if the strain of his narrative was making great demands. "Pretty damnable hole it was. Seedy looking men and the usual women. Full of smoke, and some ass put a penny in a blasted automatic piano." He gave his curious laugh again. "It was all as dull as a night club. Still, I didn't care a damn because I was pretty drunk."

He lit another cigarette and stared at the smoke as if he had forgotten my presence.

"Well, then a man came up to my table. He was quite different from the others. Well-dressed and distinguished-looking. He sat down and we began to talk. He rather fascinated me. Anyway I went on drinking. Then—as far as I remember—I started to talk. I've a kind of feeling that I said a hell of a lot. Probably all frightful nonsense!" he exclaimed angrily. "I half-believe I told the story of my life. People usually do if they begin to talk when they're drunk. Anyway I know I cursed everything pretty thoroughly. Then this man I was with began to talk again. Can't remember nearly all of it, but it was pretty acid and unlike anything I'd heard before."

Again he broke off and there was a long silence.

"Then I seem to remember having a row with some dago. Anyway, it was pretty late when we came out. The man I was with put me into a taxi, but first he gave me his card. I only found the card yesterday and then I saw that his name was Scrivener and that he lived here. I was bored to-night, so I came round. Rather wanted to find out what I'd told him. Also whether he'd actually said some of the things I remembered, or whether I'd dreamt them."

He flung his cigarette into the fire and ran his hands through his hair.

"And you were surprised to see that he had a place like this because you'd met him in a hole in Soho?"

"Yes," he replied, "seems a bit of a contradiction. When did he go away? Or I suppose you don't know."

"About a fortnight ago. He must have left very soon after you met him. He may return any day."

"I'm not keeping you up?" he asked suddenly.

"Not at all. You might let me have your address. Or of course you can look in whenever you want to."

"I'd like to see him again," he said slowly. "He was damned queer. I thought I was tolerably bitter till I met him. He's got it all pretty set, I give you my word: the whole blasted outfit, women included."

"You gathered he didn't care much about women?"

"Care much about them!" he exclaimed. "No, he did not. Said they were the vultures of civilization."

"Not its victims?"

"Victims! He said—or I dreamt it, God knows which!—that the Trinity in which women believe consists of clothes, comfort, and luxury." He laughed again. "But what I really want to know is: what did I tell him? Expect I made an awful ass of myself. It's pretty damnable to feel you've blurted out all sorts of rot to a complete stranger."

Although he had talked all the time, it was clear that temperamentally he was exceedingly reserved and that it embarrassed him to discuss himself. On the other hand it was equally evident that he was disturbed by the recollection that he had given Scrivener his confidence.

"I expect you're pretty intrigued by your own position, aren't you?" he asked suddenly.

"It's very unusual of course," I replied, "but probably Scrivener's return will make everything clear."

"He must be pretty well off," was Middleton's comment. "Somehow I never expected to find a show like this, though I'm not really surprised to find that he's read a deuce of a lot." After a pause he went on: "I've met most sorts, knocking about the world, but he's a new type to me."

"In what way?" I asked.

"You feel that he *gets you* pretty completely. Sums you up, if you like. I've only met him once in my life and I feel that he knows all about me, and I know damn-all about him. I keep remembering things I said to him—things I hadn't told anyone. Wonder what kind of a man he is really? Know any of his friends?"

The question was answered in a somewhat dramatic manner for the door opened and Pauline came into the room. She was in evening dress and I guessed that she had run in to see me on her way home after the theatre. Seeing that I was not alone, she stood motionless by the door.

"I'm disturbing you," she said.

"No, not in the least," I answered. "Please come in and sit down. I must introduce you: Miss Mandeville, Mr. Middleton. You both know Mr. Scrivener, which is perhaps a second introduction."

I took her cloak and she sat by the fire. Her beauty was heightened by her evening clothes, but again it seemed to me that her beauty was remote even from its most intimate surroundings. Francesca's clothes were part of her personality; Pauline's were merely a veil before an altar.

"You are a friend of Mr. Scrivener's?" She turned to Middleton as she asked the question.

"I've met him once," he said awkwardly, not looking at her.

"He's not returned then?"

"No," I replied. "I had a letter from him, but it was silent as to the date of his return."

There was a long silence which I could see did not trouble Pauline, but which Middleton found very difficult. It was broken by a ring on the telephone. I took up the receiver.

"Yes!"

"Mr. Wrexham?"

"Speaking."

"It's Mrs. Bellamy. Have you forgotten me?"

"I'm quite sure you did not ring up to ask that," I replied.

I heard her laugh.

"You're rather a strange person, but I suppose we shall understand each other one day and then there'll be no point in our meeting again. No news of Jonathan?"

"None."

"You never ask questions and your answers are always unsatisfactory."

"What is a satisfactory answer to a question?" I inquired.

"The only satisfactory answer is a full reply to a question that has not been asked. You are rather tiresome. I really telephoned to say that I'm going away for a day or two. We must meet on my return. Do you find your life in the flat interesting?"

"Very."

"What a wretched answer! You have only one gift. Do you know what it is?"

"I have no idea."

"You give people the illusion that it is safe to confide in you. If it really were safe, it would make things very interesting. Perhaps one day you'll convince me that it is."

"I shall not try to," I replied, "but it is safe."

"Why? Aren't you interested enough to use weapons?"

"No. I am not interested enough."

"You sound as if you were an ideal spectator. What are the qualifications necessary to be an ideal spectator?"

"Am I allowed one minute in which to think?"

"One minute," she answered.

"To be an ideal spectator one's passions must not be engaged."

"Then I shall never be an ideal spectator. I shall come to see you directly I return. I've thought about you a good deal and I want to talk to you. You must come to see me at Bruton Street. Good-night."

"Good-night."

I hung up the receiver and apologized to my visitors.

The conversation did not develop easily. Middleton said nothing but I noticed that he stared at Pauline as if she were an apparition, whenever she was not looking in his direction. When she glanced at him he immediately looked down at his shoes. Ten minutes passed. It was awkward enough, but anything is better than chatter.

At last Middleton rose. "Look here," he said to me. "I must be off. It was awfully good of you to let me come in." He turned to Pauline and said good-night.

I went into the hall with him. Directly the library door was shut he turned to me with a quick gesture.

"Who is she? That's damnably rude, I suppose, but who is she?"

"She's a friend of Scrivener's," I answered.

"Impossible. A friend of yours, you mean."

"No—Scrivener's."

He looked at me in silence. Then, suddenly: "I say! I saw a latch-key in her hand."

"Yes," I said, "she has a latchkey."

"God! do you mean she's his mistress?"

"No, I don't mean that."

"How do you know she isn't?" he asked quickly.

"She told me so."

"Good Lord! and you believe it because she told you?"

"Yes, I believe it. She hasn't the face of a liar."

He looked at me with a curious smile on his lips. "No, perhaps not. We're different evidently. Once, I assumed that no one was a liar. Now I assume that everyone is."

"Then you won't believe me when I say that I hope you'll come again some time?"

He laughed his short mirthless laugh.

"You're a fool to ask me," he said.

"Why?" I inquired.

"Only a fool tells a lonely man that he'd like to see him."

"The fool might be lonely too. Anyhow, come, if you want to."

In another moment he had gone and I returned to Pauline.

She rose as I entered the library and gave me both her hands as if to indicate that our greeting when Middleton was present did not count. The gesture also conveyed that she had given me her friendship without any reservation.

"Your visitor was rather a strange person," she said in her clear, perfectly articulated voice. "He's very unhappy, isn't he?"

"How do you know that?" I asked.

"His laugh tells anyone that," she replied. "He interested me."

"Tell me why. But first sit down by the fire."

She returned to her chair and settled herself as if she had plenty of time to spend with me. It seemed strange to be alone with her tolerably late at night and to be aware of a real sense of intimacy when by all orthodox standards we were strangers. She sat very upright in her chair and there was something incongruous about the childlike gravity of her face and her fashionable evening clothes which revealed the delicate line of her neck and the rounded beauty of her white shoulders.

"Why do you stare at me?"

The question startled me as I had not realized that I had been gazing at her.

"Because you always give me the impression that this world is a party to which you have been invited. An odd enough party, I admit. You've come from somewhere else—I don't know where—but you've had to dress in the clothes of this world, as a compliment to your hosts, and you seem to be waiting for someone to call and take you back to the region to which you belong."

"Do you know," she said with a smile, "that all that reveals just as much about you, as it does about me. All the same, it is true in its way. But I was going to tell you why your visitor interested me. What is his name?"

"Andrew Middleton. Why did he interest you?"

"Because I feel that somehow he's missed his place in the world. Life ought to have been quite clear cut and definite for him, but he's—he's——"

"Missed the boat?"

"Yes—missed the boat," she repeated slowly. "There's something about this room," she went on, "which prevents you discussing those things which you came to discuss. You were talking to a woman on the telephone, weren't you?"

"Yes."

"You gave an excellent definition of an ideal spectator."

"When you have read as much as I have, Miss Mandeville——"

"Pauline."

"Thank you. When you have read as much as I have, Pauline, you often quote without knowing it."

"I did not know you had any friends in London."

"I haven't," I replied. "I was speaking to a friend of Scrivener's—Mrs. Francesca Bellamy."

I saw immediately that the name was familiar to her. She said nothing for a minute and I imagined I could see the image of Francesca by her side. I marvelled at the contrast they presented and then a thrill, not far removed from fear, possessed me at the realization that it was Scrivener who had brought such widely-contrasted types as Pauline, Francesca, and Middleton into my life. Suddenly, there seemed something sinister in the knowledge that an unknown personality was selecting my associates and determining the pattern of my life.

"*The* Mrs. Bellamy, of course?" asked Pauline.

"Yes. You didn't know that Scrivener knew her?"

"No. I tell you that I know nothing about him and I only know what everyone knows about her. I can see now that it's probable that they would know each other. How did you meet her?"

"In exactly the same way as that in which I met you."

"*Exactly* the same?" she asked.

"Yes."

She smiled, and I was interested to see how entirely she lacked jealousy on learning that Francesca was on the same terms of intimacy with Scrivener as she was.

"Then she might open the door and come in now?" she asked.

"She could, at any rate," I replied. "It's satisfactory to be able to report that Middleton does not possess a latchkey."

"What does it all mean, James?"

I cannot convey how odd it was to hear her use my Christian name.

"I haven't the remotest idea. Sometimes I think it's a farce, sometimes a conspiracy. I am certain of only one thing, and that is that you are as much in the dark as I am. Your presence carries conviction. I don't know about the others."

There was a long silence. She sat looking into the fire.

"You haven't even a theory yet?"

"No," I answered, "but it's a curious coincidence that you, Mrs. Bellamy, and Middleton have only known Scrivener for such a short time. Perhaps someone will appear soon who has known him for years."

"Or he may return," she suggested.

"Yes, any day that is possible. Tell me this: had you any particular reason for coming to-night?"

"I want you to meet my people. Would you come to dinner one night? If you would, it might save a lot of explanations. You would see my background and I would like to know what you make of it."

She spoke about them as if they were strangers and as if the life she lived with them was removed from her real activities.

"Of course I would come," I replied, "only it doesn't seem quite fair to your people. You must understand that I have no background at all. It will be awkward for them because they can take nothing for granted. I'm a person living in the void."

"I want you to come. Everyone we know has a label tied round his neck, so you will be a new experience. You see," she added, after a pause, "I might want your advice one day. It's very probable in fact, and so the more you know about me the better. I came in to-night simply to ask you if you would come, but your visitor and this room made me forget all about it."

She rose and I got her cloak, but when she was ready she still lingered as if unwilling to go.

"Do you expect Middleton will come here again?"

"Yes," I said. "I feel quite certain he will."

"It's curious," she said, almost to herself, "that everything connected with Jonathan creates another problem in my life. I must go. You will come, one night after Christmas?"

"Yes, I will come."

I telephoned for a taxi. It was raining heavily.

Soon after Pauline left, I went to bed and for hours I lay awake listening to the rain.

II

It was only a few days to Christmas. Evidence of Santa Claus, and of little else, was everywhere apparent. For three days I had had no interruptions from the outside world. Then a letter arrived from Scrivener asking me to visit Winkworth and to give him certain instructions, all of which were clearly set out in an enclosure which accompanied his letter. In fact, so clear were these instructions that the necessity for me to visit the lawyer was not easy to detect.

I rang up and made an appointment with Winkworth the day after I had received Scrivener's letter. I walked to his office in Sackville Street.

If I die to-night, I have realized one thing, if only one, about life in this world: its significance is unrelated to Time. It was only a few weeks since I had seen Winkworth, but already my life was divided into two main categories: the years I had lived in Petersham's office, and the weeks I had spent in Scrivener's flat. Mere duration signifies nothing. It is a ticking clock without a dial hand. A man is never wise because he is old.

I expected Winkworth to keep me waiting and he did. Also he omitted to apologize for the fact, and he clearly had some difficulty in remembering my name. I made no reference to my life in the flat, but restricted the conversation solely to the limits imposed by Scrivener's instructions. Seeing that I was quite prepared to regard our interview in an entirely impersonal manner, Winkworth decided to become communicative.

He rose, pushed aside the papers we had been discussing, and walked slowly to the fireplace. As on my first visit, he was sleek and well-groomed. He wore a morning coat and toyed with the pince-nez attached to a watered silk ribbon, exactly as he had done at our first interview. He kept inspecting his nails and obviously derived great satisfaction from the appearance of his rather puffy white hands.

"That concludes our business, I *think*." He passed his hand across his forehead as if to indicate that he had weightier matters on hand which would make great mental demands. "And how are you getting on in Mr. Scrivener's flat?"

"I find it very interesting," I replied.

"A man of wide culture," he said as if he were addressing an imaginary audience. "A man of brilliant achievements, a man of remarkable possibilities. A *personality*, Mr. Wrexham, a *personality*. It's a great opportunity for a man like you to be associated with him."

He paused and I said nothing. He held the lapels of his coat and stared at the carpet while he pursed his lips and seemed to be considering a subject of great complexity. "A remarkable man, a very remarkable man," he said at last.

As I felt that these remarks were not made to me, but only in my presence, I remained silent. It irritated him that it was necessary to ask a direct question, but seeing that I did not respond to generalities he was forced to yield.

"You are not lonely, I hope?"

"Not at all, Mr. Winkworth. I find my life in Mr. Scrivener's flat most interesting. I find his library——"

"Ah, yes, yes," he interrupted, "the world of the mind. I should be a great reader if my professional duties allowed, and then there's one's social life——" He broke off with an expansive gesture which suggested that it would be useless to detail to such a negligible person as myself those splendid and exclusive circles of which he was an ornament.

I began to understand Winkworth, however. I was certain that every attitude, every gesture, the very details of his dress, had been copied—each and all—from others. Thus, I felt certain, that he had been impressed by some man who had worn a pince-nez on a watered ribbon and who had toyed with it while talking. Winkworth had adopted this habit, believing that it was the secret of the other man's impressiveness. It was the reason why he kept punctuating his speech with the phrase "I *think*." Another had done it and it had impressed him. Walk, speech, clothes, everything, had been assumed as a definite policy. I felt quite convinced that long ago he had ceased to be a man and had become an anthology.

I decided it was necessary to introduce a new theme, so I said: "Not only are Mr. Scrivener's books interesting, his friends are interesting as well."

"His friends!" Winkworth looked at me severely, but I ignored both his expression and the tone of his voice.

"Most interesting," I went on. "I am discovering new horizons which is always worth while, don't you think?"

"And what friends of Mr. Scrivener's, may I ask, have you met?"

"Mrs. Francesca Bellamy, for one," I replied.

"*Mrs. Francesca Bellamy!*" Italics are inadequate to indicate the immense emphasis with which he repeated the name. "There's some mistake here, I *think*. Surely you are not referring to the Mrs. Francesca Bellamy of Bruton Street?"

"Certainly," I replied. "She has asked me to go to see her there. I have her card in my pocket, if you would care to see it."

But Winkworth was staring at me with wide eyes. "She has asked you to go to see her! This is most mysterious. Do you know, Mr. Wrexham, that Mrs. Bellamy is worth probably a million of money?"

"I knew she was very wealthy," I answered.

"Wealthy!" Winkworth emitted a noise which was a blend of a cough and a snort. "She's a woman of great influence. Really, I do not want to discourage you, but *really* I think there is some mistake."

"There is no mistake of any kind. Mrs. Bellamy called at the flat a few weeks ago to see Mr. Scrivener. Finding that he was away, she stayed and talked with me for some time. A day or two ago she rang me up and asked me if I would go to see her in Bruton Street."

"If!" exclaimed Winkworth significantly. He took hold of his lapels again and looked down at the carpet. There was silence for a minute then he returned to his desk and sat down quite near me.

"All this is very interesting, Wrexham," he said pleasantly. "I hope you didn't think I doubted your word. Not at all. When ladies cease to have whims, they will no longer be ladies, will they? Ha—ha. I seemed surprised, because for one thing, I did not know that Mrs. Bellamy was a friend of Mr. Scrivener's. That will surprise you, doubtless, but you must understand that I have not seen Mr. Scrivener for some time."

The last statement struck me as being remarkably interesting, but I was quite determined not to ask Winkworth any questions. He went on talking but clearly his thought was not behind his words. He was trying to evolve a method of finding out what he wanted to know without appearing curious.

"You know, of course," he began in the tone of a man of the world speaking to another, "that a year ago Mrs. Bellamy was the centre of considerable public interest?"

"You refer to her husband's suicide."

"Yes—his death—his death," he said quickly. "Very unfortunate—a brilliant man; a disconsolate and beautiful widow. Great wealth, great breeding. A tragedy—no less."

"The reason for Mr. Bellamy's suicide is still a mystery, I gather?" I said in order to remind him of the only fact in the situation.

"Yes, Wrexham, I suppose it is. But, between ourselves, men at the head of great affairs are subjected to a great mental strain. I know something about that, I assure you. This room has been the scene of some *pretty* big transactions in its day. Not of the magnitude of the late Mr. Bellamy's. I don't say that. But pretty big, *pretty big.*"

He lit a cigar, and offered me a cigarette, then hastily proffered his cigar case. I took a cigarette.

"I ought not to take up any more of your time———" I began.

"Please, please." He raised a restraining hand. "Our last interview was a hurried one, of necessity. I allocated a generous amount of time to this one as I wanted to discuss certain things with you.

In our different ways, Wrexham," he said genially, "we both serve Mr. Scrivener in a fiduciary capacity. We must work together, sir, we must work together."

He leant towards me with a broad smile which I had not seen before, but which revealed his fine set of very white rather large teeth. It was clearly necessary to say something.

"I am glad to hear you say that, Mr. Winkworth, because naturally it is rather strange to be employed by a man one has never seen."

"Most irregular, Wrexham. I *quite* agree with you. Most irregular and therefore most undesirable."

He pushed a bell on his desk in a manner which suggested that Scrivener would leap into view through a trap-door and remove, by his presence, all trace of irregularity. Instead of which, however, Winkworth's secretary appeared. She was rather frigid but very immaculate.

"Miss Montgomery, Mr. Wrexham and I would like some tea. I think that could be managed. And we should like it immediately."

While we were waiting for tea to appear Winkworth arranged the papers on his desk, gave some instructions over the telephone, and indicated by his whole manner that he would shortly give me the whole of his attention. On the return of Miss Montgomery with the tea, Winkworth turned to me with a smile.

"Now that the decks are clear, Wrexham, we can talk with freedom. A dear old friend of mine, and a great lawyer, once said to me, 'One thing at a time, Winkworth, and each thing done thoroughly.' I hope that the tea is to your taste. Now, sir: Mr. Jonathan Scrivener."

He leant back in his chair, clasped the lapels of his coat and stared at the ceiling with a reminiscent expression in his eyes.

"I remember the first time I saw him as if it were yesterday. He came with his father to this office when he was quite a boy. That was the first time I saw him and the last time I saw his father. He died before the year was out. Jonathan Scrivener was an only child and his mother died when he was two or three years old. His father left a certain amount of money but not a great deal, not a great deal."

"Did you know Mr. Scrivener's father intimately?" I asked, as Winkworth had paused in his narrative.

"He wasn't a man to give his confidence readily, but we lawyers get pretty quick in summing a man up. We have our methods you know, and we know what to look for. He was a curious type of man, very silent, and not very sociable, but very aristocratic in his bearing. Well, he died and his brother made himself responsible for the boy."

Winkworth stared at the glowing end of his cigar for some seconds before he continued: "His brother was exceedingly wealthy, a great traveller, and a patron of the arts. He had a magnificent house in the country full of all kinds of treasures. He had never got on very well with Scrivener's father but he was soon devoted to the boy, and I assure you that your employer owes a very great deal to his uncle."

As Winkworth continued his story, I felt certain that he was aware only of external facts relating to the Scriveners. He had never been intimate with any of them. Also I had the definite impression that he was telling me what he knew about Scrivener, not because he considered that it was necessary for me to know these details, but because he believed that he was placing me under an obligation to him by giving me information about his client. Nevertheless, I was exceedingly interested in his story as it provided a background, however shadowy, to Scrivener.

"His uncle was a bachelor and, as I told you, he became devoted to the boy. He sent him to a first-rate public school." Winkworth mentioned the name of the school in a tone which suggested that the very sound of the word gave him profound satisfaction. "There's nothing like a public school education, Wrexham, nothing! It marks a man for life. No, sir, his uncle made no mistake *there*. Later, when the boy was eighteen, he did however, in my judgment, make a serious error: he did *not* send him to the university." Winkworth swung his pince-nez to and fro, following its progress by turning his head from side to side. "I was not consulted, and so I remained silent, but that decision was an error, Wrexham. He should have been sent to the university."

Winkworth uttered this last sentence with quite remarkable emphasis.

"You think his failure to do so had serious results?" I asked.

Winkworth regarded me quizzically with his head on one side and his right eye nearly closed.

"Let me ask you a question, Wrexham. A brilliant man—I refer to the uncle—a boy of eighteen. Which is better: for the boy to follow the tradition of his class and go to the university, or to spend three years travelling all over Europe, imbibing the opinions, and perhaps the eccentricities, of a brilliant and disillusioned man like his uncle? I posit the question, Wrexham, but we will not answer it. Let us confine ourselves to facts. A dear friend of mine, Sir Peter Bray, said to me—before he became Attorney General— 'Winkworth, to be a good lawyer, three things are essential: to know where to go for facts; to know how to marshal facts; and to know which facts to present.' A profound observation, Wrexham, most profound. Especially the third essential: *to know which facts to present.* But I'm telling you the tricks of the trade—I *should* say the subtleties of the profession. Now, where was I?"

I reminded him that he had decided to restrict his narrative to the facts concerning Scrivener.

"Ah, of course. From eighteen till twenty-one he travelled extensively with his uncle. I know little of that period. It must have been rich in cultural opportunities for your employer. A dramatic event brought that epoch to an end. Scrivener's uncle died suddenly. He left the whole of his fortune to his nephew. At the age of twenty-one, therefore, Jonathan Scrivener found himself the possessor of great wealth and absolute freedom. He was extraordinarily handsome and remarkably gifted. The world was at his feet."

Winkworth put his cigar into an ash-tray, rose, crossed the room and stood with his back to the fire.

"I yield to no man in my admiration for the world of the mind. For literature, for the arts, for culture, I have—I assure you—a genuine respect. But—I—do—say—that a knowledge of these things is not an adequate equipment for a young man of twenty-one—a young man of birth and wealth. No, sir! A practical knowledge of the world is essential. I do not suggest that the young man in question could be expected to possess that knowledge, but I do say that he should have availed himself of the advice of an older man and been guided by his judgment. I am making no complaint, you understand, I am stating an opinion."

Winkworth surveyed his nails with the appreciation of a connoisseur. It was some moments before he continued:

"You will understand, Wrexham, that there was no economic necessity for Scrivener to follow a career. You will appreciate that most doors were open to him. Now, sir, if I am to continue, it must be understood that I am in no sense criticizing my client."

"I think I understand perfectly," I said, as he waited for a reply.

"That reassures me considerably. In one sentence, then, Scrivener did not use any of the great advantages he possessed in any of the recognized ways. He did not become a great figure in the fashionable world, neither did he seek eminence in politics or in any of the professions. He sold the house in the country and, although I am given to understand that he could have made a considerable reputation in one or other of the arts, he appears always to have lost interest in any activity at the precise moment when he was about to obtain mastery. He has remained an experimentalist or, if you will, a dilettante."

Winkworth returned to his seat near me. I fancy that his love of hearing himself speak had involved him in a more detailed account of Scrivener's affairs than he had contemplated originally. Also it was quite evident that he was annoyed to discover that the subject he really wished to discuss was receding into the background. He looked at me intently as if anxious to ascertain my reaction to his narrative. I felt it necessary to relieve his mind so far as I was in a position to do so.

"I am grateful to you for giving me the general outlines of Mr. Scrivener's life. As I told you, it is natural that I should want to know something about him. I hope you understand that I realize that we are talking in confidence."

"Perfectly, perfectly. Moreover—and this is a subject to which I shall have to return—if you are meeting certain of Scrivener's friends, it is essential that you know something about him. From time to time, rumours have circulated concerning my client. That may surprise you, but it is true. It is certainly more desirable that you should learn about Scrivener from me than that you should pick up odds and ends of scandal concerning him."

It was plain by now that Winkworth was in deep waters. He was attempting success on too many levels in this conversation which he had started so light-heartedly. He was somewhat in the position of a man who was trying to dance on a tight-rope and attempting to perform a number of difficult conjuring tricks at the same time. It is not easy to wish to tell a man nothing and yet create the impression that you are giving him the whole of your confidence. If, in addition to this, you wish to convey that you know much more than you actually do, and simultaneously you are seeking to impress him with your own importance, while wishing fervently that you were discussing an entirely different topic, you will find—as I am sure Winkworth found—that you are engaged on an undertaking of considerable difficulty.

"Now, Wrexham, from the necessarily brief account I have given you of your employer, you will see that eccentricity was part of his inheritance. Both his father and his uncle were eccentric in their different ways. I will make no attempt to disguise the fact that on occasions Scrivener has chosen his associates from persons not of his own class—artists and people like that. He's accepted *nothing*. That's the trouble! And the secret of life, Wrexham, is to accept. To accept the standards of one's class and the conditions one finds in the world: to accept them and to use them. You say nothing: possibly you do not agree with me."

"I have always been an outcast," I replied, "the result was that there was nothing ready-made for me to accept. You have to be in a tradition to accept it."

"That's very true, very true. You have to be in a tradition to accept it. Very well expressed: very apt and pithy. And I may say that you have to *be* a lawyer before you become one. Some of these clerks who are given their articles prove the truth of *that* statement. I tell you frankly that Scrivener moved in many circles at one time which were not worthy of him. It gave his inferiors the opportunity to spread rumours about him. Not that he was ever faithful to anyone or anything for long. When he gets tired of his surroundings, he simply disappears."

"Disappears!" I repeated.

"You may well be surprised, Wrexham. But such is the fact, I assure you. When Scrivener becomes weary of the circle in which he has been moving, he simply goes abroad for some time and on his return becomes interested in an entirely different activity which brings him into touch with new associates. That is my reading of the situation. He has never told me that this is a deliberate policy on his part. It is, however, the only explanation of his sudden enthusiasms and equally sudden disappearances."

There was a long pause. I found this theory of Winkworth's very interesting, since it provided an explanation of Scrivener's absence. On the other hand it was significant that those of his friends whom I had met had known Scrivener for only a very short time.

"You think, then," I said, "that your theory may provide an explanation of why Mr. Scrivener left London without seeing me?"

"I think it remarkably likely, Wrexham. But, to be quite frank, I have no theory which will furnish any explanation as to why he engaged you as his secretary."

"I have thought about that for so long, with so little effect," I replied, "that I have now assumed that time will provide an explanation."

I rose, but Winkworth restrained me.

"One minute, if you please. Should you hear any rumours about Scrivener, you will understand that his eccentric conduct is liable to give rise to comments by mischievous or malicious people. Doubtless he has been indiscreet on several occasions, but that is only to be expected. He is young and wealthy. One word more: you mentioned Mrs. Francesca Bellamy. Should you meet her again, I hope you will mention my name to her. I have met her once or twice."

My expression must have indicated surprise for Winkworth added hurriedly:

"I did not mention it before because the circumstances were so trivial. After her husband's unfortunate death, she came here on a matter of business relating to his affairs. She has been once or twice on very minor matters. In fact, our interviews have been so hurried that I do not think she even realizes that I am the senior partner of this firm. It would be pleasant to meet her again. A charming woman, a brilliant woman, and a woman of remarkable power and influence. You are very fortunate to have made her acquaintance."

He broke off though it was clear that there was a great deal more he would like to have said. After some hesitation, he held out his hand.

"Now, do feel, Wrexham, that you can consult me at any time. Simply ring up or, if necessary and you would do me the honour, perhaps you would spend a week-end with me at my little place at Chislehurst. I do not want you to feel that you have no friends in London."

I thanked him, and the interview ended.

I walked home. It was a clear, frosty evening. The lights of the cars flashed past: workers were hastening homeward and seekers after amusement and pleasure were beginning to take possession of the West End. But I felt isolated from my surroundings and walked back to the flat like a man in a dream.

CHAPTER V

To know the facts is one thing; to know the truth is another. Facts are to the truth what dates are to history—they record certain events but they do not reveal the significance of those events. I discovered that although my conversation with Winkworth had yielded considerable information regarding the externals of Scrivener's life, it had not enlightened me concerning essentials. I now knew that he was an only child; that both his parents were dead; that a bachelor uncle had taken charge of him on his father's death; and that he was alleged to be fickle in his enthusiasms and impulsive in his actions. In one sense, therefore, Winkworth had told me much about Scrivener; in another sense he had told me nothing.

It is important to make this clear. We talk lightly of "knowing" someone, when in reality we know nothing of the quality of that person's life. As a rule we know only his or her circumstances. Winkworth's information had revealed no more to me than if he had pointed to half a dozen houses in various places and said: "Scrivener has lived in each of these houses in turn." To know where a man has been tells you little. It is what a traveller becomes on his pilgrimage which is important, not where he has lodged on the way.

Nevertheless, although I was still ignorant of essentials, I now possessed a background of some kind to Scrivener, and if I had known what significance to attach to Winkworth's use of the word "eccentric," I should have had some idea of my employer's psychology. At our first interview, Winkworth had said that Scrivener was eccentric; at our last meeting, he had used the same word when referring to Scrivener's father and uncle. It was quite possible, however, that Winkworth regarded everyone as eccentric if their values conflicted with his. The terms we use to describe others usually reveal little concerning them, and much concerning ourselves.

I spent a solitary Christmas trying to eliminate the important from the irrelevant in the mass of details Winkworth had disclosed. Rightly or wrongly I decided that his statement that Scrivener frequently disappeared when bored by his activities or his associates was probably the most illuminating. This, of course, was only Winkworth's theory, but it was certain that Pauline, Francesca, and Middleton, had all come to the flat expecting to find Scrivener. On the other hand, he had met them only recently, and not one of them seemed very surprised to learn that he had left England. But as I was far from certain that Francesca and Middleton were not playing parts which had been assigned to them, the evidence of two of my chief witnesses was suspect.

Directly Christmas was over, fog invaded London. The city

loomed out of shrouded desolation like a vast sepulchre. All day the yellow lights of the street lamps shone like spectral stars over the chaos of the traffic. When night intensified the gloom, the muffled silence was disturbed by sudden shouts which rose angrily through the darkness. An icy dampness penetrated everything. I saw no one till, just after ten on the third night of the fog, Middleton called again.

It was evident that he had had several drinks and he was very apologetic about disturbing me. He wandered up and down the library:

"God! What a town! It looks like a city of the damned. I've been tramping about all day in this hell."

He began to look at the titles of the books on the shelves; suddenly he broke into his short nervous laugh.

"Here you are! This is the book for a night like this!" He took down a volume and exclaimed: *The City of Dreadful Night.* Again, he laughed. "Let's try a bit of this."

He opened it at random and read:

> *"Some say that phantoms haunt those shadowy streets,*
> *And mingle freely there with sparse mankind;*
> *And tell of ancient woes and black defeats,*
> *And murmur mysteries in the grave enshrined;*
> *But others think them visions of illusion,*
> *Or even men gone far in self-confusion;*
> *No man there being wholly sane in mind."*

"That's not too bad anyway," was his comment. "I'd begin seeing phantoms like that if I wandered about for a few more days in that cursed fog." He looked at the book again, then turned a couple of pages. "Listen to this.

> *"The chambers of the mansions of my heart,*
> *In every one whereof thine image dwells,*
> *Are black with grief eternal for thy sake."*

He shut the book and turned to me almost fiercely:

"What the devil does a man want to write that stuff for?"

"He gives his reasons in the first few verses of the poem," I replied.

"Well, I shan't read them. He wasn't the first to have a hell of a time in this world, anyway." He put the book back in its place. "Scrivener has an odd taste in books," he muttered.

He continued to wander about the room. It was obvious that he had only come because he was lonely and it embarrassed him to discover that he had nothing whatever to say. I felt sorry for him, but I knew instinctively that to question him would be useless. After a long silence, he asked abruptly:

"Haven't you any idea yet when Scrivener will return?"

"None," I replied. "I have heard from him since I saw you, but he wrote only about some legal business. I know no more about his intentions than you do."

"I want to see him, and I don't want to see him," he said slowly.

"Then you like him, and you don't like him," I suggested.

"Exactly! How the devil did you know that? He caught me off my guard. Perhaps some time I'll explain that more fully. I've been thinking a good deal about that conversation I had with him in Soho."

"Have you been in London over Christmas?"

"No, I haven't," he said with a sneer. "I spent Christmas with the only relative I have in England and a very unpleasant experience I found it. I'll tell you about it, if it won't bore you."

"It won't bore me."

He lit a cigarette and stared into the fire. "I stayed with my brother. He has quite a big place in the country. He was in the army before the war and soon after the armistice he married a woman with money. She has social ambitions and they go on as if they were county people. They hunt and shoot and are more Tory than the Diehards. Their whole atmosphere suggests that their lives are bound up intimately with Court circles. I can reel all this off because I've been analysing them all day." He broke off with a laugh, then continued: "My brother was a damned good fellow before he married. But that's not the point. *This* is the point;

I stayed with them when I was home three years ago. They were just the same then, but they did not irritate me."

"And now?" I asked.

"Now they infuriate me. I've just spent four days with them and some friends of theirs. Well, they just seem to me to be a pack of people who know that they're all playing a game of make-believe. Just a stupid crowd who are hanging on to a type of existence which ceased to have any meaning long ago. I sat and watched them, waiting for one of them to laugh, or scream, or go mad. But no! On they went with the farce like a pack of bad amateur actors. And so the unpleasant truth was borne in on me that it is I who have changed. And, which is worse, I believe I envy them."

"Why?"

"Because I can't find a part to play—that's why." He flung his cigarette into the fire. "I tell you," he said slowly, "I came here to-night because I simply could not stand wandering about alone any longer. You're the only human being I could go to see in London, so I came. And for the love of God, don't imagine that I'm trying to make out that I'm a personality, or anything exceptional. I'm an ordinary man, that's my tragedy."

"That doesn't tell me much," I said, "unless you give me your definition of an ordinary man."

"I can't define anything," he began irritably. "I've done nothing but talk when I've been with you so you'll find it difficult to believe that I'm naturally very reserved. When I say I'm an ordinary man, I mean it. I used to believe in all the things that a moderately decent man believes in. And I've discovered that all those things are just a pack of lies and that the people who serve them are just a pack of fools. That discovery is made usually only by exceptional people, and it doesn't hurt them because they have gifts which create ways of escape. I'm a hewer of wood and a drawer of water, and I've seen the futility of both activities. I say!" he exclaimed suddenly, "can I have a drink?"

"Of course! I'm sorry I forgot to ask you."

"I've had a good many, as a matter of fact. I shouldn't have come if I hadn't."

I handed him a whisky and soda.

"Thanks. Coming back to what I was saying. Scrivener is an example."

"You mean that, being exceptional, he could get on without any belief in ordinary standards."

"Yes, I do. I wish to God I had told him so. He's queer, he's devilish queer." Then, after a pause, "I don't quite know how he gets through the world, all the same. There's something I want to ask you."

"What is it?"

"Has that woman been here again? Pauline Mandeville?"

"No, she has not been here again but she has asked me to her home."

He went on as if I had not answered his question:

"I cannot imagine what she is doing with Scrivener. The way he talked, I shouldn't have thought there was a woman in his life at all. I've never seen anyone in the least like her." He paused and looked at me intently.

"Go on," I said with a smile.

"So you guessed that I hadn't finished. You're right. I can't make you out either. Is it true—really true—that you've never seen Scrivener?"

"It is really true," I answered.

"Never had any dealings with him of any kind?"

"Never."

"And that woman, Pauline Mandeville, simply opened that door one day and came in and that was the first time you had ever seen her?"

"Yes," I replied.

"'Um," he said gruffly. "I'd like to be frank."

"You can be," I said. "You can say anything you like."

"Well, then, what is your game?"

"I haven't one," I answered. "I won't give you all the reasons why I took this job. It would take too long, and the real reason would not be among them. The reasons which can be stated are always secondary. But I'm playing no game. I sit here and await events and I do not know, any more than you do, why Scrivener made me his secretary."

There was a long silence. Middleton rose and wandered about the room again. Possibly five minutes passed. Then he mixed himself another drink and returned to his chair.

"I'll tell you this," he began slowly. "I don't know that I'd like to be in your shoes. I'm not at all sure that I want to know Mr. Scrivener any better than I do. Anyhow, I'd like to feel that I could drop him whenever I wanted to. He's probably got some game on with you and he certainly has with that woman. I don't envy her. But she must take what's coming to her like we all do sooner or later." He laughed his short mirthless laugh and lit another cigarette. "It's a pity you don't drink," he added abruptly. "I've only started to drink regularly during the last few months and now I understand why drunkards object to being with people who don't drink. Their abstinence is such a subtle form of criticism."

"Then I'll have a drink with you," I said. "You interested me and so I forgot, and let you drink alone."

"Do you mind if I get drunk?" he asked quite seriously.

"No. Do what you like. You find it helps things if you get drunk?"

"It might help me to tell you something if I got drunk," he replied. "And it's something I must tell you, or not come here again." He paused, then said nervously: "You're not a fool. You can see that something's happened to me, can't you?"

"I can see that you've taken a punch," I replied.

"Exactly. Well—do you know this—I was pretty tight when I came to see you last time, when that woman came in. If I hadn't been, I shouldn't have said a word. I'm only free when I've had a few drinks—do you know that? I can talk then. I'm ashamed afterwards to remember what I said, but that's not till to-morrow. And the whole problem of life is how to get through to-day."

Often there is a silence just before one person confides in another. Middleton and I both recognized that if he continued, our acquaintanceship would be ended and the responsibilities of friendship would begin. Let the mask be removed, be it but for a second, and relations are altered for ever. And it matters little if what is said is not the whole truth. Which of us can tell the whole truth about himself? It is the attempt by one person to tell the truth about himself to another which binds both of them. The responsibility of listening is as great as that of speech, for to receive a confidence is to share a burden.

Nothing was audible in the library except the ticking of the clock. Middleton sat with his head resting on his right hand. Except for the unnatural brightness of his eyes, he looked a perfect example of the better type of Englishman, the type which died by thousands in the war. Lean, wiry, afraid of his emotions, fiercely orthodox, modest, brave, and normally almost wholly inarticulate. Glancing at him, I felt convinced that he had spoken the truth when he had said his tragedy was that he was an ordinary man. It is typical of the Middleton type to believe that others are like them but, this apart, it was clear to me that it was some exceptional experience which had turned Middleton from an excellent example of his type into an impotent revolutionary who spent his days drinking—in the attempt to cheat loneliness.

"How the devil shall I begin?" he asked suddenly.

"I believe I could supply the preface," I said slowly.

"You! What on earth do you mean? You know nothing about me." He looked at me half angrily.

"All the same, I'm willing to have a shot at the preface," I said.

His expression changed to one of great perplexity. "All right," he grumbled at last, "go ahead. I'd much rather listen than talk, but I fail to see how you can know anything about me."

"It's only a leap in the dark, of course. I know nothing about you but I feel that I know something of the type to which you belong. Was your story something like this? You went to a public school where you didn't do much work because you were too keen on games. You went to the university but it was only another school for you. When you had to go into the world, you didn't know what you wanted. All you knew was what you did *not* want—and that was to go into an office."

"How the hell did you know that?" he interrupted.

"It's written all over you. So you got a job abroad—cotton or tobacco growing—anything, it didn't matter what, so long as it was in the open. Then the war came and you returned like a flash because you love England——"

"Love England!" he exclaimed.

"Yes, desperately, deeper than anything else. You love your dream of her and if the reality conflicts with the dream, you see only the dream. You don't question her, you don't criticize her——"

"Don't I, by God!" he interrupted.

"You didn't at the time of which I am speaking. When the war came, you had one wish—to die for her. In the same way, you have one regret now—that you did not die for her."

I looked over at him, but he looked away.

"That was the type to which you belonged. It's an English type although it's not understood in England, and it does not understand the English. Shall I go on about it? Shall I tell you what I believe about it?"

"Yes, go on." He was staring at me with a curious expression.

After a pause I continued:

"It is a type which is only at home in action and therefore it is superb in emergency. It credits others with its own decency. It is a type which produces Empires as a by-product of its adventurous spirit. It can conquer, but it is too restless to administrate and so demagogues and bureaucrats enter into its labours. Men of this type died by thousands in the war while placemen intrigued for power behind their backs. Men of this type are deceived, cheated, and despised by the smooth sleek men who can persuade with oily eloquence. I say that it is to this type that you belong."

He was looking at me now in amazement, very much as a child watches a conjuror. His comment on what I had said was so typical that I nearly laughed:

"I say, you don't write, or anything like that, do you?"

"No," I replied. "I don't write. I have no gifts."

"And—and you say that men of this type are not understood by the English?"

"Not in the least," I answered, "and least of all by those authors who pretend to portray it. Men of the type I am discussing are rarely credited with idealism, and the poetry inherent in them is usually overlooked. Their idealism is not perceived because they are inarticulate, and the poetry latent in them is not recognized as it is expressed only in action. But, in order to finish my analysis, I must confess that I believe that the type is rapidly dying out. Those who were not killed in the war have become——"

"Like me!" he interrupted. "That's to say, they've seen through the whole thing."

"But not as a result of logic," I went on. "Men of your type only learn through concrete experience. I believe you wanted to tell me of an experience which had happened to you."

He rose and helped himself to another drink.

"Look here," he began, "a good deal of what you said is true. How you knew it, I'm damned if I know. Anyway, roughly, I was of the type you've described. A very indifferent specimen, I admit, but still of that type. You *have* saved me the preface. Now I'll tell you what happened to me since the war. Don't expect anything much, or you'll be disappointed. I'm keeping you up damnably late. Do you mind?"

"No, of course not."

"It's odd, isn't it?" he went on, "that here we are, you and I, in Scrivener's flat, and if it hadn't been for him, we should never have met."

"And you have met him once, and I have never seen him," I added after a pause.

"Has Miss Mandeville known him for a long time?"

"About two or three months, I understand."

Middleton said nothing, but stared at me gloomily. It was obvious that his reference to Scrivener had been made only to gain time. His fear of making himself ridiculous was pathetic.

He rose suddenly and wandered about again. Then he returned to his chair. "Thank God for drink!" he exclaimed. "It wakes another man in me. Not a 'lower self' or any of that rubbish. It's myself, all right—the self which is usually made dumb by nerves.

Now, listen. I want to get this over. After the war, I was completely at a loose end. You know what things were like here. Well, I got a job of sorts in Canada. Then I was in the States for some time. I did anything that turned up. Later, I drifted back to England. Then two things happened."

He ceased abruptly and his face worked convulsively. It was a few moments before he continued:

"One was that I heard of a decent job in South America, the other was that I fell in love. That hadn't happened to me before. Love was a word like any other to me. Suddenly it became *life*. Do you understand that?"

"Yes," I said, "I can understand that."

"It got me at the right time. I was beginning to be pretty tired of most things, pretty certain that all the things I had taken for granted were not what I had imagined them to be. Suddenly, *she* came along, and everything became true again. I can't explain it better than that. Perhaps you can fill in the gaps."

"I think I know what you mean," I said. "You were able to believe in things in spite of the appearance they presented."

"Yes, that's it. I felt that somehow life was founded on a rock. I can't forget those weeks. I often think of them now. It was enough just to be alive and to walk about looking at life. Everything seemed clean, if you can imagine that. We became engaged. I don't think her people were too enthusiastic, but they consented, and I got that job in South America."

He stopped speaking. He seemed to have forgotten me. He sat, gazing into the fire as if he could see a pageant of the days he was describing. His whole expression had altered—as often occurs when a man speaks of a time when he had been happy. His voice was low and there was a new note in it. He looked years younger as he sat leaning forward, studying the flames.

"I centred everything in that woman. She may have found me dull—I don't know—but her very presence gave me something. What was it? Can you tell me what it was?"

"Perhaps it gave substance to your hopes."

"Yes," he said, almost to himself, "that's not a bad definition of happiness." A pause, then he said with a grin, "Perhaps you can give an equally good one for misery."

"Anything that gives substance to your fears creates misery. But never mind definitions. Tell me everything you want to tell me."

After a pause, he went on: "I can't tell you what I experienced in those weeks because I can't use words. I'd heard often enough about people being in love but I had never known what it meant. I think the supreme thing about it for me was that it included everything. There were no irrelevant details in my life. Everything became related to something. That was the miracle. But what the devil does all this matter! We're only concerned with the sequel."

He frowned, and immediately he became angry and nervous again. He moved restlessly and fidgeted with his hands. It was dramatic to see how perfect was the correspondence between his emotions and his gestures. Memory had transformed him momentarily; now the present claimed him again and moulded him to its mood.

"Let's make this short," he exclaimed. "It was arranged that we should marry when I came home on leave. It meant waiting three years, but I could stand that. I went to South America. I wrote every mail and I heard from her by every mail. No other woman existed for me. The future seemed to be mine. It was a map with which I used to play. I gave it frontiers and possessed it imaginatively. God Almighty! What a fool I was! And what hell it is not to be a fool! I was happy enough during those three years. I wrote her everything that I had never dared to tell anyone else. I used to talk aloud in those letters. I lost the fear of being ridiculous. I worked hard all the time, but it wasn't like work. My activities ceased to be work; they seemed like a series of deeds. I saw the beauty of earth for the first time. I wasn't ashamed of my emotions. I even found words for them. The memory of that time is finding words for me now. I put everything I felt into those letters I wrote to her."

Again the past had captured him. It was more real than anything in the room. He had forgotten himself and so words presented themselves readily to express his emotions. In describing the supreme experience of his life, he grew to the stature he had known then. And thus it was that this man who normally hesitated and fidgeted, now sat motionless and spoke simply, sincerely, evoking by some power the miracle of that serenity which love had kindled in him. The library ceased to be a room: it became a world. We did not speak. We had sat silent before, but on this occasion the silence was different.

"I had made all my plans. My leave was nearly due. In a few weeks I should sail for England. I did not hear from her during the last week or so but I paid no attention to that, thinking that she had not written because we were to meet so soon. Two days before I sailed I had a cable from her. It simply said that our engagement was over. When I arrived in England, I discovered that she had married a City man who was very rich and twenty years older than she was."

He began to drink again. After a long silence, he continued:

"I did not go to see her. I wrote to her once and left it at that. At first I just wandered about feeling as if I had been stunned. That passed after a time. Then I seemed to stand apart from my life, to watch it as if it did not belong to me. Have you ever done that?"

"Often," I replied.

"I soon ceased to blame her. She was what she was. I saw that, always, I had been a fool. Just that—no more. I'd believed all sorts of things—I'd served a number of things—simply because it was the tradition to do so. I began to examine those things and I found they weren't worth a damn. The England I had believed in did not exist. It may have once—I don't know—it doesn't now. As to the woman I had loved, I soon realized that she was infinitely less than the things she had evoked in me. All this sounds like the complaint of a schoolboy. I know that damn well. My only chance of any happiness was to remain a grown-up schoolboy. The only men of my type who are happy are simply grown-up schoolboys. You agree to that?"

"Yes," I replied, "I agree with that entirely."

"Well, I lost a creed. It was a lie, but what did that matter? Most creeds are lies but they help to get weaklings and schoolboys through the world. I'm looking out for a new lie. Perhaps you can help me to find one. Any rubbish will do, so long as I can believe in it."

"Is this what you told Scrivener?" I asked.

He was about to light a cigarette when I put the question. He paused, and the match burnt low. He threw it away, then said slowly:

"Yes, and a lot more. How much I don't know. It's what I want to find out. I believe I started to curse the whole universe from God downwards. I know I got involved in a row with some dago in that hole in Soho. And I remember that some of the things Scrivener said froze me."

"What do you mean by that?" I asked.

"I can't explain properly. He had an icy contempt for life on this planet which made my outburst seem childish. Besides, I was only complaining because I had been hurt in a common enough way. But he hadn't. There was little feeling behind his contempt. In fact, if half I seem to remember him saying was what he actually said, then I don't see how he lives from day to day. But I probably got it all wrong. If that fog's cleared, I'd better go. You know what's happened to me now, and you know the type I am. That's something, anyhow. I'd like to come again because I can't stick this eternal loneliness. It's weakness, I know, but I can't stand it."

I rose in order to see if the fog had cleared. This conversation had convinced me of Middleton's sincerity. I was certain now that he had met Scrivener only once and that there was no question of Middleton being his accomplice.

I parted the curtains. The fog had disappeared entirely. I could see the stars, and the moon rode high in the heavens. The clock at St. James's Palace struck half-past eleven. The silvery tones seemed to hover on the air like a benediction. I was about to tell Middleton that the fog had vanished when I noticed that he was leaning back in his chair, listening intently.

"What is it?" I asked.

"Didn't you tell me that your servant slept out?"

"So she does," I replied. "Why?"

"There's someone in the hall," he said.

"Impossible! There can't be anyone."

I was just going to return to my chair when the door opened and Francesca Bellamy walked into the room. She was wrapped in a fur coat and was as self-possessed as ever. She stood looking from one to the other, evidently amused by our attitudes. She held her latchkey in her right hand.

"I will not apologize," she said to me. "I've not been out for three days and when I saw, an hour ago, that the fog had gone, I decided I would walk round and see if you were still here. I'm disturbing you, I see."

"No. This is a friend of Mr. Scrivener's. Mrs. Francesca Bellamy—Mr. Middleton."

I saw immediately that her name was familiar to him. There was silence for a moment. I took her coat and she sat down by the fire. Her entry was so dramatic that Middleton was too surprised to speak. He watched her, however, as she sat in the firelight, and it was evident that her beauty impressed him.

"You've no news of Jonathan?"

"None," I replied. "I thought perhaps you had heard from him."

"We never write to each other."

She turned to Middleton.

"You know Mr. Scrivener well?" she asked.

"I scarcely know him at all," Middleton muttered. "I've met him only once. We—we picked each other up one night."

"It's an odd thing," she said lightly, "that I never meet anyone who knows him really well. Which reminds me: did Jonathan warn you that I had the key of his flat?"

"He did not," I answered. "He gave me no warnings of any kind and very few instructions."

She laughed, and turned again to Middleton. "Mr. Scrivener provides me with mysteries, do you know that? He's a mystery himself, and his secretary, Mr. Wrexham, is just as mysterious in a different way. But probably Mr. Wrexham is an old friend of yours."

Middleton twisted in his chair. "No, not at all; on the contrary," he stammered. "This is the second time we've met."

She looked at him surprised. "Then you came here expecting to find Mr. Scrivener?"

"Yes—exactly."

"And you found Mr. Wrexham, just as I did, and I daresay he told you that he had never seen Mr. Scrivener."

"Yes, that's right," said Middleton. He was staring at her. She was dressed in black and looked extremely attractive as she sat cross-legged, one hand held out towards the fire.

"What he tells us is quite true," she said. "That's disappointing in one way, but it makes things even more mysterious. You are interested in Mr. Scrivener?"

He did not reply for a minute, then I saw an angry light flash in his eyes.

"Is this some joke?" he asked gruffly.

"Joke!" Francesca looked at him surprised.

"Yes—joke!" he repeated angrily. "It's scarcely likely that a man engages a secretary whom he has never seen and that a woman, who has a key to his flat, knows nothing about him."

Francesca ignored the insulting tone in which he spoke and laughed softly.

"You feel that there is a plot, Mr. Middleton. I sympathize with you. I often feel the same. I admit that my possession of a latchkey suggests intimacy, but I assure you that I am not Mr. Scrivener's mistress and even if I were, I might know very little about him."

But I could see that Middleton was still angry. He rose awkwardly:

"I think I'll go," he said thickly, then added: "I was probably a fool to come."

He bowed to her and left the room. I followed him into the hall. He turned on me almost fiercely.

"Have you lied to me? Do you know Scrivener well?"

"I have not lied to you about anything," I said.

He looked at me searchingly for a minute. "Well, I believe you. God knows why, but I believe you. But I don't believe a word that woman says—not a syllable. She's *the* Mrs. Bellamy, isn't she?"

"Yes, she's *the* Mrs. Bellamy."

"I'm not surprised her husband shot himself. So she has a key and so has Miss Mandeville. Scrivener does not object to women apparently—whatever he may say. Do they know each other?"

"No," I replied, "they don't know each other."

"What a power!" he muttered to himself, as he got into his overcoat. "That type of woman puts the wind up me. Still, perhaps it's better than the Mandeville type. You cannot have any illusions about the Mrs. Bellamys of this world. I'm afraid I was rude," he said abruptly.

"It doesn't matter," I replied.

"As long as you don't mind, it's all right. Look here, dine with me one night, will you?"

"I'd like to very much."

A moment later he went, and I returned to the library.

"Now, please, tell me the truth about your friend who has drunk too much and who was very rude." She seemed very cool and adequate—a total contrast to the chaotic Middleton.

She took the cigarette I offered her.

"There's nothing more to tell you," I began. "Middleton has met Scrivener once, and this is the second time I have seen him. I'm sorry he was rude, but after all, the circumstances were unusual."

She sat and smoked while she studied me narrowly through half-closed eyes. It was a searching scrutiny and I felt that it would penetrate most disguises. I had nothing to conceal, however, so I returned her gaze, noting the dark fire of her eyes and the luxuriance of her jet-black hair.

"Never mind Mr. Middleton, for the moment," she said. "There's something else I want to discuss with you. I've found out that you've told me the truth."

"I hope I shall make the same discovery about you," I said lightly.

"You have doubts?"

"Certainly," I replied.

She laughed gaily. "I haven't told you any lies yet, anyway."

"That's scarcely the same thing. But it shall be as you like, Mrs. Bellamy——"

"I always allow anyone who interests me to call me Francesca."

"Then I will call you Francesca so long as I interest you, which probably will not be very long."

"Why not?"

I did not reply immediately. I had to make up my mind whether we were to continue to fence whenever we met, or whether I should make an attempt to reach an understanding with her. I felt that, underneath, she was genuinely interested in Scrivener and I knew that it was this interest which prompted her to see me. I had no objection to this but I was determined that she should admit it, if it were the fact. I had a basis now with Pauline and with Middleton and I was determined to establish common ground with Francesca. I knew that in her case it would be more difficult because, unlike the others, she carried the weapons of this world and knew how to use them.

"I asked you a question just now. Won't you answer it?"

"Tell me this:" I began, "why do you come here?"

"Why?"

"Yes—why?"

"I have told you that you interest me." She threw her cigarette into the fire and looked at me with simulated innocence.

"Listen to me, Francesca. I am a nobody. I have no gifts. I am not amusing. I have lived most of my life alone. You are wealthy, beautiful, and you know all kinds of interesting people. What possible interest can you have in me? Let us be frank, or do not let us meet. It's not worth while fencing together. If you still imagine that I am playing some part, you are wrong. I'm not interested enough in anyone or in anything, to lend myself to any deception. Let us have the cards on the table, or finish the game."

"Why did you take this job? Tell me that."

She shot the question at me and, after my plea for frankness, it put me at a disadvantage. It required an answer, and there was no adequate answer.

"The question stands, doesn't it?" she went on. "I assure you that I want to be quite certain about you. Perhaps you'll know why later on."

"I cannot tell you why I took this job," I said. "Or if I told you, I should not be able to convince you."

"What does that mean?" she asked curtly.

"I became Scrivener's secretary for no logical reason whatever. I suddenly became aware that a change was imminent in my life. With that certainty upon me, I saw his advertisement in *The Times*, and answered it."

"And why, do you imagine, he chose you for the position?"

"That is as much a mystery to me as it is to you."

"Very well," she said with a laugh. "I will believe you, but you must admit it's an act of faith. I wanted to be certain. I've another question: have you any reason to think that Jonathan knew your parents or anyone connected with you?"

"No, I think it's quite impossible. I'd thought of that. I'll make a confession to you—I am determined to discover exactly why Scrivener brought me here."

"Ah! I've been waiting for you to say that!" She rose swiftly and came over to me, then sat on a sofa which was near to my chair. "I've been waiting for you to say that," she repeated. "I want to go into partnership with you."

"Partnership!" I exclaimed.

"Yes. I want to work with you to solve the mystery of Jonathan."

"He's my employer, you know," I said with a smile.

But she was entirely serious. "Those considerations do not apply where he is concerned, and you know it. You know no one in London?"

"Not a soul."

"So much the better," she said almost to herself.

She sat motionless, her chin in her hand. I was amazed at her intensity. I could see that her thoughts were racing and I recognized that my appeal for frankness was destined to create a much deeper intimacy than I had anticipated. Yet, strangely enough, as I watched her, I could imagine that she was a great actress who had just read a part which gave her greatness scope.

"A partnership," she repeated. "Do you know that I've tested your story so far as I could?"

"You've *tested* it?" I said.

"Yes, I've confirmed that you *were* at Petersham's office all those years. And I've seen Mr. Winkworth."

"Mr. *Walter* Winkworth?" I inquired.

"Certainly. Surely he's the only one! Yes, I've seen him. He confirmed the details you told me as to the manner in which you became Jonathan's secretary."

"In my opinion, he is completely in the dark about the whole affair. Was he glad to see you?"

"Terribly! His portrait would make a perfect frontispiece to a book on Etiquette! Never mind him. I only tell you that I've checked up on you—as the Americans say—to prove that I'm in earnest about being able to trust you."

I did not reply and for several minutes we remained silent.

"I really came to ask you to dinner," she said suddenly, "but I've changed my mind. You must come to supper. Come to-day week, will you?"

"Thanks very much. Is that invitation a sign that we have become partners?"

"Perhaps. I will give you a theory which you can think over during the week. It's a theory about Jonathan and it covers most of the facts." She took another cigarette. "Yes, I'll tell it to you first and then ask you some questions."

"Does it explain the mystery of my engagement?" I asked.

"It provides a possible explanation. Perhaps the mystery of Jonathan is no more than this: *he experiments on others*. Had you thought of that?"

I had thought of a great number of things but I told her that this possibility had not occurred to me.

"Well, think of it now. Let us apply it to you: it interested him to take you out of the life you had known; to bring you here, knowing you would meet some of his friends; to leave you alone here and then, later, to return to see what you had made of entirely new surroundings and somewhat difficult circumstances. Might that be the explanation?"

I saw that she was entirely serious and, after all, this explanation fitted the facts better than any I had evolved.

"And Middleton? Do you suggest he picked him up in Soho in order to experiment on him?" I asked.

"It sounds fantastic, you mean? But tell me this: did Middleton seem impressed by Jonathan? Is he interested in him? Would you say that Jonathan had influenced him?"

I imagined that my expression answered her questions, for she went on:

"Perhaps the theory isn't so fantastic after all. Why has Middleton been here twice to find Jonathan? If you had a talk with a stranger in some café, would you call twice on him if he hadn't interested you?"

"You are making a good case," I said, "but you could easily make a better. You could apply the theory to yourself. Do you think Scrivener is experimenting on you?"

"I *know* it," she replied in a tone of finality. "We are fighting a duel."

"He has had the courage to run away," I said with a smile.

"His last remark before he went proved his skill as an antagonist," she replied enigmatically. "Still, think over my theory before we have supper together."

"You had some questions to ask," I reminded her.

"Yes, one is about Middleton. Will you bring him to see me?"

"I'm not certain," I replied, after a pause, and much to her amusement.

"One more question, and I must go," she announced. "Have there been any other visitors?"

"Yes, one."

"A woman?" She looked at me intently.

"Yes," I replied.

"Tell me about her."

"She came into this room just as you did."

"You mean—she has a latchkey?"

"Yes."

She stared at me with inscrutable eyes.

"Is she beautiful?"

"Yes."

"Dark?"

"No—fair."

"Young?"

"Yes."

She moved nearer to me. The atmosphere had become tense, dramatic.

"What is her name?"

"I cannot tell you that."

There was a pause and I hoped her cross-examination would stop. I was separated from a dilemma by a sentence or two.

"Did you tell her that another woman had a latchkey?"

"Yes."

"Did you tell her *my* name?"

"Yes."

"But you will not tell me hers!" she exclaimed passionately. "And when you told her, she said '*The* Mrs. Bellamy, I suppose?' Just as Middleton probably did when you saw him out. You imagine that if you told me *her* name, it might injure her reputation. But you knew that telling her *my* name could not injure mine! My God! I thought you—"

"I was utterly in the wrong. Her name is Pauline Mandeville. I should not have told her your name but having done so, I must tell you hers. You must forgive me—and I shall ask her to forgive me."

She stood looking at me in amazement. My revelation of the other woman's name, although it conveyed nothing to her, had taken her completely by surprise. Her mood changed like lightning.

"I forgive you," she said softly, "and so will she. Will you get me a taxi? And come to supper to-day week?"

CHAPTER VI

I

THE most difficult habit for modern people to break is that of dividing up their days into allotments, assigning an hour to this activity, another to that, as if Time were an enemy in ambush and one only to be defeated by cunning and endless vigilance. We have heard so much about the necessity for concentration that we have become its slaves, and most of us are more concerned about the quantity of our activities than their quality. We plan everything in advance. We make up our minds with such determination that, say, to-morrow, between three and four, we will do our accounts; that we not only do them, but would continue to do them if a messenger from God Himself tapped on the windowpane to attract our attention. We regard each day as a draughtboard, divided logically into squares, on which we must make our little moves and win our little prizes, and we continue to do this although we know perfectly well that our best ideas are never the result of conscious thought, and that our only chance in a sudden crisis is to act as the genius of the vital second prompts us.

I know all this—I have known it for years—but the fact remains that directly I woke on the morning after the visits of Middleton and Francesca, I proceeded to map out my day with ruthless logic. In the first place, I decided that I would see no one. I had enough to think about and it was essential to be alone. Secondly, I decided that I would telephone Winkworth as it seemed desirable to let him know that the visit Francesca had paid him was in no sense the result of anything I had said to her concerning him. Finally, I wanted to devote most of the day to considering whether there was anything in Francesca's theory that Scrivener experimented on others, and I also wished to review my whole attitude in regard to Scrivener's friends. Although conventions count for little with me, I have my standards. I was accepting Scrivener's money and at the same time I was discussing him freely with all his friends. I would give the day to considering these things.

Having shackled my soul with the armour of these resolutions, I went in to breakfast. The first thing I encountered was a miracle in the form of a letter. It had been re-directed from Petersham's office and it informed me that a man called Rogerson had recently died in Australia and had left me five thousand pounds. An extract from his will was given to the effect that many years ago my father had done him a great service. Rogerson had become successful since my father's death and therefore he left this sum to his son—the only surviving relative.

I had never heard of Rogerson, but there was the letter. It was written by a firm of solicitors in Lincoln's Inn Fields. I went on mechanically with my breakfast, trying to determine the chief effect of this miracle on my present circumstances. It took me an hour to discover the obvious. It meant that I was free, and that if I continued in Scrivener's service, I could make it clear to him that I was bound by none of the usual restrictions and that if his friends chose to become also friends of mine, I must meet them in my own right and not merely as his secretary. The alternative was my resignation. Rogerson's legacy had made me independent.

So at ten-thirty, I found myself writing at length to Scrivener. I pointed out that I was becoming intimate with his friends and that if he had any objections, which would be perfectly understandable, then I must resign, but that I should always remain his debtor since, through him, the horizons of my life had widened. I was not satisfied till this letter was in the post.

I then rang up Winkworth, but he had relapsed into the Winkworth of our first interview. He had difficulty in remembering my name. When I attempted to point out that Francesca's visit to his office was an independent act on her part, he swept the subject aside with the statement that he had had the honour to act for Mrs. Bellamy before in a professional capacity and that doubtless he would do so again in operations of some magnitude. He ignored entirely our discussion at our second meeting and when I referred to that interview, it was evident that his memory had failed him. At this point, however, I introduced a new theme:

"One thing more, Mr. Winkworth."

"My time is valuable, you know, Mr. Wrexham."

"I'm certain of it and I shall not detain you. I wonder if you would act for me in a small matter."

"Act for *you*." (The emphasis was annihilating.)

"Yes. I had a communication from Hargreaves, Grunt and Hardcastle this morning."

"The Lincoln's Inn people?" Winkworth inquired with a faint note of interest in his voice.

"Yes," I replied. "They tell me that I have been left the sum of——"

At this point we were cut off. The usual technique in such circumstances having been performed, the receiver having been replaced and so on, we were connected again about five minutes later.

"We were cut off," I began.

"You were saying that you had been left the sum of——"

"Five thousand pounds," I announced.

"Really, Wrexham, *really*. Not a fortune, of course, but a nice nest egg, sir, a nice nest egg. Come now, five thousand pounds. Not a life interest? Comes to you absolutely?"

"Absolutely," I replied.

"Ah! With judicious management and a little knowledge one can do something with five thousand pounds, I *think*. A dear friend of mine once said to me, just before he was made a baronet, 'Winkworth, the basis of my success was saving the tips my uncles gave me when I was at school.' Of course, Wrexham, I should be most happy to act for you. Not the first time, sir, that this house has had dealings with Hargreaves, Grunt and Hardcastle of Lincoln's Inn."

So it was left and in due course Winkworth transacted my business, such as it was.

It was now twelve o'clock. The day I had mapped out for myself had become only a memory. I decided that I would lunch out and a few minutes later I was about to leave the flat, when Matthews appeared and informed me that a Mr. Antony Rivers had called and had asked for Mr. Scrivener or, if he had not returned, he would like to see Mr. Wrexham.

"He's evidently a friend of Mr. Scrivener's," I said to Matthews, as I was anxious to know if she knew Mr. Rivers.

"Yes, sir. He has been here before."

"Please ask him to come in."

A moment later an immaculately-dressed young man appeared. He was the only man I have ever seen who looked elegant in modern clothes. The best that most of us achieve is to be well-groomed. He was about twenty-five, tall, very fair; he had a pink and white complexion and was easy and effervescent in his manner.

"Hullo! Scrivener not back then? Too bad. Never mind. You must be Wrexham. He told me about you. My name's Rivers— Antony Rivers."

We shook hands.

"So this is the mystery room. Never been in here before."

"Had you any reason to expect Scrivener to be here?" I asked.

"Said he might be, but you know what it is. He thought of returning a fortnight ago."

"You've seen him recently?" I managed to ask.

"Oh, yes, ran across him in Paris. Which reminds me, I've left some books in my taxi. It's outside. I'll get them. Or, perhaps your servant would."

Matthews went for the books while Rivers glanced round the library. He moved so gracefully that I thought he was about to dance. He hummed lightly while he examined the volumes. He was very good-looking in rather a pretty way which was some-what contradicted by the set line of the mouth. Every article of his attire—suit, shirt, tie, links, shoes, socks—was unique, and you knew for certain that you would not see a duplicate of any one of them on another man. Each was distinguished, and suited him to perfection, and you marvelled as to where such individuality was to be obtained.

Matthews returned with a small parcel of books and gave them to Rivers, who said to me:

"I told Scriv I'd bring these. Save him sending them. I'll put them there. I'm glad you were in. I was thrilled to find that Scriv had a secretary and I wanted to meet you."

"Well, sit down, if you're not in a hurry."

"Oh, not a bit," he raced on. "I've nothing to do, thank God! I tell you what, though. Scriv used to have a priceless sherry. Shall we have some? I'm sick of cocktails, except a new one I had in Paris called Chaos."

Matthews produced the sherry and I waited for inspiration to instruct me how to deal with Antony Rivers.

"Have you known Scrivener for some time?" I asked.

"Oh, yes," he exclaimed in the same light tone. "Three years off and on. I keep drifting into him, you know. I amuse him, I think. Several people think Scriv a bit odd but that's all nonsense. Matter of fact he's very like me."

This was an unexpected solution to the problem and possibly my expression indicated as much, for Rivers went on:

"Out for a good time, that's what I mean. We go for it in different ways, of course, but we're very much the same. By the way, do you dance a lot?"

"Not at all, I'm afraid."

"Pity! I wanted to rope you in for a new dance club. Can't be helped. Scriv doesn't dance either. What the devil does he want all these books for? This room always used to be locked. So much so, that I thought he must have murdered a rich uncle and kept the corpse here."

He lit a cigarette and went on talking. I did not hear half he said though the gleam in his attractive eyes told me that he was thoroughly enjoying himself.

Rivers was an entirely new experience for me. Not only had I never met anyone remotely like him, but I had never imagined such a person as a possibility.

But at last a definite question emerged from the froth of anecdote and scandal with which Rivers was amusing himself:

"What on earth do you and Scriv talk about when he's here? I always call him Scriv because it's so utterly incongruous. What do you talk about, though?"

"Didn't Scrivener tell you that he and I hadn't met?" I asked.

"Good Lord, no! Haven't you?"

"No."

"That's too marvellous. I can dine out on that. That's a real thrill. Engage a secretary you don't know! Damned good start for a thriller! I wrote a thriller once, by the way. Least, I began one. Promise me you're not joking."

"I'm not joking—I can promise you that."

He looked at me and for one second he was silent.

"Brilliant of him not to tell me. He's got one incredible gift—he makes you feel that he's shown you his soul. D'you know what I mean? You feel thrilled, honoured, and you have that lovely little quiver which goes right through you when you feel that someone is in your power. Then you wake up the next day and find you know nothing about him whatever."

"Except that he's out for a good time," I put in, as he paused.

"Oh, yes, except for that of course. But he wouldn't be modern if he weren't out for that, and he's a modern all right. I ought to see more of him," he went on. "He beats me at my own game. Yes, I really ought to see more of him." His tone indicated clearly that, in his judgment, there was only one side to this question.

He finished his sherry. "I want you to lunch with me," he announced. "You must come. There's a lot to discuss. It's not too early for you, is it? That's splendid. I'll take you to a little place just off Soho."

I felt much as a leaf must feel when it falls into a waterfall. The instant gratification of each mood was so imperative to Rivers that I let him sweep me away to lunch, thereby leaving the day I had planned in irreparable ruin. He got my hat, he put it on, he took my arm, and I danced down the stairs with him. When we reached the street, however, he stopped dead.

"Hullo!" he exclaimed. "That's my taxi. I'd forgotten all about it. What a compliment to you! Jump in. May as well drive as it's

still here." He gave an address and we got in. "Good thing I didn't
send this taxi away," he said in his amazingly rapid way. "Look!
there's my umbrella."

"And here are your gloves," I said picking up a superlative pair
from the floor.

"You see," he went on, "it *pays* to be extravagant. That's what my
uncle won't see." He dropped his voice to a whisper. "Of course,
between ourselves, a Victorian uncle is *the* most hopeless—Look!"

He threw himself half out of the window and began waving to
a lady in a large car at the top of St. James's Street who regarded
him with dignified amazement.

"Thought that was Monty, but it wasn't," he explained as he
returned to his seat. "Never mind." He dismissed the subject for
ever with a wave of his hand.

Now it does not occupy much time to drive from the top of St.
James's Street to the outskirts of Soho, even allowing for being held
up by the traffic. In the space of ten minutes, at the most, Rivers
told me his age; where he had been educated; the fact that his father
was dead; where his mother and brother lived in the country; that
he had a bachelor uncle who lived in Albany; that he—Rivers—had
a private income of three pounds a week and that he took on a job
occasionally, but that in no circumstances was it his intention ever
to do any work. He was one of those people—a modern type—
who, during a first meeting, tell you everything about themselves.
So much so that you cannot decide whether you will ever really
know them or whether there is anything really to know. He was
about to enlighten me as to his views on sex, when the taxi stopped
in a narrow street outside a forbidding-looking restaurant.

"Here we are! Never been here? Oh, it's great fun. Japanese
food. You'll love it."

I followed him through a dimly-lit room in which jet-black
tables were dotted about. The walls, too, were black and apparently the food was served in curious black bowls. Rivers stopped at
two tables to greet people he knew, then piloted me to a table by
the window. Whereupon he passed me a menu which conveyed
absolutely nothing to me. I indicated as much.

"Quite," was his comment. "They do a lunch here. I always have it. I like this food. Of course, if you *like*, you *can* have English food." This concession was made in such a disparaging tone that he might have been offering me poison.

"No, I'll have the lunch," I said, with the courage of the ignorant.

"I brought a man here who had lived in Japan and *he* said that this is the stuff all right."

But I had decided that I must take the conversation in hand, so I said to him:

"Do you mind if I talk about Scrivener for a bit?"

"No. Go ahead. Betty!"

The last word was a shout, and was directed towards a young woman who was looking round the restaurant. She came over to our table. She was remarkably pretty but her thoughts were clearly occupied with something remote from her surroundings.

"Hullo, Ant," she said, absent-mindedly. "Have you seen Ike?"

"No, heard he was dead," replied Rivers briskly.

"When? Not to-day?"

"Oh, no, about a month ago."

"That's all right then," said Betty with no great enthusiasm, "because I was with him yesterday. Can't remember whether he said *here*, or the *Chinese*, or the *Indian*—Oh, there he is! Bye-bye!"

"Now that girl's got brains," Rivers began, but I reminded him that we were going to discuss Scrivener.

"Quite! Go ahead."

I explained that I was naturally interested in Scrivener and asked if Rivers had spent much time with him in Paris.

"Oh, not much," he rattled off. "I wanted a free fare so I undertook a small commission for someone here. The man paid my fare and expenses. I had to give some documents to a woman. I called and there was Scriv."

"I have a reason for asking—was the lady beautiful?"

"Was she hell!" exclaimed Rivers with great emphasis. "Eyes like an oyster and you could have struck a match on her voice. My God! she carted us off to a psychic to have our fortunes told. I ought to have been paid to listen to mine, instead of which it cost me six hundred francs. Scriv seemed amused and I'm damned if the next day we didn't all go to a séance. Ever been to one?"

I said that I had never been to a séance.

"They're not bad," he said lightly, as if they were a drink of some kind. "Still, we got into touch with some pretty dreary spirits, I thought. One spirit in particular bored me. She was telling a fat Englishman who was present all about the next world. I gathered the man had once been her husband. She kept saying that she was happy and that Aunt Laura was with her. I soon saw that death has a sting all right. When it was over, I asked Scriv what he thought of the Laura stuff, and what he thought of the spiritualists."

"What did he say?" I inquired not without interest.

"He said that the spiritualists suburbanized the cosmos. It took me two days to see how this remark embraced Aunt Laura, and as I was in mid-Channel when I saw its application, I wasn't too interested."

It was at this point that the first course appeared. It consisted of odds and ends of dry, very dead-looking things. I tried one which looked like a mushroom of great antiquity, but it turned out to be raw fish. To my amazement Rivers ate this quite cheerfully while launching out on a theory concerning birth control. I tried something else which looked like ginger. I took a good bite of this hoping to banish the memory of the fish. There was a kind of explosion in my mouth; the next second it was full of acrid dust. After these two experiments, I dared not continue. Rivers did not notice, however, for he had left the subject of birth control and was discussing modern décor. He paused only to demolish two good sections of the edible which looked like ginger. After which he leant back in his chair and lit a cigarette.

My eyes had now become accustomed to the dimness of the room and I could see its occupants plainly. They were all English, or at any rate Europeans, and were somewhat eccentric in clothes and manner. They all talked loudly and everyone seemed to know everyone else. The only Japanese were the waiters. Curiously enough, I happened to look out of the window and saw four or five Japanese, but they all walked resolutely past the restaurant. I was considering this anomaly deeply when the soup arrived.

It was neither hot nor cold, clean nor dirty, thick nor clear, and it had long weeds in it which looked rather like serpents who had died in youth. Rivers started gaily enough, however. It is curious what cowards we are when we are guests. Had I been the host on this occasion, I would have sent this soup away immediately, but, as it was, I decided that I must try to get through it. . . . It tasted exactly like the old Aquarium at Brighton used to smell.

"Some people don't like this soup," said Rivers.

"I'm afraid I don't much," I said apologetically.

"Pity! Never mind. There's lots of other dishes coming. Try the things floating about in it. They're great fun."

But an interruption saved me. A very tall, lank man came up to our table. He placed both hands on it, leant forward heavily and said, "Hul-lo." These two syllables fell from him like two weights. After which he remained silent, staring at the tablecloth with lifeless eyes. His mouth was half-open and a strand of dank hair divided his forehead.

"Good Lord, Sep," exclaimed Rivers. "Thought you were in America."

"No." There was a pause after this statement. Then our visitor said playfully, yet wistfully, to Rivers:

"You're always deserting us, bad boy."

He then assembled himself and returned to a table the other side of the room.

"Of course you know who *that* is?" murmured Rivers respectfully.

"No, I'm afraid not. Who is he?"

"Why, my *dear* fellow," he explained, "that's Septimus Heron. You must have read his books. Surely! Don't you remember one was banned recently? It was called *Illicit*, I think. Anyhow, I've got a first edition. He's one of these marvellous, depraved, cultured people. Brilliant conversationalist! *Terribly* sensitive. I used to know a whole lot of artists once. But tell me this: I want your views on——"

I could easily believe that Rivers had met a great number of people in his day for he was able to talk superficially on every subject and had a theory for the solution of every problem. Each topic apparently had the same significance for him, since he gave the same emphasis to each in turn. In his manner of discussing things there was an implication that the inhabitants of the earth were simply an impossible lot of idiots and that, if they really wanted to put things right, they had only to carry out the very simple and obvious remedies which Rivers was letting off like so many fireworks. So infectious was this manner that, listening to him, one was almost hypnotized into believing oneself to be a very exclusive and highly privileged person.

He had touched lightly on prohibition, religion, science, the decay of Western civilization, and the absurdity of marriage, when the next course arrived. Simultaneously he said to me quickly, "Don't look up! There's Otto Strong."

"What is the matter with him?" I inquired.

"Oh, he used to be a charming person, but now—!" He made an expressive gesture. "He's been cured of his inferiority complex with the result, of course, that now he's terribly aggressive. He used to shiver and now he shouts. Thank God, he hasn't seen us!"

Personally I would rather have been seen by Mr. Otto Strong than have been obliged to look at the contents of the black bowl which had been placed in front of me. Although it resembled spaghetti, recent experience had proved that in this restaurant things were not what they seemed. Nor did the fact that one solitary prawn crowned the writhing pyramid inspire me with any confidence.

"Looks like spaghetti," said Rivers, "but it isn't."

I waited, hoping he would say what it was, but he began to eat in the manner of one performing a rite. Also he manipulated with great dexterity some remarkable instrument with which he conveyed the food to his mouth. I demanded a fork, although I realized that by so doing I was placing myself irredeemably.

I discovered that the thin white worms were seaweed of a notable antiquity. The fork fell from my hand. I watched Rivers,

who was eating rapidly, with genuine admiration. Then a doubt
crossed my mind: perhaps his was different from mine; perhaps
his was fresh and mine was bad. However, they looked exactly the
same. I had to admit that.

"You leave the prawn till the end," said Rivers as if he were
instructing a child. Then he went on, "The prawn acquires an
extraordinarily subtle flavour after you've finished this stuff."

I decided to lie, and I therefore began with the time-honoured
formula: "To tell you the truth, I'm not very hungry. I had a late
breakfast."

"Quite! Pity! Never mind—you can try some odd things they
usually serve after this."

But I lit a cigarette with an air of finality and glanced round the
room. Several people were eating the white seaweed, pausing only
to smoke or talk. I noticed that every one of them left the prawn
till the end. But again the voice of Rivers claimed me.

"See that girl over there? No, the one by the door in the black
hat and the yellow scarf. She's Pepstone's new model. Vital, isn't
she? I danced with her the other night. She has practically all her
meals here."

I was about to comment on this last statement when Rivers
began to rattle on again. He launched a long theory concerning
naval disarmament and having indicated in a few bold strokes
the simple method by which this could be achieved, he ended by
saying, "I admit the Japanese are a menace." After which he took
another large helping of seaweed.

It was only necessary to give Rivers half my attention, as he
rarely waited for comments and as I watched him and listened to
him, it crossed my mind that possibly at last I had met a specimen
of "modern youth," concerning whom the newspapers print so
many articles. It was clear, at any rate, that Rivers lived only for
pleasure, that his life had no backgrounds of any kind, and that
although he had nothing but contempt for his elders, he had no
objection whatever to living on them.

Feeling that I could be quite frank, I suggested this last point to
him.

"You mean I live on my mother and my uncle? Yes, of course. How odd you should say that! Scriv told me that I denied the past and yet lived on it. He said that I was therefore a good European, because Europe is living on the past and America is living on the future. I don't know what he meant about America—perhaps he was referring to the hire-purchase ramp out there. I hope everything goes smash, don't you? Such *fun*."

I brought him back to the point. He was only interesting to me when he was discussing himself, which, fortunately, was his favourite subject.

"My philosophy is very simple," he began. "I do not intend to work. I like parties, dancing, change, and amusing people. I can get along without working so why should I? It wouldn't be fair to the unemployed. If I get a job, someone who is only fit to work would have to go without one." He lit a cigarette with a generous gesture. "I'll tell you my secret, if you like. It explains me and the most modern advanced people."

I told him that it would interest me very much.

"Then listen, my dear fellow. I belong to a generation which is determined not to suffer. That is the secret." He flicked the ash off his cigarette triumphantly. "I admit," he went on, "that that phrase isn't mine. I saw it in a sixpenny highbrow paper, but directly I read it, I knew that it was true about me. Now, I'm probably a new type to you."

"I've met a number of people who had endured agonies in their determination not to suffer," I replied.

"Quite! Bad technique. They probably accepted responsibility for all kinds of rubbish. I do nothing of the kind. I shall never be old. I shall be exactly the same when I'm sixty as I am now. I don't want to sound arrogant but I do really think that people of my type are the one significant product of the war. You see, we've seen *through* so much and we have had the courage to accept futility."

"That's a new idea to me," I said perfectly truthfully.

"To accept futility? But, of course! Everyone who isn't a fool knows that everything is futile, so why not accept futility and amuse yourself?"

It may have been the food, or the atmosphere of the restaurant, but as Rivers continued to explain his philosophy, his voice seemed to grow thin as if it came from a great distance. I ceased to listen to him for I was now fairly certain that each and every subject he introduced only interested him in so far as it served as a background to himself. Also I was convinced that most of his statements he had picked up from others. This was the reason why he propounded theories of genuine originality with precisely the same flippancy as he employed when advancing intricate rubbish.

At this point some dainties were put on the table which resembled small, petrified bats. Rivers took four and there was a lull during which he ate slowly. Fortunately he did not notice that I ignored their presence. When he had eaten two, a friend came and engaged him in a whispered conversation, which gave me an opportunity to sort out my impressions. In my outlook, the most important fact concerning Rivers was the gulf which separated him from the other visitors to the flat. Although Pauline, Francesca, and Middleton had little enough in common, it was possible to conceive that an unusual man might have all three as his friends. But Rivers! It was impossible! It was intriguing that although Rivers had known Scrivener for a much longer period than the others, he could tell me less about him than any one of them. Also I was impressed by the fact that Rivers, knowing him not at all, found little mystery in him. Or was it that he was not prepared to admit it, lest the conversation should centre round Scrivener? I decided to have one more attempt to get him to discuss the subject which now interested me more than any other.

His friend retired. Rivers leant over the table and said:

"I don't introduce you to all these birds. Such a business! What? Quite! Knew you'd understand. Anyway I don't know that fellow's name who's just gone. Don't believe I've ever met him in my life. But one meets so many people, you know what it is."

"There's a question I want to ask you," I began hastily, while I had an opportunity. "I've met one or two of Scrivener's friends——"

"Do tell me their names," he interrupted. "I've no idea what crowd Scriv knows in London nowadays. Sorry to interrupt, but I really would like to know."

I hesitated for a minute but it was clear that only by answering this question could I keep the subject on Scrivener.

"Well, there's a man called Middleton—Andrew Middleton—but I don't suppose you've met him."

"No, never heard of him. Any women?"

"There's one you will have heard of, I expect, although you may not have met her, and that is Mrs. Francesca Bellamy."

"Good God!" There was vitality and genuine surprise behind that exclamation. "You don't mean that? It's impossible, my dear fellow. Why, damn it all, I talked about her to Scriv when I was in Paris and he made no comment of any kind."

"Then perhaps I was wrong to mention her name," I said slowly. "But I did not know there was any secrecy in the matter."

But Rivers was not listening to me. His whole attitude had changed. For the first time, I saw the mood in him which corresponded with the hard line of his mouth. At this moment he might have been a keen man of business. Everything about him suggested alertness and concentration. His eyes were fixed on mine and his cigarette was allowed to burn itself away neglected in an ash-tray.

"Look here, I've got to get this right. Scriv knows Mrs. Francesca Bellamy. You're *certain*?"

"I'm quite certain," I said with a smile.

"Why?"

"Well," I said, after a pause, "she's told me so. That may not be conclusive evidence, I admit, but——"

"Then *you* know her!" He leant across the table and threw the sentence at me.

"Certainly. Of course I know her. I've met her twice."

He made a sudden movement with his hand. "We'll have to go into this thoroughly. This is really damned important. Directly I saw you I knew we had something to say to each other. Now, you're not in a hurry? Good! Well, have some coffee?"

As tactfully as possible I inquired whether coffee in this restau-

rant in any way resembled the beverage usually associated with
the word. On being assured that it did, I accepted a cup. It was
coffee. I drank it quickly, fearful that its surroundings might per-
vert it.

Rivers lit another cigarette, put his elbows on the table, and
stared at me for a minute before he began to speak. An action which
informed me that, this time, he was marshalling his thoughts—
conclusive evidence that he had an end in view.

"I'm afraid, Wrexham—I can call you Wrexham? Good!
Thanks!—I'm afraid you'll think I'm cross-examining you."

"You needn't worry about that. If I don't answer, you'll understand that in my position——"

"Quite! Absolutely! What I want to know *most particularly* is
whether you met Mrs. Bellamy through being Scriv's secretary?"

"Yes, I did."

He was obviously disappointed. His glance fell and he drummed
on the table with his fingers. He was silent for a minute, then he
asked hopefully:

"All the same, you said you'd met her *twice*, didn't you?"

"Yes, twice."

Again he was silent. Then his whole manner altered and he
exhibited a charming side to his nature which had not emerged
previously. It is not easy to describe, but it enfolded you and made
you feel that he was only happy when he was with you. You smiled
immediately and felt that you would do anything he wanted, and
at the same time you realized that this engaging manner was
entirely conscious on his part. Nevertheless it was a formidable
social weapon. Even his voice changed. It had a caressing note and
he spoke much less rapidly.

"My dear fellow, what will you think of me? It's really *too* wonderful the way you answer my questions without asking me why
I'm so rude, and curious, and excited. I'll explain everything, but
somehow, with *you*, I feel that explanations are unnecessary. I
believe you understand. You're a psychologist, and that's such a
help."

I took the cigarette he offered me and had another cup of coffee. I reflected that I should need to be a good psychologist if I were ever to make anything of the maze in which I was at present hopelessly lost. I smiled at him encouragingly and he went on:

"You've met her twice. *Do* forgive me but—was she pleasant to you?"

"Very pleasant indeed," I replied, wondering what would come next.

"Then you *might* see her again?"

"I am quite certain I shall," I said. "There's no doubt about that."

"Well, then, look here. I can trust you, can't I? I mean, really trust you, because it's pretty important."

With some difficulty I answered him perfectly seriously that he could trust me. Effective as it was, there was something ludicrous in his complete change of manner, though I did not overlook the fact that the questions he had asked were far from unintelligent— not only individually, but the sequence in which he had placed them was skilful.

He leant over and said in a whisper: "I've been trying to get to know Mrs. Bellamy for over a year." He was entirely serious and spoke with great emphasis.

"It really would interest me to know why," I said.

He looked at me as if, temporarily, I had lost my reason:

"*Why?* Good Lord, Wrexham, if I knew her, and her crowd, I'd be made. She has not only great wealth but great influence *and*, my dear fellow, influence with the kind of people I want to get in with. No, it's no good, if you don't know the town as I do, I can't make you understand. But I'm not wrong—you can take that from me."

I could see that the adventurer in him had flamed into life. He was looking over my shoulder and scheme after scheme raced through his brain and was reflected in his eyes. He moved restlessly, then ran his hand through his thick fair hair.

"Look here," he said at last. "I'm going to leave this to you. I want to know her. See if you can manage it for me, there's a good fellow."

"Very well," I said. "We'll leave it like that. But I must say it seems remarkably strange to me that Scrivener was silent when you mentioned her name."

"Don't let that bother you," he said, returning to his light, airy manner. "Scriv's pose is to be mysterious." A sudden thought occurred to him. "By the way, does he know that *you* know Mrs. Bellamy?"

"He does," I replied.

"You're certain?"

"I wrote and told him so at any rate," I said a trifle irritably.

"Then it *is* odd. Never mind. We understand each other, that's the great thing. I am glad we met. Must you go? Really? Well, I shall look you up before long."

We left together. I can give no better indication of the atmosphere prevailing in that restaurant than to state that when I found myself outside it, in the sunlight, breathing the crisp, cold air, I was quite surprised to discover that the every-day world still existed; that men and women were hastening to and fro on their affairs; that I was in London; and that certain of the shop windows contained familiar objects which I could recognize definitely as food. I was prepared to believe everything that Rivers had told me, with one important exception: I did not believe that the girl, who he said was an artist's model, had practically all her meals in that restaurant. She was strong, she was beautifully made and—I did not believe it.

II

To solve any problem you must have all the data or none. If you have all, ingenuity may succeed. If you have none, inspiration may triumph. I recognized this after I had left Rivers and walked back to the flat. Information of so many kinds from such different sources was reaching me in regard to Scrivener that to seek to analyse it, or to see it in perspective, was as hopeless as to attempt to assign frontiers to chaos. One of life's secrets is to know when not to think and I decided to see what the days brought me, believ-

ing that Time—the supreme anthologist—would sift out the irrelevant and reveal the significant. Also I counted on three events to
furnish me with information of a more fundamental order than
any I had yet received. One was Scrivener's reply to my letter; the
next was my visit to Pauline's home; and the third was the supper
to which Francesca had invited me.

Possibly someone reading this book might be inclined to say:
"What the devil does this fellow Wrexham want to bother about
Scrivener for? He's got a soft job out of him; he's meeting his
friends. Why doesn't he wait till Scrivener turns up and then discover whether he's a lunatic or a philanthropist?" Legitimate questions all. And logically they all stand. But logic is an infinitesimal
part of life, and there was something in me, far deeper than logic,
which *knew* that my life was bound up with Scrivener's, that it
was not accident which had brought us into such a curious relationship, and that other lives besides ours were involved. How did
I know these things? How do you know that one hour is more
important than another? How do you guess the approach of The
Hour, amid the long file of lean nondescript hours, which holds in
its infinite compass Past, Present, and Future—The Hour which
finds you a slave and leaves you the shadow of God? Did no sudden
silence enfold Saul when he said to himself: "To-morrow I go to
Damascus"? We all know more than we dare to admit. In the least
of us there is a knowledge of which the greatest of us is afraid.

As I returned to the flat after leaving Rivers, inserted the key,
opened the front door, and passed through the hall into the library,
a sense of wonder possessed me. I looked round. I realized that I
was in another man's home. All round the walls were the books he
had made his during the last twenty years. There they stood—the
milestones of his mental life. Who was this man? What had I to do
with him? What unknown, what unimaginable law of attraction
had drawn us together—he from his world and I from mine? Habit
grows like a weed that is unobserved, and already Habit had accustomed me to accept as commonplace the miracle of my presence
in Scrivener's flat but, at this moment, habit obscured the truth no
longer and I saw myself as the stranger I was to all that surrounded

me. I stood motionless. The library was silent as ever. The memory of all the years I had spent in Petersham's office flashed in a second of time before me. Then one by one, I saw Pauline, Francesca, Middleton, Rivers—the other characters in this strange drama in which I had become involved—a drama which developed on the background of an invisible presence. I should never have entered this library if it had not been for Scrivener: not one of those people would have come here except for him. Was I destined to know something of the lives of each one of them? to penetrate into the hidden life of each? and, therefore, to be revealed to each in some degree?

There was something in me which wanted to evade the issue which I knew confronted me. Had it not been my dream for years to escape to a solitude beyond the reach of the world's clamour? to live my life apart and alone, a spectator, not a combatant? Was it not even possible that I had imagined that to become Scrivener's secretary would provide me with just such a hermitage?

I knew now that to stay was to surrender that dream—and I also knew that not to stay was impossible. It is at that moment when we reject life, once and finally, that it claims us, bends us to its will, and makes us serve ends of which we know nothing.

As I stood looking round the library, a new thought presented itself. What, *exactly*, had I written to Scrivener when I answered his advertisement? The question had the force of a blow. I found, to my amazement, that I could only remember that I had written at some length, but the precise contents eluded me. I had written so many drafts before composing the final letter; I had written the actual letter so hastily and with such a disregard of convention, confident that it would lead to nothing, that now I could remember little of its contents. I had, I knew, written about myself, but what had I actually revealed? I tried again and again to recapture what I had written, but I found that whereas my memory served me perfectly as to what I had stated in the draft letters—and there had been several—it failed me in all important particulars so far as the actual letter of application was concerned.

For over an hour I tried to solve this new enigma. I failed.

I set out the fact here because it belongs here and because it is important to remember that the very act which had obtained me my position with Scrivener had become vague to me. One thing I did remember: Winkworth had not seen the letter. That was certain.

III

London contains many worlds: there are slums within a short distance of its most aristocratic quarters, and deep solitudes within a few strides of its busiest thoroughfares. It was my visit to Pauline's home which made me aware of the second fact.

One afternoon, a day or two before I went to dine there, I walked over to see where she lived. Hence my discovery.

Holland Park is an inferno of traffic equalled only by that of Kensington High Street which is parallel to it. Between the two is an eminence. Narrow lanes and roads rise sharply at intervals from Holland Park to span this height. I made my way up one of the lanes. At each step the roar of the traffic grew less. The boughs of trees met above my head. Before long the roar of the main road ceased. I stood still, amazed by the silence. Over the high fences on either side of the lane were spacious-seeming woods. A bird sang. I imagined that enchanters were as busy with me as they used to be with Don Quixote.

But it was all true. Often since then I have stood in that lane at night: overhead, a copper-coloured moon looked through the branches, and in the tangled darkness of the wood an owl hooted. But on my first visit the sun shone and the afternoon stillness of deep country cradled the air. At the top of the eminence are great gates leading to a half-hidden house. You peer through the Ironwork. You behold a lawn of green velvet, a terrace, a wall rich in memories, beloved by moss, which curves lazily as if to indicate that Time has leant against it long enough. And over all is the atmosphere of an old country house, dreaming in its park, while beauty and the years weave silent magic. You pause and wonder and perhaps, carelessly, you continue to follow the lane which now leads downwards. The inferno rises to meet you for, at the bottom, is Kensington High Street.

There are squares perched on the side of this eminence, and in one of these Pauline lived.

As I dressed to go to dine with her people, and in the taxi as I drove to Holland Park, I foresaw that the evening might be a very difficult one. I knew that her father was a general, and I imagined that neither he nor his wife would be particularly interested in meeting a nobody, and a nobody with a somewhat doubtful background. After all, an introduction such as the following is not inspiring: "This is Mr. Wrexham. No one knows what he was before, but he is now Mr. Scrivener's secretary although he has never seen him." As the taxi drew near its destination, I decided that my visit was Pauline's doing and that she must accept the responsibility for the evening. I felt sorry for her parents, nevertheless.

I rang the bell. I heard my name announced, and Pauline rose to greet me. I imagine that I looked relieved to find her alone, because she laughed on seeing me.

"Nervous?"

"A little," I replied. "Perhaps you don't realize that I haven't visited a house such as this for twenty years."

She looked at me in astonishment. "You're not serious," she said.

"It's literally true."

We stood facing each other for about a minute.

"It's a shock to find that I know nothing about you," she said at last.

"You couldn't have realized it at a worse moment," I said with a laugh. "Let me disappear while there's time," I went on. "Let me glide out of the house, into the night, and you tell your people that it's all a mistake, that you only dreamt that I existed."

But she was looking at me with an air of perplexity, and was not listening to a word I said.

"I know you, but I know nothing about your life. It's usually exactly the other way round. Tell me, whom did you meet during those years?"

"I will explain another time, if it interests you," I said. "Tell me this: is to-night fair to your people?"

"We may as well sit down," she said. "I have no choice: if they don't see my friends they complain, and if they do——"

"They are horrified," I added, as she did not finish her sentence.

"I don't say that," she said quite seriously, "but they don't like them as a rule. I don't think they like Jonathan."

I saw my one background swept into oblivion, and began to feel slightly apprehensive. I glanced round the long, rather low-pitched, beautiful room. It had that intimacy which is only acquired when a family has lived in the same house for a number of years. I was not surprised, therefore, to learn that Pauline had been born in this house and had known no other home.

I did not speak again as she appeared to be thinking, and I did not want to disturb any plan she might be evolving for the salvation of the evening. It was not reassuring, therefore, when she said:

"Have you seen Middleton again?"

I told her that I had and tried to bring her back to the present emergency, but she waved it aside.

"It will be all right. Something will turn up to talk about. Anyhow, I have often been wearied by their friends."

And then, as always happens with me in the end, all nervousness left me. I had surrendered myself to something I did not understand when I became Scrivener's secretary. That "something" must pilot me through this evening and through everything else I was destined to encounter in his service. I banished the future and lived in the present. And the present was Pauline.

She was sitting on a low couch opposite me. She sat erect and alert, and there was something in her attitude which suggested that she was awaiting a summons. Her arms were thin as wands and again I marvelled at her tiny wrists and the hair which circled her head with fire. To see her was to understand the lines:

> . . . . *and so distinctly wrought*
> *That one might almost say her body thought.*

A few minutes passed, during which I gathered from Pauline that she had arranged that we should go out together after dinner. Then Mrs. Mandeville appeared. She was about forty-five, and so like Pauline, and yet so unlike her, that I found it difficult not to stare at her. She was slightly nervous, but clearly determined to adapt herself to the strange ways of the younger generation. The result was that I did not meet *her* because she was not herself. She was like a person playing a part who was ignorant of her lines. It is impossible to make concessions to something you do not understand, for the simple reason that you probably concede something that is not required.

However, there is always the weather. First to-day's, then yesterday's, then to-morrow's, and "no wonder people are ill," and "then look at last summer," and "still, we mustn't forget that we're getting through the winter," and so on and so on. And, if hard pressed, there's always the awful condition of trade to get dreary about. In the middle of these and other futilities I was asked if I would care to join the general for a glass of sherry before dinner.

I found him in his own room. A rather bare, intensely masculine room, with two chairs for comfort and everything else severely for use. He was a spare upright man, clean shaven, swift in his movements, with a tightly shut mouth and steel-grey eyes. He was fifty-eight and looked forty-five.

"How do you do?" he asked, looking me straight in the eyes and holding out his hand.

I said I was very well and there the conversation ended and the sherry was produced. There were no concessions here and no fear of silence. He gave me a cigarette and left it at that, thereby gaining my respect whether he wanted it or not.

I should say the silence lasted for two or three minutes. First he sipped his sherry, then I sipped mine. We smoked and looked at the fire. A painting of a soldier on the wall looked down on us.

I have always found that frankness is possible with decent people; it offends only charlatans. I decided to be frank now.

"I know it's awkward for both of us," I began. "It was a caprice on your daughter's part to invite me here, and very kind of you to let me come, although possibly it's embarrassing for everyone."

"I will be equally frank with you," he said in his clear even voice. "Pauline is not interested in our friends and so, rightly or wrongly, we try to be interested in hers." He paused, then added: "I don't pretend to understand modern ways and I don't like them. In the old days if your children didn't agree with you, you thrashed them till they did. That was wrong: this is wrong: and that's all there is to be said about it. The question of progress doesn't enter in. Both ways were wrong. But I tell you this, Mr. Wrexham," he said, with telling emphasis, "and I do not care one damn whether it sounds old-fashioned or not. It's one thing for a man to go his own way and another for a woman. And it will be so to the end of the chapter. Even if they give women votes the moment they're born."

The last sentence represented an extension of the democratic principle which had never occurred to me, but the general was in his stride and went on for some time. He ended by saying: "If Pauline had been a man she could have gone to the devil if she had wanted to. But she is a woman, and a damned attractive one. And that worries me. No," he said looking at me again straight in the eyes, "I'm glad you came to-night."

"You mean it's better to know the worst," I said, by way of a weak jest.

"When you have had to deal with men all your life, as I have, it tells you something to see one," he said enigmatically.

Then, suddenly, as happens sometimes apropos of nothing, I discovered that I liked this man very much. It did not matter that I knew we should agree about little, it was deeper than all that. I liked him and I knew that he, too, was alone as he sat there in his chair—just as much alone as I had ever been, no matter how different our lives had been externally. I looked at him as he sat smoking in the firelight and for some reason I thought of my father. He might so easily have been like Mandeville.

"Well, I don't know if you'd like to know anything about me," I said after a long silence. "I was at ——" I mentioned the name of a public school.

In an instant he was on his feet.

"What! At ——!" he repeated. "Good God, my dear fellow, why didn't you say so before! I was there myself! Have another glass of sherry? Why, fancy Pauline not telling me that! Women tell you everything except the essential. Good Lord, that's devilish interesting. Introductions be damned! So you were at ——"

When we went into dinner we were like schoolboys spending the holidays together. All problems had vanished, there were no silences, the weather ceased to exist, the condition of trade did not matter. And Mrs. Mandeville, seeing that all was well with her husband, became herself—a woman of great charm and considerable penetration. Pauline sat and watched the three of us with the eyes of a stranger. But she contrived to whisper to me:

"How on earth did you manage it?"

"I didn't," I replied. "We both went to ——"

"Ah!" she said softly.

And, since that night, when I hear people question the power, the might, the supreme and everlasting importance of a public school education, I too murmur: "Ah," softly, and think of General Mandeville.

It is unnecessary to discuss that evening at length. But one fragment of the conversation needs to be reported.

After nearly all the famous people who had been educated at —— had been discussed, which took some time, I thought it desirable to introduce another theme, since Pauline clearly had not the interest in that almighty institution which her father had. Consequently I said that I understood that they had met Mr. Jonathan Scrivener and I should be interested in their impression of him for obvious reasons. This simple request immediately produced a silence that could be felt. I knew instinctively that the weather wouldn't get us out of this.

"He was brought here one night," the general said at length in a tone which suggested the impartiality of an historian, "by Sir Mortimer Dankin. By the way, Dankin was at —— Did you know?"

"No, I didn't know that," I said.

"Well, he was, and of course he was a great sportsman before he went on the stage. *He* brought Scrivener." Another long pause.

"Well, I can only say, Wrexham, that Scrivener discussed all sorts of topics in a manner such as I have never experienced before or since. But if you criticize him, you're told he's an artist, and what the devil can you say to that?"

I admitted that it was difficult.

"He's remarkable to look at and a great personality, but I shouldn't care to be influenced by him, and I should say that he had influenced a number of people. I asked Dankin what he thought of him and he said he was a 'spiritual Bolshevist,' if that tells you anything."

But at this point Mrs. Mandeville adroitly turned the conversation and Scrivener's name was not mentioned again.

Soon after nine, on the pretence that we were going on somewhere, Pauline and I left the house. She gave the taxi-driver an address and we drove off.

After we had gone a few yards I said to her: "Where are you taking me?"

"To your flat," she replied. "Do you mind?"

"Of course not."

"It was better to get away. I wanted you to come—anyhow once—as you'll understand some things better, which I may tell you later."

In twenty minutes we were seated in the library.

"You saw my father's enthusiasm about public schools," she said suddenly. "It's an example of how we differ. He imagines that I will marry and live just such a life as my mother has lived. He thinks that's possible because he is determined to go on as if everything were the same as it was thirty years ago. If anyone tells him the fact that Eton and Harrow are kept going by Jews nowadays, he goes purple. You see what he said about Jonathan. I tell you that Jonathan's conversation that night was a revelation to me."

"In what way?" I asked, keenly interested.

"Perhaps it wasn't so much what he said, but his whole attitude suggested that you could make something of life if you had courage and dared to assert yourself. Listening to him, I felt there were an endless number of doors where I had believed there was only a prison wall. We talked together a lot that evening. When it was over, I felt that something had been solved. And yet, I don't know," she added, "I wish he'd come back."

She told me a great deal about her people. She explained how the antagonism between her and her father had resulted in a kind of armistice, each side retaining its own opinion and each maintaining silence on certain subjects. This was the real meaning, she explained, of her statement at our first meeting that she had freedom at home. She had her way but she was always aware of unspoken criticism.

"I think my father is afraid that I shall take a job and become the modern independent woman he dislikes so much. But I am not deceived by that type of freedom. Women have gone into the market thinking to find the freedom of men, instead of which they now share men's slavery. I would work, if it were necessary, but I should not deceive myself that it were an end in itself. I want neither the life my mother has had nor the lives of the women I see every day. If that is the choice, there is no choice. There must be something else. I am going to find something else."

She spoke with quiet intensity. Middleton came into my mind as I sat listening to her. By strangely different roads they had arrived at the same destination. It is true that he was angry, hurt, fiercely rebellious, and that she was calm and remote, but each of them, it seemed to me, had arrived at a frontier. Behind them were roads, rules, traditions, and in front of them was the unknown. . . .

They were examples of the revolt in the world. That revolt shows itself in every sphere of human activity. It is idle to deny it, and it is idle to assign superficial causes in order to explain it. It is not to be suppressed by any of the old methods. It is not a question of class; it is to be found in every class. At its best it is a determination to achieve a new consciousness; at its worst it is a determination to destroy. At its highest, it respects nothing but the true; at its lowest, it respects nothing but the strong. It is present in a thousand forms and, as a result, Certainty has vanished. To be aware of this spirit of revolt it is not necessary to have thought. Most people are afraid of it—in themselves and in others. They seek to evade the knowledge of it: some by a fanatical worship of the past, others by an hysterical descent into the pleasures of the present. But raise what battle-cry you will, every echo has only one answer—and the answer of each echo is *Change*. For the old order has failed and the new order is in the agony of birth. . . .

For some time Pauline sat talking in her soft perfectly articulated voice. She talked to me as if she were thinking aloud, and much that she said was as familiar to me as if my own emotions had attained suddenly the gift of speech. Then returning to the subject of her parents, she said:

"It is amusing in its way. I think my father is really afraid that I might run off with someone. It's on those levels that he worries about me. He doesn't see that all that has nothing to do with it. It's a different life I want from anything I have known. All words like 'worse' or 'better' do not apply. It must be *different*. It must serve other ends, it must be differently based. I can't tell him so, but his gods to me are simply mouldering mummies. I don't blame him for dreaming, but I cannot share his dream. My mother is neutral. She is so neutral that I think she understands something of what I feel. My father doesn't."

As I listened to her, I could see her father quite plainly as he had sat in the firelight. And it seemed to me that to agree with one or the other had little meaning. We are attracted to those whose state of consciousness is related to our own, and we are repelled by those whose state makes no contact with ours—or we are indifferent to them.

"I want you to tell me something," she said. "You told me to-night that you had not been in a house like ours for twenty years. Whom did you meet during all that time?"

"You must remember," I began, "that my father's death cut me off from the life I had known. I had to get a living. His friends had begun to drop him for some years before his death. He was an eccentric man. But why do you want to know? What does it matter?"

"Tell me; it interests me," she said. "I want to know more about you."

"I knew no one in one sense. I picked up people—when I couldn't stand my loneliness any longer. I didn't much mind who they were—strangers in public houses, women of the streets, anybody. I hated my life, my work, everything, during most of those years, and I tried to live through books. Which is the reason why I read so seldom nowadays."

"I can see why Jonathan chose you for his secretary," she said slowly.

I was about to reply when there was a ring at the bell. It was Middleton. He seemed more nervous than ever and to my surprise, he was evidently glad to find that I was not alone. He was awkward when he greeted Pauline. Underneath, I could see that he was very excited and I noticed that on this occasion, as on the former one, he stared at Pauline whenever she was not looking in his direction. His face was heavily lined and I could see that he was still drinking a good deal.

"Since coming to this place," he announced jerkily, "I've begun to read. Effect of all those books, I suppose."

"What have you been reading?" Pauline asked.

He gave his short staccato laugh. "Oh, novels and some plays, but better class ones than my usual dope. I've made one discovery about 'em, only one."

"What's that?" I inquired.

"These cursed novelists only write about people of leisure. It's the same with the dramatists. What's the idea? Snobbishness?"

"It's inevitable," I said.

"Inevitable! I don't see why. Why shouldn't the hero of a novel be a plumber?"

"There's no reason whatever," I replied, "but the book would have to be concerned with him when he was not plumbing, or the book would be a technical work on that activity—and so not a novel."

He pondered over this for a minute, then said: "I'm damned if I get you. Perhaps you'll explain. Tell me if this bores you," he said to Pauline.

"Why should it bore me? Go on," she said, turning to me.

"People are only interesting when they are free. It is what people do with their leisure that reveals them. We do not want to know what they do under compulsion, because it tells us nothing about them."

Middleton lit a cigarette and appeared to be thinking deeply. I could see that he did not like my theory.

"What about a man in prison then?" he asked. "He couldn't be interesting. Is that it?"

"Only his thoughts would be interesting, because only in them would he be free," I answered. "Besides, novelist and dramatist alike have to depict the emotional life of their characters. So if the hero were a plumber, the author would have to deal with him in his leisure hours. Nobody, I take it, could plumb emotionally."

Pauline laughed, but Middleton wasn't satisfied.

"Then *I'm* more interesting than if I got a job, worked from nine till nine, had a meal and went to bed. Is that so?"

"You certainly would make better material for a novelist as you are now," I said with conviction.

"All very interesting," he said slowly, "and it's curious but I asked Scrivener something about leisure, and got very much the same answer, plus a number of paradoxes which were beyond me."

"I'm glad you came in to-night, Mr. Middleton." Pauline's voice was a remarkable contrast to his. "I want to meet everyone who knows Jonathan. You know him. Mrs. Bellamy knows him, I hear. By the way," she said suddenly to me, "is there anyone else?"

"There is a gentleman called Mr. Antony Rivers. I have met him only once, but he tells me that he has known Scrivener for some time."

"Will you see him again?" she asked eagerly.

"Yes, I am quite certain I shall. I will introduce you both to him. Middleton has met Mrs. Bellamy. Did you know that? He met her here."

"Yes, I've met her," he muttered.

They stayed for an hour longer, then left together. I discovered later that Middleton saw Pauline home.

CHAPTER VII

I

THERE are flowers which open only at night, and there are
people who should be seen only at night. Francesca was one
of them. Night was her element. Her passion, her pride, her magnetism were intensified; the facets of her personality became more
vivid; the secret of her mystery more obscure. Jewellers do not err
when they exhibit brilliants on a setting of black plush.

It struck eleven as I entered her house in Bruton Street. Though
there was no ostentation, an atmosphere of wealth immediately
enveloped me. Nothing proclaimed it, yet everything suggested it.
I felt that I should have guessed that this was her home had I been
brought to it blindfold with no knowledge that it was hers. It was
haunted by her personality in the same way as Scrivener's library
was haunted by his.

These thoughts possessed me while we had supper. She was
gay and flippant and there was little need for me to speak. She
indicated that the real reason why she wanted to see me would be
made clear after supper. She was excited, and her excitement was
infectious. There was something in her attitude which made me
certain that she had made some decision—a decision which had
been long in the making, but which was now absolute.

But as I listened to her, as I admired again the beauty of her
shoulders, which resembled fine marble, the long dark eyes and
the provocation of the red mouth, suddenly I thought of Bellamy.
I looked round the room. It was Bellamy who had provided this
luxury. I wondered what his thoughts had been that night in
Paris—the last night he had known. I glanced at her. She was
laughing: there was not a line, not a shadow on her face. She radi-
ated a fierce, passionate love of life and I felt certain that death was
the only tragedy she could imagine.

"Why did you look at me like that? You weren't listening to me. You looked at me to confirm your own thoughts."

"How quick of you!" I said immediately in order to gain time. "Incidentally you are entirely right. I am making a psychological study of you."

"Tell me what you've made of me. You'll need all your knowledge of psychology for Jonathan, I promise you that. Let's go into another room and then you must tell me."

I followed her into a small room on the ground floor. It was lit by candles and a great fire was burning.

"You must sit there," she said. "I want to be able to see you. I am going to take a risk with you to-night. But, first, I want to hear your analysis."

Fortunately I had thought much about her and so I was more or less prepared. I took the cigarette she offered me.

"You won't expect much, I hope. Anyway, this is my first draft. You are a being of this world, wholly concerned with it, and conscious of the power of your weapons. You are capable of passion, but unaware of the havoc your caprices might cause in the lives of others. You are dangerous, because you are what you are, not by reason of malignant ends. You are naturally perverse, naturally exotic, and naturally selfish. You are a stranger to conscience, remorse, problems. In another age, you might have been the centre of great events but, if you had, you would have been aware only of the personalities surrounding you, not of the issues involved. Your perceptions, your intuitions, your inspirations are always in regard to persons, not things. You know your enemies and your slaves instantly. You accept tributes as if you were conferring favours. To know you is an opportunity: to love you would be hell."

I was about to end this tirade with a joke when I saw that she was staring at me with fascinated eyes.

"But it's—it's impossible!" she stammered.

"Yes, of course," I said, "it's probably all nonsense——"

"It's true! Every word of it is true! How did you know?" She had risen and was looking down at me.

"You told me a good deal about yourself when we first met," I reminded her, "and your appearance tells everybody something."

But she was not satisfied.

"*You do know Jonathan.* I am certain of it. You couldn't have guessed all that."

"You know that I do not know him. You have verified my story. Anyone could reel off that string of sentences about you. You have said each one of them yourself in different words."

She sat down again, then her red lips curved into a challenging smile.

"Very well, let it pass. It's a brilliant analysis all the same, and it makes things easier." She paused, then announced lightly: "Your friend Middleton came to see me a few days ago. Did you know?"

"Middleton!"

I was amazed and must have shown it.

"Ah!" she exclaimed in triumph. "Your psychology failed you there! Yes, Middleton came here to see me."

"What on earth for?" I asked, only half-believing what she said.

"To apologize for his rudeness. You remember how rude he was."

I did not reply, but sat gazing at her. Instinctively sometimes you feel that two persons should not become intimate and I never was so convinced of it as in this instance. Francesca enjoyed my perplexity.

"He's an interesting man, isn't he? He talks quite surprisingly if he is a little drunk. I can see why Jonathan picked him up. Incidentally, I learnt more about Pauline Mandeville from him than I did from you. I've told him to get to know her better. You look quite angry."

I did not answer her and she leant back and laughed softly. Her amusement was real. I found it impossible to imagine Middleton with Francesca, but now I understood why he had been glad that I was not alone when he called. He wanted me to find out about his visit to Francesca, thinking that it would simplify explanations.

"You're not very amusing," she said. "Did you want to keep Jonathan's friends to yourself?"

"The best answer I can give you to that," I said, "is to tell you that I have just met another friend of Scrivener's who is most anxious to meet you."

"A man or a woman, and—if the latter—has she a latchkey?" she asked.

"A man, Antony Rivers. Young, good-looking, and amusing. Shall I bring him to see you? He has known Scrivener, off and on, for two years. He has just returned from Paris where he spent some time with Scrivener. Apparently they went to a séance together. That's the best catalogue I can give you."

She was looking at me with considerable interest.

"A *séance*! You're joking."

"Not at all," I replied. "Why shouldn't Scrivener go to a séance? Someone told me once that he had known a man who founded an occult order of some kind——"

"He told me about him," she interrupted. "Gesler was his name. Jonathan said he was a spiritual *arriviste* and that the pride of the saved was more deadly than the pride of the damned. But send your Mr. Rivers along. I want to meet him."

She took a cigarette and I felt that we had reached a frontier in our discussion. For several minutes there was silence, then she turned and looked at me fixedly.

"I'm going to tell you something about myself," she announced.

"Why?" I asked before she could continue. "As a prelude to our partnership?"

"Yes, partly," she replied. "But I trust you not to let me go on if you have met Jonathan, or have any understanding with him."

"Neither the one nor the other. I know nothing whatever about him. You can believe that absolutely and finally."

She clasped her knee with her hands and leant back. The firelight illuminated the long line of her beautiful legs. The silence seemed to thicken about us.

"He has not written to you about me, or Middleton, or Pauline Mandeville?"

"Not a word," I replied.

Her next question was utterly unexpected.

"Did you wonder why my husband shot himself?"

"Surely everybody wondered that," I answered.

"Is it such a mystery to you now that you have met me?"

I had never expected anything like this, and I had no time in which to think.

"I can imagine a man who loved you committing suicide," I replied. "I take it you want me to be frank."

"I will tell you about it but remember I have told no one this. But Jonathan may know something."

"What makes you think that?"

She gave a kind of shudder and changed her attitude. "You remember that I told you that his last remark before he went away revealed his skill as an antagonist? He let me know that he had seen my husband in Paris on the morning of the day on which he shot himself. No!" she exclaimed quickly, as I was about to speak. "Ask me nothing, because I know no more than that. It may have been no more than a clever move in the game between us."

"And what is that game?" I asked.

"Wait! I believe that Jonathan *did* see him. I did not know that they knew each other. In fact that meeting may have been their first."

She rose impulsively with a fluttering gesture of her hands as if to banish the subject. I could see she was thinking of Scrivener. It was the fact that he had seen her husband in Paris which occupied her thoughts far more than her husband's suicide. Everything about her proclaimed it, and I began to understand the extent to which she was obsessed by Scrivener. I felt unwilling to share her secrets, and yet fascinated by the intensity and the passion of the world in which she lived. At this moment it claimed her so completely and she yielded to it so absolutely, that it made the everyday world seem a colourless drab affair. She invested her world with drama to such a degree that I was drawn into it as a chip of wood is swept into a vortex.

"I am the illegitimate daughter of an Italian actress. Did you know that?" She was still standing and she said the words as if she had rehearsed them.

I looked up at her as I asked, "How do you think I could know that? I know only what the papers revealed at the time of your husband's suicide. That was little enough about him, and less about you. There was a lot of hysteria about his wealth and your beauty, but that did not tell anyone much. I do remember now that it was stated that you met him in Italy."

After a silence she went on: "My father was an Englishman, wealthy and, I believe, well-born, but I do not know, because I never knew his name and so far as I know I have never seen him. My mother died when I was fifteen and then a mysterious English woman appeared to look after me. She was sent of course by my father. Later I travelled for some years with her. She had been well chosen and she revealed nothing. When I was twenty-one I returned to Italy. I met Stanley in Rome."

She stopped speaking and stood gazing in front of her as if she were seeing the past on some distant horizon. How much those few sentences had explained to me! But what was the real reason why she was telling me this? I waited for her to continue, knowing definitely that, whatever her motive, she was telling the truth.

"It doesn't matter how I met him," she went on. "He fell passionately in love with me. And I with him—as I understand love. I told him about myself. He cared nothing about that. He did not want to hear. He was used to having his wishes gratified and he wanted to marry me immediately. Nothing existed for him but that. I loved that impetuosity in him, for it is how I have always seen life. To take—now!—while the desire burns in you! There is only To-day! Yesterday is a ghost and To-morrow a dream."

She drew a cushion to the fire and sat down. Her head almost touched my knee.

"My companion, as I will call her, wrote to England, but we were married before any reply came. Then she disappeared and I have never seen her again. We went to Paris and later we came to London. I know now that he had only two things in his life: his passion for me and his passion for money. He was thirty-six when he married me and he was wealthy then."

Again she was silent. No matter what the subject may be, there is something awe-inspiring about the truth. For, whatever the level, where there is truth there is holy ground. And sentence by sentence the truth came from her.

"Probably it will explain everything to you," she went on, "when I say that it never occurred to me to be faithful to him. Can you understand that?"

"Yes," I answered, "I can understand anything about a human being. You do not need to have looked deeply into yourself in order to be able to do that."

"And it never occurred to me that he would be faithful to me. A fool would ask: then why marry? You marry because the world is the world and because you are fonder of one man than any other. Had I known that he expected fidelity, I should have hated him." She paused and gazed into the fire. "I thought there was an unspoken understanding between us. He went away frequently on his business deals. He was wealthy. It never occurred to me that he was faithful. How should it?"

There was a long pause.

"If love is what the world thinks it is," she went on with passionate emphasis, "then I am incapable of it. It is monotony, and I loathe monotony more than anything else in the universe. To live with a person, year in, year out; to see that person at nearly every meal; to hear his opinions again and again! My God, is *that* what they call love? I call it death! I need passion, colour, the unexpected—the romance of the unknown!"

She ceased speaking but the vibration of her voice still quivered in the room. She was leaning forward towards the fire. She seemed to be speaking to it, rather than to me.

"For seven years we lived like that. He was very successful. I cared about him much more than any other man. I loved his love of power, his daring, his ambition. Older men used to warn him about his recklessness, but he only laughed. It was the excitement, the suspense, which fascinated him. Money? I could have the money—anyone could have the money! He only wanted the adventure. I loved him for that."

"You had several lovers during those years?" I asked.

"Yes, several. I was often alone. I, too, wanted excitement. *He* should have known that. Passion was my type of speculation. Then—the end. The tragic, ludicrous, unnecessary end."

She turned to me with a quick movement. Whenever I think of her, I see her face as it was then: tense, dramatic, the dark eyes on fire, the red lips slightly parted.

"Do you believe that the dead survive?"

"Yes," I replied.

"That they remember, that they still love, hate, and suffer?"

"I imagine," I said slowly, "that for most of us the death of the body cannot affect the essential in us. Why should it?"

She gave a short laugh. "You are not sentimental. You do not believe that we rise blissfully to heaven."

"Why should death be a short cut? Nothing is easier than to die."

She did not reply. A coal burst into a sudden frenzy of flame and the shadows of things flitted over the walls. When she spoke there was a new note in her voice.

"He discovered the night he went to Paris. He had left the house. I was to join him in a week. After he had gone, I remained in the room in which we had said good-bye. I had had a letter from my lover. He had broken my rule, which was that he was never to write to me. I was furious with him. I read the letter again and decided I would ring him up before he telephoned me, and refuse to see him because he had written. I put his letter in the book I had been reading and left the room. I returned perhaps five minutes later. My husband was in the room. He had come back because he had forgotten his passport. The letter was in his hand. He looked like a ghost."

Silence, so profound that it seemed like a presence in the room.

"He read the letter to the end. It fluttered out of his hands. I can see now the line it made as it eddied through the air. I can hear the odd little crisp noise it made as it reached the floor. It fell at my feet. He did not move and I couldn't. The telephone bell began to ring in my room. He knew, and I knew, that it was my lover. He went out of the room as if he were in a trance. He passed quite near me. I couldn't stretch out my hand. I couldn't speak. I saw him go through the open door and I knew I should never see him again. I tried desperately to call, to run after him. Impossible! I heard the car drive away. The telephone was still ringing. I had told my maid that I was expecting a call and would answer it myself. It rang and rang and it sounded to me like a funeral bell."

Again she rose with that strange fluttering gesture of the hands. She moved about the room, paused to alter the position of a flower, touched familiar things as if to prove their reality.

"That's all," she said at last. "You know the rest. But one thing I must tell you. I did not tell my lover that Stanley had found his letter. Later, I lied to him and he believed me. It was easy to convince him that our affair had nothing to do with Stanley's death. *He* wasn't the type to kill himself about a woman. So it was easy for him to believe that Stanley wasn't."

"And now," I said, surprised by the sound of my own voice, "why have you told me this?"

She gave a short laugh. "You're fascinating. You accept life so strangely—no criticism, no comments, just acceptance. I have told you for two reasons, my friend. I have wanted to tell someone the truth ever since I heard that Jonathan met Stanley in Paris. I do not know what Stanley told *him*—or if he told him anything. But I have told you the truth—all of it—and *not* in answer to anything my husband may have said. I believe that never, unless I ask you, will you repeat a word of this to a living soul."

"You can count on that absolutely," I said. "And the second reason?"

"I want you to know what I am, what I have been. One last thing: after Stanley had gone that evening, I thought all through the night. I could not blame myself. I could not then, and I do not now. He loved a woman who didn't exist." A pause. "I will give you a drink and we will change the subject."

It was not difficult to believe that her mother had been an actress. I am inclined to believe that she had been a great one and that her daughter inherited her temperament. Francesca had lived again through her husband's tragedy, called it from its grave, given it life. Now, in an instant, she banished it and she became the woman I had known. The curtain had fallen on a scene from her memories. The play was over and the actress resumed her own individual life. Voice, attitude, gesture, everything indicated that our conversation was to enter a new phase. She gave me a drink, lit a cigarette, and sat down in a low chair by the fire.

"I want a rest," she said. "You talk."

"Why didn't you go on the stage?" I asked.

"You've the oddest idea of conversation! I ask you to talk and you immediately ask a question. Answer your own question, but answer it out loud and I'll listen."

She settled herself comfortably in her chair and inhaled the smoke of her cigarette.

"I can't answer it. I'll make a few guesses to amuse you. You have inherited your mother's histrionic power but, for you, the mimic passions and emotions of the stage are inadequate. Your nature demands drama in the terms of actual life. Is that any good as a beginning?"

She regarded me doubtfully. "It's a little too good, my friend. But you can go on."

"Your mother was a great actress——"

She interrupted like a flash. "When did I say she was a *great* actress?"

"Let us assume it," I said. "Now I shall have to start again. Your mother was a great actress. Great parts were therefore essential to her. They confirmed her belief in herself. She realized herself through them. But your world is your stage and you require perpetual evidence of your dominion. That evidence is to you what applause was to your mother. It convinces you of your power in the same way as applause convinced her of hers. Your mother portrayed the emotions of others, you dramatize your own."

I could see from her expression that several of these shots in the dark had reached their mark.

"You're a little disturbing," she said slowly, "but you save me a lot of explanations. I would like your assurance, however, that you have never known *anyone* who knows me."

"Never."

"I cannot think why I believe you. But you told your friend Middleton just what you told me about yourself. I did find that out," she added with a provocative smile.

"Let us discuss him another time. I want to discuss Scrivener with you."

She gave a triumphant laugh. "The partnership!" She rose quickly. "We will drink to our partnership. I have decided to trust you, so I will tell you everything. You have a mystery to solve. That's true, isn't it?"

"Perfectly true."

"And I have a mystery to solve. We will solve them together."

We drank to each other with due solemnity.

She was called away to speak on the telephone and I was glad to be alone. My mind was still dominated by that last scene with her husband. It had all the clarity and fixity of a tableau. Not a word had been spoken, yet in that timeless silence each had been revealed to the other. Revealed, so completely, that the will to act and the power to speak had been paralysed. Logic, abuse, entreaties only have a part to play if a man believes that a woman has been false to herself. But to discover, as Bellamy had done, that she was utterly remote from his conception of her, is to realize the futility of speech. That moment had been Bellamy's real death. He had left the house, a ghost, and all that night she had called herself to judgment—and her verdict was "not guilty."

Was it true that she had told me all this because she believed that Scrivener had seen her husband in Paris? I was inclined to believe it. Now, at any rate, there was someone who knew her story, and, as she had pointed out, a story not designed to answer anything that her husband might have said to Scrivener. Was she afraid of Scrivener? I remembered the shudder which had passed over her when she had told me of his meeting with her husband. And she could imagine that this meeting had been purely an invention of Scrivener's! Whether or not that were true, it was significant that she could imagine him capable of deception of such an order. I pointed this out to her on her return.

"I can imagine anything about him," she replied. "It is one secret of his attraction. I prefer the cruel to the sentimental."

"And you have a theory," I reminded her, "that he experiments on others."

"It is obvious. For three or four years I had heard of him. He was almost a legend in my life. I kept hearing his name; I kept meeting people who had known him. When I asked to meet him, I was always told that they hadn't seen him lately, or that he had gone away." She paused, then added; "And one or two of them evidently did not wish to discuss him. But one thing was clear: he had left his mark on every one of them."

She spoke excitedly and watched me narrowly as if to read my thoughts, then continued:

"Do you think I am deceiving myself? Do you imagine that I haven't met a great number of alleged personalities and the so-called famous? He is different from them all. He has some secret, and it gives him power."

I noticed again how different she was when Scrivener was being discussed and, unlike Pauline, she invested him with a sinister significance. It was almost as if she were discussing a different man who happened to bear the same name. It was interesting that I had experienced this sensation when Rivers had discussed him. And yet had I not also felt that the man Middleton had met in the café in Soho was a stranger to the one Pauline knew? As I sat silent opposite Francesca I began to realize how intricate was the mystery which surrounded me.

"You say nothing," she said irritably. "Have I convinced you?"

"That he experiments on others?" I inquired. "No, not yet. It stands as a general theory but you have given no individual applications."

She laughed joyously. "You're getting dull. And what do you imagine is his interest in Miss Pauline Mandeville? Your friend Middleton gave me an excellent description of her. It evidently amuses Jonathan to experiment on her. She is clearly attractive, spirituelle, virginal. He descends into her life. He is utterly different from anything she has ever known. She is indecisive about everything. An idealist, perhaps. He meets her on her own ground. Platonic affection—and a latchkey!"

She laughed again, then took a cigarette. "Yes, a latchkey," she repeated. "Then, slowly, subtly he begins to captivate her—fascinates her, dominates her. Everyone else begins to bore her. She does not detect the process. To her, everything is on an extremely elevated level. Two souls seeking salvation—a road through the world, and all that. Jonathan is weary of the worldly woman. And how will it end? She will crawl on her knees to him and offer herself."

I said nothing, which irritated her.

"You don't believe a word of it?" she asked.

"Number one," I replied. "Now—Middleton."

"You want to discover what he has told me? I don't mind telling you. Middleton! Rather interesting—don't you think—for Jonathan to discover such a traditional type suddenly at such odds with his world? To study Middleton's impotent rebellion against all the gods he used to worship. And then, having heard his passionate indictment against a world that has let him down, to reveal to him an icy contempt, infinitely beyond Middleton's frontiers, and by so doing send him deeper into the abyss. To hand him a scourge of scorpions to replace the whips which have caused him so much suffering. Don't you think Jonathan might find all that quite amusing?"

"I think that Middleton had been drinking quite a lot before he came to see you," I said quietly.

"You know that unless he had he would not have had the courage to come. You're not a fool. Well, tell me if I have made a good case."

I rose and stood by the fire. She looked up almost angrily and I was amazed to see the depth of her interest in everything that related to Scrivener. Also her interpretation of Scrivener's relations with Pauline and Middleton—theatrically as she had expressed it—had taken me somewhat by surprise.

"Do answer!" she exclaimed. "Have I made a good case?"

"How can I tell you that, Francesca, when it isn't complete?"

"Not complete?"

"Certainly not!"

We looked at each other in silence.

"How irritating you are!" she exclaimed.

"How dull you are!" I replied.

"Ah! I see." She rose impulsively and stood by my side. "You mean I've omitted——"

"Francesca! Exactly! I asked you to apply your theory to yourself once before—but you evaded the issue."

She was standing quite near me and I could feel her quick, eager breath on my face. There was a long silence, then she said:

"You must sit down again."

I went back to my chair, but she remained standing.

"I told your friend, Winkworth, when I saw him recently, that I thought of going into partnership with someone and I asked him what was the basis of partnership."

"Really! And what did he say?"

"He said that the essence of partnership was mutual trust," she replied in a tone which mimicked Winkworth's perfectly.

"All of which means that you are going to tell me the experiment which Scrivener has reserved for you?"

"Yes, but I would emphasize the word 'mutual' in Winkworth's definition."

Again she drew the cushion to my feet and sat down. But it was some time before she began, a fact which suggested certain mental editing.

"Tell me, is this fantastic? Jonathan knows exactly the type of woman I am. He knows that I am proud; he knows that I love power. He knows that I am admired, that I have influence. He knows my world and what it means to me. And he knows that passion and independence are body and soul to me. In fact, strangely enough," she added with emphasis, "he knows all that *you* included in your catalogue."

I decided to ignore the emphasis, despite the long pause she allowed for comment. She laughed, then continued:

"And shall we imagine that he has not found his world? He could have entered into many, and by right of conquest. But just as he was about to accept his dominion, he looked round and discovered that he could see the frontiers too clearly. And so he abdicated and left a mediocrity, or a charlatan, to scramble on to the throne. And out he went into the wilderness again. Shall we imagine that?"

For some ludicrous reason the question which Middleton had asked me came into my mind and I decided to pass it on:

"You don't write, or anything like that, do you?"

"Idiot!" she exclaimed. "You know he hasn't found his world. You *know* of his extraordinary disappearances. Winkworth told you about them."

"I surrender," I said. "Go on."

"But he sees *me* satisfied with my world. It would be amusing for him to take me as his lover. To respond to the passion which he knows he awakes in me. And to make me *loathe* that world of mine and then to watch disillusion creep over me like a leprosy. That is his experiment with me." A pause. "I long for him and I am afraid to give myself to him."

The last sentence was a whisper and, once again, I knew that it was true if all the rest were moonshine.

"Well?" she said looking up at me. There was a weary note in her voice and the animation had left her features. Then her glance fell and she bent her head. "My God! why doesn't he come back! I want him! When you told me about that Mandeville girl, I could have killed her. Now, I'm sorry for her. But I will not let him experiment on me. Whatever it costs, the duel shall go on." Then with a rapid transition to her challenging mood she exclaimed: "You're terribly dull. You say nothing. I'm waiting for you to criticize my theory."

"Then I must have a cigarette. But before the criticism, I must remind you that you have to fit Rivers into your theory."

"Did Jonathan *tell* Rivers to come to see you?" she asked.

"He did, and although Rivers mentioned your name to Scrivener, he did not tell Rivers that he knew you."

"You'll send Rivers along soon, won't you?" was her very practical comment. "And now—your criticism."

"You suggested this theory of yours at the flat, if you remember. I have had time to think it over. Winkworth did tell me that Scrivener wearied of people suddenly and then went abroad. But if your descriptions of his relations with you, Pauline Mandeville, and Middleton are true, then he seems to have deserted you all at the moment when, from his point of view, things were exceedingly interesting."

"He may have wearied of all of us."

"In which case the experiments are at an end," I pointed out, "and we must evolve another theory. But, assuming that you are right, despite his departure, you still have to explain why he chose me for his secretary. You gave an explanation when we discussed it before, but I don't think it's sound and, anyway, according to you, he had enough experiments on hand."

"*You* are the supreme mystery," she admitted. "It will be explained when he returns. But I stick to my theory. I know it's the explanation."

"One last thing, and I must go, Francesca. Do you attach any significance to the fact that he never received his friends in his library, yet gives a complete stranger the run of it?"

"I don't understand it. Sometimes I think I know nothing about him whatever."

The same words, almost, that Pauline had used.

"By the way," I said as I rose to go. "How long have you had your latchkey?"

"You remember our first meeting?" she said. "That was the first time I had used it. He gave it to me as a joke. He took it out of his pocket and gave it to me a day or two before he left England." Then she added, "I meant to tell you that before."

"And you had no idea he was going?" I asked.

"None."

We talked for perhaps ten minutes longer and then I left her and walked back to the flat. The moon was shining amid a host of stars.

II

Two days later I received Scrivener's reply to my letter. It was as follows:

"MY DEAR WREXHAM,

"I congratulate you on your good fortune. I have always regretted that you were not financially independent, and I am delighted that this is no longer the case. I wish you to feel under no restraint in your relations with my friends. Meet them in your own right and do not feel any obligation to render me an account either of your words or your actions. That you should be free, is what I desire above anything else.

"Should a man named Denvers call, will you kindly tell him that I am no longer interested?

"I had been thinking of returning to London, but have decided not to do so yet. It is immaterial to me where I am since, as you know, the temptation in all places and at all times is to see life with the eyes of a ghost.

"Yours sincerely,

"JONATHAN SCRIVENER."

PART TWO

CHAPTER VIII

THREE months went by in a whirl of activity. Three months packed with experiences so removed from any I had known, that my old life soon became as vague as the memory of a memory. Once, I had known only loneliness; now, I rarely possessed an hour's solitude.

It is no longer possible to record individual events as and when they occurred, and if it were possible the history of those three months would still be incomplete. I can only set down what that period meant to me, the life I lived, and the discoveries I made.

In an early chapter of this book I tried to explain that, allowing for obvious differences, I was somewhat in the position of a novelist whose characters suddenly became living human beings, independent of his will, who went their ways irrespective of any limitations imposed by an arbitrary plot. I added that the novelist thereupon became simply an additional character in a series of scenes and situations not of his contriving. A slight extension of that comparison will illuminate my present difficulty.

A novelist is aware of each thought and act of every one of his puppets. No two of them can meet unless he sanctions the tryst and is present at it. He has difficulties enough, I have no doubt, but at any rate his characters cannot go behind his back. They cannot establish relations of which he is not fully cognizant.

I have no such authority. During the three months which followed my visit to Bruton Street, Pauline, Francesca, Middleton, and Rivers became intimate. Naturally they met frequently when

I was not present and I learnt just so much of developments between them as each chose to tell me.

During the period covered by the first part of this book, I was in a strategical position in that I could see the moves of my "characters." I was an onlooker, if not a creator. In this second part, I am chiefly a detective, and one concerned with several problems, for Scrivener's friends not only shed little light on the mystery surrounding him, but were themselves mysterious. But the whole point, at this stage, is that it did not matter how many problems I had to solve, for the adequate reason that I had no time in which to think. I now had four friends in London and I soon possessed a host of acquaintances.

Before explaining, however, the manner of my life during those three months, it is necessary to say this: to present an adequate record of that period it would be essential for Pauline, Francesca, Middleton, and Rivers, each to write a book. And, possibly, Scrivener. . . .

It has been said of London that the world does not contain a worse city in which to be friendless. I believe it. If I had not made friends of my visitors, I am quite certain I could have lived in Scrivener's flat for half a century and never have known a soul. Pauline, Francesca, Middleton and Rivers, however, were not just four persons—each was an entrance to a world. I entered the world of each one of them; I became familiar with it and its inhabitants. Frequently, in the space of an hour, I passed from one of those worlds to another.

I saw much of Middleton during this period, but the library soon ceased to be our background. He began to drink more and more seriously and gradually he drifted to others who did the same.

"Come out with me," he used to say. "You've sat long enough with those damned books. Come and see where I spend my time when I'm not here. I only care about people like myself, nowadays. You know, men and women who've fallen out of that disciplined army which marches monotonously down the highroad, determined to believe that it's on the way to somewhere. Yes, I'm interested in what they call the failures. I drink with them, listen to them, study them. Or I would study them if I didn't get so damned drunk. Come along and have a look at them."

I used to go with him. When he had been drinking, he was amazingly talkative and often interesting. When he was sober, he would sit silent and stare at his shoes with angry eyes. He took me to out-of-the-way pubs which seemed to depend entirely on their own customers. There was little or no chance trade. I visited one of these very often with Middleton. It was in a blind alley and was in reality a small hotel. Several of the men we met in the bar had rooms upstairs and apparently drank the whole time they were awake.

On our first visit, Middleton informed me that they were a "Bohemian bunch." Then he explained: "You know the type: old lyric writers who can't get a job, theatrical hacks, and dramatic critics on some wretched twopenny weekly of a sporting nature. One of the barmaids told me all about them a month ago. I know most of them now. Dud serial writers, poster artists, who were successful once and who now do nothing but drink. God in Heaven knows where they get their money from!"

Middleton's description was accurate enough. He introduced me to a curious assortment of derelicts. There is no room in the modern world for the old-time Bohemian. Success to-day demands discipline, but these men were incapable of adjustment to the new régime. Their conversation consisted entirely of reminiscences, anecdotes, and pathetic boasting about the golden glory which would be theirs tomorrow or the day after, or—at the latest—next month. There was a conspiracy to regard themselves as the wits of the town, and the possessors of great influence in the theatrical world. Yet they were lovable, amusing, and generous to the pitch of genius. They were like a pack of lost dogs, each one of which pretended to have a good home. Listening to them, the electric light seemed an anachronism. There should have been flaring gas jets. When one left them, one should have encountered hansoms and horse-buses in the streets, not taxis and motors. They always addressed each other as "old boy," or "old man," and there were usually two or three geniuses present.

I never went into the bar without seeing a man who looked like a degenerate Punch. He was dramatic critic to a gutter sporting weekly entitled *They're Off*. To watch him drink whisky after whisky, hour after hour, was to know fear. I wondered how the barmaid dared to serve him. But I never saw him drunk. He became absolutely motionless and the expression in his eyes became more and more fixed. That was all. He was a man of principle, however, and on countless occasions I heard him say:

"I made up my mind when I became a dramatic critic that I would never write for the stage. Never! And I never have, and I never will." After this announcement he would turn his head very slowly and look intently at each of his listeners in turn.

There was another habitué of the place, a small man who never wore an overcoat and always had a bowler on the back of his head. He had a grey moustache, into which he always spoke, and a permanent smile frozen on his lips. Long years ago he had had a hand in several successful musical comedies. Very occasionally nowadays he got the job of writing "gags" into a comedian's part. Under their glaze, the eyes were still intelligent and he was very gentle in his movements and scrupulously polite. He objected strongly if anyone addressed coarse remarks to the barmaids. He had a room upstairs and apparently never ate. He slept from four in the morning to mid-day. Everyone loved him. He explained to me that everything was relative and added: "Give you an example. I have to start the day with ten drinks in order to get normal. Must be normal, old man, must be normal. Secret of success is to be normal." He was always taking you on one side and saying: "Tell me, old man, is this funny?" Some nonsense or other would follow, then he would say: "There's a laugh in that, don't you think?" He dealt in "laughs." But he had a philosophy and a remarkably simple one. It was this: there was one essential in life—to possess a top-hat. You could not go quite under if you had a top-hat. Apparently he had not possessed one for some years.

There were a few tables round the walls of the room, occupied generally by couples. Usually at one of them was a man with a big head who leant forward heavily. His name was familiar to me and he was always with a large, blowzy woman. An interminable argument was invariably in progress between them. The theme of this argument never varied. At eight o'clock the woman said they ought to go—and they argued till one in the morning as to whether they should go or not. When he wanted a drink, he banged on the table with his stick. On the rare occasions when he lurched over to the bar, he was treated with immense respect by everyone. He looked from face to face with great haunted eyes as if he were forced to seek someone of whom he was afraid.

Drinking in this pub was not restricted to the sessions imposed by law, since residents could drink all night if they chose, and evidently it was this fact which induced a number of men to make the place their headquarters. The bar was shut at closing-time and thereafter drinks were obtained from the night porter. I never discovered who owned the place but it must have been worth a fortune.

"Well, what do you think of it?" Middleton asked during my third visit. He did not wait for my reply but went on: "I like these fellows, do you know that? Yes, I like them. A year ago I'd have called them a pack of wasters. But that's just a phrase."

He was fairly intoxicated, and after a brief pause he went on:

"These fellows haven't gone to the devil because they're weaker than the normal respectable type. Not a bit of it! They're stronger."

I told him that was an interesting theory and so he developed it. "Course they're stronger. The others are so lacking in vitality that they can live without a dream. These fellows *demand* a dream. They can't live without it. This world refuses them one, so they create an artificial one. They're in revolt—they don't know it—but they are. Every one of them would rather go mad than become a machine." He gave his short, staccato laugh, then added: "There's more real faith in the pubs than there is in the churches. Not that that is saying much."

Although I saw a great deal of Middleton, and although he was very talkative as he was drinking heavily, he rarely referred to Scrivener. That was strange enough, but what was more remarkable was the fact that although I knew that he was seeing Pauline and

Francesca—and although he knew quite well that I was aware of the fact—he seldom referred to either of them. His silence, however, only concealed his thoughts. By many signs it was obvious that his emotional life was in a state of chaos.

Middleton was one world: General Mandeville another. To go from one to the other was to realize the drama of opposites.

I met General Mandeville frequently during the early part of the period I am now describing. Pauline and her mother were away, and he seemed to want to see me. I gathered that my frankness at our first meeting had appealed to him. At any rate, he turned up at the flat one morning and that meeting was the prelude to many. We dined together several times. I lunched at his club, and I met a number of his friends. Perhaps Mandeville's description of his world gave the secret of its attraction for him. "You know where you are with these people," he said to me once, "you know where you are."

It was a world rich in assumptions, rigid in its code, and jealous of its prerogatives. It assumed that everyone who was anyone was well-dressed, well-fed, well-housed. If you were a man, it was assumed that you had been to a public school, that you were intensely interested in sport, that you had travelled, that you were a Conservative, and that you disliked America. It was assumed that, in given circumstances, you would die for a given number of things. The only criticism permitted was criticism of those who criticized the immutable value of those things. It was assumed, as a matter of course, that you made all these assumptions. If you were a woman, it was taken for granted that you regarded your highest function to be the production of children who would be worthy upholders of the tradition. As to the code of this class, it consisted almost entirely of what you should *not* say and what you must *not* do. Everything of any importance had been settled, and rightly settled, long ago. Your duty was to conform and to serve. You were "the right type," or you weren't. Money did not affect the issue one way or the other. And there weren't problems. Democracy was responsible for all social and political evils. As to individuals, if they did not fit into a perfectly clear-cut scheme of things, they were "cranks." As Mandeville said, "you knew where you were."

If you met these people on their own ground they were friendly and hospitable. The men were either healthy grown-up school-boys, who discussed nothing but sport, or they were irritable old men who cursed their ailments with well-bred fluency. Many of them possessed great ability, but it related only to their work. They had brains, rather than minds. The women were either extremely dowdy or very distinguished in appearance, and they ordered every detail of their husbands' lives—although the latter never suspected the fact for a single second. In everything the wives implied that the husbands were the masters, and the husbands believed it and felt protective.

One night I dined at Mandeville's house with several of his friends. I had spent the afternoon with Middleton and some of his acquaintances, and the swift transition from one group to the other had been a little disconcerting. Yet dining with Mandeville and his friends, I realized that it was to this type that Middleton really belonged. I saw how easily their mode of life might have been his and I understood how headlong is the descent of the traditional type who leaves the main road. This discovery disturbed me, for I was fond of Middleton, and once again I wished fervently that he had not met Francesca. But I had little time in which to think, for the actor, Sir Mortimer Dankin, was among the guests and was evidently interested in me.

"Mandeville tells me," he said, "that you're Scrivener's secretary. I have only seen him once during the last two or three years. I used to see a lot of him. What's he doing with himself?"

I explained my relations with Scrivener. Dankin listened attentively. He was a distinguished-looking man, extremely polished, and spoke with an air of easy assurance.

"Queer fellow," he said when I had finished. "Makings of a great actor, you know. Mandeville doesn't like him. I know what he feels. There's something rather sinister about Scrivener. You discover the significance of his remarks about twenty-four hours after hearing them. I told him once that he was always acting, and he told me to take a leaf out of his book." He laughed lightly, then added. "You hear a lot of queer stories about him, but I always ignore that sort of thing. Still he *is* odd."

The conversation became general. Service appointments were discussed and then the question of naval armaments. Just before I left a man who had said little during the evening came over to me.

"Pardon my curiosity," he began, "but I think I heard you discussing a man called Scrivener with Dankin. Do you mind telling me if you were talking about *Jonathan* Scrivener?"

"Yes, we were," I replied. "Do you know him?"

"I knew him five years ago in Rome." He paused. "I am not particularly anxious to renew our friendship."

I quote these incidents, not because of their individual importance, but because they were typical of the kind of comment which Scrivener's name evoked in Mandeville's circle.

People are usually better than their creeds and more decent than their opinions. If this were not so, civil warfare would be the monotonous characteristic of national life. Thus, the opinions of Mandeville and his friends were mainly the logical expression of their fears and prejudices, but their actions were not based on their opinions. In all their actual personal relationships they were considerate, even imaginative, and it was only when they became theoretical that they ceased to be human. It is so with most of us. And whatever criticism is directed against Mandeville's class, it has to be conceded that its members are prepared to die for their beliefs. Although it is easier to die for something than to live for it, nevertheless physical courage has a positive value. Ordeal by performance is the test of pretensions.

As I saw it, everything was fixed in Mandeville's world—opinions, incomes, beliefs, everything—and therefore it was a total contrast to the world into which Middleton had drifted. Yet, for different reasons, the inhabitants of both these worlds looked at the present with aversion and at the past with affection. In Mandeville's group, as in Middleton's, "the good old days" were over. There was no doubt about that. Mandeville's group defined the destroyer as "Americanization"—and Middleton's group drank far too deeply to indulge in the luxury of definition.

Near them in space, utterly remote in terms of values, was another group—Francesca's. It consisted of the financially successful. In it I met newspaper magnates, financiers, theatrical bosses, dramatists, big business people and so on. An aura of affluence invested each one of them. They lived in the limelight; their most trivial actions were regarded as news by the press. They were the aristocrats of democracy. They supplied the middle classes with scandals, thrills, drama. For some of them money was simply the prize in an exciting game; for others it was the supreme end of existence—the terms in which every man and everything were to be assessed.

Francesca insisted that I should enter this world.

"You'll understand Jonathan's attractions for me if you meet these people," she said rather enigmatically.

"Why?" I inquired.

"Because he could have played their game so much better than they do—if it had interested him."

"And their game is?" I asked.

"Money, power, influence, notoriety," she replied, "the obvious and the tangible. For most of them, wealth is slavery because they worship it. For me, it is freedom because I use it. But I won't tell you about them, you must meet them."

I went to several receptions at her house. I saw at close quarters people whose names I had known for years. It was interesting to see a little bent man with a large head, who was a famous newspaper proprietor, and who suffered from megalomania to such a degree that it was embarrassing to be in his presence. It was instructive to overhear the theories of an eminent barrister on the drama; and to listen to the legal opinions of a famous dramatist on a sensational trial which had just ended. It was a revelation to realize the complexity of the amorous affairs of well-known people and it was a matter for speculation as to what could remain secret when so many intimate details were regarded as common knowledge. But on those rather rare occasions when conversation became focussed upon one theme, the extent and diversity of the knowledge revealed in discussing it were remarkable. Moreover, nearly always there was one or another person present who could offer a unique contribution to whatever subject was under review. Usually, however, the guests were dotted about in small groups, and I felt that in many of them deals were being discussed and plans elaborated. Others consisted of miniature courts where homage was paid to the beauty of a woman, or the wit of a reigning theatrical favourite. One or two people, like myself, were solitary. Notably a Jew of about fifty who apparently never became involved for long in any conversation. But he had a look about him which suggested that he had earned the right to be present and he watched the scene before him as if he were studying a balance sheet. On one occasion we left at the same time. An enormous car awaited him.

Francesca ignored me at these receptions as if anxious that I should make my own discoveries. She was amused, however, at my becoming friendly with the famous novelist, Archibald Stenning. She asked me what I made of him and I told her that he had a genius for listening. According to her, before he became successful, Stenning had been a brilliant talker, a master of repartee and a creator of epigrams. Directly he had established a great reputation with the public, however, he ceased to exploit his social gifts. He told Francesca that it was no longer necessary for him to be a "mental mannequin." He listened. He reserved all his energy for his work. He used to sit with me and seemed like a vast sponge absorbing everything that was going on round him. He watched the young literary men, who were reeling off theories on every subject, with the eyes of a veteran. Why he singled me out for attention was a mystery until our fourth meeting when he said casually:

"Francesca tells me that you are Scrivener's secretary. It's rather odd, because I was attracted to you directly I saw you."

"You know Scrivener well?" I asked.

"No, not well, and yet I owe everything to him."

I imagine that I looked interested, for he went on:

"Yes, that sounds intriguing I admit. Francesca also tells me that you never chatter about people, so I do not mind being frank. I knew Scrivener five years ago. He had written one or two books, not under his own name, which impressed me very much. I got an introduction to him."

A lady appeared at this point and paid Stenning some graceful compliments on his last book.

"Clever woman," he remarked, when she had gone. "You noticed that her flattery did not necessarily involve any knowledge of my novel. Where was I?"

"You got an introduction to Scrivener," I prompted.

"Oh, yes! I asked him why he did not devote himself to litera-ture. He did not answer the question, but he gave me a remarkable criticism of my own work and he outlined a programme for me which, he said, would bring me success. He was entirely right. It was masterly advice. Then he went abroad and I haven't seen him for years. I tell you this partly for your own sake. You are secretary to a very remarkable man."

Just before I left that evening, Francesca summoned me to her side with an imperious gesture.

"Stenning has taken a great fancy to you. Have you told him that you've never seen Scrivener?"

"Yes," I replied, "I have told him."

"He'll use it, he uses everything. You'll find yourself in his next novel."

I did not appear in his next novel, though possibly I shall recognize myself in the one he is writing now. But there was a passage in the novel he has just published which proved to me how observant he was, although his eyes always seemed to be half-closed as if he were about to fall asleep. The passage described just such a reception as the ones I had attended in Bruton Street. A few impressionistic sentences gave the setting: the room was nearly full of men talking in little groups; the hostess was not present; deals, schemes, scandals were being discussed with animation. The cosmopolitan atmosphere, the type and appearance of the guests, the decoration of the room, were vividly presented. Then

Stenning explained the effect created by the entry of the hostess. He described how the appearance of this beautiful woman, half-naked in her ultra modern evening clothes, entirely altered the vibration of the room. Men who had their backs to her knew instinctively that she had appeared. Each man seemed at pains to hide the effect which this instinctive knowledge produced in him. Conversations were continued, but the centre of interest had changed. Attitudes altered, groups disintegrated. There was a subtle rivalry in manœuvring for strategical positions in the new balance of power now in process of formation. Stenning indicated brilliantly the tactics of different types—one man turned impulsively and pretended to be surprised to discover his hostess; another remembered that he had a message for her. And then followed a paragraph in which Stenning analysed the power of beauty. He said that it was the supreme power for it alone conquered simply by its presence.

This passage impressed me for I had seen Francesca's entrance produce just the effect Stenning had described in his novel, but I could never have translated my impression into words as he had done. . . .

Francesca's world was the third, then, into which I entered. But there was a fourth, and it was Rivers who initiated me into its mysteries. With Rivers for guide, I entered chaos.

He would arrive at the flat at any time, day or night, alone or with others, and hurry me off to a restaurant, a theatre, a cinema, a party, a concert, or a café. He introduced me to literally hundreds of people. To be his friend was to solve the problem of perpetual motion. He had a genius for entering into easy and pleasant relations with any number of men and women in every sphere of society. He had vitality; a passion for pleasure; the world was his playground, and the instant gratification of every whim was his religion. He borrowed, lent, obtained credit, but always had money to spend. His lyrical lightness of touch extended to his amorous affairs. His love of variety and adventure caused him to pass from lover to lover easily, naturally, and each lady in turn remained his friend after she had ceased to be his mistress. It never seemed to occur to him that he might become deeply involved, and by some miracle he never did.

"Everything is perfectly simple, my dear fellow," he was always saying to me, "perfectly simple. All people who are decent want to give. You have only to ask in the right way. Besides, asking in the right way *is* giving. Here's an example. I met a marvellous girl at supper three nights ago. I drove her home. Naturally, I suggested that we should become lovers. That is, I gave her the opportunity of collaborating with me in the creation of beautiful memories. She's thinking it over. She's intelligent. She'll see that I'm right."

I do not know why Rivers took me up with such enthusiasm and every day I expected him to drop me. But week after week passed and I saw him almost daily. In everything, with one exception, he was a total contrast to Middleton. They had this in common. Almost from the day on which they began to meet Pauline and Francesca independently of me, they both became very reticent in regard to them. It was this silence which convinced me that there was a good deal which could be said. I knew positively that Rivers met Francesca frequently and his secretiveness in regard to her was curious, particularly when contrasted with his frankness about her at our first meeting. However, it is necessary to explain that although I saw a great deal of Rivers at this time, we were seldom alone.

An outing with Rivers was never an incident in one's life: it was a series of explosions. Thus, at six-thirty one evening the telephone rang. I picked up the receiver.

"Wrexham? Rivers. Listen! You've got to dine with me to-night. You must, I want you to. I've seats for *The Log Cabin*. Musical comedy. American. Not too bad, and something will turn up afterwards. Dine early, of course, have to, so dress now. With you at seven."

Down went his receiver before I had time to say a word. In half an hour he arrived, immaculate from top to toe. With him were two vivacious young women. He had forgotten to mention that they would be present. The three of them drank Scrivener's sherry, smoked, laughed, shouted—simultaneously. I was swept into a taxi; out of it; into a restaurant. A chaos of conversation;

another taxi; the theatre. A huge theatre, whose name is world famous. It was once a temple dedicated to drama, now——

The curtain went up and the enormous audience became silent. Almost immediately a tune writhed seductively in a sugary spiral from the orchestra. I had heard it on barrel organs for the last three months and was destined to hear it twenty-four times during the performance. The words were of secondary importance, but their dominant theme was that "The Old Log Cabin Still Stands." The Log Cabin was revealed from every possible angle in a series of spectacular scenes. Curious instruments wailed plaintively in the orchestra, an army corps of chorus girls drilled with Robot precision, while the enormous audience swayed to and fro in a transport of affection for the Old Log Cabin, and generally evinced a rhapsodical determination to take up the Black Man's burden.

In many ways, however, this musical comedy was representative of the age. Mechanically it was a triumph. It possessed every conceivable device for an elaborate presentation, but it had nothing to present. The book contained neither wit nor humour; the music was an enervated lament. For three hours sex and sentimentality fought for supremacy, and both won at eleven o'clock.

"What do you think of it?" Rivers asked in an interval during which everyone hummed "The Old Log Cabin Still Stands."

I told him.

"Ah, my dear fellow," he said with an airy wave of the hand, "you mustn't listen to this music with your ears. You must listen with your solar plexus. A show like this is most instructive. I've analysed it. Everyone is tired, everyone wants to escape, everyone wants to forget. This show is a debauch for the weak, the starved, and the weary. In the next half, a nigger sings a song called 'There's a Great Deep Sleep Comin' Soon.' Why, damn it, you can hear a pin drop!" At this point Rivers began to sing:

> Good-bye, earth, good-bye, sun;
> Good-bye, good-bye, great round moon:
> Ole man nigger's nearly done—
> There's a great deep sleep comin' soon.

I returned to my seat in a state of anticipation, qualified by apprehension. . . .

When, at last, the performance was over, Rivers evidently regarded the evening as about to begin. The two young ladies left us, as they had a supper engagement, and Rivers reviewed the relative merits of different schemes for our entertainment.

"Care to drop in on a bunch of highbrows?" he inquired. "It's quite near. You've heard of Ursula Umbrage, of course."

"No, I'm afraid not," I replied.

"Surely! Sallow, tall, dark. Will wear brown. She's the centre of a group. They meet on Fridays and spend hours assessing the significance of the intellectual heavyweights of the day. You ought to meet Ursula. She admits she's a highbrow, unlike most of them."

"Does she write?" I asked, anxious for further information before committing myself.

"Does a bit of everything, my dear fellow. She claims to be the intellectual barometer of Europe. For about two years her mercurial nature registered 'Very Stormy,' but lately it's stuck at 'Very Dry.' It may be because of her husband's death. He was a critic. You won't believe it, but he was found dead in the country—sitting on a fence. It's a fact. I told Ursula that the manner of his death was symbolic, which didn't go too well. I don't think we'll see her, after all. It's a bit depressing. You know what I mean. Sort of 'Die, and let die' atmosphere. I tell you what we'll do. We'll go to Pride's."

He took my arm and piloted me through the streets. It was a very cold, clear night. Theatres and picture palaces were emptying and the pavements were thronged. Commissionaires shouted; cars, taxis, and buses hooted. Everyone was in a hurry.

"It's nice to get into the warm streets after the icy cold of the theatre," said Rivers, adjusting his scarf. "The English will stand anything. They've no sense of pleasure. They pay sixteen shillings for a stall, sit and shiver in their overcoats, watching a show which is a frost. Yet people write articles about the future of the theatre! The future of the theatres is simply this: very shortly Lyons will take them over and use them as cold storage depots."

A pause, a very short one.

"In fact, Wrexham, life in England is one desperate attempt to find warmth. Icy as the theatres are, they are not so cold as the stately homes of England. I penetrate occasionally to certain country houses, so the Ice Age has no secrets from me. Your very thoughts become icicles. And if you ever hear that anyone is having a fire in his *bedroom*, you know that the end is near. The search for warmth! Why do people go to the pictures? Warmth! Why do they dance? Warmth! Why do they play games? Warmth! Why do they flirt and sleep together? Warmth! Why has the Church had to drop the idea that hell is literally a riot of writhing flames? Because the English were beginning to look forward to going there."

Another pause, another very short one.

"Idiots boast about the glories of this age," he began again, "but it's all nonsense. This era will be known eventually as the Influenza Age. We all have influenza in England because our rooms are so cold; and all the Americans have it because theirs are so hot. Why not have the vision to see the opportunity provided by this mutual inheritance? Let us stop being sentimental about *The Mayflower* and take our stand on Influenza. That's common ground."

He was still talking when we reached Pride's.

It was a restaurant in a modest side street. Externally, it had no pretensions. You entered a narrow doorway, passed down a long passage, and found yourself in a large, low-pitched, oblong room. The walls were hung with sporting prints, old playbills, and framed menu cards adorned with the signatures of a number of notabilities. The tables were solid, the chairs spacious. Everything was reminiscent of Dickens—except the electric light, the patrons, the food, and the prices. Successful artists—and those who wanted to be thought successful—supped here nightly: revue stars, actors, dramatists, and so on. The proprietor was a great favourite and made his customers feel that they were his guests, which possibly was the explanation of the remarkable legend that the place was not expensive.

Rivers selected a table in a strategical position and distributed nods to his friends.

"Rather a dull bunch to-night," he announced. "Sometimes it's amusing. You want to know this place, or it's easy to drop bricks. For instance, you see that empty table over there? Well, you couldn't go and sit at it, even if you wanted to."

"Why not?" I asked. It was the first time I had spoken since we left the theatre.

"That's Tenterton's table. He's rather a dud actor, but he's amusing enough. That table is always reserved for him. There he is! And, good Lord, there's Hysterical Harry with him!"

"Who, exactly, is Hysterical Harry?" I asked.

"You must know that, my dear fellow. He's Podger—that dreadful person who foams each week in *The Sunday Recorder*. A staunch upholder of cowardice, which he nicknames morality. His pet subject is the pornographic nature of modern literature. He attacks every novel which mentions sex and, therefore, has created more best sellers than any man in London. Harry is a joy. Sunday is bearable because of his article. He only attacks sexy fiction. The thousands of novels which are concerned wholly with murder, criminals, abduction, Sadism, and so on, he evidently regards as good clean fun and wholesome entertainment for the young. And that outlook, my dear Wrexham, is not restricted to Hysterical Harry. It is that of the Home Office and all the societies which are concerned with public morals. And I'm not prejudiced. Sex novels bore me. I get no thrill from the ravings of the impotent. But if you believe that the young *are* influenced by books, then why not attack all this muck which revels in crime? Why only sex?"

A man crossed the room and began to talk with Rivers. I had time to look round. The restaurant was pretty full now and I recognized several people I had seen on the stage. The man who had joined us was talking about the theatre; the people at the table next to mine were doing the same; a man and a woman who were standing near me, looking for a table, were also talking about theatrical affairs. Everyone was discussing the same subject. When we were alone again, I mentioned the fact to Rivers.

"All talking about the stage? Of course they are! They always do.

That's the charm about theatrical people and the reason why they are so boring."

I pointed out the contradiction in his last remark, but Rivers raced on:

"It's charming to be with these people when you want to escape from the horror of the world. For them, nothing exists but the theatre. They are interested in nothing else. Nothing has any reality for them except their little world of make-believe. That's why they're charming and that's why they're boring. It depends on your mood. Besides, they are so absurdly personal: if they are doing well, everything is marvellous. If they are doing badly, everything is done for. They have no critical faculty whatever. They hypnotize themselves, their friends, and their backers. I love them."

He went on talking. People came, people went, but Rivers never ceased to comment on any and every subject. As it was now nearly one in the morning, I suggested that we might go home.

"Home!" he exclaimed. "Not on your life! There's sure to be a party somewhere. We'll go to it. Wait a minute and I'll find out what's doing." He rose and made a tour of the tables. He was welcomed everywhere with enthusiasm. When he returned, he leant towards me and said confidentially: "There's an orgy at Burton's, but they're always dull. Freddie is reading his new play at Brice's, but I think we'll go to Gaby's. She's a party on, and it may be amusing."

In a few minutes we left with several others and drove away in taxis. The party was extremely noisy. Dawn was breaking when I said good-bye to Rivers. We stood chatting at the bottom of St. James's Street.

"Interesting evening, don't you think?" he asked. "Interesting to me, at any rate, but then I'm a student."

I looked at him as he stood there, immaculate, with no visible sign of fatigue, and asked him to define the nature of his studies.

"I study a dying civilization, my dear fellow. Decay interests me more than growth. Fortunately I was born in this age. Do you know how I see all our present-day activities? I'll tell you. Politicians, parsons, patriots, artists—they're all doing the same thing.

Each one still beats his drum in front of his booth, and urges the public to witness the splendour of the show. And there isn't a show. That's the joke. It's all become meaningless. But they go on beating their drums. Habit dies hard. Besides, not one of them dares to admit that the show doesn't exist any longer. And——"

But I interrupted:

"Does Scrivener beat a drum?" I asked.

He looked at me sharply before he replied:

"I've made a discovery about him recently. It's this: I thought I knew him, and I find that I know nothing whatever about him. But I'll say this: he doesn't beat a drum. Perhaps that's his tragedy. Good-night, my dear fellow."

I have set down the incidents of this particular evening, not because they are important in themselves, but because they were typical. To know Rivers was to enter not merely one world, but several, and it was through my association with him that I met several people who had known Scrivener at some time or other.

It is difficult to describe the life I lived during these three months. Thought was impossible because solitude was unknown. The days passed in a ceaseless whirl of activity. Superficially, I became more intimate with Pauline, Francesca, Middleton, and Rivers, yet the more frequent our meetings, the more I suspected the existence of complicated relations between them of which I was ignorant. But that was not all. During this period I made many discoveries about myself, and one of fundamental importance.

Before I became Scrivener's secretary, I believed that I had renounced the kingdoms of this world. It is an error frequently made by those to whom the world offers nothing. It is arrogance masquerading as renunciation. My father's death had left me stranded; my life in Petersham's office had consisted of long years of impotent revolt; all roads were barred—there was no way of life for me and yet I had to live. It is true that a change came to me; it is true that I became reconciled to being a spectator in life, but the fact remains that there were a number of temptations to which I had not been subjected. Imaginatively, however, I rejected what I had not been offered. The change which had come to me was more in the nature of a substitute for life than a fulfilment of life. Pride hid this fact from me at the time, but later it became clear. And it was chiefly my experiences during the three months I am now reviewing which forced me to see the past in perspective.

But what surprised me above everything else was that I did not hear a word from Scrivener during this period. I forwarded letters, I wrote to him once or twice, but no sign came from him. More than once the fantastic theory occurred to me that he knew the manner of life I was leading, and that his knowledge was not derived from the letters of others. I had the curious sensation that he was aware of the type of developments which must ensue between me and those friends of his with whom I had become so intimate. I felt that he understood each one of us; that it had interested him to bring us together; and that now he remained silent while he waited to see what the results of our association would be. I even felt that he had deduced those results and was waiting for events to confirm his deductions. Again and again I told myself that all this was nonsense and yet as the weeks went by and no word came from Scrivener, I became dominated by the mystery surrounding him. I realized too that each of the others, in his or her way, was counting on him for something, and the further fact that not one of them wished to discuss him impressed me considerably. I felt that all of us were flies snared in the same invisible net.

At last I determined to make an attempt to discover what had happened to Scrivener. I rang up Walter Winkworth. That gentleman was remarkably dejected. He informed me that he had telephoned on several occasions, but apparently I was never in the flat. He explained that he had heard nothing from Scrivener for many weeks although he had written to him frequently on matters of considerable importance.

"A man in his position, Wrexham, has social obligations which cannot be ignored in this manner. He should marry—there's no doubt about that—he should marry. A man wants a woman in his life, sir—a *woman*. It gives him balance and a background. The late Lord Chief Justice said to me: 'Winkworth, behind every successful man there is a woman.' A penetrating statement, Wrexham.

And all the more remarkable as it came from a bachelor. Do please come to see me soon. There are matters we should discuss. I am very disturbed, very disturbed indeed."

Winkworth knew nothing and I had no other source of information.

The weeks passed and no letter came from Scrivener.

CHAPTER IX

I HAD dined with Francesca and Rivers. It was the first occasion on which I had been with them alone, and it had interested me to note the efforts Rivers had made to be amusing. I had said nothing, Francesca had said little, but Rivers had staged a display of mental fireworks for our entertainment. It seemed to me that his endeavour to be brilliant resulted in his being less amusing than usual. Francesca watched more than she listened. The hint of an enigmatic smile curled her lips and to my surprise I discovered that I felt a little sorry for Rivers. He was working so hard, was evidently so satisfied with the result, and clearly quite unaware of the reservations and criticisms implied in Francesca's expression and attitude.

In the middle of one of his most amusing anecdotes she turned to me and said:

"It's very nearly time that we saw each other alone again, don't you think?"

"It's not happened for three months," I replied.

She brought Rivers into the conversation with a little wave of her hand.

"This may be a warning to you. When I last saw Mr. Wrexham we were exceedingly confidential. Naturally, we've avoided each other ever since. That is true, isn't it?" she asked, turning to me.

"Not a word of it," I answered. "We have not met alone since that night in Bruton Street because you——"

"Have discovered the fascination of Mr. Scrivener's other friends," she interrupted. "That's perfectly true. I only met them through you, however. I think it's time we had a long talk together."

I decided to ascertain whether either of them knew anything about Scrivener.

"Has either of you heard from Scrivener?" I asked. "I have heard nothing from him for three months."

"*You* have heard nothing from him!" exclaimed Rivers.

I shook my head, then glanced at Francesca.

"I have no news from him," she said, "but possibly I have learnt a little about him lately. I told you long ago that we never write to each other. Has Pauline Mandeville heard from him?"

"I have not asked her," I replied.

"Nor Mr. Middleton?" she inquired with ironic insistence.

"No. Scrivener's name has not been mentioned between us for a long time."

There was a pause. Francesca evidently decided it was time to go, but before she rose she sent Rivers on some errand, then turned to me impetuously.

"Hasn't this farce gone on long enough between us?"

"What farce?" I asked with genuine surprise.

She looked at me intently. "We have been collecting data independently. Isn't it time we compared notes?"

"I've discovered nothing," I replied, "except one or two things about myself which are of no interest to anyone. It is you who have made discoveries, and kept them to yourself. Have you proved your theory?"

"What theory?" she asked.

"That Scrivener experiments on others. You remember that you believed that he was experimenting on Pauline."

She looked at me with a curious expression. I could see that she was very excited.

"I know nothing whatever about him," she said slowly. "Nothing whatever."

"Rivers made the same confession to me recently," I said impartially.

"Rivers!" Her tone was cold with contempt. "He only said that because I showed him the absurdity of his so-called knowledge about Jonathan. But he amuses me—and so does your friend, Mr. Middleton. Has either of them discussed me with you?"

"You know quite well they haven't. I believe you have ordered them not to."

She laughed gaily. "And you imagine that they would obey my orders?"

"Yes."

Again she laughed. "Well, at any rate I am quite certain *you* wouldn't."

"You are quite certain?"

"Of course," she said, after a pause. "Why, you never even praise my appearance. I have no power over you."

"That's not true," I replied. "It would have been only too easy to become completely fascinated by you."

"You've never given me a thought," she said decisively.

"Often," I replied. "Even before I met you. Even before I knew you existed. What man escapes you wholly?"

She studied me narrowly for some seconds.

"Wouldn't that be equally true if you said it to Pauline Mandeville?"

"Yes," I replied, "it would be equally true."

She rose. "Remember, I am coming to see you soon and I must see you alone. Why do you look at me in that strange way?"

"You're tired of the game you have been playing, Francesca."

"You don't know what the game has been—yet."

"Perhaps you are going to leave me with the casualties," I suggested.

"Hush! Here he comes. Remember, I am coming to see you. I have a proposal to make to you."

I left them and walked through St. James's Park on my way home. We had dined late and had sat on talking for some time. It was now nearly eleven o'clock. The air was fragrant with the promise of spring and even in the city one was aware that earth was stirring with the passionate pulse of life. There was a brilliant moon. I walked on slowly. The noise of the traffic in Piccadilly dwindled to a muttering menace. Then, dotted about on a knoll ringed by trees, I saw a group of sheep. They were motionless in the moonlight as if the waving of a magic wand had conjured them into existence and left them spellbound. For several minutes I stood watching them. London no longer existed; the sense of my own identity vanished; the veils of Time had fluttered apart, revealing a glimpse of a patriarchal world.

I did not hurry home and it was nearly a quarter to twelve before I reached the flat. I found Middleton sitting on the stairs. He had evidently been waiting for some time and had grown tired of standing. His appearance disturbed me: his face was haggard, his eyes were too bright, and he had obviously been drinking heavily. He gave his short laugh and rose unsteadily to his feet.

"Couldn't go home, old boy. That's why I'm here. Ever felt like that? Ever felt you couldn't go home?"

I opened the front door and we went in together. Directly we were in the library Middleton helped himself to a drink while he continued to talk excitedly.

"Time's a damned funny thing, isn't it? I've got a theory about it—a much better one than this high-hat scientific stuff. Time, old man, only exists for the lonely. Tell you something else too. Once there was no such thing as time—then a lonely man invented it."

He rambled on. I hadn't seen him for ten days, and I began to realize how greatly he had altered since I first met him. Little things revealed it. To give one instance, his phraseology was now that of his Bohemian associates. Every other sentence was punctuated with "old boy" or "old man."

"You've been away since I saw you last, haven't you?" I asked.

He lit a cigarette, then laughed unpleasantly. "I've been away, all right. Been staying with the county, but I shan't be asked again. Tell you all about it. You listen to this carefully."

He paused and looked round the room quickly as if to satisfy himself that we were alone.

"You remember I told you about my brother. Damned good fellow till he married a woman with money who likes to be thought a somebody. Right! I went to stay with 'em. Well, the day before yesterday, after dinner, they and their friends began to discuss a great problem. Guess what it was."

I suggested the first things which came into my head. "Unemployment? Foreign affairs? Election results?"

"Not on your life! This, my boy, *this*. A man called Robinson and his wife have just taken a biggish house near them. Well, should people call on them? *That* was the point. They went on and on about it. Who was the man? Who was his wife? *Could* she have been one of the Berkshire Dinnots? Was he one of the Rutland Robinsons? It went on and on and then I began to laugh. I began to laugh like hell."

He rose and made a wide sweeping gesture with his hand. "Imagine the scene. There they were in a circle, staring at me. And the more they stared, the more I laughed. There was a doddering old parson there with a face like a tombstone. It told you when he was born and when he died and nothing else. God! I'll never forget it."

"How did it end?" I asked.

"Well, I stopped laughing and then got angry. Their owlish faces made me furious. I turned on 'em. Asked 'em if they'd ever thought whether the Robinsons wanted to know *them*. Asked them what was the use of the whole blooming lot of us. Told them they were a pack of fakes and twisters, trying to live on the past—like worms live on a corpse. There was hell's own scene I tell you. Course I was drunk. Yes, old boy, the lone wolf squealed at last and the pack didn't like it."

He dropped into his chair again and threw his cigarette away. He mixed another drink, then scowled angrily at the fire. Neither of us spoke for some minutes. Everything proclaimed that he was in a state of extreme nervous irritation, but whether its true cause would emerge was a matter for speculation.

He began to mutter to himself, then took up the thread of his narrative again.

"I cleared out that night. Went to my room and packed. Walked in to the station—four miles—carrying my bag. That's the end of that. And do you know what really worries me? You'd never guess. It's this."

He leant forward and spoke with great intensity. "Suppose that woman I told you about hadn't turned me down. Imagine that I had married her. Well, then, my brother and his crowd wouldn't have irritated me. I should have thought that they were just decent normal people. Good God! I should probably have been one of them."

There was a long pause, then he went on:

"That crowd my brother's married into are an interesting study, old man. They've got the wind up all right. They all think there's going to be a revolution. A revolution!" He laughed mirthlessly. "Why, damn it, there isn't enough vitality in this country to stage a revolution. Anyway, if there's one, it will be engineered by the upper classes."

"That's an interesting theory," I said.

"Of course it will! The Tories have been telling the Socialists for years that they must be constitutional. Well, soon it's going to suit the Socialists to be constitutional. Then you'll see what will happen. The Tories will kick the constitution to hell and demand a dictator. They're only for law and order so long as it suits *them*."

He began to mutter to himself again.

"Why do you bother yourself about all these things?" I asked.

"Because it's these things which used to deceive me. Damn it all! I believed in these people once. I made my religion out of the things they pretend to worship. And now I see clean through them. God! You should have heard them talking about America. The Americans are such materialists! The Americans only care about money! The Americans are a menace to civilization! That's what they said. And *they* talk about nothing but food and money and they don't care a damn about civilization. I told them that there was one difference between the Americans and them and that it was this: the Americans are out for money, admit it, and work for it. And my brother's bunch only want money, won't admit it, and don't mean to work for it. The result will be that in a few years we'll be just a suburb of America. The Americans will not be such fools as the Germans were. They'll be content with commercial dominion."

He paused, then added: "I told them the simple facts that English economic supremacy had gone and that naval supremacy would follow it. We've got to get used to not being boss."

He filled his glass again. I said nothing. It was so clear to me that the indictment he had hurled at his relatives represented only a projection of his own unhappiness, that I decided that I would not discuss in impersonal terms an issue which was wholly personal. He was utterly pathetic and I felt terribly sorry for him.

"You're a queer bird," he announced.

"In what way?" I asked.

"*You* say nothing, old boy. Others tell me not to do this, not to do that—to give up drink and so on. You don't say a word. No reason why you should, of course, still it's odd. Give me some advice. I can't go on like this, anyway."

"I've only one thing to say. It's this. You must accept what's happened to you."

"Accept!"

"Yes," I went on. "Accept the fact that your engagement was broken off. Accept the fact that your life has been jerked out of the traditional rut. Accept your loneliness in fact."

He stared at me. "And what the hell happens then?"

"Then," I replied, "it would be possible for something to happen."

"Might go mad, for instance?" he suggested with a sneer.

"Possibly," I answered. "But it would be your own madness. It would belong to you. You're just as traditional to-day as you were a year ago."

"What in God's name are you talking about?" he asked irritably.

"It's quite simple, Middleton. You took a punch and it knocked you clean out of the life of your type. What have you done? You've accepted the traditional way of dodging things. That is, you've begun to drink heavily and to mix with people who do the same. You don't belong to them and you know it."

He sat leaning forward, staring at me. "Go on," he said at last.

"You won't solve a problem by going below it. I admit that you're up against a conflict. Every man is who has watched his world crumble before his eyes. But you're taking on a conflict which doesn't belong to you. Why were you furious with your brother and his crowd? The truth is that you were furious with *yourself*. You transferred that fury to them. Why did you turn on them and insult them? You wanted to destroy the world in which they live. You wanted to bring them into *your* position—the position you are afraid to face. You like to think you were possessed by righteous indignation. You weren't. You wanted to drag them into your own hell."

There was a long silence, then Middleton said: "It's all perfectly true: how did you know?"

"You're not the first to hit blindly at everything just because you've been hurt. London's no good to you. Why don't you cut your leave and get back to your job?"

"Job! Oh, of course, you don't know. I've chucked the job. Don't look so surprised, old boy. Did you think I was going back there with dead dreams for company? Not on your life! I've just enough to live on. I'll stay here and drink till Scrivener turns up. I want one good long talk with him. I reckon he owes me that. I met him at a crisis in my life."

"You haven't mentioned him lately," I said somewhat pointedly.

"We'll come back to him—perhaps. Can I have another drink? Good! I'm not worrying really. Something will turn up—another war or something."

I said nothing, and after a pause he went on:

"Talking about war, have you noticed that the last war is just beginning to reach civilian England? People are just beginning to feel it. Perhaps, in a different way, I'm finding out what it did to me, too."

"I don't understand," I said.

He took a pull at his drink, then went on: "I didn't feel it when I was out there. My nerves held. It didn't seem to affect me. Course it was bloody, but I believed in all sorts of dope, and I got through all right. Well, you'll scarcely believe it, but I've begun to dream about it lately."

He rose impetuously and began to walk up and down the

room. "Yes, I've begun to dream about it. Only recently—just the last month or two. I wake up sweating with fear. It's damned odd, because I didn't get the wind up out there. It all seemed like a dream then—and now I dream about it and it's hell." He laughed shamefacedly. "Why, damn it, sometimes I'm afraid to go to sleep."

He continued walking up and down talking about himself, the war, and the life he was leading. It was clear that he wanted to cheat loneliness by staying with me and it was equally clear that there was a subject he wished to discuss, yet feared to introduce. Always he was haunted by the fear of making himself ridiculous, yet it was evident that the need to confide in someone had become imperative.

He returned to his chair and began to drink again. The room seemed more silent than ever—an ominous prophetic silence.

I looked at Middleton and our eyes met. He had evidently been gazing at me for some seconds. Anger and perplexity were pretty evenly balanced in his expression. He began to talk again:

"You're just as queer as Scrivener in your way. Do you know that? I'll tell you this, anyway: I wish to God I'd never come to this flat! I was a damned fool. My talk to Scrivener in that hole in Soho wasn't so elevating that I had any excuse for looking him up. Don't want to be rude, old boy, but I wish to God I'd never met you, or any of the people I've met in this flat! It was difficult enough for me before I met Scrivener, but it's been much worse since." A pause, then speaking in a low voice which vibrated with anger: "Besides, he's a hypocrite. Do you know that? Just a hypocrite and a poseur. I'm waiting till he returns to tell him so. I've found him out, and he's going to know it."

"You're excited," I began, but he interrupted me.

"Excited be damned! I tell you he was bitter as death when we talked that night in Soho. God knows I had reason enough to be bitter about women, but you should have heard Scrivener! All lies! I come here and find that he's intimate enough with two women who——"

It was my turn to interrupt.

"Wait a minute, Middleton. How did Scrivener know you'd come here at all?"

He looked at me almost condescendingly before he replied:

"If you meet a man who is utterly lonely in London, talk with him, give him your card, it's probable, isn't it, that he'll look you up?"

I had to admit that it was probable. Then he went on:

"And he saw deep enough into me that night to know that it would be some days before I called on him. He knew perfectly well that I should be ashamed of revealing myself to a stranger. He totted up everything—*everything*. He knew that I shouldn't turn up here till he'd gone."

"Well, if you're right, what was his motive?"

His anger had died down and he looked at me gloomily. "It would puzzle the devil to answer that question, but one thing is certain: he wanted me to meet those women, and he wanted you to meet them. Also he knew that *we* should meet. He has some game on. I hope it's amusing him, because it's playing the devil with me."

Again he rose and began to walk about the room. I was glad he was silent for a new idea had occurred to me. To-night, for the first time for three months, Middleton had discussed Scrivener intimately with me. Was it simply coincidence that to-night Francesca had said that she wanted to see me alone? Was I about to learn something of the relations which had been established between my four visitors during the past few months? I glanced at Middleton. It was easy to see that something had precipitated a crisis in his life. I decided to risk a long shot, so I said to him:

"I dined with Francesca to-night."

"I knew you were going to," he replied.

"Did she know you were coming here?" I asked.

He turned suddenly on his heel and faced me:

"She told me to come here. We may as well be frank, Wrexham. I know you've noticed that I've not discussed Scrivener with you lately. Well, I'll give you one explanation which will cover fifty. I'll have a drink first though. Have one with me for God's sake!"

I mixed two drinks. He returned to his chair and lit a cigarette. Suddenly he began to laugh:

"Don't look so surprised," he exclaimed, "you'll be laughing yourself in a minute. When I came here first, I was in hell because I loved a woman who'd turned me down. You remember that, don't you?"

"Of course, I remember," I replied.

"Well, now I'm in love with two women. Yes, don't stare at me. *In love with two women.* I'm quite an interesting study, I assure you. I knew I'd tell you this to-night. I tried like hell not to come, because I knew I'd tell you."

He broke off and was silent for a minute. His face was working convulsively and I could see that he did not know how to express what he wanted to say.

"Pauline Mandeville." He half whispered the words. "I'm afraid to love her. Do you know why? I should love her as I loved the other one. Do you think I'm going to risk loving like that again? Go back to old dreams, believe again in all the things I used to believe? Never! And yet—she's the only person who could help me. I *know* it. But I'm afraid of her—I'm afraid of what she wakes in me. But that's not all. There's your friend, Francesca. I despise her. She's everything that stirs my contempt. But—but she's beautiful. She's got that damnable type of beauty which maddens the blood. I'm her slave, and she knows it, although I've never said a syllable to her about her attraction for me. I—I——"

He made a gesture as if to indicate the inadequacy of words.

It was some time before he continued, then I learnt all that the past three months had meant to him. It was a complex, chaotic confession, full of repetitions, a strange mixture of self-pity and bitter denunciation. I was amazed by the intensity of the inner drama which was making his life an impossibility. Pauline had awakened everything which he had believed was dead in him; Francesca had made him a stranger to himself, for under her influence he had become aware of passions and desires of which he had been ignorant, and of which he was afraid. These two women constituted the foreground of the drama within him and each was poised on the background of the mystery of Scrivener.

But, above all, it was the futility of the drama which tormented him. Pauline represented a challenge to which he had once responded, and it was that response which had occasioned all his subsequent suffering.

"A man can't go back," he exclaimed. "I should have met her a year ago, or I should never have met her at all. I don't believe that she is what she appears—I daren't believe it. Nowadays, I prefer weeds to flowers—weeds proclaim their origin. Besides, what's my feeling for her worth, when at the same time my senses ache for another woman?"

"There may be another explanation," I said. "Your real mistake was chucking your job."

"You mean loneliness? I've thought of that. It's a disease—I know that well enough. It's not listed as one, but, nevertheless, it's the most prevalent of all modern diseases. But no one will admit it. I'd never have met either of those women if I hadn't been lonely. I shouldn't have met Scrivener. But the point is: what the hell am I to do?"

"There are many solutions," I said. "For instance, Rivers manages to fill up his days and nights."

Middleton smiled grimly.

"I've seen a good deal of Rivers lately. That's a pretty significant fact in itself. I'll only say this: Rivers isn't so adequate to life as he thinks."

A pause, then he continued:

"What weaklings we all are! I come here, get drunk, and tell you that I'm in love with two women. Also I ask for advice. Advice! My destiny is clear enough. I shall drink myself slowly to death like those men I meet at the pubs. That's what will happen to me. And the more I drink, the more I'll humiliate myself. It's interesting to see so clearly that I'll become everything I have always despised. One last drink, old boy, and I'm off."

He rose and went over to the table. He was fairly drunk by this time and had to lean against a chair to steady himself.

"You tell old Scrivener when you write that I'm drinking a hell of a lot of his whisky."

He reeled back to his chair, holding his glass. For five minutes we sat in silence and then he made a pathetic attempt to go.

"I'll smoke one cigarette, then I'll be off," he said.

Suddenly he leant forward and began to talk in quick, feverish sentences.

"She sent me here to-night. She knew I'd drink and tell you everything. She knows I'm in love with Pauline, just as she knows that I want her. I've never told her—but she knows." Then angrily, passionately, "And I swore to myself that I wouldn't tell you! I made up my mind I wouldn't! But I have. And I've made a vow that I'll never *tell* Francesca that I want her as the damned want deliverance. But I shall tell her. I'll drink till I've got the courage and then I'll tell her. By God, Wrexham, I can't go on like this. But my will is paralysed and I can't act. I *must* see Scrivener. He's responsible, damn him, and I must see him! . . . No, that's no good! I mustn't see any of you again. It's the only way. I must learn to be alone. Promise me this—don't tell Pauline about to-night. Don't tell her. . . ."

I walked home with him through the silent, deserted streets. Neither of us spoke. The clock at St. James's struck three just as I returned to the flat.

CHAPTER X

I

Two days after Middleton's visit I was sitting in the library reading. I had spent the morning alone and it seemed probable that at last I was going to have a day to myself. I was tired, not a little depressed, and my thoughts were in a state of chaos. I needed solitude. The life I had lived recently had made great demands, and I was exhausted mentally and emotionally. I was very irritated, therefore, when the telephone bell rang.

It was Mr. Walter Winkworth. I gathered he had telephoned frequently during the last day or two. He reproached me for not keeping in touch with him. I reminded him that we had spoken on the telephone quite recently, but his tone implied that we had been great friends for a number of years and that I had neglected him without cause. But, above all, he was extremely mysterious. He hinted that he knew dark secrets which I must share, and generally conveyed the impression that there were matters urgently needing discussion which could not even be hinted at over the telephone.

"I want your advice, Wrexham. I *need* your advice, and I have a proposition to make to you."

The proposition was so unexpected that I assented to it immediately. It was this: Winkworth suggested that I should join him at his office at five o'clock and spend the night at his house in Chislehurst.

"Certain of the things I wish to discuss, Wrexham, demand the privacy of one's own study. In this office interruptions are inevitable and frequent. I shall convince you, I *think*, of the necessity for caution. Now, may I expect you at five o'clock?"

I arrived at his office in Sackville Street as five was striking. The immaculate young man in the outer office piloted me immediately to Winkworth's room where I received an effusive welcome.

"To the minute, Wrexham, to the minute! Ah, my dear sir, if only everyone were punctual! Do sit down. I shall not keep you long. A heavy day's work and a lot of letters to sign."

He seated himself at his desk. His secretary stood by his side holding a tray containing a sheaf of letters, which required his signature. It was easy to see from Winkworth's attitude that this ritual symbolized the end of the day's work. He leant back in his chair, took each letter in turn, regarded it through his pince-nez—which he used as if it were a lorgnette—and read each word with evident satisfaction. When he had completed his scrutiny, he placed the letter on the table, leant forward, closed his eyes for a moment, then took a pen and signed his name. He performed this act with such deliberation that I felt I was watching Destiny at work.

In course of time the last letter was reached. Winkworth read it aloud. "A sound piece of construction, Wrexham, eh?"

"Admirable!" I replied.

"And sound law, too. Now I am at your disposal."

His secretary assisted him with his overcoat and we left the office together.

Winkworth's car was waiting. The chauffeur helped him in and adjusted the rug. As we made our way through a crowded Piccadilly, Winkworth explained to me that he was about to purchase a much more expensive car and asked my advice as to the respective merits of several aristocratic models. As we approached Chislehurst, he was at some pains to point out that in the near future he was going to buy a much larger house in a more distinguished situation. In fact, he conveyed the impression that everything he now possessed represented simply a temporary expedient and that, very shortly, the whole manner of his life would be elevated to a more luxurious and appropriate level.

On arrival, I found an attractive house, set well back from the road, surrounded by a spacious well-kept garden in which a number of flowers were ranged with the precision of soldiers on parade.

Winkworth threw open the front door with a gesture, and his wife appeared immediately. The reception she gave him could not have been more affectionate if he had just returned from a voyage round the world. She fussed round him, took his hat and overcoat, inquired about his health, asked if he had had a strenuous day, and behaved generally as if he had just recovered from a serious nervous breakdown. She kept giving me little glances which seemed to imply that she knew that I recognized, as she did, how important and wonderful he was. She was a rather stout, untidy woman, with weak watery eyes, extraordinarily alert in her movements, and obviously very good-natured.

She led us into a sitting-room. Winkworth's slippers were reposing against the fender. Two evening papers stood on a little table within reach of his armchair. A bowl of gay flowers was perched on the mantelpiece, just underneath Winkworth's portrait.

"Now, I hope, Mr. Wrexham," began Mrs. Winkworth, shaking her head from side to side and speaking in a coy admonishing falsetto, "I hope you are not going to discuss any business with Walter. He never thinks of himself—never! It's always his horrid clients."

"My love!" exclaimed Winkworth in a tone which administered a reproof to her levity.

"They *are* horrid," she replied with elephantine girlishness, "but you men will go your own way."

She chattered on for a few minutes, then left us together.

"The ladies will have their say, Wrexham, but—there!—I don't know what we should do without them."

There are houses which it is only necessary to enter in order to find oneself in the atmosphere of another age. After I had been in Winkworth's house for a quarter of an hour I was certain that Victoria was on her throne; that the South African War had yet to be fought; and that fashionable women resembled elaborate bundles. The illusion would have been maintained if it had not been for dinner.

I had expected that meal to be plain, ample, solid. It was nothing of the kind. It consisted of a large number of pretentious and diminutive dishes, elaborately served and indifferently cooked. I discovered that Mrs. Winkworth was one of those women, common enough in the country, who seek to combine excessive frugality with ostentatious display. It was not her fault, however. Winkworth clearly belonged to the type of man who believes that a pound goes five times as far in housekeeping as it does in any other activity, and his wife was evidently determined to prove that he was right. Fortunately they had no children and it was certain that Winkworth's sleek and well-fed appearance was due to the excellent luncheons he procured in London. If the dinner was not a success, however, the conversation was quite revealing, although it consisted almost entirely of a monologue by Winkworth.

"I frequently tell my wife, Wrexham, that it is not the work at the office which tires me. It's *worry*. Practically each day and every day I interview client after client and each one, sir, wants me to do the same thing—to raise money."

He put down his knife and fork and regarded me mournfully. "Money! Mine is an old-established family practice. I number among my clients many of the oldest families in England. I am proud of the fact. They all want money, Wrexham. Taxation, death duties, and so on, make it impossible for them to live as they have been accustomed to live—as they *ought* to live, in my opinion. No wonder that their treasures are going to America! No wonder that many great houses in the country stand empty! I'm not a politician myself, but——"

His wife interrupted:

"Oh, Mr. Wrexham, if only Walter would go into Parliament! I am always telling him it is his duty to do so. He could save England—I know he could—because, in one way, he *is* England."

"My dear!" Winkworth raised his hand as if to shield himself from temptation.

"He ought to be Home Secretary," his wife insisted. "I am always telling him so, but he won't listen to little me. Walter is always explaining exactly what is necessary to put England on her feet. I sit and listen and I think to myself: he ought to be saying this in the House of Commons."

"Really, my dear!" expostulated Winkworth weakly.

"It's true, Walter. I *will* speak up. It's true. You should be Home Secretary." She then gave a list of the qualities her husband possessed, all of which she considered essential in a Home Secretary. She was evidently a traditionalist and a Home Secretary was closely associated in her mind with an old woman.

"A great friend of mine," said Winkworth impartially, "and a man who held high office under Baldwin, said to me: 'Winkworth, we need men like you in Parliament.' And do you know what I said to him? I said this: 'And my clients say to me: we want a man like you in Sackville Street!' And that is my answer to you, my love. It is not always a question of capability: it is often a question of duty."

Having made this statement with immense dignity, Winkworth proceeded to give a survey of home and foreign affairs. It lasted for a considerable time and ended on rather a pessimistic note. It was difficult for me to escape the impression that a loud speaker had been switched on. His wife, however, listened with such adoring eyes that I began to realize just how serious it can be when the English wife is not lost in the English mother.

Dinner ended at last, and coffee was served in the lounge. Mrs. Winkworth then related every detail concerning her neighbours' affairs which she had collected during the day: the maid at the

Johnstons' had given notice; Mrs. Fitzjohn's baby had not arrived yet; the Trouts had a new car; the vicar's hat had been blown off as he was crossing the High Street; and so on. Winkworth listened and occasionally nodded his head majestically. I could see that this account of the day's doings was a regular after-dinner event. During the meal, Winkworth delivered the monologue on his day and the world at large. After dinner, it was his wife's turn. Presumably they never conversed: first one made a report, then the other.

At ten o'clock Winkworth interrupted his wife's narrative by waving his forefinger waggishly at her and remarking: "Ten o'clock, I *think*," whereupon his wife rose immediately and went to bed. An inflexible routine obviously governed their companionship.

"Now, Wrexham, we'll make ourselves comfortable in my study. I have a brandy, sir—well, you'll see for yourself."

I followed him into the study. The room seemed surprised at our appearance: its atmosphere proclaimed that it was rarely used, and everything frowned at us. I felt that we were entirely excluded from the room's confidence. I glanced at the bookshelves: the classics, elaborately bound, were ranged solidly in mass formation as if to defy assault.

"No man is fonder of the society of the ladies than I am," Winkworth announced, "but there are matters which it would be injudicious to discuss before them. *Injudicious*, Wrexham—that's the word."

He stirred the fire, produced his liqueur brandy, lit a cigar, and seated himself comfortably in an arm-chair.

Parenthetically, it is worth observing that though I had only spent a few hours with the Winkworths, I gathered that after thirty years' intimate companionship, Winkworth still regarded his wife as an example of "the ladies," and she considered him to be a superlative specimen of a strange species which she referred to as "you men." I can only say that this was my impression. It may well have been false, for the reality underlying any human relationship is always a profound mystery.

Winkworth began to talk again. He was an expert in working up an atmosphere. By hints, unfinished sentences, and expressive gestures he succeeded in waking my curiosity as to the subject he was approaching in such a mysterious manner.

"Let me break off at this point, Wrexham, in order to ask you a question: how long, exactly, have you been in Scrivener's flat?"

I told him the date upon which I had gone to the flat.

"Ah!" he exclaimed, "Now, before I introduce the very serious subject of to-night's discussion, would it not be as well if you gave me *your* impressions of the whole situation? A most unusual situation, sir, *most* unusual! And I dislike any departure from normality more than I could ever express adequately."

I decided to put my case to him more fully than I had yet done.

"Have you ever put yourself in my place—imaginatively?" I asked.

"Put myself in *your* place?" he inquired with a touch of dignity.

"Yes. I came from a life of utter solitude. I saw you. I obtained the position of secretary to Scrivener. I went to his flat. Months go by. I meet many of his friends, become intimate with them. Scrivener never appears; he ceases to write to me. Try to imagine yourself in my position."

He looked at me with an expression of perplexity which was rather ludicrous.

"Go on, Wrexham, go on," he said at last, "all this clears the ground for what I have to say."

"My first impression, after I had been in the flat for a day or two, was that I was in a trap of some kind."

"A trap!" He almost shouted the words.

"Yes," I answered quietly, "a trap. Then Scrivener's friends began to turn up. The manner of their appearance in some cases was suspicious. Each one was remarkable in his or her way. Each expected him to be in London: none had known him for long. Each was desperately interested in him: not one has received any communication from him. What was I to make of all this?"

Winkworth sat staring at me rather mournfully, but said nothing. After a long pause, I continued:

"You were the only person to give me any details of Scrivener's past: his friends seem ignorant of any facts relating to him."

At this point, he asked me to give him a fuller account of my visitors. I gave him a rough impression of Middleton, Rivers, and Pauline. He was interested in the last, as General Mandeville's name was known to him. I said little about Francesca, as I deemed it superfluous. An omission which disappointed him. I ended by saying:

"I want you to realize that these people were strangers to one another. I was the means of making them acquainted. I have become intimate with each one of them. I believe, although I have no definite evidence, that complex relations have become established between these people. I am so interested in each one of them, in different ways, that I frequently forget Scrivener's existence. Then, suddenly, I remember that he is the link between all of us. And I feel this, strongly: *all that has happened has been deliberately willed by him.* It is his motive which is the supreme mystery."

Winkworth had listened with great attention to my long speech, his eyes had not left mine for a second. When I ceased, he still continued to stare at me. At last, with an obvious effort, he asked this question:

"You say you have also met a number of people who have known Scrivener at some time or other?"

"A considerable number," I replied. "They may be divided into two categories: those who are still interested in him, and those who do not care to hear his name mentioned."

"A strange man," he said at length, "a strange, inscrutable man. A restless, devastating mind. An *insatiable* mind! When I think of his opportunities and then think of his life, I am haunted by a sense of loss. He could have done anything—anything!"

"That seems the prevalent opinion," I said with some emphasis. "However, I am really interested in one thing—and one only."

"And what is that?" he asked.

"Why did he choose me to be his secretary? I ask you to tell me frankly."

"Tell you!" He looked at me round-eyed. "I wish I could! I haven't the slightest idea. That action was unprecedented in my experience and I claim to be a man of some experience."

"You can't help me, then?"

"No, sir. I cannot unravel the mystery of your engagement. But I have a suggestion to make as to Scrivener's silence. It's merely a guess on my part—and a most sinister one. It is what I want to discuss with you."

He rose and stood with his back to the fire. The loud ticking of the clock on the mantelpiece made the ensuing silence dramatic.

"Has it crossed your mind as a possibility, Wrexham, that Scrivener has committed suicide?"

"Committed suicide!" I exclaimed. Of all possible explanations this was the only one which I had not imagined.

"I do not put forward such a theory lightly, I assure you. The fact that I mention it now is evidence of the confidence I place in you."

I could see that he would continue in this way for some time, so I interrupted:

"But have you any reason to think——"

"Wait, Wrexham, wait." He sat down again and took a sip of brandy. Then in his best legal manner he outlined his case.

"During the last two or three months I have written to Scrivener on matters of considerable importance—financial matters and others, which demanded his serious and prompt attention. I have received no acknowledgement of these communications."

"Have the letters been returned?" I inquired.

"No. I attribute little importance to that fact, however. You'll appreciate why, later. I am speaking now in *absolute confidence*, you understand."

He paused and I nodded.

"I explained to you, some time ago," he went on, "that Scrivener has frequently disappeared. But, sir, the manner of his last disappearance, the duration of his absence, and his refusal to communicate even with his lawyer, are without precedent."

"Surely," I began, "you have more definite——"

"Wait! I also explained to you some time ago that Scrivener often became involved with a type of person far removed from his own station. When he wearied of such associates he dropped them by the simple expedient of going abroad. I feel that on the last occasion he was *compelled* to disappear. I believe that he had become enmeshed in some dangerous or scandalous affair. His flight was dictated by circumstances outside his control. And *that*, I believe, is the reason why he left London without seeing you."

He re-lit his cigar and leant back in his chair. I was far from convinced that he had told me everything and I asked him a number of questions, but his replies elicited little additional information. A statement, volunteered by him, however, interested me very much.

"I cannot give details, Wrexham. You will, I *think*, appreciate that. This, however, I can tell you. In the past I have had to effect a settlement on Scrivener's behalf in certain affairs not to his credit. Those affairs, sir, were not the normal excesses of a young man of wealth and breeding. They—were—not—normal—sir."

The pause which followed these individually emphasized words was remarkably eloquent.

"Now," he resumed, "it's only too easy for me to imagine some affair of an even more degenerate nature which would place Scrivener in a position of grave personal danger. I tell you, Wrexham, I believe one of two things: either he has committed suicide, or he has been murdered."

The fact that Winkworth—the sober, solid, respectable Winkworth—could imagine such an alternative impressed me profoundly. I decided not to reveal the effect which his words had produced.

"If there is anything in your theory," I said with a smile, "why were you surprised when I told you that after I had been in Scrivener's flat for a day or two I felt that my engagement was in the nature of a trap?"

"Because you had had an interview with *me*, sir," he replied with Olympian dignity.

"At which you had indicated," I pointed out, "that you had merely followed your client's instructions and, if I remember, you disassociated yourself entirely from your client's decision to employ me as his secretary."

"True, true," he replied meditatively, but it was quite clear that he was thinking of something else.

"Anyway," I went on, "if he's dead, surely we should have been informed of the fact?"

"This is my belief. Follow me closely. We have simply the address of his banker in Paris. Heaven knows what low haunts he has been visiting! He's probably been far distant from Paris. He might have been murdered, or have committed suicide, in some wretched out of the way place where his identity was quite unknown. Unfortunately I know too well the type of place he sometimes visits on his travels. He's been *hiding*, Wrexham. Why, good God, sir, do you imagine I would discuss a client of mine like this, even with you, unless I were pretty certain that he was dead? The relations between client and lawyer are sacred, and my conduct would be reprehensible in the highest degree if I were not almost convinced that Scrivener has paid the price of some desperate folly."

He leant back, took hold of the lapels of his coat, and contemplated the ceiling for some time. Then he turned to me. A slow, rather sad smile, revealed his large white teeth.

"I'm afraid I'm right," he said ponderously. "You raised the point about my letters not being returned. They've probably been forwarded to some wretched hole where they have been ignored, or possibly Scrivener gave instructions to the Bank that they were not to be forwarded. I'm afraid I'm right," he repeated.

"I hope you're wrong," I said with emphasis. "I want to meet Scrivener as I have never wanted to meet anyone."

Neither of us spoke for some time. Winkworth's theory that Scrivener was dead oppressed me considerably. Till this moment, I had always believed that eventually the mystery of Scrivener would be solved. Was it conceivable that he was dead, that I should leave the flat in Pall Mall, and that all the strange experiences of the last few months would become simply a fantastic episode in my life? It seemed impossible, but Winkworth was not an imaginative man, and, therefore, his belief that Scrivener had committed suicide compelled attention. During our conversation I had realized that, although he would not admit it openly, Winkworth's interest in Scrivener was not restricted within the narrow limits of a professional relationship.

The silence continued. A new speculation flashed into my mind. Hitherto, in discussing Scrivener with those who had met him, I had naturally considered myself at a grave disadvantage in that I had never spoken to him. But did these people know any more about him than I did? Also was it not very remarkable that after all the conversations I had had concerning him with Pauline, Francesca, Middleton, Rivers, and Winkworth, I did not possess any definite impressions as to the type of man he was? Did not their descriptions of him cancel out? All these people were vitally interested in him, but was not the centre of interest different in each case?

At this point, however, Winkworth broke the silence:

"The more I consider the question, the more convinced I become that I am right. I will only say this: if Jonathan Scrivener is dead, what a tragic commentary his whole life has been on what I can only describe as the modern spirit!"

"I'm afraid I don't understand you in the least," I said, as he glanced over at me impressively.

"Listen, Wrexham. Birth, breeding, brains—Scrivener had all three. If I wished to extend the alliteration, I might almost add—beauty. His appearance was very remarkable. But he did not come into line with the ways of the world. Something kept him aloof from his fellow-men. He wanted to create his own standards, Wrexham, and really, you know, a man cannot do that. In one word, he would not accept."

"Perhaps he couldn't," I suggested, as he evidently expected me to say something.

"The world is old," Winkworth replied emphatically, "it's old, and its boundaries are established. Scrivener experimented in everything and many of those experiments were unworthy of him. A dear old friend of mine, now unhappily no more, met Scrivener some few years ago. I do not know what subjects they discussed but my friend said to me: 'Winkworth, that fellow could do anything, but what he *will* do is to go to the devil!' Scrivener accepted nothing, and the younger generation to-day accept nothing. Why, good God, man!" he exclaimed explosively, "if everything is to be probed and examined, nothing will be left standing."

He would have gone on indefinitely, but I slipped in a question: "Do you feel that you understand him?"

"There's a side to him which I do not want to understand," he replied somewhat grimly, "otherwise, we lawyers are pretty quick—we have our own methods, you know. Yes, sir, I do under-stand him. At least I think so. His father was queer; his uncle was a disillusioned eccentric man, and his influence upon Scrivener must have been very extensive. We will discuss this no further now, but I am afraid he has destroyed himself."

He paused, then after a long rigmarole I gathered that he had seen me with Francesca when we were leaving the restaurant with Rivers. Winkworth explained that he had spent that night in London. With immense circumlocution, he indicated that he was very anxious to meet Francesca again and he even hinted, with great delicacy, that to serve her in a professional capacity would be an honour. He ended by saying:

"Please mention my name to her. Ah, my dear Wrexham, consider, I beg of you, how much she has in common with Scriv-ener, and contrast her wisdom with his folly. She, too, has brains, breeding, beauty. But she has accepted the world as it is. She has compelled its respect and its admiration. The result is that she has influence and power."

"She's very interested in Scrivener, all the same," I said pointedly.

"God bless my soul! Is she? You don't say so. *Very* interested?"

"It must have occurred to you that she has no other reason for seeing me."

"Of course! Just so! Well, mention my name to her, Wrexham. A charming woman, a remarkable woman! So distinguished, so aristocratic! What a figure! What wealth! . . ."

II

An incident occurred, a day or two after my visit to Winkworth,

which corroborated certain of his statements in a curiously effective manner. Before I relate it, however, it is necessary to explain
that although Winkworth had stated on two different occasions
that Scrivener had associated with people of a degenerate type, I
personally had not encountered any examples. As it was obvious
that Winkworth was a snob in these matters, I thought it probable
that he had exaggerated. I found I was wrong.

It was mid-day and I was alone in the library. I had been speculating why Rivers had deserted me. Since the night on which I had
dined with him and Francesca, no sign had come from him. It was
also a fact that Middleton had left me alone, but I knew him well
enough to understand that after his recent confidences it would
be some time before he had the courage to call. No such reason
applied to Rivers, and his silence surprised me.

The door opened and Matthews appeared.

"Mr. Denvers has called, sir. He wants to know if Mr. Scrivener
is at home. He says he wants to see him urgently."

The name was vaguely familiar. Suddenly I remembered that
Scrivener had mentioned the name of Denvers in the last letter
I had had from him. I found the letter and read it again. "Should
a man named Denvers call, will you kindly tell him that I am no
longer interested?"

"You told Mr. Denvers that Mr. Scrivener was away of course?"

"Yes, sir," Matthews replied. "But he said he wanted his address
and——"

"What's the idea of hiding yourself away like this——?"

Denvers appeared on the threshold. He was evidently so amazed
at seeing a complete stranger, when he had so confidently expected
to find Scrivener, that he stopped short and stood motionless with
his mouth open.

I dismissed Matthews and looked at my visitor with some
curiosity.

"Who the hell are you?" he asked in a thick unpleasant voice.

I did not reply but studied him closely. He was short, thick-set,
and had the smallest eyes I have ever seen in a human being. The
face was rather puffy and resembled moist india-rubber. There

was cruelty in the thick, rather twisted mouth and brutality in the large, misshapen hands. Nevertheless, the dominant impression he produced was of something amazingly mean and sordid. He was probably about forty.

"Haven't you got a tongue in your head? Who the hell are *you*?"

"I am Mr. Scrivener's secretary," I replied.

"That's a lie, anyway," was his comment, but there was no fire behind the words.

"You imagined you were being told a lie when you were informed that Mr. Scrivener was away. You were wrong then—you are wrong now."

He looked at me suspiciously. "Come on, out with it, what's the game?"

I crossed to the writing-desk and sat down. There was something much more repulsive in this puffy unhealthy man in his shabby respectable clothes than in the traditional underworld types—something essentially mean, flabby, and inert. His attempt to use the language of a bully was a total failure, and yet I felt that he could be more dangerous than twenty bullies. Anger was possibly the only thing of which he was incapable.

"I asked you what your game was?" he said heavily.

"You're wasting your time here, Mr. Denvers. Do you imagine I am going to answer your questions? I've answered one and been called a liar for my pains. You'd better go."

He came over to me. He moved slowly and there was something in his gait which gave me the fantastic impression that it was not normal to him to walk upright. This idea was so ridiculous that I smiled involuntarily.

"You're going to tell me where Scrivener is," he announced.

"You're quite wrong there," I said quietly.

"I'm going to know where he is before I leave this flat. He can't drop me when it suits him. I know too much about him for that."

The words were commonplace enough, but something in his manner carried conviction.

"And *you* can't bluff me either," he added, with heavy insolence.

I rose impetuously. I was irritable before he came, and was in no mood to put up with threats.

"Look here, we'll settle this question of bluff once for all," I began. "I am not going to give you Scrivener's address, and you will not stay here just as long as you choose waiting for it. I'll have you put out, if you don't go."

"You're being a damned bad friend to Scrivener," he said grimly.

"I'm not a friend of his at all. I'm his secretary. I carry out his instructions, but I do not allow a stranger to walk in here and call me a liar. You can get out. I am not in the least afraid of you."

He stood staring at me with his tiny eyes. There was no hint of anger in them—they were just cold and calculating.

"I see," he said at last. "Very well, have it your own way. So you're his secretary. He's given you a nice room to work in. I hope you've been through *all* his books. Just tell me this: you forward his letters, I suppose?"

"Naturally."

"Well, you'd do him a service if you suggested that he answered *some* letters he's received—and answered them pretty quick too. You think I'm no one, don't you? You think I couldn't have anything in common with your aristocratic master. You're wrong. We've tastes in common—secrets in common. We've done quite a lot together, on and off, the last five years or so."

I said nothing, and he continued to stare at me. "Just one thing before I go," he went on. "I'll go all right, and you'll lose your job because of the way you've spoken to me. I'll see to that."

"You are making yourself quite ridiculous," I replied. "It's a matter of absolute indifference to me whether I keep this job or lose it."

"You're very certain of yourself, aren't you? Well, you carry out Scrivener's instructions, you say. Has he given any in regard to me?"

I picked up Scrivener's letter which was on the desk. "Yes, he has. Shall I read what he says?"

"That would be really nice of you," he replied with weighty sarcasm.

"He says this: 'Should a man named Denvers call, will you kindly tell him that I am no longer interested?'"

"No longer interested," he repeated, after a long silence. "Well, *I am*. And that fact is going to make him *very* interested. I promise him that. There'll be a letter here for him in the morning. I'm sure you'll forward it."

I did not reply. After a pause, he turned slowly and walked out of the room. I went to the front door with him and watched him go slowly down the stairs. I immediately asked Matthews if she had seen him before, and learnt that he had visited Scrivener on several occasions—usually at long intervals.

It was in this manner that some of the sinister hints given by Winkworth received such unexpected confirmation.

It was days before I could begin to rid myself of the impression created by Denvers. In the first place he was utterly removed from every imaginative scheme into which I had tried to fit Scrivener. What could the dull, almost lifeless Denvers have in common with the brilliant and fascinating Scrivener? And yet I was compelled to believe every word that Denvers had said and, therefore, I did not find it difficult to imagine that Winkworth might easily have been right when he had said that Scrivener's last disappearance had been compulsory, and that in reality he had been in hiding ever since I became his secretary.

But the immediate impression Denvers created was this: I had seen a commonplace, rather stout, ungainly man, dressed respectably, if shabbily; a man whose attempt to ape the behaviour of an underworld crook had been almost a ludicrous failure; a man who weakly abandoned his strategy immediately he saw that it did not work; a man incapable of anger. Yet I felt that he was essentially sinister; narrowed to one objective; the possessor of only one weapon, but one which in some diabolical way would penetrate below Scrivener's defence. And, above all, I was certain that Scrivener's pride would not allow him to recognize Denvers as an adversary.

CHAPTER XI

I

T HE cheapest form of adventure in London is to board the first
'bus which passes you, secure the front inside seat on the top
deck, and say to the conductor: "All the way," when he asks you for
your fare. To do this is to make more discoveries in a shorter space
of time than any other activity affords. You learn, almost simultaneously, that you know nothing whatever about London, that the
number of green open spaces is remarkable, and that solitude is
not necessarily loneliness. Also, that the conductor regards you in
an entirely different light from the other passengers: they are only
fares, but you are a fixture.

One afternoon, very shortly after Denvers' visit, I indulged in
this form of recreation with a view to sorting out my impressions.
For some months I had been hopelessly lost in an intricate maze,
and all my endeavours to reach its centre had served only to com-
plicate my predicament. It was essential to remain stationary, to
forget what I was seeking, and to ascertain precisely where I was.

Now, all sorts of things have been done on the top of a 'bus:
plays have been written, visions have been glimpsed, new phi-
losophies have been evolved. Anything and everything has been
done—with one exception. No one has ever given a thought to the
problem the consideration of which was the sole motive for board-
ing the 'bus. I, too, failed. I had intended to think about myself. I
immediately began to think about Scrivener, and thence—by an
inevitable progression—I found myself speculating on the nature
of Mystery.

I soon satisfied myself that the mystery of Scrivener was a genuine one. Where a problem is simple, the ascertainment of each
and every relevant fact narrows the field of inquiry. A solution is
possible in the terms of mere knowledge. But where the problem

is so profound that it enters the domain of Mystery, the emergence of each additional fact serves only to reveal the magnitude of the inquiry. The telescope did not enable man to solve the riddle of the stars. It illumined his ignorance by revealing the necessity for "thinking again the thoughts of God."

This is the wisdom of the Sphinx—she only yields her secret to the wise.

The 'bus went its way and my thoughts went theirs. Winkworth's belief that Scrivener had committed suicide had the effect of centering all my thoughts in him again. Recently, I had been so concerned with his friends that he had slipped into the background, but Winkworth's theory, and Denvers' visit, brought Scrivener dramatically to the forefront of my speculations. . . .

An argument about a fare developed just behind me. A woman said the fare was twopence: the conductor said it was threepence. The woman said she had made the journey every day for three months and only paid twopence, whereupon the conductor worked out how much she owed the company. The woman said she wanted none of his lip. He replied that he wanted an extra penny. The discussion progressed somewhat in these terms:

"You got on at the *Bull and Cow.*"

"Not me!" retorted the woman. "I got on at *The Pig and Whistle.*"

"Don't matter. It's only acrost the road. And you want to get orf at *The King's 'ead.* Thruppence—see?"

"Tuppence, I tell yer. Ain't I done it day in, day out——"

"Done the company, yer mean."

Pause. Then in a tone of icy impartiality, the woman asked:

"Nu on this route, ain't yer?"

"Nu, but not green," replied the conductor with scientific detachment.

"It ain't the penny I'm arguin' about, young feller. But right's right the world over."

"I tell yer it's *thruppence,*" answered the uncompromising realist.

The argument continued till the 'bus was within a hundred yards of *The King's Head,* whereupon the woman said she wasn't "paying no extra penny"—she'd rather walk.

"Saved yer penny *and* yer shoeleather." The conductor's final remark was weighted with sarcasm.

"Meet all sorts on this job," he announced philosophically to me. "All sorts. But what gets me," he added confidentially, "is the larst trip at night when you're in a 'urry to get 'ome. Lord love yer, every blinkin' one of 'em gives you 'arf-a-crown for a penny fare. And slow! Gawd! you should see the way they get on and orf! Whizz about like tortoises, some of 'em."

He retired, and I attempted to recapture my thoughts. . . .

I began to regret my treatment of Denvers. It might have proved fruitful to introduce him to the others. Middleton was so certain that he knew the real Scrivener: Francesca was equally convinced that she, and she only, knew the features of the man behind the mask. And this was true, although occasionally they said that they knew nothing whatever about him. What would they have made of Denvers? What would Denvers have thought of their conceptions of Scrivener?

As the 'bus went on its laborious way, I discovered that no simple Jekyll and Hyde theory would solve the enigma of Scrivener. Two men and two women had given me their intimate impressions of my employer. Each might have been describing a different man. I realized this for the first time and the great significance of this simple discovery overwhelmed me. After all, what was there in common between the man Middleton had described and the man Francesca had met? Only the name of Jonathan Scrivener. Why, I could almost believe they had met different men who happened to bear the same name. My thoughts began to race. Was not this also true, in its degree, concerning Pauline and Rivers? The only thing these people had in common was their interest in Scrivener, but their outlook was so different that it was difficult to believe that they were interested in the same man. Yet I was convinced that each, in his or her way, expected something from Scrivener— something of fundamental importance. No man living could satisfy these different demands. Yet each waited confidently, and I too was waiting for I knew not what.

Now Denvers had come upon the scene and had thereby indicated that any solution of the mystery would have to include him. Should I tell the others of his visit? Should I indicate the impression he had made upon me? Instinctively I knew that if I told anybody, it would be Francesca.

A wave of irritability suddenly possessed me. What was the use of thinking about these people and striving to solve a problem which had baffled me for months? One thing was certain: until I ascertained why Scrivener had made me his secretary, I should discover none of his motives. My only plan was to concentrate all my energies on this personal problem and not seek to unravel the mystery of his relations with others.

With an effort of will, I became interested in the world outside me. An hour passed and the 'bus reached its destination. I found I was near Richmond, so I walked into the Park and whiled away two or three hours. For some reason, I did not want to return to the flat. It was impossible to forget Scrivener in that silent library and I wanted to forget him. There were moments when I felt that I hated him: he had destroyed the life I had known, he had made me uncertain of the few certainties I had ever possessed, and it was through the conscious election of his will that I had met Pauline and Francesca. I am convinced that he realized some of the difficulties I should experience through meeting these women. If I have said nothing about these difficulties in what I have written, it is only because this book is concerned with Scrivener. I am merely the narrator.

I returned to London, dined alone, and went to a theatre. It was nearly midnight when I returned to the flat. Francesca was waiting for me in the library.

II

She was leaning lightly against the chimney-piece. I paused in the doorway, and for nearly a minute we looked at each other in silence. A hint of the perfume she was wearing pervaded the atmosphere. It seemed to symbolize her conquest of the room: she had found it empty and had made it hers. She was in evening dress and her beauty suggested a sword half-drawn from its scabbard.

Her dark eyes gleamed with ironical amusement.

"I've always wanted to spend some time in this room alone," she said casually, by way of greeting.

"Have you been here long?" I asked.

"Nearly an hour."

She sat down, and I sat opposite her by the fire. She lit a cigarette and seemed in no hurry to begin to talk. I noticed that several books had been removed from the shelves.

"I've been having a holiday from my world," she announced at last. "You guessed that, I suppose. I've spent a lot of time with Middleton and Rivers, and I've seen a good deal of Pauline Mandeville. I've been trying to find out what Jonathan saw in them."

"Have you succeeded?" I asked.

"Not altogether. I've discovered that they know very little about him. They're strange people—they've nothing in common that I can discover. Except perhaps this: the life of each one of them has been twisted entirely through Jonathan's influence."

I laughed and she looked at me quickly.

"That's true about us too, isn't it?" I inquired. "Still," I went on, "leave me out of it. It's true about you."

She leant back and clasped her knee with her hands.

"These people are nobodies," she said with a trace of that arrogance which belonged to her. "Why were they interested in him? I can tell you why I was—but I've told you that."

"Not very clearly," I pointed out. "Tell me exactly why you were interested."

There was a long pause, then she said: "Imagine that you were a painter—an artist of definite and recognized distinction. You were the centre of your world: you were copied, envied, flattered. You were at the height of your success, the summit of your ambition. Well, one day a man walks into your studio and begins to talk with you. You become friends. Then, later, you visit him and you find that there's a room at the top of his house in which there are a number of pictures infinitely better than anything you've ever done. You discover that they are his work. You're amazed, you ask him why he doesn't have an exhibition. And he laughs and tells you that he's not in the least interested in art. Such an experience might make you question the value of your activities, don't you think?"

"Excellent," I replied, "but you must interpret your symbols."

She rose with a sudden swift movement, as if the whole of her body had responded to the drama of her thoughts.

"Do you imagine that I reached my position easily? I had no money, no position, nothing. I had great ambitions, and only one weapon with which to achieve them. I succeeded. I have influence, power, notoriety. I loved those things—I believed in them. They were the best things to be got in a wretched, mean and sordid world. I am a greater actress than my mother was. I have to provoke cues, not merely to wait for them. Well, then I met Jonathan. And I *knew* he could have played my game even better than I had done—and it didn't interest him."

I looked up at her with a smile. "You met a greater exponent of your own philosophy."

"That wouldn't have mattered," she replied. "I could have learnt something. But to meet a greater exponent of one's own philosophy and to discover that he doesn't believe in that philosophy is very disturbing. You've seen the people I know—you've seen the quality of their lives. Jonathan could beat every one of them at their own game. But it wouldn't amuse him. I tell you, he turns one's gods into toys."

She spoke with passionate intensity. The vibrations of her voice quivered in the silence. There were two women in her: an arrogant, poised, calculating woman; and an actress of such genius that, in an instant, the world of her emotions became the supreme reality. She passed from one to the other with a stride.

"There's one thing I don't understand," I began slowly, "but I shall have to be frank if I'm to say what it is."

"You will not shock me," she said in a tone of absolute conviction.

"It's this, then. You are not fettered by any conventions and you are obviously very attracted by Scrivener. I've sometimes wondered——"

"Why we didn't become lovers?" She laughed somewhat bitterly. "I told you long ago that, from the beginning, he and I were fighting a duel. Do you imagine that I would not have given myself to him? Why, it's impossible to find a lover nowadays who doesn't bore you to death in a week. Of course I would have given myself to him, but I was determined that he should say *give*, and he was determined that I should say *take*."

"Was that the only reason?"

"It was an important one. To yield to him meant more than a physical surrender. He despised my standards and if I had become his lover, I should soon have despised them too. I am certain of it. I might have sacrificed my pride, but I would not sacrifice my world with it. What had he to offer if I gave up all that I had made mine?"

As I watched her, I wondered for the hundredth time whether she had told me everything. When she discussed Scrivener it seemed as if she believed that her destiny depended on him. His name gave concentration to all her energies and definition to all her desires.

"When I met you and the others," she went on, "I saw an opportunity to find out what *did* interest him. Everything I valued he despised, so I expected to make some remarkable discoveries. That's why I was so interested in his friends."

She paused, and I suggested that she must have been very disappointed.

She laughed. "It's my turn to be frank. I regarded *you* simply as a caprice on Jonathan's part, though I'm not so certain of that now. Then I met Middleton. I soon learnt the history of his relations with Jonathan. Well, it's clear that it amused him to complete the havoc made in Middleton by the collapse of a sentimental dream. But why? It baffles me. Then—Rivers. What is there in Rivers to interest Jonathan? Yet he has seen a lot of Rivers, was with him recently in Paris, and then sent him on to you, knowing that he'd meet Pauline, Middleton and myself. But what is his motive? Can these people interest him more than the prizes of my world?"

"You've said nothing about Pauline," I pointed out.

She looked at me with a smile.

"There's always one explanation for the interest a man takes in an attractive woman."

"And you find that explanation adequate in this case?" I inquired.

"No, not altogether," she admitted. "Your friend Pauline is as great a mystery in her way as Jonathan. She's a statue. She only wears clothes as a concession to fig-leaf morality. She gives you the eerie sensation that you are in the presence of the unborn. That's very original. Most people make you quite certain that you're in the presence of the dead."

"I had no idea you were such a psychologist," I exclaimed.

"You've always underrated me," she replied. "You find it impossible to believe that a woman with my type of attraction could really be intelligent. But, seriously, I can see something in common between Jonathan and Pauline."

"And that is?"

"He doesn't use his weapons and she doesn't use hers. All really gifted people are mad nowadays and these two are not exceptions to that rule. Look at Pauline! She has beauty, distinction, fascination. She could marry anyone and have the world at her feet. But she ignores her gifts so completely that others forget to notice them. I told her what she ought to do and she watched me with those strange eyes till I almost felt uncomfortable for the first time in my life. So, failing any other explanation as to why Jonathan is interested in her, I fall back on the obvious one."

She sat down and lit a cigarette. Everything about her proclaimed that she had lost interest in the people we had been discussing. She had hoped to use them for her own ends, to penetrate to Scrivener's secret through them. They had failed her and she was no longer interested in them. It was with a view to proving that this was so that I told her about Denvers. I explained the manner of his entrance, the effect he had produced on me, and then I gave her an account of our interview. She listened to every word and when I had finished she asked if I thought I should see him again. I told her it was unlikely, but she would not leave the subject till she had made me promise that if Denvers called again, I would arrange a meeting between them. The importance she attached to the incident astonished me. But I was determined that she should realize the implications of her recent adventures.

"You're no longer interested in Middleton?" I asked.

"Not in the smallest degree. I shall drop him. Why do you ask?"

"Has it occurred to you that it may have meant something to him to meet you?"

She looked at me as if I were talking nonsense.

"Middleton! He's fallen in love with his own suffering and drinks in order to become maudlin over his memories. He's simply a sentimentalist who cannot find anything to be sentimental about. He's beginning to blame Jonathan for his dilemma instead of the lady who wisely deserted him for a rich stockbroker. He saw me because he's interested in Jonathan, and hoped to find out something about him. You're quite wrong. Now, if you'd said the same about Rivers——"

"He can look after himself," I interrupted.

"Are you so certain?" She glanced swiftly at me. Her eyes shone with malicious amusement. "He's a better actor than Middleton, but he's just as big a fool. For the first time in his life, he had a good hand, but he lost his head and threw his cards away. He's become simply ludicrous."

"I was right, Francesca, when I told you at dinner the other night that you were going to leave me with the casualties. And, incidentally, didn't you say that you had a proposition to make to me?"

"Yes, it's this: when you're tired of being Jonathan's secretary how would you like to be mine? You interest me. You're mysterious in your way, but you would be useful to me."

I burst out laughing. "You're not serious, of course."

"Perfectly. Can't you see——"

She was interrupted by a ring of the bell. It was a long ring and it seemed to echo through the flat. Instinctively we both rose. She gripped my arm with a strength which surprised me, her eyes met mine and I saw the light of sudden fear in them. I could see she thought it was Scrivener. We stood motionless.

Again the peal of the bell echoed through the flat. Francesca moved nearer to me—I could feel the outline of her body against mine. To an onlooker we should have seemed like guilty lovers about to be discovered.

"See who it is," she whispered.

I left her and went slowly into the hall. The discovery that she was afraid to meet Scrivener had been totally unexpected and it impressed me despite the drama of the moment which had revealed it.

I opened the front door. I had been so certain that a stranger would be outside, that my features must have expressed surprise when I saw Middleton.

It was only too evident that he was drunk. He reeled into the hall and staggered towards the library without a word of greeting. I noticed, however, that his eyes flamed angrily which was unusual when he was intoxicated and his whole bearing was so desperate that I followed him into the library feeling almost apprehensive as to the effect Francesca's presence would produce.

He stood, as if transfixed, on seeing her. A great vein stood out on his forehead and his fingers twitched nervously. I guessed that he had come so late in order to ensure finding me alone. He had reached some crisis in his life and desperation had driven him to me. Now, perhaps, he was confronted by the person who more than any other was responsible for that crisis.

Francesca was standing in front of the fire. I passed Middleton and stood by the desk. He remained in the doorway.

"So you were lying," he said to her in a thick, unsteady voice. "You told your servants to say you were not at home. You've decided to drop me."

She looked at him contemptuously, but remained silent.

He ignored my presence so completely that I felt I was eavesdropping. He broke into a short laugh which ended abruptly.

"I didn't expect to have the opportunity to tell *you* what I think of you. I came here to say something else. But I'm glad you're here. You've amused yourself with me——"

"Amused!" There was infinite contempt in her repetition of the word.

He flushed with anger and shame, then took a stride towards her.

"Yes, amused! You've ferreted out of me everything you could about your friend Scrivener. You dangled your attractions before me in order to get me to relate things which you knew I did not want to tell you——"

"You're quite mistaken, Mr. Middleton."

"Don't lie!" He shouted the words. "You asked me to visit you. You saw me alone again and again. You pretended to be interested in me. In every way, you encouraged me to talk—to spread my life before you and, above all, every detail of it which related to Scrivener. You knew that I was as lonely as the damned: you knew that you attracted me——"

Her cool, silvery laugh interrupted him. "I assure you, I knew nothing of the kind."

"You traded on it like a harlot," he shouted.

I was about to interfere, but Francesca motioned me back.

"Like a harlot—which is what you are," he went on, "except that you lack the excuse of necessity. You wormed everything out of me. Every one of my memories is now sullied by the knowledge that you share it. I despise you as I've never despised anyone——"

"Then surely," she interrupted, "it was an excellent thing that I gave orders that you were to be told that I was away?"

She was cold, logical, utterly unmoved by his passion. Her attitude succeeded in making him appear ludicrous and vulgar. He was aware of it and his anger increased. It was obvious that he continued to insult her in the hope of stumbling across a phrase which would hurt her, knowing only too well that it would elude him.

"You've tricked and cheated me, filled me with disgust for myself, experimented on me because you are an utterly idle, worthless, vicious type—eager for some new distraction. When did you consider *me* in what you've done? I loathe you and my senses ache for you, and you knew it and used it. And now that you are convinced that there's nothing more to learn from me, you fling me on one side——"

"You're tiresome," she said, as if addressing a schoolboy. "I thought you were more intelligent. I imagined that we were both interested in the same person—Jonathan Scrivener. I thought we could discuss him together—compare notes, if you like. I assure you I have always been quite impersonal in my relations with you."

He stood, staring at her. He was so certain that she was lying, whereas I knew definitely that what she said was largely true. He had never existed for her in his own right. The silence was terribly oppressive.

Middleton turned as if to go, then paused. "No wonder your husband shot himself."

Her eyes flashed, and he laughed. He had succeeded beyond his expectation.

"That stung, didn't it? No wonder he shot himself! I suppose you were quite impersonal in your relations with *him*. You drove him to suicide and now live in luxury on his money."

I was going to speak, but Francesca silenced me with a gesture.

"Let him go on," she said. "It is impossible for him to be anything but ridiculous. It's his destiny."

She turned to Middleton. "Please say anything you like. You will write an apology to-morrow when you remember these insults."

"You're liars, all of you," he muttered. He turned fiercely to her again. "You're Scrivener's mistress and you've some plan between you. God knows what it is, but you've managed to ruin me between you. Did you come to chatter to Wrexham about the mystery of Scrivener? Mystery! He's a hypocrite and a liar and I have proved it. If half of what he said to me had been the truth, he'd never have known a woman like you. You are everything which he said he loathed. I'm going, and I wish to God I'd never seen any of you. I've this comfort left: I can go to hell my own way without seeing any of you again."

He reeled out of the room and a moment later the front door banged.

Francesca sat down in her armchair and laughed quietly. "I think it must be this room," she said at last. "In fact I'm certain it is. It has an odd effect on people. Middleton, for instance, is quite a different person when he is here. He interested me to-night for the first time. Why do you look so serious?"

"I lack your detachment, Francesca. It's evident to me that Middleton in his present state might do anything. I like him, and am sorry for him. If he committed suicide, which is quite possible, I should feel responsible in my degree. Unlike you, I find that disturbing."

She looked at me meditatively for a minute before she spoke. "I suppose I shall become a sentimentalist if I stay in England long enough," she announced. "Sentimentality and rheumatism are part of the national inheritance."

But I was determined to make her face the issue in concrete terms.

"Now look here," I began, "tell me this. If Middleton shot himself to-night, would it disturb you in the least?"

"No, not in the least. I am sorry to disappoint you." She lit a cigarette then went on. "Middleton will do something ridiculous and he would do it if I had never been born. All this chatter about suffering bores me. People must adapt themselves to their conditions. Middleton built a sentimental and quite unreal edifice on his feelings for some woman. It collapses. Instead of calling himself a fool, what does he do?"

"Runs into Scrivener somewhat unfortunately, as it turns out," I replied. "And Scrivener, for some unguessable reason, completes the ruin of Middleton's values."

"Exactly!" she cut in. "He amused himself. Jonathan saw, as I do, that Middleton is determined to be hurt by life and he showed him that it could be done on a bigger scale than he imagined. It's really a simple matter. Middleton can no longer believe in sentimentality and so he'll drink himself to death, or he'll marry a prostitute and try to reform her. He'd be interesting if he committed suicide."

I stared at her and she saw the question in my eyes which I hesitated to express in words.

"Yes, you've guessed it. My husband was never so interesting to me as when I learnt that he had shot himself. Wait! Wait! I've never tried to make anyone understand this, and it's difficult."

She leant forward and stared into the fire, thinking deeply. Several minutes passed, then she said: "Passion alone interests me. You must realize that. It is the only thing to which I respond. It is what makes people interesting because it reveals them. If you can find out what a person will sacrifice to obtain his or her desire, you know everything about that person. Artist, lover, statesman, fanatic—each is revealed by the extent of the sacrifice he is prepared to make in order to feed the fire on his altar." She paused, then added: "Am I boring you?"

"You're interesting me very much," I replied.

"And, incidentally, telling you everything about myself. But it doesn't matter. Middleton was interesting to-night because passion possessed him. It made him ridiculous, but it revealed him. There's something unique in everyone, but each one is afraid to show it."

She hesitated, and I wondered whether she had difficulty in expressing her thoughts, or whether she wanted to evade the explanation to which she was pledged. I said nothing, although I hoped she would continue.

The clock at St. James's struck one. The solitary note thrilled the silence like a warning.

"When I heard that my husband had shot himself, I tried to imagine being so devoted to a person that life without that person would be an impossibility. But I could not imagine that. I could not believe he had killed himself simply because he had discovered that I had a lover. It never occurred to me that he was capable of passion to that degree. I should have said confidently that his financial deals meant more to him than I did. His death told me that he was a much greater person than I was. You won't believe me when I say that in my way I did suffer when I heard of his suicide."

"Why shouldn't I believe you?" I asked.

"Because, my friend, such a theory conflicts with the well-established cliché convention as to what my emotions should have been. By all the rules of sentimental tradition, I ought to have been overwhelmed by remorse and a haunting sense of guilt. All that, however, seemed quite irrelevant to me. How could I blame myself for not being someone else? I had never known Stanley and he had never known me. That must be true of thousands of husbands and wives in London. It never occurred to me that he expected fidelity, or that he was faithful. It never occurred to him to wonder whether I was the person he imagined me to be. His suicide proved to me that we had always been strangers. Was I to suffer the remorse of the damned because he was what he was—and I was what I was? What sentimental rubbish! Cowards invent a handful of clichés and then adopt moral attitudes when life refuses to be restricted within such narrow limits."

She broke off with a laugh, then rose to go. I was about to put her cloak round her when she said lightly, "Don't worry about your friend, Middleton. Only gamblers commit suicide."

"*Everyone* commits suicide, Francesca," I replied.

"What on earth do you mean by that?" she asked.

"Nearly every face in the street proves the truth of what I say. Most of us commit suicide, but the fact is only recognized if we blow our brains out. The most tragic suicide is never the dramatic one."

We were both standing, and she looked at me with a puzzled expression in her dark eyes.

"You're rather a disturbing person," she said at last, "but there is one great advantage in you from my point of view."

"And that is?" I inquired.

"We can be friends because you are not attracted by me."

I laughed and moved nearer to her. "You believe that?" I asked. "Why, in one form or another, all my life has been haunted by you. You represent everything which has never been offered to me. You are everything which life has denied. But that's not all. You were the prize for which everyone was struggling. Ambition, power, success—these are your other names. Not to strive for one of these was not to live the life of the world. Not to serve you was to be branded as a failure. Yet to reject you—once, finally, and for ever—was difficult. It was difficult because I should have had no means of knowing whether my rejection was sincere. It is easy to reject what is not offered. Always I have been haunted by the fear that you had only to beckon and I should become your slave, like all the others."

"My dear," she exclaimed, "nothing infuriates a woman so much as to be regarded as a symbol. It reduces her to a term in a mathematical formula." She paused, then added, "You've dwindled me to an icy abstraction. I'll never forgive you. Your friend, Pauline, has the same effect on me. By the way, have you seen her recently?"

"Yes, but not alone," I replied. "Her father returned a few weeks ago and I've seen a good deal of both of them."

She put on her cloak, then said with a smile: "You are very like her. Jonathan evidently wanted you to meet her. You have no news of him?"

"None."

She held out her hand. "Good-bye. It's been interesting. I've a feeling that Jonathan will return soon. But perhaps he will wait till things are even more complicated. Remember that I want to meet Denvers, won't you?" She looked round the room and a curious smile curled her lips. "I'm afraid I haven't replaced some of the books I looked at while I was waiting for you. I was not surprised to discover that Jonathan has his degenerate moments."

CHAPTER XII

I

SOMETIMES when you go to the theatre to see an eminent actor who impressed you very much some years ago, and whom you have not seen since, you find that his performance to-day is only a plagiarism of himself during his best period. Voice, gesture, attitudes, and mannerisms do not appear to have altered, but on the present occasion they succeed only in irritating you. They are no longer indispensable and inevitable, because the inspiration which once fused them into organic unity has vanished. Formerly they were the unconscious expression of histrionic vitality: to-day, they are exploited as a deliberate policy. The actor has ceased to be an artist and has become a box of tricks.

All forms of plagiarism are depressing, but self-plagiarism is tragic. It is the last ditch of the egotist.

I was reminded of this fact by encountering Rivers. It happened like this:

I had not seen him for a considerable time and was convinced that he was avoiding me. I knew that he was still in London, that he met Middleton frequently, and I could not imagine why he had dropped me. Then, one night, I ran into him in Piccadilly.

He was as immaculate as ever. While we exchanged greetings and while I listened to his unconvincing reasons why he had not called, I again noticed the remarkable individuality of each article of his attire. An exclusive quality pervaded his clothes, compelling admiration, but at the same time proclaiming the impossibility of emulation. Such distinction was obtainable only by Rivers. Yet as he went on talking, I detected a change in him. He was still attractive enough in his rather pretty way, but the hard line of the mouth—which had impressed me at our first meeting—was accentuated, and there was a slightly strained expression in the eyes. His whole manner was a mimicry of his familiar self. It was very well done, but it lacked that quality which was the secret of his social success—spontaneity.

Many things revealed the change in him. For instance, usually he swept me from place to place, without a moment's hesitation, assuming wholeheartedly that his desire and my pleasure were one and the same thing. But on this occasion, although he assured me that we must remain together, he was vague and indecisive. He asked me where we should dine and hastened to give a list of all the most expensive restaurants which apparently bored him very much indeed nowadays. Now, I could not suggest anywhere, because once all that nonsense about "I know a nice little restaurant, *not* expensive," is eliminated, the fact remains that you can only *dine* in London at fabulous expense. You can get a meal, of course, either in the great open marble spaces, or in those pompous-looking establishments where a table d'hôte dinner is served with noisy celerity reminiscent of artillery fire. But to dine, and not ruin yourself, is a real difficulty. Consequently Rivers and I stood in the middle of the pavement awaiting an inspiration.

As one did not descend we went into a café and had a drink. I gave him every opportunity to get rid of me but as he insisted that we should remain together, and as he was normally the entertainer, I left matters largely to him.

He lit a cigarette and sat sipping a gin and Italian in a meditative manner.

"You've caught me in a philosophic mood, my dear fellow. Yes, really! Do you believe in destiny? I do sometimes. I do to-night. It was providential that I ran into you."

The same light lyrical note in the voice and yet I felt that there was not only calculation behind his attitude but a desire to gain time, as if it were necessary for him to adjust his mood to my company. I asked him in what way I had been the instrument of Providence.

"I was on the verge of committing the supreme error," he went on. "I was about to *think*. You know how parsons—and other moral deadheads—are always imploring you to stop, pause, consider, take stock, and so on? I was about to commit all those follies."

I said nothing and after a silence he added: "Yes, I was about to *think*, Wrexham. It's a damned good thing I ran into you."

I ignored the implication that Thought was an impossibility in my presence, and asked why he considered that activity to be the supreme error.

"To think, my dear fellow, is an admission that inspiration has failed you. It is a sign that you have lost your nerve. Imagine what would have happened if Joan of Arc or Napoleon at any period in their careers had paused to *think*. But they didn't. They went on in defiance of common sense, acting in accordance with the inspiration of each moment, confident of their destiny, believing in their genius. They were adventurers. Joan was a spiritual adventurer; Napoleon was a military adventurer." A pause. "I am a social adventurer."

He took another sip of gin and Italian, and regarded me somewhat ruefully. But he was not alone, the limelight was on him, and he had to play his part. He waved his hand airily then continued:

"To think is to admit the power of those obstacles which separate you from your objective. Genius ignores them; common sense measures them, accepts them and then lives a wretched little life in their shadow. Sheer cowardice! I've lost my nerve the last week or two, but I'm curing myself."

"And what is the precise nature of the cure you are taking?" I inquired.

He lit another cigarette and ordered another drink.

"I've been standing in front of a magnifying mirror. Sounds symbolic, and all that, I know, but listen. It's entirely scientific, really. I use people—you knew that, of course?"

I said that it had crossed my mind as a possibility. He regarded this comment as a compliment.

"Well," he went on, "I've been using Middleton. That's really why I've not seen you lately."

"Why Middleton?" I asked.

"Because he was the ideal cure, of course," he replied irritably. "Surely that's plain. Middleton is a romantic who ruined himself by thought, and has now taken to drink. When that woman let him down, he should have carried his illusions to another *immediately*. But he didn't. He began to think. That ruined him. Thought is not in his line. His brain's a chopper and he's trying to do fretwork with it. But there's another reason why I've been seeing a lot of him." He broke off abruptly and insisted on my having another drink.

By this time the café was full of people and smoke. It was a large place, only recently erected, where light meals could be obtained. The crowd was very cosmopolitan. If you simply looked at the people, and did not listen to them, you could imagine that you were in Paris or Berlin. There was nothing essentially English about the place or the people. A babel of conversation rose on all sides and waiters darted about frantically.

"I knew you'd been seeing a good deal of Middleton," I said. "It interested me because you're so different."

He moved restlessly on his chair and it was quite evident that under his debonair exterior he was very disturbed.

"I see him because he's a fool," he said almost angrily. "He's a warning. He's allowed life to hurt him. I'll take damned good care nothing of that kind ever happens to me." He went off at a tangent. "Look here. Let's dine in this hole. It's as good as any other."

I agreed—it was a matter of indifference to me—and he ordered himself a grapefruit, a lobster salad, and some very ripe Stilton.

The food appeared and then an unprecedented event occurred—Rivers sat silent. Two or three minutes passed and still no word came from him. He sat, playing with his food, a thin line of smoke rising from his cigarette which reposed in the ash-tray in front of him. All animation had left him and he looked tired and irritable. And so, for the first time in our relations, I felt that I must assume responsibility for the conversation.

"Have you seen Pauline Mandeville?" I asked.

He looked at me intently before he replied.

"Yes, a week or so ago. Strange creature, isn't she? People are diamond clear to me as a rule, but she isn't. I'm not going to see her at the minute," he added. "She doesn't increase one's confidence in oneself and I want all I've got and more."

I asked him to explain, but he hesitated a good deal.

"It's like this," he said at last. "You feel that she's watching you. She doesn't judge you, but she makes you judge yourself. I'd never tell her my ambitions because I'm certain that if I did I should discover that they weren't worth a damn. She makes Middleton completely inarticulate, even when he's drunk. He just stares at her, as the damned in hell would stare at an angel."

Again, a long silence. I felt the embarrassment which an audience feels when an actor entirely forgets his lines. I knew it was useless for me simply to chatter for the sake of saying something. At last Rivers said:

"Tell me, when the devil is Scriv coming back? I've *got* to see him. Damn it! If he doesn't come back soon, I'll go to Paris to see him."

"There's no reason to think he's there," I pointed out. "He doesn't write and I've no idea where he is."

A long pause, then Rivers made an impetuous gesture. "Come on," he said, "let's get out of this. It's hell's bells here. Let's go for a walk in the Park. It's still safe to do that with a man after dark."

We said very little on our way to the Park. Rivers's technique had clearly failed him, and when he spoke his attempts at brilliance became less and less frequent. I made one more effort to leave him, but he repudiated the suggestion with such vehemence that I let things take their course.

It was a warm evening and the Park was very full, but we found two seats away from the crowd and sat down. After a silence which lasted for five minutes Rivers turned to me with some of his old impetuosity:

"You're with the biggest fool in London, Wrexham. Yes, you are! There's one inch of my brain which is still detached, and by its aid I can judge myself as I would a stranger. I'm in the devil's own mess. It's a weakness to admit it but——"

I interrupted at this point. I had had all the confidences I wanted recently and I did not want to hear Rivers's difficulties. I could guess some of them, but apart from this, he was the only escape from the mystery in which my life was enmeshed. In the past he had provided the light relief in a dramatic situation and I did not want him to assume another rôle. But he had made up his mind to go on and I could not stop him.

"No!" he exclaimed, "I'm going to tell you. You're the only person I *can* tell. Listen—laugh if you want to—it's amusing in its way. Where the devil shall I begin?"

He threw his cigarette away and thought for a moment.

"I've got it! Remember the first time we lunched together? Right! You mentioned Francesca Bellamy. I'd heard of her often enough and wanted to meet her. You introduced me. That was my moment. I had the ball at my feet. I knew her crowd, and I knew I could amuse them. If you can amuse people, and are clever in other ways, they'll do anything for you. I saw my chance and jumped at it."

Much to Rivers's annoyance a man appeared and demanded money for the chairs. After his departure, Rivers wasted time and energy in cursing him fluently.

"Damn the idiot! Where was I? Oh, yes. Well, Francesca took a fancy to me. Wanted to come round to my haunts and meet all my friends and acquaintances. It was a new experience for her. She talked a hell of a lot about Scriv and was very interested to meet anyone who knew him. Bit of a bore, because I wanted to talk about myself, but there it was. Anyway, I was getting well in with her. And I met several pretty useful people at her house."

"But what exactly did you think these people could do for you?" I asked.

"My good infant," he replied with immense patronage, "everything is done by influence. Her crowd have influence. Any one of them could push me into a damned good thing. It only needed a cool head and patience to nurse them a bit and, above all, keep 'em amused. Why, I'm on the verge of getting half-a-dozen plum jobs at the present minute, but I've lost my nerve for the first time in my life and at the most important crisis of my life. I've been thinking—totting things up. It's madness! Just the courage to make one last leap—that's all I want."

"I don't understand," I said. "*Why* have you lost your nerve?"

There was a long pause. When he spoke his voice was almost a whisper.

"I've committed the incredible folly of getting keen on Francesca herself. My God! can you believe that? I wasn't aware of it till it had happened. Had no warnings. It seemed to me I was playing my hand with her calmly and coolly. Then, one night, she broke an appointment with me."

He was silent for a moment, then continued:

"Suddenly I knew that I was keen as hell on her. The knowledge surged round me like a sea. I was appalled. I was becoming a schoolboy when it was imperative to remain a strategist. Why, I was afraid to meet her again. I knew if she guessed the truth I was done for."

"You were quite certain of that?" I asked.

"Certain of it," he exclaimed contemptuously. "Yes, I should say I was! I know her. She could respect an adventurer because she is one in the true sense of the word, not the melodramatic. Good God! if she knew I was keen on her, I'd lose my background immediately. I'd become just one of a crowd. She respects only isolation, pride, and the ability to seize. Make no mistake whatever about that. I'm *afraid* to see her. I'm avoiding her till I get over this folly. I haven't been to see you because I didn't want to tell anyone this. So I fell back on Middleton."

There was another long pause. I did not want the conversation to drift to Middleton again as I did not care to be cross-examined about him. I soon saw, however, that there was little danger. Rivers was narrowed to his own problems.

"I'll tell you something else," he went on. "There's something damned queer about all this. I've been forced to think lately, and I've been going over that time I spent with Scriv in Paris. Now, I didn't want to return from Paris. I only came back because I understood from Scriv that he was returning almost immediately. That was a lie evidently. He told me to look you up. He knew that *you* knew Francesca. He never mentioned that *he* did. He guessed that I should meet her through you. Well, it looks like a plot of some kind, don't you think?"

"My dear Rivers," I said solemnly, "surely you must be able to imagine that, in my position, I've thought a good deal about Scrivener's acts and their possible motives."

"Yes, I suppose you have," he said in a tone which implied that the idea was quite a new one to him. He was a true egotist: the frontier of his world was the boundary of the universe.

He was silent for a minute then went on:

"Yes, I've been thinking a lot about Scriv. I remember he made an odd remark to me in Paris. I'd forgotten it till recently. I'd been joking with him about the way in which he dropped people, disappeared, then turned up later with a new interest and a fresh bunch of friends. I told him he was a humbug, and then he said something about he was trying a final experiment with people and that if it didn't come off, he'd become a hermit. I thought at the time it was just another pose. But I'm damned if I don't think there was something in it."

Logic has little to do with our reactions. I felt that Rivers, in quoting that remark of Scrivener's, had provided me with information of a more central order than any I had yet received. I knew that it was significant although its significance eluded me.

Rivers turned to me irritably.

"Well, you don't say anything. I've told you the fix I'm in and you sit there like a mute."

"You've also told me how you are going to get out of it," I reminded him. "You say that you're going to lie low, not see Francesca, and that then you'll pick up your cards again and go on with the game. It's only a question of waiting."

"Yes, that's true enough," he admitted, but with no enthusiasm. "The devil of it is I can't afford to wait. I may as well tell you everything. I've spent a hell of a lot of money. You can't run round with a woman like Francesca and not find it expensive. *She* thought it was all very Bohemian and cost nothing, but, naturally, money doesn't exist for her."

He was silent, and it was clear that the financial aspect of his predicament was one which he did not care to discuss. After a pause, however, he went on but he attempted one or two fireworks first as if he felt it necessary to relieve the gloom of the situation.

"A man always becomes bankrupt in courage before he goes bust on a cash basis. That's certain. I've got to live up to my own philosophy. Never think about money or you're done. Borrow, steal, live on credit—do what you like to get money—but keep your eyes fixed on your objective. I'll give you an example of what I mean. If I were to review my situation in the terms of common sense, shall I tell you how it would appear?"

"Yes, if you like," I said.

"But remember," he added with great emphasis, "I'm only telling you the *appearance* of the situation. It will be all right of course," he announced airily. "Well, on the surface, then, I owe about three thousand pounds and I haven't a bob. My uncle has let me have a lot of money because I told him I was in a business with great possibilities. Now, superficially, that was a lie."

He paused but I said nothing. I waited to hear the symbolic interpretation by which a surface lie became an interior truth.

"The business, of course, was the game I had on with Francesca's crowd," he said casually.

"Did you explain that to your uncle?" I inquired.

"Oh, dear no!" he exclaimed. "He's very old-fashioned. I simply told him that some influential people had taken me up and that I was on my way to making a fortune. I told him I had to sink a bit to keep my end up. Perfectly true, really, you know."

"I see," I said, then paused, rather at a loss how to continue. "And—and he accepted that statement without inquiries?"

"Yes—yes—that's right. Quite! You see—it's like this. Well, it's rather difficult to explain. He said some stuff about he knew I'd settle down one day. Then he went on something about he was ignorant of business—which is true enough, he's always had money of his own. Then he indulged in some sentimental chat about he was getting old and that he must trust me about details but that he'd promised my father he'd give me a hand and, if now was the time, he wasn't going back on his word. Something like that—so far as I remember. Then he wrote to my mother and said I had told him that I was going to *buckle down*—isn't that an awful phrase?—and she wrote me a rapturous letter and sent a bit of extra money."

A long pause.

"Well, that's about it—roughly. Of course, I say nothing about tailors' bills, and odds and ends I owe to several people and one or two moneylenders because all that is normal, natural, and inevitable."

Another long pause.

"But, remember," he said with studied emphasis, "that's only the *appearance* of the situation. I've told you the way you must *not* look at it."

I thought that over for some time while waiting for him to unfold the way in which I must look at it. But either he thought that self-evident, or he did not wish to reveal the secret which had baffled certain of the old alchemists so persistently.

"So, you see," he began again, "I can't really afford to wait. I must get something out of those people I've met and get it damned quick too. Look here," he exclaimed suddenly. "It's simply a question of *will*. I've got to put this nonsense about Francesca right out of my head and play my cards with an ice-cold brain. Damn it! I'm not Middleton! Anyway, there's nothing really to bother about— yet. Francesca hasn't the slightest idea that I've fallen for her. She thinks I'm out of town."

In the far distance the band began to play *God Save the King*. It seemed to suggest that the curtain had fallen on the get-rich-quick period of Rivers's career. I could not decide whether to say anything or to remain silent. Most people when they confide their difficulties usually hasten to indicate a quick and easy way out of them. They want your instantaneous agreement, not criticism. Rivers was no exception. Moreover, I had to tell him everything or nothing. Was I to tell him that his position was hopeless? that Francesca was fully aware of his infatuation and had no longer the slightest interest in him?

"Scriv would get me out of this hole," he said slowly. "He understands the 'good time' philosophy of the younger generation. He's exactly like me," he added confidentially, "only he does things on a bigger scale. Wish to God he'd come back!"

He lit a cigarette. A moment later he rose, and banishing all serious considerations became the gay, flippant person I had always known. This reversion was so unexpected, so sudden and so complete, that I half imagined some miraculous way out of all his trouble had presented itself.

We began to walk towards Piccadilly. He seemed to dance along and it was difficult to keep pace with him. He talked at lightning speed. Everything was solved, everything was simple, everyone was a knave or a fool—except Rivers. Everything existed to amuse him. He would do what he liked, where he liked, when he liked. The recipe was simple enough:—respect nothing, bow down to nothing, never admit that there ever had been—or could be—

anyone of greater importance than yourself. Great achievements were all moonshine. He, Rivers, could write like Shakespeare or compose like Beethoven—if he wanted to. Admiration of any kind was a sign of an inferiority complex. He, Rivers, was a pioneer. Yes, a pioneer. Quite! Men and women were about to become completely emancipated. They would then be just like him. History, philosophy, religion were all nonsense—they were dope demanded by weaklings. He, Rivers, did not need any dope. He was strong enough to face the horror of life. He had neither hope nor fear—he was himself. Meanwhile, in order to prove his immense superiority over others, he—Rivers—proposed to insult the things they valued, to tread their gods underfoot, and to defy their conventions. And, above all, in no circumstances whatever— come what may—would he do any work of any kind. Certainly not. The Great War had been a supreme blessing because it had made possible the advent of a new type—the Rivers type. If it had not been for the war, the world would have had to wait for the Rivers type for another century at least. Chaos would be the outstanding characteristic of the new order. But when he, Rivers, said *chaos* he meant, of course, that it would appear like chaos to old-fashioned idiots. But *really* it would be Order such as their imagination could not conceive. Of course it was a burden to be a pioneer. Quite! One accepted that—at least he did. And the most important article in the creed of the new race was *to refuse to suffer*. He, Rivers, hadn't suffered, wasn't suffering, and had no intention of doing so.

After which he paused, studied me with the eyes of a super-man, then asked if I could lend him a tenner. The atmosphere was so charged with the philosophy of "live dangerously" that I said "yes." Whereupon he pointed out that his prospects were my security. Despite this assurance, however, I regarded myself as an unsecured creditor.

In Piccadilly Circus, when we were saying goodnight, he gave me a card. "This is my address for the minute," he informed me. "I'm in hiding, so to speak. If Scriv writes or returns, let me know."

He waved his hand and disappeared.

I walked home slowly.

The butterfly was putting up a gallant struggle, but nevertheless it was in the net.

II

The car threaded the darkness swiftly, speeding down the spectral avenue created by the headlights. A tree, a house, momentarily claimed recognition, then flashed into insatiable obscurity. Shapes died as they were born. Only the white road, endlessly vanishing, endlessly renewed, rushed out of the darkness to serve us.

Pauline drove the car with that precision and concentration which distinguished all her actions. There are people who reveal their individuality in every trivial occupation. She was one of them. She accorded to each act precisely what was essential to its perfect execution, and consequently her every action—no matter how commonplace in itself—achieved the quality of a deed. Nothing existed for her but the thing she was doing, and nothing less than its perfect performance would suffice.

At last we were alone together. Although I had seen her frequently during the last two months, her father had usually been with us. He had not been well—his wife was away—and we had kept him company. Now he was better and had joined his wife abroad.

This midnight drive into the country was Pauline's idea and I imagined that she had proposed it in order to celebrate her freedom. She was not wearing a hat and again I noticed the beauty of her hair and the perfect poise of her head.

All day a blazing sun had made the city intolerable and even now the air seemed to vibrate with heat. The earth lay exhausted under a moonless and starless sky as if eager to rest before the return of the all-subduing sun.

We reached a village and Pauline stopped the car. We walked for some distance in silence, then followed a lane which rose sharply and led to a wood. There was not a sound. It was so dark that I could scarcely see her.

"It's ages since I was with you alone," I said at last. "I've been less fortunate than the others."

"My father did not care about them," she replied, "but when he knew I was seeing you, it was different. There's something I want to ask you," she continued, "have you seen Middleton?"

I told her of his sudden appearance and of the way in which he had insulted Francesca. She was anxious to ascertain the precise date of this meeting and whether I had seen him since.

"No, I've not seen him again. And I don't think I shall—anyway for some time."

There was a pause, then she said:

"He came to you straight from me, did you know that?"

"No. I guessed that he'd come to tell me something, but I'd no idea what it was."

We discovered a fallen tree and she sat down. The place, the solitude, the darkness, all conspired to create the impression that this meeting was part of a dream. I felt that at any moment the sound of her voice would cease, the scene vanish, and I should find myself alone in the library.

"He'd come to you straight from me," she repeated, articulating each word and so transforming it. "He rang me up that afternoon and asked me to see him. I told him I was going to a theatre. He begged me to go in afterwards if only for a few minutes."

"You mean to his flat?" I asked.

"Yes, I went there after the play. He'd been drinking and he talked incoherently about Francesca. He was obsessed by her. He had called, but had been told that she was away."

"Why did he want to tell you about all that?" I asked.

She did not reply immediately. Somewhere in the wood a bough fell to the ground. For some seconds everything seemed to listen.

"I do not know," she said at last. "He went on for some time, then he came over to me and suddenly, without any warning, he seized me in his arms and kissed me again and again."

"And then?" I asked.

"He wasn't responsible, he didn't know what he was doing. He tore my dress off my shoulders. He was like a madman. He——"

"But what did you do?" I interrupted. "Weren't you frightened?"

"I did nothing," she replied. "I wasn't afraid of him. I was sorry for him—I have been terribly sorry for him for a long time. If I had resisted he would have torn all my clothes off. As I didn't, he stopped. He stood and stared at me, then suddenly he implored me to go. He evidently went straight to you."

The drama of this incident was heightened by the manner in which she related it. She conveyed the impression that she had witnessed the scene, not participated in it.

"Do you understand Middleton?" I asked.

"Yes, in a way. His tragedy is that he does not realize the type of man he is. He deceives himself about everything. He's in love with his memories." She rose and we walked on slowly.

"And Francesca?" I asked.

"In some ways I envy her," she replied. "Middleton does not know what he wants, but Francesca knows exactly. I'm certain that even when she was a child she knew just what she wanted from life and she's got it. She simply *takes*, and ignores the consequences." She was silent, then added. "If she were less intelligent, it would be easy enough to understand her. As it is, she's a mystery to me."

"As you are to her. I've a theory about her type," I went on. "She's an avenger. All the nameless nondescript women who are bullied and humiliated by men obtain a vicarious revenge through the Francesca type. Instinctively she knows that she must be either a victim or a victor. She goes forth conquering and to conquer. The obscure sufferings of multitudes of anonymous women have forged her into a weapon of revenge. Her beauty is that of a dagger. Pity, regret, remorse do not exist for her. She is spared everything except the bitterness of victory."

She did not reply and we walked on. We emerged from the wood and climbed to the summit of a hill. She took my arm and we stood motionless, looking down into the darkness. Below, to the left, the light of a swiftly-moving car defined the sinuous curves of an invisible road. On and on it went, threading obscurity like an inspired thought. Then it rose in a long straight ascent and vanished.

"Why is it," she said almost in a whisper, "that I know for certain that I shall never forget how we stood here and watched that light glide through the darkness and disappear?"

"I shall never forget it either," I answered. Then, almost involuntarily, I took her in my arms and kissed her lips. They were cool as a flower and I could feel the caress of her hair upon my forehead. She neither moved nor spoke, but her great eyes shone in the darkness and seemed to be seeking something. Although her body yielded to my embrace, physical proximity made her even more elusive: it added nothing to that intimacy which had been established at our first meeting. Her kiss was that of a child, and so it wakened wonder, not passion. I understood why Middleton had begged her to go after he had torn her dress from her shoulders. Francesca's beauty had maddened him, but Pauline's had cooled him. Francesca's body was a flame: Pauline's a stream.

We walked slowly back through the wood and she began to talk about Rivers. Although he had not confided in her, she had guessed his predicament. It was evident that, to her, he was simply a child who had been hypnotized by the tinsel of life and that he was about to fall into the deep gulf which separated his theories from the actualities of existence.

Somewhat to my surprise, I discovered that she thought Middleton and Rivers were very much alike, despite all the superficial evidence to the contrary, and she did not agree with me when I said that Middleton was capable of tragedy whereas Rivers was not.

But what really interested her about them and Francesca was the fact that although each of them was so concerned with Scrivener, not one of them in her judgment knew anything about him. She told me that she had discussed Scrivener at length with all of them and she had been amazed to discover the profundity of their ignorance. Then she explained to me how, when she met Scrivener, she encountered someone for the first time in her life whose problems resembled her own. She had difficulty in expressing her meaning but I gathered that in the same way as life offered him a number of things, none of which could hold him, so she was offered a number of things, none of which evoked a response from the whole of her. It did not matter that his possibilities were widely different from hers: it did not matter that others fervently desired the things they were offered. There was something else—some different way of life—and it was that which Scrivener was seeking in his way, just as she was seeking it in hers.

"I see the lives of the women I know," she added, "I could not live as they do. I feel that I have lived such a life thousands of times. I do not believe that is arrogance. It is not a question of being better than they are, or any rubbish of that kind. If I were to accept their values, I should only *watch myself trying to live*. I should hear my own voice when I spoke and wonder who the stranger was who had stolen it. Does all that sound utterly fantastic to you?"

"No, not in the least," I replied. "You are a voice in the darkness and so am I. We can say what we like. Tell me this: *why* is Scrivener interested in these people?"

"It is a mystery," she replied, "because he is a mystery. I believe he will return soon. Things are rapidly approaching a crisis between all of us and I feel that he has plotted that crisis and when it emerges, he will appear."

We had reached the car, but we stood and talked for some minutes before returning to London.

"You've no definition to cover Scrivener, then?" I asked.

"None," she answered, "unless he's the pilgrim of an inward Odyssey."

"That's a strange phrase," I said. "Did you invent it?"

She laughed. "Of course not. I saw it in one of his books."

We got into the car, and drove back to London in silence.

CHAPTER XIII

I

THREE days later, feeling restless, and experiencing that nervous tension produced by the premonition that a crisis is imminent, I went to lunch at the café I had visited so recently with Rivers. With some difficulty I found a table and, ignoring the surroundings, I read a paper during my meal. Half an hour later, just as I was about to leave, I looked round half hoping that I should discover someone with whom to spend the afternoon. Seated at a table only a few yards from me I saw Rivers and Middleton.

They were not talking. Middleton was sitting sideways with his hands clenched, gazing at his shoes. He looked as if he had not slept for nights. Rivers was looking vacantly at an ash-tray while he drummed the table with the fingers of his right hand. Two or three minutes passed. They did not speak: their attitudes remained the same. I sat watching them, wondering whether I should join them or not. Gradually I became aware that there was some change in Rivers. For some moments I was unable to define it, then I realized that he was less smart than usual. Compared with Middleton, who was extremely shabby, he was still the glass of fashion but, judged by his former impeccable standard, something was lacking. He was no longer immaculate.

I thought of the first time I had met him. I remembered how he had danced into the flat, expecting to find Scrivener, and the tempestuous way in which he had swept me off to lunch in that Japanese restaurant. How careless, confident, and certain he had been! Life for him was simply an affair of glittering ideas and abstract theories with which he juggled brilliantly, displaying all the easy dexterity of a social showman. And now, only a few months later, he sat in silence—with a dull companion—drumming his fingers on the table. . . .

And Middleton—I remembered the first time he had come to the flat: his curious laugh, his nervousness, and his sudden flashes of irritability. But, despite these, his appearance had proclaimed the type to which he belonged. His figure had been that of an athlete, and you knew instantly that he was an Englishman, the product of a long-established tradition. And now, only a few months later, he sat half-stupefied—with a companion who represented everything he had once despised—bereft of every distinguishing characteristic, staring at his shoes with sodden eyes.

Judged by the evidence, Francesca was responsible for the change in them, but I did not think of her as I sat watching them. I thought of Scrivener. They were his work, not hers. He had contrived that they should meet her, foreseeing the result of that meeting. Why had it interested him to break a sentimentalist and a butterfly on the same wheel?

I rose and went over to them. My reception was not enthusiastic. Middleton scowled and said nothing. I had not seen him since the night on which he had insulted Francesca, and doubtless he guessed that I knew the details of his last meeting with Pauline. He ordered another drink and ignored my presence. As to Rivers, he looked up apprehensively when I approached, but seeing who the intruder was he seemed relieved. I knew his secret and therefore my presence did not necessitate any acting on his part. He gave me a cigarette, but said little.

A quarter of an hour passed. Middleton drank, Rivers smoked, and I watched the people near me. The depression was almost tangible. I soon realized why they spent so much time together: each of them for different reasons was desperately lonely. Middleton had failed to find forgetfulness, and Rivers had been wounded by the weapon he had hoped to use. Yet I felt that there was no confidence between them. They only met because each was afraid of being alone with his own thoughts.

When another ten minutes had passed, I tried to leave them, but Rivers immediately asked where I was going. I told him that I should return to the flat and he suggested that they should come with me. The prospect of an afternoon in their company rather chilled me, but it was difficult to refuse. Middleton went to the bar to get some cigarettes and I took this opportunity to ask Rivers how his cure was progressing.

"It's not," he replied curtly. "I'm in the devil's own fix. It looks like a finish this time. I *can't* see her! I'm mad about her! It gets worse every day. Wish to God I'd never met her! She still thinks I'm away, that's one thing. Look here," he added in a low voice, "things are pretty desperate. I've *got* to pull something off in a fortnight—at latest. And my nerves aren't worth a damn."

We walked slowly to the flat. When we were settled in the library we must have looked like waxworks. No one said a word. Time attained a new significance: it became an implacable enemy waging a war of attrition.

But a dramatic change was imminent. Just as I had decided that it was impossible to endure this depression for another minute, the door opened and Francesca and Pauline appeared.

We rose awkwardly: each one a study in embarrassment. In an instant the atmosphere became electric. Middleton was utterly humiliated by the presence of these women, each of whom he had insulted in such strangely different ways. Rivers found himself confronted by the person he had not dared to meet. The knowledge that a supreme effort was necessary, if he were to retain even the shadow of the background he thought he possessed, robbed him of all initiative. He stared at Francesca with the eyes of an infatuated schoolboy. As to Pauline, she was so aware of the intricacy of the issues involved in this unexpected meeting that she became a spectator. But Francesca was smiling. She seemed to prolong the silence deliberately. She alone had the power to end it, and her refusal to do so confirmed her dominion over a situation concerning which the rest of us were impotent.

"I thought you were out of town," she said to Rivers at last.

He gave a long unconvincing explanation of his sudden return to London. It could have deceived no one and he must have known it.

She listened to him with exaggerated attention and her ready acquiescence to every improbable detail in his story only accentuated its absurdity. It evidently amused her to make him ridiculous and she succeeded in humiliating him thoroughly. Long before the process was complete, I felt more sorry for him than for Middleton. When she had reduced him to a state bordering on stammering imbecility, she turned away with a little shrug of the shoulders and began to study the books on the shelves.

Several minutes passed. We all sat motionless. Small-talk was impossible—silence unbearable. The persons present were neither strangers nor friends. Then, with a swift transition of mood, Francesca again accepted the social responsibilities of the situation but, on this occasion, she ignored Rivers and addressed no one in particular. I do not know whether her motive was deliberately malicious, but she elected to be amusing and succeeded admirably in beating Rivers at his own game. Sometimes a burlesque is better than its original, and it was so in the present instance. It was as if she were determined to complete Rivers's present humiliation by robbing his past triumphs of their laurels. She adopted his light lyrical manner, his nonchalant detachment, his egotistic philosophy, and his theoretical fireworks. It was a remarkable improvization. Her range was wider than his; her technique more flexible. She made Rivers, the raconteur, seem merely a clever amateur.

The effect on Rivers was utterly unexpected. Apparently he regarded her display as a challenge, and at the earliest opportunity he tried to emulate it. A cripple's attempt to dance would have been less painful.

By an effort of will I did not listen to him but studied Francesca. Something in her manner convinced me that she was amusing herself with all of us for the last time. We had failed her. She had hoped to learn something from one or other of us concerning Scrivener. She had taken each of us up in turn and examined us under a microscope. She had discovered nothing to her purpose and this meeting was her farewell. Her experiment was at an end and she did not give one second's thought to the suffering it had caused. Middleton and Rivers were equally ridiculous and she was no longer concerned with them. Pauline was a mystery but not one in which she was interested. She was narrowed to Scrivener and I knew definitely that if she continued to keep in touch with me, her sole reason for doing so would be that I was nearer to him in one sense than any of them.

But the surprises of this impossible afternoon were not yet at an end.

While Rivers's lamentable attempt to be amusing was still in progress, there was a ring at the bell. I was grateful for any opportunity to escape, and consequently I went to the door without considering who my visitor was likely to be. It was Mr. Walter

Winkworth, resplendent in morning coat and top hat. Before I had time to indicate my surprise, he took me by the lapel of my coat and drew me gently to one side.

"Wrexham, my dear fellow," he said almost in a whisper, "a word in your ear. I must be brief or your absence will occasion comment. I was passing this building, sir, when I noticed a magnificent car outside. It occurred to me that it might be Mrs. Bellamy's. Now, was I right?"

"You were quite right," I answered, "Mrs. Bellamy is in the library. And not only Mrs. ——"

But he interrupted me:

"I *felt* I was right, Wrexham, that's why I decided to call. It seemed to me that it would be a natural and convenient manner for me to encounter that charming woman again. I suggest—I only suggest, mind—that she be allowed to consider my call a pure coincidence. There are occasions, Wrexham, when I say to myself: 'A little diplomacy is needed here, I *think*,' and I believe the present is just such an occasion."

I led the way into the library, feeling that Winkworth would probably need all his diplomacy. Rivers's attempt to be brilliant had petered out and the four sat in gloomy silence. Apparently, however, Winkworth was only aware of Francesca whom he greeted with elaborate courtesy.

"My *dear* Mrs. Bellamy," he exclaimed, "this is an unsought, an unexpected, and an undeserved pleasure for me. How do you do?"

They shook hands.

"I rang the bell of this flat with a mind intent on certain dry business matters which I wished to discuss with our good friend Wrexham. What was my surprise—my *delight*, if you will allow the word—when he told me that *you* were in the library!"

Francesca listened to him graciously, although an ironical smile curled her lips.

"Your visit was providential, Mr. Winkworth. It was all that was necessary to complete one of the most interesting afternoons I have ever spent. I am leaving London almost immediately and am so glad to have seen you before I go."

The effect of this announcement on Rivers was devastating. The game was over, and he had lost. The last flicker of hope was extinguished.

Winkworth, however, was rapturously happy. He began an animated conversation with Francesca as if they were alone together, till she adroitly indicated the social obligations of the position.

"Mr. Wrexham must introduce you to his friends," she said gaily, "and incidentally they are all friends of Mr. Scrivener's."

Introductions were effected. Winkworth entirely ignored Middleton and Rivers. They might have been a couple of schoolboys for all the attention he paid to them. Pauline, however, was another affair.

"Naturally, your name is known to me, Miss Mandeville," he said with a bow. "Every Englishman must respect the name of Mandeville. The Empire owes much to men like your father."

From this point onward, Winkworth dominated the proceedings. He was obviously quite unconscious of the atmosphere of constraint which hung like a threatening storm over the party. He was satisfied that he was making a huge success with Francesca and the delight which this knowledge evoked reduced everything else to insignificance. On one occasion, when Rivers volunteered a remark, Winkworth snubbed him promptly and effectively. He ignored Middleton so absolutely that I had to glance occasionally in Middleton's direction to assure myself that he was still there. Every now and again Winkworth recognized Pauline's presence by a graceful wave of the hand. He was neither friendly nor distant with me but maintained a neutral attitude and I could see that he wished to observe Francesca's relations with me before definitely committing himself.

He stood with his back to the fireplace and discussed current topics with a spacious air of well-bred tolerance. A General Election was imminent and he favoured Francesca with his views on the subject.

"I am all for democracy, Mrs. Bellamy. I am a believer in the democratic principle. But, as a dear friend of mine, and a captain of industry, said to me recently: *There are limits*. A profound observation! The qualification for a vote is not age, my dear Mrs. Bellamy. No, it is not age and it is not sex. The essential qualification is *a stake in the country*. A vote is a responsibility, or it is nothing. Being a responsibility, it should only be vested in responsible persons. When I consider the magnitude of the issues now before the country, and when I consider the quality of those persons who form the electorate, I am frequently very disturbed—very disturbed indeed. I am all for progress, I assure you, but only so far as progress is consonant with the dictates of Safety First. When I scan the frontiers of this far-flung Empire——"

His voice went on and on. Its effect became almost hypnotic. It produced the sensation that always, all one's life long, one had been listening to Walter Winkworth, and that for ever and ever, world without end, one would sit there listening to him. It ceased to be a voice, it became one's pulse—a relentless rhythm throbbing monotonously through one's whole being.

I glanced furtively at the others. Middleton had discovered that the whisky was within reach of his hand and had helped himself generously. He was nearly buried in a huge armchair and was scowling impotently at Winkworth. Rivers was gazing at Francesca with imploring eyes. Pauline sat as straight as a lance on her high-backed chair and seemed to be watching something which was taking place in the far distance. But Francesca was listening attentively to Winkworth, an appreciative smile on her lips. The very curve of her body as she sat looking up at him was indicative of respectful interest. Being thus encouraged, Winkworth became over life-size.

"Were I to become a Member of Parliament, my dear Mrs. Bellamy, a course of action which I have sometimes contemplated." He paused, and Francesca intimated that it was clearly his duty to go to Westminster without further delay. "Thank you, thank you," he exclaimed, evidently extremely flattered. "If ever I became a Member of Parliament, I should try to make my constituents realize the responsibilities involved in the possession of a great fortune."

Francesca indicated how much she would value his views on this subject.

"Forgive me, then, if I become personal," Winkworth said with great delicacy. "Let me apply my theory to *you*. The ignorant conception of such a life as yours would be that your days and nights consisted of one long round of amusement and excitement. Now, what are the facts?"

Francesca evidently preferred that he should state them, which Winkworth hastened to do.

"First, Mrs. Bellamy, you have to protect yourself against the wiles of unscrupulous adventurers. Are the ignorant aware of *that* fact? Only too many rogues, I fear, would regard you as a short-cut to affluence. It might be argued," he went on in his best legal manner, and entirely unconscious of the bricks he was dropping, "it might be argued that you can buy expert advice. For instance, it might be suggested that I—or some member of the profession to which I have the honour to belong—might stand as a bulwark between you and the unscrupulous. The argument is unsound. It is unsound because I cannot think for you. I often explain this to my clients. 'You must decide' I say to them. '*You* must decide. It is for me to give legal expression to your decision.' And that, Mrs. Bellamy, is the true relationship—as I see it—between a lawyer and his clients."

Endlessly, monotonously, the voice went on. All his mannerisms were exploited: the pince-nez was swung to and fro on its ribbon; every fifth sentence was punctuated by "I *think*"; quotations from eminent friends were plentiful; his nails were inspected frequently; and he managed to convey the impression that we were only a handful among a great audience he was addressing.

It amused Francesca, however, to encourage him. I had always known that hidden in the depths of her complex nature was a vein of cruelty, but I had not realized its dimensions till the present occasion. She had been merciless to Rivers and now she exulted in causing Winkworth to make himself ridiculous. If she spared Middleton, it was not because she pitied him. He had humiliated himself so abjectly, and was so conscious of the fact, that her imagination could not devise any indignity which he had not imposed on himself. She was having her revenge for the time she had wasted with them. By an adroit manipulation of her conversation with Winkworth, however, she contrived to deliver some final blows on her two victims. In this she eventually succeeded beyond her expectations.

It was necessary for her only to hint at a theme in order for Winkworth to enlarge upon it at great length and consequently it was easy for her to introduce a subject upon which his views would prove extremely irritating to Middleton and Rivers. She led him on to discuss "the rising generation" with a somewhat dramatic result.

"I have studied the rising generation," Winkworth began, "I assure you I have studied these young people deeply. I have said to myself: 'What is the matter with these young men and women? Why are they so restless, so dissatisfied, so lacking in respect?' Wherever I look I see them agitating for this, that, and the other. Either they want money without working for it, or they fling themselves into every excess with a reckless disregard of consequences. And I think to myself: what is the reason for this? Can it possibly——"

Suddenly Middleton leapt to his feet, his hands were trembling, and there was a furious light in his eyes.

"What's the reason for this?" His mimicry of Winkworth's voice and manner was ludicrously effective. "*I'll* tell you what the reason is!" he shouted. "It's—*you*! Yes, *you*!"

He reeled over to Winkworth, and for a moment I thought he was going to strike him. "You!" he hissed, "and the thousands like you—the smug, the sleek, the self-satisfied, who loll back in their armchairs and talk about England as if it were their back garden! You, my fat friend, you! A flunkey in the service of Vested Interests. *You* are what's the matter—nothing else."

Winkworth was breathing heavily and staring at Middleton with his mouth open. The latter broke into his strange abrupt laugh, then continued:

"There's only one problem for what you call the rising generation. It's this:—can they continue to bear the burden of duds like you on their shoulders? That's the only problem. God! What an exhibition you've made of yourself! How you've writhed round this woman simply because she's got money! How you've twisted, wheedled, and insinuated! And how damned dignified you imagined you were! Good God, man, there's nothing to you but your clothes and mannerisms! Well, get on with your tricks, but don't sneer at drunkards in my presence. You'd be nearer God than you are if you were one."

He turned away from him and looked round the room.

"I'm through with the lot of you. And this time I mean it. If it hadn't been for the humbug who owns this place, I'd never have met any of you."

He laughed again and reeled out of the room.

All eyes were fixed on Winkworth. He seemed to have shrunk and was trembling with agitation. Middleton's attack had been so sudden, so utterly unexpected, and so ferocious that it had annihilated him. However crude the attack may have been, it had succeeded in reducing him to agitated silence. That was not only a miracle, it was also the measure of Middleton's triumph.

Winkworth collapsed limply into a chair and stared at each one of us in turn with an expression of ludicrous perplexity. It was quite obvious that he was helpless and would have to be rescued. Stripped of his mannerisms and dignified deportment, he was rather a pathetic figure—a marionette out of action. The only person, however, who could rescue him was Francesca, but it piqued her perversity to delay taking action and consequently the situation became more embarrassing every moment. At last she decided to restore Winkworth to his pinnacle and succeeded in doing so promptly and effectively.

"You are not the first to be insulted by Mr. Middleton," she said consolingly. "Mr. Wrexham is a witness that a week or two ago he insulted me in the most outrageous terms."

"Insulted *you*." Winkworth rose, a trifle unsteadily. "My dear Mrs. Bellamy," he went on with a ghostly resemblance to his old manner, "if *that* is the case——"

He paused. He seemed to grow bigger. He threw his shoulders back. His right hand fumbled for the ribbon which controlled his pince-nez. When he spoke again his voice had practically recovered its former resonance.

"If *that* is the case, his insults become compliments."

He turned to me with an imperial gesture and demanded: "Who is this fellow?"

"He is a friend of Mr. Scrivener's," I replied.

"I am grieved to hear it," he said. "Unfortunately, Mrs. Bellamy, it is a fact that my client has a penchant for associating with his social inferiors."

He was about to continue when Francesca anticipated him.

"I felt that you could enlighten us about Mr. Scrivener. I am sure you could," she added with a smile which entirely restored Winkworth to his former glory. "I am not asking you to reveal professional secrets—I know you too well for that—but I am quite sure that you could, if you would, shed some light on Mr. Scrivener's psychology. Everyone in this room has reason to be extraordinarily interested in him."

It was remarkable how easily Francesca, in dealing with Winkworth, became exactly the woman she knew he imagined her to be. She discarded her intelligence, her critical faculty, her worldly knowledge, and became the rather silly, petted, rich society woman which Winkworth expected to find.

"Ah! if only I could speak entirely frankly!" exclaimed Winkworth with a glance at Francesca which implied that if she would grant him a private interview he would withhold nothing from her. "I have studied my client and I understand him, I *think*."

He began a mighty monologue. He told us all about Scrivener's youth. He described his father and how, when he died, Scrivener's uncle had taken charge of the boy. He recounted how the two had travelled widely together and how, at the age of twenty-one, Scrivener had inherited the whole of his uncle's fortune. Winkworth let himself go. He favoured us with long elaborate comments on each fact in his narrative, and introduced so much irrelevant matter that at one point it was not clear whether he was giving us the story of Scrivener or whether he was giving us an account of his own life. He managed to hint darkly at dangers from which he had rescued

Scrivener, and he gave his explanation of Scrivener's disappearances and eccentricities. He ended by saying:

"He is representative of his age, Mrs. Bellamy. He is restless, dissatisfied, disturbed. He rejects in turn everything he is offered. He experiments——"

"*You* think he experiments?" Francesca queried quickly.

"I fear so," replied Winkworth mournfully. "And he wearies easily of his experiments."

"Look here," said Rivers suddenly, after being silent for nearly an hour, "Middleton called Scrivener a humbug. I'm not sure he's not right. What do you think?" he asked, turning to Winkworth.

"Do you really think, Mrs. Bellamy, that we need concern ourselves with anything that individual said?" Winkworth inquired, as if Rivers did not exist.

"I don't think so," she replied with a smile and without even glancing in Rivers's direction.

Winkworth began to talk again, but on this occasion he was frequently interrupted by Francesca. She extracted almost everything he knew about Scrivener and in less than half an hour she had pumped him dry. She then brought me into the conversation and later Pauline. Scrivener was discussed from every possible angle. Then, during a pause, Pauline said suddenly: "We are talking about him as if he were dead."

Winkworth started violently. His theory that Scrivener had committed suicide was the only one he had kept to himself. But Francesca had noticed his reaction to Pauline's comment and was on her feet in an instant.

"Dead!" she exclaimed. She looked from Winkworth to me as if one of us had hidden a secret from her.

"My *dear* Mrs. ——"

"Wait!" The word rapped out like a command. "What do you know about this?" she asked me.

"Nothing," I replied. "I only know that I have not heard anything from Scrivener for months."

"And you?" she asked, turning to Winkworth.

She had become a different person so suddenly that Winkworth was mystified. The petted, fashionable lady had vanished in a flash and in her place was a passionate fierce woman whose dark eyes seemed to read his every thought.

"Why—er—well—how shall I put it?" Winkworth stammered. Francesca stamped her foot with irritation.

"Now, I beg of you," he faltered, "do not concern yourself——"

"I *am* concerned." The sentence flashed out like a dagger. "Tell me, without any flourishes—have you any reason to think he is dead?"

Winkworth looked round despairingly but Rivers and Pauline, no less than Francesca, were intent on his answer.

"I can only say this," he said at last, looking at Francesca with troubled eyes. "More than this I *cannot* say. I have frequently of late written to my client on matters of some importance. I have not heard from him in reply. That's all."

"It's *not* all." Francesca's tone implied that she was addressing a dishonest office boy.

"*Not* all?" queried Winkworth weakly. "Really! Not all?"

"Certainly not!" Francesca replied scornfully. "His former disappearances may be explained by the fact that he was bored by his associates, but that explanation does not fit his last disappearance. Why do *you* imagine he left London so unexpectedly without telling anyone?"

Winkworth fidgeted. "I think it possible—only possible, mind—that he *had* to go. But I do not *know*. I can only say this: if I do *not* hear from him shortly, I shall institute inquiries. This long silence disturbs me very much indeed."

He knew no more and Francesca realized the fact. A few moments later she left with Pauline. She was curt in her manner to Winkworth and scarcely nodded to Rivers. A moment later he went away, a study in abject dejection. Winkworth and I were left alone.

"A remarkable afternoon, Wrexham, a *very* remarkable afternoon." He mopped his forehead with his handkerchief. "I really don't quite know what to make of it." He sat down and looked round the room with unseeing eyes. "No, I don't quite know *what* to make of it. You didn't, of course, indicate at any time that it had crossed my mind that Scrivener might have committed suicide?"

"Never," I answered emphatically.

"Just so. That makes it all the more remarkable." After a pause he continued: "I dislike mysteries more than I can say. I shall have to consider my whole position in this matter and I advise you to consider yours. By the way, Wrexham, did you observe the remarkable interest which Mrs. Bellamy takes in Scrivener?"

I told him that I had noticed it on the first occasion on which I had met her, then added: "It is only because of her interest in him that she bothers about any of us."

"I would not go so far as that," he replied brusquely. "No, sir, I certainly would *not* go so far as that. In many cases, doubtless, that is so, but not in all—not in all."

We talked for a few minutes longer then, very much mystified by his experiences, he left the flat. . . .

Later, I realized that on this particular afternoon the five of us had been together for the first time.

PART THREE

CHAPTER XIV

I

I AM obsessed by an idea. Day and night it haunts me. I tell myself that it is wholly fantastic and yet the more I analyse it the more convinced I become that it represents the truth. If I express it, I may escape from it. Nothing truly exists until it is expressed.

But, first, I must explain that I am alone. The others have all left London. The departure and destination of each were characteristic. Francesca has gone abroad and proposes to travel for several months. She telephoned me the night before she left simply to ask me to wire her if Scrivener returned or if I received any news of him. Pauline has joined her parents in the country as her father is seriously ill. She left almost immediately. A day or two later Rivers came to see me. He was still very depressed and explained his position in a few disjointed sentences:

"It's all up, Wrexham," he said. "I don't know what the hell I'm going to do. There's going to be a smash this time. Damn everything and everybody! I'll have to go and stay with my mother for a bit. I can't remain in London—I owe so much that I'm afraid to go out. My uncle will have to be told everything and he'll think I've lied to him. He's as old-fashioned as the devil. I wouldn't care," he went on dejectedly, "if I could get Francesca out of my head, but I can't. She rages in me like a fever."

A long pause.

"Wonder if I'll ever see her again. Look here!" he exclaimed suddenly, "Scriv must be worth the earth. Wonder if he'd lend me a decent bit. What do you think?"

I told him that I had not the least idea, but he did not listen, and immediately began to base extravagant hopes on this new scheme for deliverance.

"Better ask him for a packet. That's good psychology. It irritates rich people to be asked for trifles. Besides it would let me down in his eyes, and—what's more—it wouldn't do *me* any good. I'll ask him for three thousand quid. If I write the letter, will you send it on?"

I promised that I would send it to the only address I had and Rivers announced that, pending a reply, he would go to his mother's place in the country and hide. He had the most amazing facility for believing what he hoped and in the space of a few minutes he hypnotized himself into the belief that his financial difficulties were at an end and that the only remaining problem was the best means of restoring his prestige with Francesca. His resolute refusal to admit any of the facts of the situation was pathetic and I was glad to lend him a fiver in order to get rid of him.

Two days later I was summoned to Middleton's flat. He had been in bed for some days and it was only too easy to see that he was beginning to pay the physical price of his recent excesses. The doctor was insistent on the need for complete rest in the country, and directly he was well enough to travel he left London and went to the coast.

Even Winkworth is away. I am alone. Day follows day and I sit in the library. Matthews continues to render her services with clockwork precision and efficiency. She gives no confidences, invites none, and evidently lives her life apart in a world of her own. We know nothing of each other.

I go out seldom. I sit in the silent library. The books look down on me from their shelves and I remember how, when I first came to the flat, I thought of studying them systematically in the hope that they would yield the secret of Scrivener. Only a few months ago I had planned to do this, but now it seems a lifetime since that theory presented itself. Yet—in another mood—it is the events of these last few months which seem unreal—the crowded canvas of a vivid dream—and I half-believe that Francesca, Pauline, Rivers, Middleton, and all the adventures I have had with them, are only shadows which have haunted my sleep. I feel that scarcely a week has passed since I came to live in Scrivener's flat, and that I am a stranger to London and its ways.

I have recaptured my solitude. For long years it was normal for me to spend my days alone. Now, it is strange. I am surprised as hour succeeds hour that no one appears. The very silence is different, because I have changed.

I am alone with only an idea for company—an idea which continually expands and develops, till it seems as disproportionate to its origin as an oak tree is to an acorn.

II

When all one's thoughts have revolved round a specific subject for a considerable time, it is sometimes difficult to remember the precise incident which caused that subject to assume such central importance. I am reminded of this fact by the difficulty I have had in remembering exactly how this idea first presented itself to my mind. Even now, I am not certain, but there is little doubt that the receipt of a strange communication was largely if not wholly responsible. It happened like this.

Towards the end of my first week of solitude, a large envelope, which had been posted in Paris, and which was addressed to me in an unfamiliar handwriting, arrived by the last post. It contained various documents, but there was no covering letter to explain why they had been sent to me. I looked at them in turn but most of them related to business matters concerning which I knew nothing. Amongst them was a sealed envelope which bore the inscription: "The Will of Jonathan Scrivener." I was turning over paper after paper in the hope of discovering some explanation of the mystery, when I suddenly caught sight of a long letter in my own handwriting. It was my letter of application for the post of secretary to Scrivener.

Directly I recognized it I recalled vividly the circumstances in which it had been written. I remembered that Saturday afternoon on which I had seen the advertisement in *The Times*, and my instant determination to apply for the position. I remembered how, on the following day, I had drafted letter after letter until, almost in desperation, I destroyed my former efforts and wrote rapidly an account of my life and why I had decided to apply for the post. I remembered how I sealed the letter, without even reading it through, and posted it that night. Simply to see it again brought back all the weariness of the years I had spent in Petersham's office. The room in which I had written the letter rose before me. I could see the ugly furniture, the gap in the badly-fitting curtains, and I could hear the melancholy monotony of the church bells ringing for evening service. My God! the horror of that sitting-room, in somebody else's house, where I had lived for years, and in which I had been utterly lonely! I could see that room and feel it. Its *atmosphere* was more substantial to me than any article of furniture it had contained. It is interesting that one can shudder at the memory of a room. . . .

I sat down at the desk and read the letter through carefully. At last it fell from my hand. I had written *that*. I experienced such a sensation of shame that I wanted to burn the letter, to watch it shrivel and blacken before my eyes, so that never would it be read by me or anyone again. It was utterly false and its falsity was intensified by the fact that, superficially, every word it contained was true. It is essential to explain this, yet it is almost impossible to explain.

What is so unfamiliar as a letter you wrote some time ago? It comes again into your possession and as you read it through you almost wonder who wrote it. You feel that it was written by some stranger—a stranger who has counterfeited your handwriting. You rebel at the thought that this letter will always be associated with you. The person who wrote it no longer exists. It is a subtle type of forgery. You experience these sensations even when the letter in question is of a comparatively trivial nature but the letter with which I was concerned was not of this type for it did not record simply the external circumstances of my life. Usually when we write an account of ourselves, we restrict our narrative to the narrow limits of times and places, but I had ignored those settings and had tried to reveal something of the history of my thoughts and emotions. I had attempted to depict the interior drama of my life, not the scenery which had served as a background.

This letter revealed the bitterness I had known when my father's sudden death had banished me to Petersham's office. It indicated the suffering of those long years of impotent rebellion which had made my life an impossibility. It hinted at the scorn and hatred which had possessed me during this period and it revealed the attempt I had made to make books serve as a substitute for life. All this I had written at white heat. The writing of it had stirred those passions which slumber in the volcano of memory. To have revealed all this to a stranger was bad enough but what followed was worse.

In the first chapter of this book I hinted briefly at the unhappiness I had experienced during those years in Petersham's office, and I added that then something happened which made me content to become a spectator of life. The second part of my letter of application attempted to describe the experience which had effected this transformation. To re-read this part of the letter, after a lapse of several months, made me blush with shame. It was pretentious, arrogant, rich in false assumptions, steeped in spiritual pride. It conveyed the impression that by some sudden act of renunciation I had rejected the lust of the flesh, the lust of the eye, and the pride of life. It asserted that I had found within myself a power which enabled me to live secure and apart in an interior world of my own and that, therefore, the desire, the dreams, the ambitions, and the hopes of other men had been revealed to me as so many vanities and vexations of spirit. It implied that I had refused the kingdoms of this world, and the glories thereof, because I had glimpsed the eternal frontier of the Kingdom of God. When I wrote it, I have no doubt that I believed it to be a declaration of faith. As I re-read it, I realized that it was an indictment of myself, and one which only I could have written.

I read the letter for the third time, then put it down on the desk and began to pace the room restlessly. So *this* was what I had believed to be the truth of myself! I had dreamed that I was self-sufficient, that I could live alone, that life had yielded its secret to me! I had dared to dream that the things of this world had ended for me! This letter was a mirror which reflected the image of my arrogance. When I wrote it I believed I was recording the truth about myself. Only a few months have elapsed, but I now know that it is false, pretentious, *theoretical*.

Imaginatively, it is quite easy to triumph over all kinds of temptations. We say to ourselves: "if I were rich, I would commit none of the follies of the wealthy and I would indulge in none of their vices." And we believe it, and feel virtuous. It is the same with worldly success. We are convinced that, if only it would come our way, we should demonstrate conclusively that we should continue to see ourselves in perspective and be guilty of none of the extravagancies and vain posturings of those whom the world has crowned. We are quite certain of it. We thrill with pride at the thought of our humility. In fact we are amazed that, being so eligible for worldly honours, Providence does not promote us immediately to the chief seats in the synagogue. Can it be that the All-Seeing has failed to observe the obvious?

It is remarkably easy to gain a theoretical triumph over an imaginary temptation. So easy, in fact, that our speculations as to what we should do, or should not do, in any given circumstances are not worth anything at all. Ordeal by experience is the only test.

I believed that this world held no prizes for me. Rubbish! Theoretical cant and hypocrisy! Good God! Life had only to beckon with her little finger in order to make me forget all about my renunciation. I was in the race again like a flash—pushing, struggling, shouting, with the best of them. And I imagined that I had rejected everything! The simple truth was that *I had not been offered anything*. No, not even a villa, an adoring wife, and the chance of being a little somebody at the local tennis club! Having nothing, I made a virtue of necessity and decided that I had refused everything. I gave away the fortune I did not possess. I looked down on the world with a pitying smile from the top of my tower of Babel. I felt lonely, isolated, important, tragic, and immensely superior. I even began to think in a language I had invented. I judged everything and everyone by a theoretical standard of excellence.

Then came swift and dramatic Change. I saw Scrivener's advertisement in *The Times*. I became his secretary. I found myself in entirely new surroundings. I had money, leisure, a great city to explore, a mystery to unravel, friends, acquaintances, amusements, and adventures of all kinds. I shed my pretensions as easily as a snake sheds its skin. I discovered that I had an immense zest for life, a passionate interest in the lives of others, and a determination to immerse myself in the life which seethed round me. The necessity for my old type of existence had vanished. I became a different person. The man who had written the letter was a stranger to me, yet one whom I was forced to recognize. He was what I had once imagined myself to be. . . .

I ceased to pace the room and returned to the desk. I read the letter again more impartially. One fact dominated everything else—this letter had triumphed over all other applications. It had secured me the position. It had been read only by Scrivener and it was the sole evidence on which he had based his selection. It *must*, therefore, have appealed to him. Something in him must have responded to the writer of that letter. Because of it, he had chosen me as his secretary. *Why* had it appealed to him? That was the question I had to answer.

I studied the letter minutely for over an hour. I ignored my personal reaction to it and tried to regard it with scientific detachment. By a feat of imagination, I put myself in Scrivener's place and attempted to read the letter with his eyes. Then—slowly and obscurely at first, but later with ever-increasing clarity—a possible solution presented itself. It was this. Although what I had written was not the truth about me, *it might be the truth about him*.

That sounds ridiculous, but it is worth consideration. Of all the information I had collected about Scrivener, which was the one fact concerning which everyone agreed? This: that he refused to claim the eminence to which he was entitled. Everyone admitted that he could have been successful in a number of activities. Francesca, Pauline, Winkworth, and many others, had stressed that fact repeatedly. But Scrivener had rejected every throne which had been offered to him. *My* rejections had been theoretical, but *his* had been actual. Unlike me, he had been offered much, and had refused everything. Was *that* why my letter had interested him? Did it reveal to him that I understood—if only theoretically—the problem which was so real and actual for him? And that problem was this: the discovery of an Activity which would include, and give meaning to, *all* activities? He had failed to find it, and he had been unable to devote his life to a substitute. He was aware of the possibility of this supreme Activity and consequently he was not dazzled by the glittering prizes which blinded other men. My letter would have revealed to him that I was aware that such a problem could exist, even if it were not mine.

The more I considered my letter the more convinced I became that this was what Scrivener had seen in it, and it was because of this that he had chosen me to be his secretary. As it is essential to make my meaning clear, I will express it from another angle. If my opportunities had been in any way comparable with those of Scrivener; if my rejections had not been theoretical but actual; then my problem would have been his.

In one sentence: Scrivener was myself magnified.

I began to pace the room again. I felt strangely excited. Yes, here at last, was the truth. I was certain of it. Scrivener was myself magnified.

Then, suddenly, like a flash of lightning in my brain, I realized a fact of even greater significance—*everyone thought this about him.* Pauline, Francesca, Middleton, Rivers, each and every one of them, saw in Scrivener their own image magnified.

I stood motionless in the library. I had discovered the obvious and so I could not believe it. I *knew* that I had my finger on the pulse of the mystery which had baffled me for months. I was about to understand, and I was half afraid to understand.

III

At last I had a general principle to which to relate all the data I had amassed about Scrivener. If each of his friends saw in him a magnified image of himself or herself, an explanation of many of my difficulties would be available. I decided to apply this general principle to those of his friends whom I knew most intimately. I began with Francesca.

What was Scrivener's attraction for her? She had realized her ambitions. This fact separated her from the others. She had always known what she wanted and had organized her life to obtain her desire. Money, position, influence—these were the only things she valued. She possessed all of them. She had sacrificed everyone and everything to obtain them and she had entered into her kingdom. Then Scrivener had appeared. She told me that, long before she had met him, she had heard a great deal about him. He was almost a legend in her life. *She* had contrived that they should meet and, from the outset, she realized that they were antagonists.

I recalled Francesca's first visit. I remembered how she had said to me: "He could be famous as a pianist if he wanted to be, or a writer, or an actor." Then, much later, when I had visited her in Bruton Street, and seen the types with which she associated, she had told me that Scrivener could have beaten every one of them at their own game. It was *this* which fascinated and intrigued her. He could have occupied a greater position in her world than she did, and it did not interest him. It was his refusal to accept which made her question the value of those things for which she had sacrificed so much. If she had had any doubt as to his ability to triumph in the sphere in which she had succeeded, she would have ignored him as easily as she had dismissed Rivers. But she had no doubt. He was an invitation and a challenge—an invitation to her passion; a challenge to her values. She was afraid to become his lover. She dare not say *take*, and she knew he would never say *give*. Also she recognized that to become his lover involved more than simply another passionate episode in her life. I remembered the very words in which she had expressed her dilemma to me: "He sees me satisfied with my world. It would be amusing for him to take me as his lover. To respond to the passion which he knows he awakes in me. And to make me *loathe* that world of mine and then to watch disillusion creep over me like a leprosy. This is his experiment with me!" How well I remember the night she said that!

This is what haunted Francesca: if she had been greater, if she had demanded more from life, her problem would have been Scrivener's. The pottage for which she had sold her birthright did not even tempt him. Everything she possessed lost some of its lustre because she knew it was dross to him. *What* was it that he demanded? *What* was it he was seeking? If she were greater, would not his quest be hers also? He was a mirror in which she saw herself magnified.

But the Scrivener whom Middleton had met was an entirely different person. One night Middleton had encountered a stranger in a café in Soho. He had been interested in him, and it was only after they had parted that Middleton had discovered that the stranger's name was Jonathan Scrivener. Middleton knew nothing of Scrivener's past, his achievements, or his reputation. He had met him only once, but that meeting had been an epoch in Middleton's life. It had occurred at a critical time for him. He had centred all his hopes of happiness in a woman and she had deserted him. The whole of his mental and emotional life was in a state of chaos—suffering was a new experience for him—he was disillusioned, bitter, impotent. He had been drinking heavily and had gone into that Soho café because he was intolerably lonely. Then, suddenly, a stranger had approached him, a man different in every way from the other occupants of the place. They had begun to talk and Middleton had told this stranger about himself and the manner in which his life had suffered ship-wreck. He could not remember exactly how much he had revealed, but he knew that he had given this stranger his confidence and had stammered out a passionate indictment of a world which had hurt and humiliated him.

Then Scrivener began to talk and Middleton learnt that there was a bitterness and a scorn in him which made his outburst seem that of a schoolboy. Here was an icy intellectual contempt which was not the result of the collapse of a sentimental dream. It was the rejection of every standard known to Middleton. It was the statement of a man who had sought harmony, on levels unknown to Middleton, and who had abandoned his search. Middleton had railed with passionate incoherence chiefly against women, but Scrivener's revolt had been absolute. One had lost a woman; the other a world. If Middleton had possessed knowledge, insight, experience, comparable with Scrivener's he would have known a greater wilderness than the one in which he was lost.

They had parted and later Middleton had found Scrivener's card in his pocket. He had called at the flat because he was fascinated by this man whose philosophy frightened him. He had expected to find something approaching a hermit's cell. He found luxury, refinement, wealth. He had assumed that no woman had any part in Scrivener's life. He discovered that he was intimate with two women of exceptional beauty. He was utterly bewildered. The whole setting of Scrivener's life seemed to deny the values of the man he had met in that Soho café. Yet he clung to the belief that the man he had met was the real Scrivener and even when drink, loneliness, and his complex relations with Francesca and Pauline had reduced him to a state of utter humiliation, the charge he lev-elled at Scrivener was that of hypocrisy—thereby implying that Scrivener had been false to himself, and that the real Scrivener was the one he had met in the café. Middleton had emphasized this when I saw him in his flat just before he left London. He was certain that Scrivener was only amusing himself with Pauline and Francesca. "They are to him what drink is to me," he had said with that strange abrupt laugh of his. "But I know the real man, and they don't, although I've met him only once. He was himself in that café. I took to drink because I dared not face the possibility of becoming like him. If I'd had brains and courage, I *should* have been like him."

Middleton—magnified. That was his conception of Scrivener.

And Pauline? I write her name, and her image rises before me. She stands like a statue and her eyes are studying something which

I cannot see. She is a stranger to the passions which dominate the lives of Francesca and Middleton. She was born with a knowledge which they do not possess. Their problems do not exist for her and hers are unknown to them. They live on this planet; she is a visitor. I love her so wholly that I cannot imagine how I lived before I knew her.

Judged externally, what link can she have with Scrivener? He has every background which she lacks. He is brilliant, witty, accomplished. A potential leader in many activities. He knows everything concerning which she is ignorant. She has no choice except to wait, and he has no problem except to choose. Yet they are intimate, as though each recognized that development was only possible through the other.

But, in Scrivener, Pauline sees her own problem intensified. She is offered the traditional life of the class to which she belongs, but she knows that she cannot accept it. It does not belong to her. She must find a life of different hopes, different desires, different objectives. She scans the horizons, seeking this way of life. She can only watch and wait. She meets Scrivener. She sees that although he is offered infinitely more than she is, yet he too cannot accept; he too is seeking a life outside the rut of tradition. Her problem is his, although his possibilities are greater. If she had been more gifted, she would have been in his position. He may amuse himself with others, try to escape from his quest, but she knows where the issue lies for him. She knows him, because he is herself—magnified.

Then—Rivers. The first time I met him he announced that he was like Scrivener and that he understood him. Although these statements were made lightly, it was evident that Rivers believed them. To him, Scrivener was a modern, an exponent of the "good time" philosophy, and possibly rather a poseur. Rivers had known him on and off for some years and was quite certain that he understood him thoroughly. He realized that Scrivener got a better time than he did as Scrivener could enter intellectually into spheres which were closed to him. Once Rivers had confided to me that "Scriv gets a greater kick out of more things than I do because he's a hell of a highbrow in his way." Nevertheless Rivers was confident that Scrivener was simply a super Rivers. . . .

It is obvious that each of them regards Scrivener as a magnifying mirror. It has been obvious from the beginning but I have only just seen it and now, for the first time, I begin to understand.

IV

I have re-read the last section and I know that to many people it will be no more than the description of a hypocrite. But hypocrisy is always motivated by self-interest. If Scrivener had deliberately deceived these friends of his, he had gained nothing by it. The real explanation lies deeper than this.

Nearly all of us have a rough and ready-made theory that there are two sides to our nature. The parable of *Dr. Jekyll and Mr. Hyde* is designed to illustrate this belief. It is a clear-cut and convenient conception, but it is utterly inadequate. We are as many persons as we have friends. Before you repudiate that statement, review your relations with your friends and you will find that you are a different person with every one of them. The difference may be slight, but it is there. It is inevitable, for friendship is the fusion of two enthusiasms, and no two of your friends possess the same enthusiasm in precisely the same degree.

It is through Scrivener's friends that I must discover his secret and I have learnt that to each he is a different person. That fact does not necessarily stamp him as a hypocrite. On the contrary, it may be an indication that his nature is so rich that it is responsive to each and every appeal. Indeed all the facts of his life, as known to me, support this contention.

I try to imagine him as a child. There is no doubt that he was extraordinarily handsome, a compelling personality, a leader, even as a boy at school. I try to imagine his life with his father—the man whom Winkworth described as eccentric and silent. Then, later, when he was seventeen, and after his father's death—I wonder which quality in him made his uncle devote his life to him. According to Winkworth's account they must have seemed an ill-assorted pair: a youth on the threshold of life and a disillusioned, queer, wealthy bachelor—a great traveller and a patron of the arts. For four years they had wandered about the world together. Winkworth knew nothing of that period. The uncle was as great a mystery to him as the father had been. But the experiences of those years must have had a profound effect upon Scrivener. What had his aims and ambitions been then, and what share had his eccentric uncle had in defining and influencing them? There is no direct evidence on which to base even a guess: the uncle is dead and Scrivener has been silent concerning that period of his life. But possibly his subsequent actions may furnish a clue.

At the age of twenty-one he found himself alone in the world, the possessor of experiences wholly unusual in a man of his age, and a fortune of very considerable dimensions. Birth, beauty, gifts, breeding, wealth—all were his. In Winkworth's phrase, the world was at his feet. I try to imagine him then, but it is a formidable task. I try to endow myself with his experiences and gifts and strive to imagine the aspect the world would have presented. Surely the horizons must have seemed limitless: the possibilities infinite. The chance of even one modest career has been denied to me, but Scrivener had a dozen from which to choose. How he must have been sought after, flattered, tempted! Youth, distinction, beauty, wealth, and a bachelor—what a destiny! How many hopes and ambitions must have centred in him! How many times he must have been married in the fond imaginations of designing mothers! How many subtle schemes must have been elaborated to relieve him of the burden of his wealth! What scope had been his for the gratification of every passion!

He had everything that most of us desire but—for many of us—to gain our desires would involve our destruction. He had avoided all the customary snares designed to deceive a man in his circumstances. Winkworth had complained that he, Scrivener, had not availed himself of the benefit of his professional advice, but possibly Scrivener's uncle had explained the type of temptations by which he would be surrounded and had provided him with the knowledge necessary for his protection. In any event Scrivener had stood alone and from that day to this he had been a mystery to everyone who had encountered him.

His first act after inheriting his uncle's fortune was a definite indication that he had renounced social glory. He sold the great house in the country which contained so many treasures, and ignored all the social responsibilities of his position. Doubtless this offended a number of people very much indeed. A man is expected to do exactly what the herd does of which he is a member. If you belong to a family whose supreme pleasure is hunting, you are expected to hunt—and to evince a delirious passion for that activity. If you don't, there's something wrong with you. And not only that. Your refusal is regarded by the members of your family as a criticism of them. It's no good saying you don't hunt because you don't like it, for the interpretation given to that statement is that you mean that *they* ought not to like it. If you persist in your refusal, it is either assumed that you have a secret vice, or that you are a Bolshevik in close touch with Moscow. Argument is useless. Either you must adhere to your refusal and accept ignominy, or you must leap on to a horse and pursue a tiny and terrified animal in company with other sportsmen.

In precisely the same way a number of assumptions were made about Scrivener. He was well-born and wealthy. Very well then. He would immediately adopt the type of life lived by those so circumstanced. He would entertain and be entertained. He would adopt with enthusiasm that mode of life which consists of doing the same things, with the same people, at the same places, at the same periods, year in, year out, world without end, till gout or death do them part. That is, he would become a member of the fashionable world.

He did nothing of the kind. Immediately, he was regarded as "odd." Immediately, it was remembered that his father was mad and his uncle eccentric. People shook their heads and talked about "heredity." It is the custom of slaves to praise independence, but on the rare occasions when they encounter it they become extremely angry. "This man doesn't need *us*? He can't be out of the top drawer!" One must never doubt the supreme value of the activities of one's class. It's not done.

From all the odds and ends of information I have been able to collect, it is quite certain that Scrivener spent the next nine years in studying one or other of the arts. I have it on indisputable authority that as a writer, or a musician, or an actor, he could have achieved eminence. In fact, there is a greater measure of agreement concerning this than in any other particular relating to him. Naturally, during this period his associates were those who shared his enthusiasms. At that point, however, at which he was about to obtain mastery in any one of these activities, his interest vanished. When the crown was offered, he could not accept it. Winkworth had told me this, but he had failed entirely to suggest any explanations. I am groping towards one.

The younger generation of to-day contains a number of persons who affect to despise what they cannot obtain. By the adoption of a few simple formulae they convince themselves of their spiritual superiority over others. Necessarily, the chief article in their creed is that anyone who is successful cannot be any good. That is their fundamental and essential belief, for all their other dogmas depend on it. These persons usually live in rather stark and severe surroundings and they manage to convey the impression that "we could, if we would, but we won't." They all have private incomes, and believe in revolution. They have gestures, attitudes, and passwords of their own. They are terrified of being understood. They have a slightly conspiratorial air, and they chatter eternally about Life. They have a knack of intimidating their superiors.

If Scrivener had been one of these articulate mummies, and had merely rejected what he had failed to win, he would have been of no interest whatever. But it was definitely established that he had refused, again and again, the prizes which belonged to him by right of conquest. Indeed it was this fact which made him a mystery to everyone. Did he realize at that moment when he was about to enter the kingdom he had won how narrow and sharply defined were its frontiers? Did he shrink from the knowledge that the acceptance of leadership in any given activity involved the rejection of a part of himself for ever? Or did he instinctively loathe everything directly it was within reach of his hand?

There is a legend that Michelangelo possessed a statue from which he refused to be separated. It depicted a man with his adversary helpless beneath him. The hand of the conqueror was raised to strike the final blow. It was his moment of triumph: the moment of which he had dreamt. For years the thought of victory had hung like a star over the darkness of his anger. Now, he holds his enemy at his mercy, his hand is raised—but he is not looking at his victim. He is looking backward with a strange haunted expression. The great moment has come—and it is nothing. His desire is granted—and it is dust. He looks behind him into vacancy, afraid of the silence, afraid of the emptiness in his heart. He has attained the summit of his hopes, and the terror of attainment numbs him.

Which of us has not experienced this in his degree? Our desire, like a butterfly, is alluring only while it eludes. Captured, it is a dead thing through which we stick a pin. We multiply our wants because each possession in turn disappoints us, yet we lack the courage to admit the futility of the chase. The Failure becomes bankrupt in that he loses his hope; and the Successful knows the bankruptcy involved in the attainment of his desire. Neither will admit it and so the frenzied farce goes on.

Doubtless when Scrivener rejected the social glory that was offered him, he turned with exultant anticipation to the arts. In one or other of them he would find fulfilment. He would realize himself in creation, inhabit an ideal world, reveal his secret in images and symbols.

His life between the ages of twenty-one and thirty was occupied wholly by the study of one or other of the arts. I have verified from a hundred sources how unsparing was his devotion to his work during this period and how speedily he gained recognition as an artist of force and originality. After he was thirty, however, his disappearances became more frequent and from the age of thirty-three he appears to have lived in solitude. I have learnt little concerning this epoch of his life, but it is clear that he abandoned all his ambitions and avoided all his former associates. The only coherent incident I know relative to this period is worth quoting. It was told to me by a man named Fraser whom I met one night at a party to which Rivers had taken me. Fraser began to talk about Scrivener directly he learnt that I was his secretary.

"Since he became thirty-three the devil knows what he does with himself!" he exclaimed. "I knew him well once, saw a lot of him. Then he began to live like a hermit. Well, one night in Paris, I ran into him. It was pretty late and at first I was certain I was mistaken. He was shabbily dressed, unshaven, and he was bent as if the world were on his shoulders."

"You're sure it was Scrivener?" I asked.

"Damn it, of course I am! I spoke to him. It was Scrivener all right. Couldn't believe it at first because usually he is so elegant in appearance, don't you know? Well, he gave no explanation. Stood there with a damned unpleasant smile, and a worse light in his eyes, and just exchanged inane comments with me. But the uncanny part of it was that I *daren't* question him. I was bursting to ask him why he'd chucked everything, but I daren't. He's got the will of the devil. That's the last I saw of him."

I could learn no more from Fraser but all my investigations concerning Scrivener at that time indicated that he remained in this solitude until he became acquainted with Pauline and Francesca. Indeed, it may well have been Francesca's letter which caused him to abandon his solitary existence. I believe that he decided to try one last adventure before confronting the problem which had driven him to loneliness, and of which he was afraid.

Rivers told me, when I was with him that night in the Park, that Scrivener had explained to him in Paris that he was trying one last experiment and that if it failed he would become a hermit. Rivers had attached no significance to that statement, but I am certain that it affected not only him, but Pauline, Francesca, Middleton, and myself. But the experiment was instituted for Scrivener's benefit, not for ours. It is difficult to explain this theory of mine but it is essential to make it clear, for I believe that it is the truth concerning his relations with all of us. It explains why each one of us has a definite conception of his character and why each conception is fundamentally different.

He had failed to find an activity which could hold him. He

was unable, unlike the majority of us, to continue to race round a revolving cage. He had refused all substitutes for life. He was alone, inactive, yet aware of the immense possibilities within him. His rejection of the world's prizes was actual, not theoretical. He had a magnificent equipment and no medium through which to express himself. Then, in the loneliness of his solitude, he caught a glimpse of the only way of life for him, but he shrank from this vision. To accept it, involved the sacrifice of everything which he had built up. He decided to evade this issue—to try one last flirtation with life, one final experiment. He returned to the world.

This, I believe, was his final experiment:—he would yield to another that side of his nature which responded to that other's influence. But, in yielding, he would not surrender himself. He would be to another what that other evoked in him. His theory, as I conceive it, was a simple one. The richest intercourse between two human beings proceeds from the response by one to the other's enthusiasm. *Scrivener decided that he would be to another just what that other awoke in him.*

Is that fantastic? Isn't it what we all do, in our degree? I meet you and gradually we become friends. You tell me your hopes, your fears, your secrets. If I respond to these things, can I be a stranger to them? Even to *listen* is sometimes a confession. Will not the quality of my response be the measure of the intimacy between us? Will it not be the means of establishing the common elements in our experience? And will not the development of our friendship depend on the number of enthusiasms which we share? And then, shall I not feel that I *know* you, and will you not be convinced that you *know* me? And, normally, each of us will be right. But suppose that one of us is Scrivener. What then? Suppose, that is to say, that one of us has had experiences in regions of which the other is entirely ignorant. What then?

Why, good God! had you and I been alive in Shakespeare's day, and met him several times in a tavern, drank with him, laughed with him, told him our joys and sorrows, and never known who he was—we should have imagined that we *knew* him. He would have understood us so perfectly, reacted so wholly to our enthusiasms, responded so unerringly to our appeals, that we should have been quite convinced that he was just a damned good fellow and so one of us. He wouldn't have been such a fool as to want to impress us with his importance. Good Lord! What for? *He knew what he was.* Only the poseurs, the halt, the lame, the uncertain, and the blind require admiration. They can only believe in themselves if the half-witted believe in them. Shakespeare would have accepted us as we were, identified himself with our projects, *known* us, perhaps even loved us. (Yes, he might have been great enough even for that!) But—and this is the point—we'd have been quite certain that we knew *him.* And there would have been no arrogance in that belief. You can always tell when you are with your superiors—they give you the illusion that you are their equal. That's why you like them. Conversely, your inferiors always try to indicate their superiority. That's why you loathe them. Shakespeare would have made us feel quite at home with him. We should have found the reflection of our little experience in the myriad-sided mirror of his mind. And we should probably have mistaken that reflection for the whole man. That's why we should have thought that he was just one of us.

I am not suggesting that Scrivener was a Shakespeare, but I do know that his experience was far wider and far deeper than that of his friends, and I am certain that he identified himself with the central activity of each of them. He reflected it and each one of them mistook this reflection for the whole man. It is the reason why each one in turn imagined that he or she knew the true Scrivener. Francesca is one example. Despite her worldliness, she was capable of passion and Scrivener allowed the passion of his own nature to respond to her magnetism. In his response she discovered a passion greater than her own and one which held and hypnotized her. But though he yielded to her appeal, he did not surrender himself. He isolated for her benefit that side of himself which she evoked. For him to have surrendered would have been a denial of all that in him which was outside the frontiers of her influence. Hence he was a mystery to her, although she clung to the belief that she understood him. She did not appreciate that he had gone further down her road than she had—and knew the vanity of her destination. His friends were enigmas to Francesca for they represented alien aspects of his nature, the existence of which was unknown to her. She thought that he was a straight line—he was a labyrinth.

Then—Pauline. In every way she was a contrast to Francesca. The latter knew exactly what she wanted—Pauline only knew what she did not want. She was not deceived by the tinsel triumphs which fascinated Francesca. She was one of those rare beings who are *born* with experience. Most of us have to make fools of ourselves before we have any understanding of the nature of folly, but persons of Pauline's type are born with that knowledge. Hence her appeal to Scrivener was of an entirely different order from Francesca's. He was aware of Pauline's problem, for he too had no continuing city. There was in him a questing spirit which had wandered from illusion to illusion seeking the shadow of reality. He reacted to Pauline's appeal, just as he responded to Francesca's magnetism, and there was no hypocrisy in this dual response. Two sides of his nature had been evoked—he denied neither and each was allowed its expression.

The same principle applies to Middleton and Rivers. The deepest thing in Middleton, and the most vital, was his rebellion against his destiny. It was this revolt in him which poised him on a different background—it individualized him, isolated him, gave him colour. It inspired him with a fiery eloquence; it was the quick of his mental and emotional life. If rebellion—the sudden rage born of finding oneself hopelessly at odds with the world—wakes no response in you, what could you have had to say to Middleton? You had to meet him in chaos, or not meet him at all. Scrivener had responded to him by revealing a bitterness that Middleton could never have known. That is, he revealed to Middleton exactly that side of his nature which Middleton called forth.

It was the same, though less dramatically, with Rivers. Rivers was an adventurer and, to him, Scrivener was simply a greater adventurer. That was all. Scrivener was a mirror in which each of his friends found the image he or she evoked.

And Denvers was the living equivalent to certain of the books on Scrivener's shelves. He was the slave of perversities which once had interested Scrivener. . . .

All roads had become barred to him: he had tried all things and each one in turn had failed him. Deep in him he knew that his salvation consisted in rejecting all that he had created; to put aside all the ambitions he had ever known; to enter the wilderness and to have the faith and courage to wait until it was revealed to him what he had to do. But he shrank from this abdication. He tried a final experiment in the hope of evading the surrender of his personality. He was a chameleon. He would exploit his friends. He allowed others to evoke different sides of his nature, half hoping that he would find satisfaction in one or other of those things he had served in the past.

My letter of application told him that I understood—if only theoretically—the problem which was so actual and urgent for him. He made me his secretary and by so doing he put me in a position in which it was possible for me to discover his secret. It may even be that he wished one human being to know him as he was, and it intrigued him to choose a stranger. This, I believe, was the reason why he had placed at my disposal those rooms in his flat from which his friends had been excluded. That act was an indication that I should have access to certain aspects of his life which he had hidden from others. He knew that it was inevitable that I should meet his friends and that each of them would be an entrance into a world in which I should learn about him. He guessed that Winkworth, when he discovered that I was friendly with Francesca, would tell me the external facts of his life. But he realized that Winkworth, like Matthews, knew nothing of the labyrinth in which he had wandered. My letter had convinced him that I was capable of solving his secret and he wished it to be solved—and by a stranger.

V

It is late at night. I am alone in the library. All the thoughts, all the speculations and theories, I have had about the man who owns this room, seem to flit to and fro in the silence like invisible bats. . . .

Who is he? What is he? At moments he ceases to be a man and attains the stature of a symbol. He is everything that each one of us at some period of our lives has served or worshipped. He is everything which we believed could bring us harmony. He is riches, culture, personality, art—all the idols before which we have knelt. Everything which life has denied to us it has offered to him. All those prizes for which we would have bartered ourselves have been rejected by him. He stands at the end of those roads, down which we hasten so eagerly, gazing at a desert. He is at one and the same time our aspiration and the death of our hope. Either we must have the courage to follow him and enter the wilderness; or we must have the courage to renounce him—and all that he represents.

He has taken those things to which we render lip service and sought to make them the substance of his life. He has dared to believe in our gods and to base his life upon their reality. He has accepted their promises as truth and has built his life upon them. One by one they have failed him, as they would fail us if we had the courage to live them. We have only praised the beauty of a mirage; he has dared to attempt to make it his habitation. He is alone, inactive, impotent, not because he is less than we are but because he is greater. Our ideals, for us, are only the toys with which we play for an idle hour, but he dared to make them his daily bread and they turned to dust in his mouth. He was too great to accept a lie because it was hallowed by age and tradition. He was impelled to test it and, having proved its falsity, he refused the tinsel crown which the world offers to its princes as the price of their silence. . . .

Jonathan Scrivener. I repeat his name aloud. I say it again and again. The sound of the words hypnotizes me. It seems in some utterly fantastic way that he is myself. All the dreams, all the hopes, all the ambitions, which have haunted my solitary life, seem to have been realized in the life of this stranger. Had God granted the prayers I never had the faith to utter, I should have been him. His opportunities, his freedom, his gifts, would have been mine. All my life I have lied to myself. I have pretended that I did not want what I could not obtain. I have been a slave to the subtlest form of pride—that pride which evades action in order to avoid failure so abject that it would have to be admitted. But if all my repressed desires could have found expression, I should have been a Jonathan Scrivener, and I should have gone forth into the world conquering and to conquer. So, in this sense, *his* failure is *my* failure, for if I had had his equipment, his gods would have been my gods—and one by one they would have crumbled to dust before my eyes, as they have crumbled before his.

And yet, I wish to God that his present problem were mine! I wish I had been offered all that has been offered to him and known and proved the vanity of all of it. *Then* my rejection could be a true rejection, like his. As it is, I am haunted by the thought that were I to be offered anything at all I would accept it, believe in it, become smug, self-satisfied, important, opinionated, respectable, confident, happy—and go to my grave certain that God Himself would welcome me with all due honors and appropriate solemnity in the very centre of His highest heaven. I know the value of *theoretical* rejections. They are the triumphs of weaklings to whom the devil won't offer even half-a-crown, so they take their revenge by asserting that they have refused all the kingdoms of this world and the glories thereof . . .

But I have solved the riddle of Jonathan Scrivener. I am certain of it. And I am equally certain that he willed that I should solve it. In experimenting with us, he is experimenting with himself. We represent different aspects of his nature—the warring elements in him which he has failed to harmonize. We are the outward and visible representatives of his inward invisible strife. I do not know how long his experiment will last, any more than I know when I shall end this book. Probably I shall end it when a point is reached beyond which it would be *impossible* to continue it. Perhaps the same applies to Scrivener's experiment.

VI

Day after day passes. I spend each one in solitude. Except for a brief line from Pauline in which she told me that she had found her father seriously ill, I have heard from no one. Francesca, Middleton, Rivers—silence. They have vanished and some instinct tells me that I shall not see them again. I summon up memories of the adventures I had with them and I seem to be watching incidents in some half-forgotten film. Then, once again, the suspicion wakes in me that they were Scrivener's accomplices, that they have now played their parts in some plot of his contriving and one quite outside the range of my imagination. Yet one glance at the facts reveals the impossibility of this theory. Whichever way I turn, I am forced in the end to believe that my estimate of Scrivener's motives is the true one.

If Winkworth is right—if Scrivener is dead—what then? Presumably I shall remain in this flat until the fact of his death is established, then I shall leave here and all the circumstances of my engagement, all the events which have happened since, will remain mysteries for ever. I should never *know* whether my solution of the riddle is the true one or moonshine. I should not know where to go, or what to do. I cannot imagine my life apart from Scrivener and, as I write the words, I know that I must be little removed from a madman to be able to state that I cannot imagine what I should make of my life if I learnt that a man, whom I have never seen, was dead. My God! I could almost wish that everything I have written in this book were only the record of a strange and vivid dream; that I could wake up and find myself in my old lodgings; and discover that I am still a clerk in Petersham's office. I am weary, utterly weary, of the mystery which envelops me and I am beginning to be afraid of this silent library which waits with timeless patience for the return of its owner. Its owner, who may be dead! I cannot endure this solitude which is rendered more impossible by the fact that I have only to open the door to find myself in the roaring whirl of London. Even in the thronged streets, I am conscious of this library and it draws me back to it by some unholy spell. Everything in it is dead and I have the ridiculous suspicion that if I took a book from the shelves, I should discover that it is a dummy. My nerves are failing me. Everything is becoming distorted. I find something sinister even in Matthews— something inhuman in her lack of curiosity, and in the Robot-like precision with which she carries out her duties. Always punctual, always silent, always efficient. I lunch and dine out in order to see less of her, because the insane suspicion sometimes possesses me that she, and she alone, knows the truth about Scrivener and the real reason for my engagement. All the others have spoken—she has said nothing. She has never even asked for the slightest concession—never wanted to leave early, never suggested that she should have a day off. How can such a person exist in an age like this! I believe that if I touched her, I should find that she is cold.

No, I cannot live like this much longer. I am risking my very reason. I will give myself a time limit. I will fix a date and if something has not happened by then, I will write to Scrivener and resign. . . .

I look at the calendar. Exactly seven months ago to-day I came to this flat.

CHAPTER XV

A HEAVY, dull, lugubrious day. One of those sunless summer days when the atmosphere is oppressed by the menace of thunder. It has not rained for weeks and the city is dusty and airless. Every noise seems to be accentuated; everyone is irritable, restless. Life is reduced to the level of a vast mechanism. It yields a soulless obedience to the rigid laws of a relentless routine. It has no sparkle, no animation.

I went out early and spent the day by the river, returning to London in time for dinner. A curious excitement possessed me, born of a presentiment that I was on the threshold of sudden and unimaginable change. I experienced that mood in which one seems to be looking at everything for the last time.

It was nearly ten o'clock when I walked back to the flat. There was a lurid light in the west and I felt that the storm grew nearer every moment. The atmosphere was tense, electric, and instinctively I kept glancing at the darkening sky. I was tired and eager to regain the solitude of the flat, but directly I found myself in the library I began to wish that I had remained in the streets. I could not read, sleep was an impossibility. I began to wander about the room, waiting for I knew not what.

I suppose an hour passed. Then, just as I was wondering whether I would go out again, there was a ring at the bell. It was a long peal and it echoed like a challenge through the silent flat.

I stood motionless in the middle of the library. No one had called for days. My brain was numbed and I could not even guess at the identity of my visitor. After a moment, however, I decided that either Middleton or Rivers had returned, and a wave of weariness passed over me at the thought that another act in the drama was about to begin. But perhaps this was some new friend of Scrivener's, some stranger with whom I was destined to become intimate, and who would intensify the mystery which surrounded me. I stood irresolute, feeling that I could play my part no longer.

Again the sound of the bell pealed through the silence. I went to the front door mechanically, watching my own actions as one watches oneself thread the maze of a dream.

A man stood on the threshold. I stared at him in silence. He was tall and powerfully built. He held a soft black hat in his left hand. His head was that of an emperor and I was held by the power of the most remarkable eyes I have ever seen.

He did not speak and I remained silent. For nearly a minute we stood looking at each other.

"You are James Wrexham."

The voice was deep and vibrant. It dominated my whole being and I could not speak. After a long pause he continued:

"Shall I introduce myself? Or is it unnecessary?" He held out his hand. "I am Jonathan Scrivener."

ALSO AVAILABLE FROM VALANCOURT BOOKS

Lightning Source UK Ltd.
Milton Keynes UK
UKHW010628220520
363663UK00003B/993